The Lucky One

NICHOLAS SPARKS

The Lucky One

SPHERE

First published in the United States of America in 2008
by Grand Central Publishing
First published in 2008 by Sphere

Copyright © 2008 by Nicholas Sparks

The moral right of the author has been asserted.

*All characters and events in this publication, other than those
clearly in the public domain, are fictitious and any resemblance
to real persons, living or dead, is purely coincidental.*

All rights reserved.
No part of this publication may be reproduced, stored in a
retrieval system, or transmitted, in any form or by any means, without
the prior permission in writing of the publisher, nor be otherwise circulated
in any form of binding or cover other than that in which it is published
and without a similar condition including this condition
being imposed on the subsequent purchaser.

A CIP catalogue record for this book
is available from the British Library.

ISBN 978-1-84744-114-0

Printed and bound in Great Britain by
Clays Ltd, St Ives plc

Papers used by Sphere are natural, renewable and recyclable
products made from wood grown in sustainable forests and certified
in accordance with the rules of the Forest Stewardship Council.

Mixed Sources
Product group from well-managed
forests and other controlled sources
www.fsc.org   Cert no. SGS-COC-004081
© 1996 Forest Stewardship Council

Sphere
An imprint of
Little, Brown Book Group
100 Victoria Embankment
London EC4Y 0DY

An Hachette Livre UK Company
www.hachettelivre.co.uk

www.littlebrown.co.uk

For Jamie Raab and Dennis Dalrymple

A year to remember . . .
and a year to forget.
I'm with you in spirit.

Acknowledgments

Writing is never a solitary effort, and as always, there are many people I have to thank for having the energy and ability to complete this novel. There are many ways to honor these people for their efforts, of course, so I thought I'd throw in a few different ways to say thank you—at least according to the list I "Googled" right before writing this. (Without looking them up, can you name all the languages offhand?)

At the top of the list, of course, is my wife, Cathy. More than anything, she keeps me centered and focused on all the things in life that are really important. I tell my sons they would do well to marry a woman much like her one day. *Thank you!*

The kids come next: Miles, Ryan, Landon, Lexie, and Savannah, all of whom have been immortalized (in a teeny-tiny way) as the names of characters in my previous novels. To receive their hugs is to receive the greatest gift of all. *Muchas gracias!*

And then? My literary agent, Theresa Park, always deserves my gratitude. The agent-author relationship can be tricky at times— or so I've heard from other agents and authors. In all honesty, for me it's been nothing but fantastic and wonderful to have worked with Theresa since we first spoke on the phone way back in 1995. She is the very best; not only is she intelligent and patient, but

she is blessed with more common sense than most people I know.
Danke schön!

Denise DiNovi, my friend and movie-accomplice, is another
of the many blessings in my life. She's produced three of my
films—including *Nights in Rodanthe*, *Message in a Bottle*, and *A
Walk to Remember*—which makes me one of the most fortunate
authors in the world. *Merci beaucoup!*

David Young, the fabulous CEO of Grand Central Publishing,
has been nothing but supportive, and I'm lucky to work with him.
Arigato gozaimasu!

Jennifer Romanello, a publicist and friend, has made publicity
an endlessly interesting and enjoyable experience for the past
thirteen years. *Grazie!*

Edna Farley, my telephone friend, schedules nearly everything—and handles every problem that crops up—while touring.
She's not only fantastic, but endlessly optimistic, something I've
grown to cherish. *Tapadh leibh!*

Howie Sanders, my film agent and friend, is another member
of the "I've worked with that author for a long time" club. And
my life is better for it. *Toda raba!*

Keya Khayatian, another of my film agents, is terrific and always generous with his time. *Merci!* or, if you prefer, *Mamnoon!*

Harvey-Jane Kowal and Sona Vogel, my copy editors, are in-
credibly patient, considering I'm always so far behind on deadline.
They have to catch all the little errors in my novels (okay, sometimes biggies, too), and unfortunately, I seldom give them much
time. So if you find an error (and you might), don't blame them.
Blame me. They're fantastic at what they do. To the both of you:
Spasibo!

Scott Schwimer, my entertainment attorney, is one of those
guys who make you frown at lawyer jokes. He's a great person and
an even better friend. *Liels paldies!*

Many thanks also to Marty Bowen, Courtenay Valenti, Abby

Koons, Sharon Krassney, Lynn Harris, and Mark Johnson. *Efharisto poli!*

Alice Arthur, my photographer, is always ready at a moment's notice and takes a fantastic photo, for which I'm always grateful. *Toa chie! Or Xie xie!*

Flag has yet again designed a wonderful cover. *Shukran gazilan!*

Tom McLaughlin, the headmaster at The Epiphany School—a school that my wife and I helped found—has made my life richer and more full since we've been working together. *Obrigado!*

And finally, to David Simpson, my fellow coach at New Bern High—*Mahalo nui loa!*

P.S. The languages are: English, Spanish, German, French, Japanese, Italian, Scottish Gaelic, Hebrew, Farsi (Persian), Russian, Latvian, Greek, Chinese, Arabic, Portuguese, and Hawaiian. At least according the site I found on the Internet. But who can believe everything there?

1

Clayton and Thibault

Deputy Keith Clayton hadn't heard them approach, and up close, he didn't like the looks of them any more than he had the first time he'd seen them. The dog was part of it. He wasn't fond of German shepherds, and this one, though he was standing quietly, reminded him of Panther, the police dog that rode with Deputy Kenny Moore and was quick to bite suspects in the crotch at the slightest command. Most of the time he regarded Moore as an idiot, but he was still just about the closest thing to a friend that Clayton had in the department, and he had to admit that Moore had a way of telling those crotch-biting stories that made Clayton double over in laughter. And Moore would definitely have appreciated the little skinny-dipping party Clayton had just broken up, when he'd spied a couple of coeds sunning down by the creek in all their morning glory. He hadn't been there for more than a few minutes and had snapped only a couple of pictures on the digital camera when he saw a third girl pop up from behind a hydrangea bush. After quickly ditching the camera in the bushes behind him, he'd stepped out from behind the tree, and a moment later, he and the coed were face-to-face.

"Well, what have we got here?" he drawled, trying to put her on the defensive.

He hadn't liked the fact that he'd been caught, nor was he pleased with his insipid opening line. Usually he was smoother than that. A lot smoother. Thankfully, the girl was too embarrassed to notice much of anything, and she almost tripped while trying to back up. She stammered something like an answer as she tried to cover herself with her hands. It was like watching someone play a game of Twister by herself.

He made no effort to avert his gaze. Instead he smiled, pretending not to notice her body, as if he bumped into naked women in the woods all the time. He could already tell she knew nothing about the camera.

"Now calm down. What's going on?" he asked.

He knew full well what was going on. It happened a few times every summer, but especially in August: Coeds from Chapel Hill or NC State, heading to the beach for a long, last-chance weekend at Emerald Isle before the fall term began, often made a detour onto an old logging road that twisted and bumped for a mile or so into the national forest before reaching the point where Swan Creek made a sharp turn toward the South River. There was a rock-pebble beach there that had come to be known for nude sunbathing—how that happened, he had no idea—and Clayton often made it a point to swing by on the off chance he might get lucky. Two weeks ago, he'd seen six lovelies; today, however, there were three, and the two who'd been lying on their towels were already reaching for their shirts. Though one of them was a bit heavy, the other two—including the brunette standing in front of him—had the kind of figures that made frat boys go crazy. Deputies, too.

"We didn't know anyone was out here! We thought it would be okay!"

Her face held just enough innocence to make him think, *Wouldn't Daddy be proud if he knew what his little girl was up to?* It amused him to imagine what she might say to that, but since he was in uniform, he knew he had to say something official. Besides,

he knew he was pressing his luck; if word got out that the sheriff's office was actually patrolling the area, there'd be no more
coeds in the future, and that was something he didn't want to
contemplate.

"Let's go talk to your friends."

He followed her back toward the beach, watching as she tried
unsuccessfully to cover her backside, enjoying the little show. By
the time they stepped from the trees into the clearing by the river,
her friends had pulled on their shirts. The brunette jogged and
jiggled toward the others and quickly reached for a towel, knocking over a couple of cans of beer in the process. Clayton motioned
to a nearby tree.

"Didn't y'all see the sign?"

On cue, their eyes swung that way. People were sheep, waiting
for the next order, he thought. The sign, small and partially hidden by the low-slung branches of an ancient live oak, had been
posted by order of Judge Kendrick Clayton, who also happened
to be his uncle. The idea for the signs had been Keith's; he knew
that the public prohibition would only enhance the attraction of
the place.

"We didn't see it!" the brunette cried, swiveling back to him.
"We didn't know! We just heard about this place a couple of days
ago!" She continued to protest while struggling with the towel;
the others were too terrified to do much of anything except try to
wiggle back into their bikini bottoms. "It's the first time we've
ever been here!"

It came out like a whine, making her sound like a spoiled soror-
ity sister. Which all of them probably were. They had that *look*.

"Did you know that public nudity is a misdemeanor in this
county?"

He saw their young faces grow even more pale, knowing they
were imagining this little transgression on their record. Fun to
watch, but he reminded himself not to let it go too far.

"What's your name?"

"Amy." The brunette swallowed. "Amy White."

"Where are you from?"

"Chapel Hill. But I'm from Charlotte originally."

"I see some alcohol there. Are y'all twenty-one?"

For the first time, the others answered as well. "Yes, sir."

"Okay, Amy. I'll tell you what I'm going to do. I'm going to take you at your word that you didn't see the sign and that you're of legal age to drink, so I'm not going to make a big deal out of this. I'll pretend I wasn't even here. As long as you promise not to tell my boss that I let you three off the hook."

They weren't sure whether to believe him.

"Really?"

"Really," he said. "I was in college once, too." He hadn't been, but he knew it sounded good. "And you might want to put your clothes on. You never know—there might be people lurking around." He flashed a smile. "Make sure you clean up all the cans, okay?"

"Yes, sir."

"I appreciate it." He turned to leave.

"That's it?"

Turning around, he flashed his smile again. "That's it. Y'all take care now."

Clayton pushed through the underbrush, ducking beneath the occasional branch on the way back to his cruiser, thinking he'd handled that well. Very well indeed. Amy had actually smiled at him, and as he'd turned away, he'd toyed with the idea of doubling back and asking her for her phone number. No, he decided, it was probably better to simply leave good enough alone. More than likely they'd go back and tell their friends that even though they'd been caught by the sheriff, nothing had happened to them. Word would get around that the deputies around here were *cool*. Still, as he wove through the woods, he hoped the pictures came out. They would make a nice addition to his little collection.

All in all, it had been an excellent day. He was about to go back for the camera when he heard whistling. He followed the sound toward the logging road and saw the stranger with a dog, walking slowly up the road, looking like some kind of hippie from the sixties.

The stranger wasn't with the girls. Clayton was sure of it. The guy was too old to be a college student, for one thing; he had to be late twenties, at least. His long hair reminded Clayton of a rat's nest, and on the stranger's back, Clayton could see the outlines of a sleeping bag poking out from beneath a backpack. This was no day-tripper on the way to the beach; this guy had the appearance of someone who'd been hiking, maybe even camping out. No telling how long he'd been here or what he'd seen.

Like Clayton taking pictures?

No way. It wasn't possible. He'd been hidden from the main road, the underbrush was thick, and he would have heard someone tramping through the woods. Right? Still, it was an odd place to be hiking. They were in the middle of nowhere out here, and the last thing he wanted was a bunch of hippie losers ruining this spot for the coeds.

By then, the stranger had passed him. He was nearly to the cruiser and heading toward the Jeep that the girls had driven. Clayton stepped onto the road and cleared his throat. The stranger and the dog turned at the sound.

From a distance, Clayton continued to evaluate them. The stranger seemed unfazed by Clayton's sudden appearance, as did the dog, and there was something in the stranger's gaze that unsettled him. Like he'd almost expected Clayton to show up. Same thing with the German shepherd. The dog's expression was aloof and wary at the same time—*intelligent,* almost—which was the same way Panther often appeared before Moore set him loose. His stomach did a quick flip-flop. He had to force himself not to cover his privates.

For a long minute, they continued to stare at each other. Clayton had learned a long time ago that his uniform intimidated most people. Everyone, even innocent people, got nervous around the law, and he figured this guy was no exception. It was one of the reasons he loved being a deputy.

"You got a leash for your dog?" he said, making it sound more like a command than a question.

"In my backpack."

Clayton could hear no accent at all. "Johnny Carson English," as his mother used to describe it. "Put it on."

"Don't worry. He won't move unless I tell him to."

"Put it on anyway."

The stranger lowered his backpack and fished around; Clayton craned his neck, hoping for a glimpse of anything that could be construed as drugs or weapons. A moment later, the leash was attached to the dog's collar and the stranger faced him with an expression that seemed to say, *Now what?*

"What are you doing out here?" Clayton asked.

"Hiking."

"That's quite a pack you've got for a hike."

The stranger said nothing.

"Or maybe you were sneaking around, trying to see the sights?"

"Is that what people do when they're here?"

Clayton didn't like his tone, or the implication. "I'd like to see some identification."

The stranger bent over his backpack again and fished out his passport. He held an open palm to the dog, making the dog stay, then took a step toward Clayton and handed it over.

"No driver's license?"

"I don't have one."

Clayton studied the name, his lips moving slightly. "Logan Thibault?"

The stranger nodded.

"Where you from?"

"Colorado."

"Long trip."

The stranger said nothing.

"You going anywhere in particular?"

"I'm on my way to Arden."

"What's in Arden?"

"I couldn't say. I haven't been there yet."

Clayton frowned at the answer. Too slick. Too . . . challenging? Too something. Whatever. All at once, he knew he didn't like this guy. "Wait here," he said. "You don't mind if I check this out, do you?"

"Help yourself."

As Clayton headed back to the car, he glanced over his shoulder and saw Thibault reach into his backpack and pull out a small bowl before proceeding to empty a bottle of water into it. Like he didn't have a care in the world.

We'll find out, won't we? In the cruiser, Clayton radioed in the name and spelling before being interrupted by the dispatcher.

"It's Thibault, like T-bow, not Thigh-bolt. It's French."

"Why should I care how it's pronounced?"

"I was just saying—"

"Whatever, Marge. Just check it out, will you?"

"Does he look French?"

"How the hell would I know what a Frenchman looks like?"

"I'm just curious. Don't get so huffy about it. I'm a little busy here."

Yeah, real busy, Clayton thought. Eating doughnuts, most likely. Marge scarfed down at least a dozen Krispy Kremes a day. She must have weighed at least three hundred pounds.

Through the window, he could see the stranger squatting beside the dog and whispering to it as it lapped up the water. He shook his head. Talking to animals. Freak. Like the dog could understand anything other than the most basic of commands. His ex-wife used to do that, too. That woman treated dogs like people, which should have warned him to stay away from her in the first place.

"I can't find anything," he heard Marge say. She sounded like she was chewing something. "No outstanding warrants that I can see."

"You sure?"

"Yeah, I'm sure. I do know how to do my job."

As though he'd been listening in on the conversation, the stranger retrieved the bowl and slipped it back into his backpack, then slung his backpack over his shoulder.

"Have there been any other unusual calls? People loitering around, things like that?"

"No. It's been quiet this morning. And where are you, by the way? Your dad's been trying to find you."

Clayton's dad was the county sheriff.

"Tell him I'll be back in a little while."

"He seems mad."

"Just tell him I've been on patrol, okay?"

So he'll know I've been working, he didn't bother to add.

"Will do."

That's better.

"I gotta go."

He put the radio handset back in place and sat without moving, feeling the slightest trace of disappointment. It would have been fun to see how the guy handled lockup, what with that girly hair and all. The Landry brothers would have had a field day with him. They were regulars in lockup on Saturday nights: drunk and disorderly, disturbing the peace, fighting, almost always with each other. Except when they were in lockup. Then they'd pick on someone else.

He fiddled with the handle of his car door. And what was his dad mad about this time? Dude got on his nerves. Do this. Do that. You serve those papers yet? Why are you late? Where've you been? Half the time he wanted to tell the old guy to mind his own damn business. Old guy still thought he ran things around here.

No matter. He supposed he'd find out sooner or later. Now it was time to get the hippie loser out of here, before the girls came out. Place was supposed to be private, right? Hippie freaks could ruin the place.

Clayton got out of the car, closing the door behind him. The dog cocked its head to the side as Clayton approached. He handed the passport back. "Sorry for the inconvenience, Mr. Thibault." This time, he mangled the pronunciation on purpose. "Just doing my job. Unless, of course, you've got some drugs or guns in your pack."

"I don't."

"You care to let me see for myself?"

"Not really. Fourth Amendment and all."

"I see your sleeping bag there. You been camping?"

"I was in Burke County last night."

Clayton studied the guy, thinking about the answer.

"There aren't any campgrounds around here."

The guy said nothing.

It was Clayton who looked away. "You might want to keep that dog on the leash."

"I didn't think there was a leash law in this county."

"There isn't. It's for your dog's safety. Lot of cars out by the main road."

"I'll keep that in mind."

"Okay, then." Clayton turned away before pausing once more. "If you don't mind my asking, how long have you been out here?"

"I just walked up. Why?"

Something in the way he answered made Clayton wonder, and he hesitated before reminding himself again that there was no way the guy could know what he'd been up to. "No reason."

"Can I go?"

"Yeah. Okay."

Clayton watched the stranger and his dog start up the logging road before veering onto a small trail that led into the woods. Once he vanished, Clayton went back to his original vantage point to search for the camera. He poked his arm into the bushes, kicked at the pine straw, and retraced his steps a couple of times to make sure he was in the right place. Eventually, he dropped to his knees, panic beginning to settle in. The camera belonged to the sheriff's department. He'd only *borrowed* it for these special outings, and there'd be a lot of questions from his dad if it turned out to be lost. Worse, discovered with a card full of nudie pictures. His dad was a stickler for protocol and responsibility.

By then, a few minutes had passed. In the distance, he heard the throaty roar of an engine fire up. He assumed the coeds were leaving; only briefly did he consider what they might be thinking when they noticed his cruiser was still there. He had other issues on his mind.

The camera was gone.

Not lost. *Gone*. And the damn thing sure as hell didn't walk off on its own. No way the girls had found it, either. Which meant Thigh-bolt had been playing him all along. *Thigh-bolt. Playing. Him.* Unbelievable. He knew the guy had been acting too slick, too *I Know What You Did Last Summer*.

No way was he getting away with that. No grimy, hippie, dog-talking freak was ever going to show up Keith Clayton. Not in this life, anyway.

He pushed through branches heading back to the road, figuring he'd catch up to Logan *Thigh-bolt* and have a little look-see. And that was just for starters. More than that would follow; that much was certain. Guy plays him? That just wasn't done. Not in this town, anyway. He didn't give a damn about the dog, either. Dog gets upset? Bye, bye, doggie. Simple as that. German shepherds were weapons—there wasn't a court in the land where that wouldn't stand up.

First things first, though. Find Thibault. Get the camera. Then figure out the next step.

It was only then, while approaching his cruiser, that he realized both his rear tires were flat.

"What did you say your name was?"

Thibault leaned across the front seat of the Jeep a few minutes later, talking over the roar of the wind. "Logan Thibault." He thumbed over his shoulder. "And this is Zeus."

Zeus was in the back of the Jeep, tongue out, nose lifted to the wind as the Jeep sped toward the highway.

"Beautiful dog. I'm Amy. And this is Jennifer and Lori."

Thibault glanced over his shoulder. "Hi."

"Hey."

They seemed distracted. Not surprising, Thibault thought, considering what they'd been through. "I appreciate the ride."

"No big deal. And you said you're going to Hampton?"

"If it's not too far."

"It's right on the way."

After leaving the logging road and taking care of a couple of things, Thibault had edged back to the road just as the girls were pulling out. He'd held out his thumb, thankful that Zeus was with him, and they'd pulled over almost immediately.

Sometimes things work out just like they're supposed to.

Though he pretended otherwise, he'd actually seen the three of them earlier that morning as they'd come in—he'd camped just over the ridge from the beach—but had given them the privacy they deserved as soon as they'd started to disrobe. To his mind, what they were doing fell into the "no harm, no foul" category; aside from him, they were completely alone out here, and he had no intention of hanging around to stare. Who cared if they took their clothes off or, for that matter, dressed up in chicken costumes? It wasn't any of his business, and he'd intended to keep it that way—until he saw the deputy driving up the road in a Hampton County Sheriff's Department car.

He got a good look at the deputy through the windshield, and there was something *wrong* about the guy's expression. Hard to say what it was, exactly, and he didn't pause to analyze it. He turned around, cutting through the forest, and arrived in time to see the deputy checking the disk in his camera before quietly shutting the door of his cruiser. He watched him slink off toward the ridge. Thibault knew full well that the deputy could have been working officially, but he looked the way Zeus did when he was waiting for a piece of beef jerky. A little too excited about the whole thing.

Thibault had Zeus stay where he was, kept enough distance so the deputy wouldn't hear him, and the rest of the plan had come together spontaneously after that. He knew that direct confrontation was out—the deputy would have claimed he was collecting evidence, and the strength of his word against a stranger's would have been unassailable. Anything physical was out of the question, mostly because it would have caused more problems than it was worth, though he would have loved to go toe-to-toe with the guy. Luckily—or unluckily, he supposed, depending on the perspective—the girl had appeared, the deputy had panicked, and Thibault had seen where the camera had landed. Once the deputy and the girl headed back toward her friends, Thibault retrieved the camera. He could have simply left at that point, but the guy needed to be taught a lesson. Not a big lesson, just a lesson that would keep the girls' honor intact, allow Thibault to be on his way, and ruin the deputy's day. Which was why he'd doubled back to flatten the deputy's tires.

"Oh, that reminds me," Thibault volunteered. "I found your camera in the woods."

"It's not mine. Lori or Jen—did either of you lose a camera?"

Both of them shook their heads.

"Keep it anyway," Thibault said, putting it on the seat, "and thanks for the ride. I've already got one."

"You sure? It's probably expensive."

"Positive."

"Thanks."

Thibault noted the shadows playing on her features, thinking she was attractive in a big-city kind of way, with sharp features, olive skin, and brown eyes flecked with hazel. He could imagine staring at her for hours.

"Hey . . . you doing anything this weekend?" Amy asked. "We're all going out to the beach."

"I appreciate the offer, but I can't."

"I'll bet you're going to see your girlfriend, aren't you."

"What makes you say that?"

"You have that way about you."

He forced himself to turn away. "Something like that."

2

Thibault

It was strange to think of the unexpected twists a man's life could take. Up until a year ago, Thibault would have jumped at the opportunity to spend the weekend with Amy and her friends. It was probably exactly what he needed, but when they dropped him off just outside the Hampton town limits with the August afternoon heat bearing down hard, he waved good-bye, feeling strangely relieved. Maintaining a facade of normalcy had been exhausting.

Since leaving Colorado five months earlier, he hadn't voluntarily spent more than a few hours with anyone, the lone exception being an elderly dairy farmer just south of Little Rock, who let him sleep in an unused upstairs bedroom after a dinner in which the farmer talked as little as he did. He appreciated the fact that the man didn't feel the need to press him about why he'd just appeared the way he had. No questions, no curiosity, no open-ended hints. Just a casual acceptance that Thibault didn't feel like talking. In gratitude, Thibault spent a couple of days helping to repair the roof of the barn before finally returning to the road, backpack loaded, with Zeus trailing behind him.

With the exception of the ride from the girls, he'd walked the entire distance. After dropping the keys to his apartment at the manager's office in mid-March, he'd gone through eight pairs of shoes, pretty much survived on PowerBars and water during long, lonely stretches between towns, and once, in Tennessee, had eaten five tall stacks of pancakes after going nearly three days without food. Along with Zeus, he'd traveled through blizzards, hailstorms, rain, and heat so intense that it made the skin on his arms blister; he'd seen a tornado on the horizon near Tulsa, Oklahoma, and had nearly been struck by lightning twice. He'd taken numerous detours, trying to stay off the main roads, further lengthening the journey, sometimes on a whim. Usually, he walked until he was tired, and toward the end of the day, he'd start searching for a spot to camp, anywhere he thought he and Zeus wouldn't be disturbed. In the mornings, they hit the road before dawn so no one would be the wiser. To this point, no one had bothered them.

He figured he'd been averaging more than twenty miles a day, though he'd never kept specific track of either the time or the distance. That wasn't what the journey was about. He could imagine some people thinking that he was walking to outpace the memories of the world he'd left behind, which had a poetic ring to it; others might want to believe he was walking simply for the sake of the journey itself. But neither was true. He liked to walk and he had someplace to go. Simple as that. He liked going when he wanted, at the pace he wanted, to the place he wanted to be. After four years of following orders in the Marine Corps, the freedom of it appealed to him.

His mother worried about him, but then that's what mothers did. Or his mother, anyway. He called every few days to let her know he was doing okay, and usually, after hanging up, he would think that he wasn't being fair to her. He'd already been gone for much of the past five years, and before each of his three tours in Iraq, he'd listened as she'd lectured into the phone, reminding him not to do anything stupid. He hadn't, but there had been more than a few close calls. Though he'd never told her about them, she read the papers. "And now this," his mother had lamented the night before he'd left. "This whole thing seems crazy to me."

Maybe it was. Maybe it wasn't. He wasn't sure yet.

"What do you think, Zeus?"

The dog looked up at the sound of his name and padded to his side.

"Yeah, I know. You're hungry. What's new?"

Thibault paused in the parking lot of a run-down motel on the edge of town. He reached for the bowl and the last of the dog food. As Zeus began to eat, Thibault took in the view of the town.

Hampton wasn't the worst place he'd ever seen, not by a long shot, but it wasn't the best, either. The town was located on the banks of the South River, about thirty-five miles northwest of Wilmington and the coast, and at first glance, it seemed no different from the thousands of self-sufficient, blue-collar communities long on pride and history that dotted the South. There were a couple of traffic lights dangling on droopy wires that interrupted the traffic flow as it edged toward the bridge that spanned the river, and on either side of the main road were low-slung brick buildings, sandwiched together and stretching for half a mile, with business names stenciled on the front windows advertising places to eat and drink or purchase hardware. A few old magnolias were scattered here and there and made the sidewalks swell beneath their bulging roots. In the distance, he saw an old-fashioned barber pole, along with the requisite older men sitting on the bench out in front of it. He smiled. It was quaint, like a fantasy of the 1950s.

On closer inspection, though, he sensed that first impressions were deceiving. Despite the waterfront location—or maybe because of it, he surmised—he noted the decay near the rooflines, in the crumbling bricks near the foundations, in the faded brackish stains a couple of feet higher than the foundations, which indicated serious flooding in the past. None of the shops were boarded up yet, but observing the dearth of cars parked in front of the businesses, he wondered how long they could hold out. Small-town commercial districts were going the way of the dinosaurs, and if this place was like most of the other towns he'd passed through, he figured there was probably another, newer area for businesses, one most likely anchored by a Wal-Mart or a Piggly Wiggly, that would spell the end for this part of town.

Strange, though. Being here. He wasn't sure what he'd imagined Hampton to be, but it wasn't this.

No matter. As Zeus was finishing his food, he wondered how long it would take to find her. The woman in the photograph. The woman he'd come to meet.

But he would find her. That much was certain. He hoisted his backpack. "You ready?"

Zeus tilted his head.

"Let's get a room. I want to eat and shower. And you need a bath."

Thibault took a couple of steps before realizing Zeus hadn't moved. He glanced over his shoulder.

"Don't give me that look. You definitely need a bath. You smell."

Zeus still didn't move.

"Fine. Do what you want. I'm going."

He headed toward the manager's office to check in, knowing that Zeus would follow. In the end, Zeus always followed.

Until he'd found the photograph, Thibault's life had proceeded as he'd long intended. He'd always had a plan. He'd wanted to do well in school and had; he'd wanted to participate in a variety of sports and had grown up playing pretty much everything. He'd wanted to learn to play the piano and the violin, and he'd become proficient enough to write his own music. After college at the University of Colorado, he'd planned to join the Marine Corps, and the recruiter had been thrilled that he'd chosen to enlist instead of becoming an officer. Shocked, but thrilled. Most graduates had little desire to become a grunt, but that was exactly what he'd wanted.

The bombing of the World Trade Center had little to do with his decision. Instead, joining the military seemed the natural thing to do, since his dad had served with the marines for twenty-five years. His dad had gone in as a private and finished as one of those grizzled, steel-jawed sergeants who intimidated pretty much everyone except his wife and the platoons he commanded. He treated those young men like his sons; his sole intent, he used to tell them, was to bring them back home to their mothers alive and well and all grown up. His dad must have attended more than fifty weddings over the years of guys he'd led who couldn't imagine getting married without having his blessing. Good marine, too. He'd picked up a Bronze Star and two Purple Hearts in Vietnam and over the years had served in Grenada, Panama, Bosnia, and the First Gulf War. His dad was a marine who didn't mind transfers, and Thibault had spent the majority of his youth moving from place to place, living on bases around the world. In some ways, Okinawa seemed more like home than Colorado, and though his Japanese was a bit rusty, he figured a week spent in Tokyo would rekindle the fluency he'd once known. Like his dad, he figured he'd end up retiring from the corps, but unlike his dad, he intended to live long enough afterward to enjoy it. His dad had died of a heart attack only two years after he'd slipped his dress blues onto the hanger for the last time, a massive infarction that came out of the blue. One minute he was shoveling snow from the driveway, and the next minute he was gone. That was thirteen years ago. Thibault had been fifteen years old at the time.

That day and the funeral that followed were the most vivid memories of his life prior to joining the marines. Being raised as a military brat has a way of making things blur together, simply because of how often you have to move. Friends come and go, clothing is packed and unpacked, households are continually purged of unnecessary items, and as a result, not much sticks. It's hard at times, but it makes a kid strong in ways that most people can't understand. Teaches them that even though people are left behind, new ones will inevitably take their place; that every place has something good—and bad—to offer. It makes a kid grow up fast.

Even his college years were hazy, but that chapter of his life had its own routines. Studying during the week, enjoying the weekends, cramming for finals, crappy dorm food, and two girlfriends, one of whom lasted a little more than a year. Everyone who ever went to college had the same stories to tell, few of which had lasting impact. In the end, only his education remained. In truth, he felt like his life hadn't really started until he'd arrived on Parris Island for basic training. As soon as he'd hopped off the bus, the drill sergeant started shouting in his ear. There's nothing like a drill sergeant to make a person believe that nothing in his life had really mattered to that point. You were theirs now, and that was that. Good at sports? *Give me fifty push-ups, Mr. Point Guard.* College educated? *Assemble this rifle, Einstein.* Father was in the marines? *Clean the crapper like your old man once did.* Same old clichés. Run, march, stand at attention, crawl through the mud, scale that wall: There was nothing in basic training he hadn't expected.

He had to admit that the drill mostly worked. It broke people down, beat them down even further, and eventually molded them into marines. Or that's what they said, anyway. He didn't break down. He went through the motions, kept his head low, did as he was ordered, and remained the same man he'd been before. He became a marine anyway.

He ended up with the First Battalion, Fifth Marines, based out of Camp Pendleton. San Diego was his kind of town, with great weather, gorgeous beaches, and even more beautiful women. But it was not to last. In January 2003, right after he turned twenty-three, he deployed to Kuwait as part of Operation Iraqi Freedom. Camp Doha, in an industrial part of Kuwait City, had been in use

since the First Gulf War and was pretty much a town unto itself.
There was a gym and a computer center, a PX, places to eat, and
tents spread as far as the horizon. Busy place made much busier
by the impending invasion, and things were chaotic from the
start. His days were an unbroken sequence of hours-long meetings, backbreaking drills, and rehearsals of ever changing attack
plans. He must have practiced donning his chemical war protection suit a hundred times. There were endless rumors, too. The
worst part was trying to figure out which one might be true. Everyone knew of someone who knew someone who'd heard the *real
story*. One day they were going in imminently; next day they'd
hear that they were holding off. First, they were coming in from
the north and south; then just from the south, and maybe not
even that. They heard the enemy had chemical weapons and
intended to use them; next day they heard they wouldn't use
them because they believed that the United States would respond
with nukes. There were whispers that the Iraqi Republican Guard
intended to make a suicide stand just over the border; others
swore they intended to make the stand near Baghdad. Still others
said the suicide stand would happen near the oil fields. In short,
no one knew anything, which only fueled the imaginations of the
150,000 troops who'd assembled in Kuwait.

For the most part, soldiers are kids. People forget that sometimes. Eighteen, nineteen, twenty—half of the servicemen weren't
old enough even to buy a beer. They were confident and well
trained and excited to go, but it was impossible to ignore the reality of what was coming. Some of them were going to die. Some
talked openly about it, others wrote letters to their families and
handed them to the chaplain. Tempers were short. Some had
trouble sleeping; others slept almost all the time. Thibault observed
it all with a strange sense of detachment. *Welcome to war*, he could
hear his father saying. *It's always a SNAFU: situation normal, all
f—ed up*.

Thibault wasn't completely immune to the escalating tension, and like everyone else, he'd needed an outlet. It was impossible not to have one. He started playing poker. His dad had taught him to play, and he knew the game . . . or thought he knew. He quickly found out that others knew more. In the first three weeks, he proceeded to lose pretty much every dime he'd saved since joining up, bluffing when he should have folded, folding when he should have stayed in the game. It wasn't much money to begin with, and it wasn't as if he had many places to spend it even if he'd kept it, but it put him in a foul mood for days. He hated to lose.

The only antidote was to go for long runs first thing in the morning, before the sun came up. It was usually frigid; though he'd been in the Middle East for a month, it continually amazed him how cold the desert could be. He ran hard beneath a sky crowded with stars, his breaths coming out in little puffs.

Toward the end of one of his runs, when he could see his tent in the distance, he began to slow. By then, the sun had begun to crest the horizon, spreading gold across the arid landscape. With his hands on his hips, he continued to catch his breath, and it was then, from the corner of his eye, that he spotted the dull gleam of a photograph, half-buried in the dirt. He stopped to pick it up and noticed that it had been cheaply but neatly laminated, probably to protect it from the elements. He brushed off the dust, clearing the image, and that was the first time he saw her.

The blonde with the smile and the jade-colored mischievous eyes, wearing jeans and a T-shirt emblazoned with the words LUCKY LADY across the front. Behind her was a banner showing the words HAMPTON FAIRGROUNDS. A German shepherd, gray in the muzzle, stood by her side. In the crowd behind her were two young men, clustered near the ticket stand and a bit out of focus, wearing T-shirts with logos. Three evergreen trees rose in the distance, pointy ones that could grow almost anywhere. On the back of the photo were the handwritten words, *"Keep Safe! E."*

Not that he'd noticed any of those things right away. His first instinct, in fact, had been to toss the picture aside. He almost had, but just as he was about to do so, it occurred to him that whoever had lost it might want it back. It obviously meant something to someone.

When he returned to camp, he tacked the photo to a message board near the entrance to the computer center, figuring that pretty much every inhabitant of the camp made his way there at one point or another. No doubt someone would claim it.

A week went by, then ten days. The photo was never retrieved. By that point, his platoon was drilling for hours every day, and the poker games had become serious. Some men had lost thousands of dollars; one lance corporal was said to have lost close to ten thousand. Thibault, who hadn't played since his initial humiliating attempt, preferred to spend his free time brooding on the upcoming invasion and wondering how he'd react to being fired upon. When he wandered over to the computer center three days before the invasion, he saw the photo still tacked to the message board, and for a reason he still didn't quite understand, he took down the photo and put it in his pocket.

Victor, his best friend in the squad—they'd been together since basic training—talked him into joining the poker game that night, despite Thibault's reservations. Still low on funds, Thibault started conservatively and didn't think he'd be in the game for more than half an hour. He folded in the first three games, then drew a straight in the fourth game and a full house in the sixth. The cards kept falling his way—flushes, straights, full houses—and by the halfway point in the evening, he'd recouped his earlier losses. The original players had left by then, replaced by others. Thibault stayed. In turn, they were replaced. Thibault stayed. His winning streak persisted, and by dawn, he'd won more than he'd earned in his first six months in the marines.

It was only when he was leaving the game with Victor that he realized he'd had the photograph in his pocket the entire time. When they were back at their tent, he showed the photo to Victor and pointed out the words on the woman's shirt. Victor, whose parents were illegal immigrants living near Bakersfield, California, was not only religious, but believed in portents of all kinds. Lightning storms, forked roads, and black cats were favorites, and before they'd shipped out, he'd told Thibault about an uncle who supposedly possessed the evil eye: "When he looks at you a certain way, it's only a matter of time before you die." Victor's conviction made Thibault feel like he was ten years old again, listening raptly as Victor told the story with a flashlight propped beneath his chin. He said nothing at the time. Everyone had their quirks. Guy wanted to believe in omens? Fine with him. More important was the fact that Victor was a good enough shot to have been recruited as a sniper and that Thibault trusted him with his life.

Victor stared at the picture before handing it back. "You said you found this at dawn?"

"Yeah."

"Dawn is a powerful time of the day."

"So you've told me."

"It's a sign," he said. "She's your good-luck charm. See the shirt she is wearing?"

"She was tonight."

"Not just tonight. You found that picture for a reason. No one claimed it for a reason. You took it today for a reason. Only you were meant to have it."

Thibault wanted to say something about the guy who'd lost it and how he'd feel about that, but he kept quiet. Instead, he lay back on the cot and clasped his hands behind his head.

Victor mirrored the movement. "I'm happy for you. Luck will be on your side from now on," he added.

"I hope so."

"But you can't ever lose the picture."

"No?"

"If you do, then the charm works in reverse."

"Which means what?"

"It means you'll be unlucky. And in war, unlucky is the last thing you want to be."

The motel room was as ugly on the inside as it had been from the outside: wood paneling, light fixtures attached to the ceiling with chains, shag carpet, television bolted to the stand. It seemed to have been decorated around 1975 and never updated, and it reminded Thibault of the places his dad had made them stay in when they took their family vacations through the Southwest, when Thibault was a kid. They'd stayed overnight in places just off the highway, and as long as they were relatively clean, his dad had deemed them fine. His mom less so, but what could she do? It wasn't as if there had been a Four Seasons across the street, and even if there had been, there was no way they could ever have afforded it.

Thibault went through the same routine his dad had when entering a motel room: He pulled back the comforter to make sure the sheets were fresh, he checked the shower curtain for mold, he looked for hairs in the sink. Despite the expected rust stains, a leaky faucet, and cigarette burns, the place was cleaner than he'd imagined it might be. Inexpensive, too. Thibault had paid cash for a week in advance, no questions asked, no extra charge for the dog. All in all, a bargain. Good thing. Thibault had no credit cards, no debit cards, no ATM cards, no official mailing address, no cell phone. He carried pretty much everything he owned. He did have a bank account, one that would wire him money as needed. It was registered under a corporate name, not his own. He wasn't rich. He wasn't even middle-class. The corporation did no business. He just liked his privacy.

He led Zeus to the tub and washed him, using the shampoo in his backpack. Afterward, he showered and dressed in the last of his clean clothes. Sitting on the bed, he thumbed through the phone book, searching for something in particular, without luck. He made a note to do laundry when he had time, then decided to get a bite to eat at the small restaurant he'd seen just down the street.

When he got there, they wouldn't let Zeus inside, which wasn't surprising. Zeus lay down outside the front door and went to sleep. Thibault had a cheeseburger and fries, washed it down with a chocolate milk shake, then ordered a cheeseburger to go for Zeus. Back outside, he watched as Zeus gobbled it down in less than twenty seconds and then looked up at Thibault again.

"Glad you really savored that. Come on."

Thibault bought a map of the town at a convenience store and sat on a bench near the town square—one of those old-fashioned parks bordered on all four sides by business-lined streets. Featuring large shady trees, a play area for the kids, and lots of flowers, it didn't seem crowded: A few mothers were clustered together, while children zipped down the slide or glided back and forth on the swings. He examined the faces of the women, making sure she wasn't among them, then turned away and opened the map before they grew nervous at his presence. Mothers with young kids always got nervous when they saw single men lingering in the area, doing nothing purposeful. He didn't blame them. Too many perverts out there.

Studying the map, he oriented himself and tried to figure out his next move. He had no illusions that it was going to be easy. He didn't know much, after all. All he had was a photograph—no name or address. No employment history. No phone number. No date. Nothing but a face in the crowd.

But there were some clues. He'd studied the details of the photo, as he had so many times before, and started with what he *knew*. The photograph had been taken in Hampton. The woman appeared to be in her early twenties when the photo was taken. She was attractive. She either owned a German shepherd or knew someone who did. Her first name started with the letter *E*. Emma, Elaine, Elise, Eileen, Ellen, Emily, Erin, Erica . . . they seemed the most likely, though in the South, he supposed there could be names like Erdine or Elspeth, too. She went to the fair with someone who was later posted to Iraq. She had given this person the photograph, and Thibault had found the photograph in February 2003, which meant it had to have been taken before then. The woman, then, was most likely now in her late twenties. There was a series of three evergreen trees in the distance. These things he knew. *Facts*.

Then, there were assumptions, beginning with Hampton. Hampton was a relatively common name. A quick Internet search turned up a lot of them. Counties and towns: South Carolina, Virginia, New Hampshire, Iowa, Nebraska. Georgia. Others, too. Lots of others. And, of course, a Hampton in Hampton County, North Carolina.

Though there'd been no obvious landmarks in the background— no picture of Monticello indicating Virginia, for instance, no WELCOME TO IOWA! sign in the distance—there had been information. Not about the woman, but gleaned from the young men in the background, standing in line for tickets. Two of them had been wearing shirts with logos. One—an image of Homer Simpson— didn't help. The other, with the word DAVIDSON written across the front, meant nothing at first, even when Thibault thought about it. He'd originally assumed the shirt was an abbreviated reference to Harley-Davidson, the motorcycle. Another Google search cleared that up. Davidson, he'd learned, was also the name of a reputable college located near Charlotte, North Carolina. Selective, challenging, with an emphasis on liberal arts. A review of their bookstore catalog showed a sample of the same shirt.

The shirt, he realized, was no guarantee that the photo had been taken in North Carolina. Maybe someone who'd gone to the college gave the guy the shirt; maybe he was an out-of-state student, maybe he just liked the colors, maybe he was an alum and had moved someplace new. But with nothing else to go on, Thibault had made a quick phone call to the Hampton Chamber of Commerce before he'd left Colorado and verified that they had a county fair every summer. Another good sign. He had a destination, but it wasn't yet a fact. He just *assumed* this was the right place. Still, for a reason he couldn't explain, this place felt right.

There were other assumptions, too, but he'd get to those later. The first thing he had to do was find the fairgrounds. Hopefully, the county fair had been held in the same location for years; he hoped the person who could point him in the right direction could answer that question as well. Best place to find someone like that was at one of the businesses around here. Not a souvenir or antiques shop—those were often owned by newcomers to town, people escaping from the North in search of a quieter life in warmer weather. Instead, he thought his best bet would be someplace like a local hardware store. Or a bar. Or a real estate office. He figured he'd know the place when he saw it.

He wanted to see the exact place the photograph had been taken. Not to get a better feel for who the woman was. The fairgrounds wouldn't help with that at all.

He wanted to know if there were three tall evergreen trees clustered together, pointy ones that could grow almost anywhere.

3

Beth

Beth set aside her can of Diet Coke, glad that Ben was having a good time at his friend Zach's birthday party. She was just wishing that he didn't have to go to his father's when Melody came by and sat in the chair beside her.

"Good idea, huh? The water guns are a big hit." Melody smiled, her bleached teeth a bit too white, her skin a shade too dark, as though she'd just come back from a trip to the tanning salon. Which she probably had. Melody had been vain about her appearance since high school, and lately it seemed to have become even more of an obsession.

"Let's just hope they don't turn those Super Soakers on us."

"They better not." Melody frowned. "I told Zach that if he did, I'd send everyone home." She leaned back, making herself more comfortable. "What have you been doing with yourself this summer? I haven't seen you around, and you haven't returned my calls."

"I know. I'm sorry about that. I've been a hermit this summer. It's just been hard trying to keep up with Nana and the kennel and all the training. I have no idea how Nana kept it up for so long."

"Nana's doing okay these days?"

Nana was Beth's grandmother. She'd raised Beth since the age of three, after Beth's parents died in a car accident. She nodded. "She's getting better, but the stroke took a lot out of her. Her left side is still really weak. She can manage some of the training, but running the kennel and training is beyond her. And you know how hard she pushes herself. I'm always worried she might be overdoing it."

"I noticed she was back in the choir this week."

Nana had been in the First Baptist Church choir for over thirty years, and Beth knew it was one of her passions. "Last week was her first week back, but I'm not sure how much singing she actually did. Afterward, she took a two-hour nap."

Melody nodded. "What's going to happen when school starts up?"

"I don't know."

"You are going to teach, aren't you?"

"I hope so."

"You hope? Don't you have teacher meetings next week?"

Beth didn't want to think about it, let alone discuss it, but she knew Melody meant well. "Yeah, but that doesn't mean I'll be there. I know it would leave the school in a bind, but it's not as if I can leave Nana alone all day. Not yet, anyway. And who would help her run the kennel? There's no way she could train the dogs all day."

"Can't you hire someone?" Melody suggested.

"I've been trying. Did I tell you what happened earlier in the summer? I hired a guy who showed up twice, then quit as soon as the weekend rolled around. Same thing with the next guy I hired. After that, no one's even bothered to come by. The 'Help Wanted' sign has become a permanent fixture in the window."

"David's always complaining about the lack of good employees."

"Tell him to offer minimum wage. Then he'd really complain. Even high school kids don't want to clean the cages anymore. They say it's gross."

"It *is* gross."

Beth laughed. "Yeah, it is," she admitted. "But I'm out of time. I doubt if anything will change before next week, and if it doesn't, there are worse things. I do enjoy training the dogs. Half the time they're easier than students."

"Like mine?"

"Yours was easy. Trust me."

Melody motioned toward Ben. "He's grown since the last time I saw him."

"Almost an inch," she said, thinking it was nice of Melody to notice. Ben had always been small for his age, the kid always positioned on the left side, front row, of the class picture, half a head shorter than the child seated next to him. Zach, Melody's son, was just the opposite: right-hand side, in the back, always the tallest in class.

"I heard a rumor that Ben isn't playing soccer this fall," Melody commented.

"He wants to try something different."

"Like what?"

"He wants to learn to play the violin. He's going to take lessons with Mrs. Hastings."

"She's still teaching? She must be at least ninety."

"But she's got patience to teach a beginner. Or at least that's what she told me. And Ben likes her a lot. That's the main thing."

"Good for him," Melody said. "I'll bet he'll be great at it. But Zach's going to be bummed."

"They wouldn't be on the same team. Zach is going to play for the select team, right?"

"If he makes it."

"He will."

And he would. Zach was one of those naturally confident, competitive kids who matured early and ran rings around other, less talented players on the field. Like Ben. Even now, running

around the yard with his Super Soaker, Ben couldn't keep up with
him. Though good-hearted and sweet, Ben wasn't much of an
athlete, a fact that endlessly infuriated her ex-husband. Last year,
her ex had stood on the sidelines of soccer games with a scowl on
his face, which was another reason Ben didn't want to play.

"Is David going to help coach again?"

David was Melody's husband and one of two pediatricians in
town. "He hasn't decided yet. Since Hoskins left, he's been on
call a lot more. He hates it, but what can he do? They've been
trying to recruit another doctor, but it's been hard. Not everyone
wants to work in a small town, especially with the nearest hospi-
tal in Wilmington forty-five minutes away. Makes for much longer days. Half the time he doesn't get home until almost eight.
Sometimes it's even later than that."

Beth heard the worry in Melody's voice, and she figured her
friend was thinking about the affair David had confessed to last
winter. Beth knew enough not to comment on it. She'd decided
when she'd first heard the whispers that they would talk about it
only if Melody wanted to. And if not? That was fine, too. It was
none of her business.

"How about you, though? Have you been seeing anyone?"

Beth grimaced. "No. Not since Adam."

"Whatever happened with that?"

"I have no idea."

Melody shook her head. "I can't say that I envy you. I never
liked dating."

"Yeah, but at least you were good at it. I'm terrible."

"You're exaggerating."

"I'm not. But it's not that big of a deal. I'm not sure I even have
the energy for it anymore. Wearing thongs, shaving my legs, flirt-
ing, pretending to get along with his friends. The whole thing
seems like a lot of effort."

Melody wrinkled her nose. "You don't shave your legs?"

"Of course I shave my legs," she said. Then, lowering her voice,

"Most of the time, anyway." She sat up straighter. "But you get the point. Dating is hard. Especially for someone my age."

"Oh, please. You're not even thirty, and you're a knockout."

Beth had heard that for as long as she could remember, and she wasn't immune to the fact that men—even married men—often craned their necks when she walked past them. In her first three years teaching, she'd had only one parent-teacher conference with a father who came alone. In every other instance, it was the mother who attended the conference. She remembered wondering aloud about it to Nana a few years back, and Nana had said, "They don't want you alone with the hubbies because you're as pretty as a tickled pumpkin."

Nana always had a unique way of putting things.

"You forget where we live," Beth offered. "There aren't a lot of single men my age. And if they are single, there's a reason."

"That's not true."

"Maybe in a city. But around here? In this town? Trust me. I've lived here all my life, and even when I was in college, I commuted from home. On the rare occasions that I have been asked out, we'll go on two or three dates and then they stop calling. Don't ask me why." She waved a hand philosophically. "But it's no big deal. I've got Ben and Nana. It's not like I'm living alone, surrounded by dozens of cats."

"No. You've got dogs."

"Not my dogs. Other people's dogs. There's a difference."

"Oh yeah," Melody snorted. "Big difference."

Across the yard, Ben was trailing behind the group with his Super Soaker, doing his best to keep up, when he suddenly slipped and fell. His glasses tumbled off into the grass. Beth knew enough not to get up and see if he was okay: The last time she'd tried to help, he'd been visibly embarrassed. He felt around until he found his glasses and was up and running again.

"They grow up so fast, don't they?" said Melody, interrupting Beth's thoughts. "I know it's a cliché, but it's true. I remember my mom telling me they would and thinking she didn't know what she was talking about. I couldn't wait for Zach to get a little older. Of course, at the time, he had colic and I hadn't slept more than a couple of hours a night in over a month. But now, just like that, they'll be starting middle school already."

"Not yet. They've got another year."

"I know. But it still makes me nervous."

"Why?"

"You know . . . it's a hard age. Kids are in that stage where they're beginning to understand the world of adults, without having the maturity of adults to deal with everything going on around them. Add to that all the temptations, and the fact that they stop listening to you the way they once did, and the moods of adolescence, and I'll be the first to admit that I'm not looking forward to it. You're a teacher. You know."

"That's why I teach second grade."

"Good choice." Melody grew quiet. "Did you hear about Elliot Spencer?"

"I haven't heard much of anything. I've been a hermit, remember?"

"He was caught selling drugs."

"He's only a couple of years older than Ben!"

"And still in middle school."

"Now you're making me nervous."

Melody rolled her eyes. "Don't be. If my son were more like Ben, I wouldn't have reason to be nervous. Ben has an old soul. He's always polite, he's always kind, always the first to help the younger kids. He's empathetic. I, on the other hand, have Zach."

"Zach's a great kid, too."

"I know he is. But he's always been more difficult than Ben. And he's more of a follower than Ben."

"Have you seen them playing? From where I'm sitting, Ben's been doing all the following."

"You know what I mean."

Actually, she did. Even from a young age, Ben had been content to forge his own path. Which was nice, she had to admit, since it had been a pretty good path. Though he didn't have many friends, he had a lot of interests he pursued on his own. Good ones, too. He had little interest in video games or surfing the Web, and while he occasionally watched television, he'd usually turn it off on his own after thirty minutes or so. Instead, he read or played chess (a game that he seemed to understand on some intuitive level) on the electronic game board he'd received for Christmas. He loved to read and write, and though he enjoyed the dogs at the kennel, most of them were anxious because of the long hours they spent in a kennel and tended to ignore him. He spent many afternoons throwing tennis balls that few, if any, ever retrieved.

"It'll be fine."

"I hope so." Melody set aside her drink. "I suppose I should go get the cake, huh? Zach has practice at five."

"It'll be hot."

Melody stood. "I'm sure he'll want to bring the Super Soaker. Probably squirt the coach."

"Do you need some help?"

"No thanks. Just sit here and relax. I'll be right back."

Beth watched Melody walk away, realizing for the first time how thin she'd become. Ten, maybe fifteen pounds lighter than she'd been the last time Beth had seen her. Had to be stress, she thought. David's affair had crushed her, but unlike Beth when it had happened to her, Melody was determined to save her marriage. Then again, they'd had different sorts of marriages. David made a big mistake and it hurt Melody, but overall, they'd always struck Beth as a happy couple. Beth's marriage, on the other hand, had been a fiasco from the beginning. Just as Nana had predicted. Nana had the ability to size people up in an instant, and she had this way of shrugging when she didn't like someone. When Beth announced she was pregnant and that instead of going to college, she and her ex planned to get married, Nana began shrugging so much that it resembled a nervous tic. Beth, of course, ignored it at the time, thinking, *She hasn't given him a chance. She doesn't really know him. We can make this work.* Nosiree. Never happened. Nana was always polite, always cordial when he was around, but the shrugging didn't stop until Beth moved back home ten years ago. The marriage had lasted less than nine months; Ben was five weeks old. Nana had been right about him all along.

Melody vanished inside the house, only to reemerge a few minutes later, David right behind her. He was carrying paper plates and forks, obviously preoccupied. She could see the tufts of gray hair near his ears and deep lines in his forehead. The last time she'd seen him, the lines hadn't been as evident, and she figured it was another sign of the stress he was under.

Sometimes, Beth wondered what her life would be like if she were married. Not to her ex, of course. That thought made her shudder. Dealing with him every other weekend was more than enough, thank you very much. But to someone else. Someone . . . better. It seemed like it might be a good idea, at least in the abstract, anyway. After ten years, she was used to her life, and though it might be nice to have someone to share her evenings with after work or get a back rub from now and then, there was also something nice about spending all day Saturday in her pajamas if she wanted to. Which she sometimes did. Ben, too. They called them "lazy days." They were the best days ever. Sometimes they'd cap off a day of doing absolutely nothing by ordering pizza and watching a movie. Heavenly.

Besides, if relationships were hard, marriage was even harder. It wasn't just Melody and David who struggled; it seemed like most couples struggled. It went with the territory. What did Nana always say? *Stick two different people with two different sets of expectations under one roof and it ain't always going to be shrimp and grits on Easter.*

Exactly. Even if she wasn't completely sure where Nana came up with her metaphors.

Glancing at her watch, she knew that as soon as the party ended, she'd have to head back to check in on Nana. No doubt she'd find her in the kennel, either behind the desk or checking on the dogs. Nana was stubborn like that. Did it matter that her left leg could barely support her? *My leg ain't perfect, but it's not beeswax, either.* Or that she might fall and get hurt? *I'm not a bucket of fine china.* Or that her left arm was basically useless? *As long as I can eat soup, I don't need it anyway.*

She was one of a kind, bless her heart. Always had been.

"Hey, Mom?"

Lost in thought, she hadn't seen Ben approaching. His freckled face was shiny with sweat. Water dripped from his clothes, and there were grass stains on his shirt she was certain would never come out.

"Yeah, baby?"

"Can I spend the night at Zach's tonight?"

"I thought he had soccer practice."

"After practice. There's going to be a bunch of people staying over, and his mom got him Guitar Hero for his birthday."

She knew the real reason he was asking.

"Not tonight. You can't. Your dad's coming to pick you up at five."

"Can you call him and ask?"

"I can try. But you know . . ."

Ben nodded, and as it usually did when this happened, her heart broke just a little. "Yeah, I know."

The sun glared through the windshield at baking temperature, and she found herself wishing she'd had the car's air conditioner fixed. With the window rolled down, her hair whipped in her face, making it sting. She reminded herself again to get a real haircut. She imagined saying to her hairdresser, *Chop it all off,*

Terri. Make me look like a man! But she knew she'd end up asking for her regular trim when the time came. In some things, she was a coward.

"You guys looked like you were having fun."

"I was."

"That's all you can say?"

"I'm just tired, Mom."

She pointed toward the Dairy Queen in the distance. "You want to swing by and get some ice cream?"

"It's not good for me."

"Hey, I'm the mother here. That's what I'm supposed to say. I was just thinking that if you're hot, you might want some."

"I'm not hungry. I just had cake."

"All right. Suit yourself. But don't blame me if you get home and realize you should have jumped at the opportunity."

"I won't." He turned toward the window.

"Hey, champ. You okay?"

When he spoke, his voice was almost inaudible over the wind. "Why do I have to go to Dad's? It's not like we're going to do anything fun. He sends me to bed at nine o'clock, like I'm still in second grade or something. I'm never even tired. And tomorrow, he'll have me do chores all day."

"I thought he was taking you to your grandfather's house for brunch after church."

"I still don't want to go."

I don't want you to go, either, she thought. But what could she do?

"Why don't you bring a book?" she suggested. "You can read in your room tonight, and if you get bored tomorrow, you can read there, too."

"You always say that."

Because I don't know what else to tell you, she thought. "You want to go to the bookstore?"

"No," he said. But she could tell he didn't mean it.

"Well, come with me anyway. I want to get a book for myself."

"Okay."

"I'm sorry about this, you know."

"Yeah. I know."

Going to the bookstore did little to lift Ben's mood. Though he'd ended up picking out a couple of Hardy Boys mysteries, she'd recognized his slouch as they'd stood in line to pay for them. On the ride home, he opened one of the books and pretended to be reading. Beth was pretty sure he'd done it to keep her from peppering him with questions or trying, with forced cheerfulness, to make him feel better about his overnight at his dad's. At ten, Ben was already remarkably adept at predicting her behavior.

She hated the fact that he didn't like going to his dad's. She watched him walk inside their house, knowing that he was heading to his room to pack his things. Instead of following him, she took a seat on the porch steps and wished for the thousandth time she'd put up a swing. It was still hot, and from the whimpering coming from the kennel across the yard, it was clear that the dogs, too, were suffering from the heat. She strained for the sound of Nana inside. Had she been in the kitchen when Ben walked through, she definitely would have heard her. Nana was a walking cacophony. Not because of the stroke, but because it went part and parcel with her personality. Seventy-six going on seventeen, she laughed loud, banged pans with the spoon when she cooked, adored baseball, and turned the radio up to ear-shattering levels whenever NPR featured the Big Band era. "Music like that doesn't just grow like bananas, you know." Until the stroke, she'd worn rubber boots, overalls, and an oversize straw hat nearly every day, tromping through the yard as she taught dogs to heel or come or stay.

Years ago, along with her husband, Nana had taught them to do pretty much everything. Together, they'd bred and trained hunting dogs, service dogs for the blind, drug-sniffing dogs for the police, security dogs for home protection. Now that he was gone, she did those things only occasionally. Not because she didn't know what to do; she'd always handled most of the training anyway. But to train a dog for home protection took fourteen months, and given the fact that Nana could fall in love with a squirrel in less than three seconds, it always broke her heart to have to give up the dog when the training was completed. Without Grandpa around to say, "We've already sold him, so we don't have a choice," Nana had found it easier to simply fold that part of the business.

Instead, these days Nana ran a thriving obedience school. People would drop off their dogs for a couple of weeks—doggie boot camp, she called it—and Nana would teach them how to sit, lie down, stay, come, and heel. They were simple, uncomplicated commands that nearly every dog could master quickly. Usually, somewhere between fifteen and twenty-five dogs cycled through every two weeks, and each one needed roughly twenty minutes of training per day. Any more than that, and the dogs would lose interest. It wasn't so bad when there were fifteen, but boarding twenty-five made for long days, considering each dog also needed to be walked. And that didn't factor in all the feeding, kennel maintenance, phone calls, dealing with clients, and paperwork. For most of the summer, Beth had been working twelve or thirteen hours a day.

They were always busy. It wasn't difficult to train a dog—Beth had been helping Nana on and off since she was twelve—and there were dozens of books on the subject. In addition, the veterinary clinic offered lessons for dogs and their owners every Saturday morning for a fraction of the price. Beth knew that most people could spare twenty minutes a day for a couple of weeks to train their dog. But they didn't. Instead, people came from as far away as Florida and Tennessee to drop off their dogs to have someone else do it. Granted, Nana had a great reputation as a trainer, but she was really only teaching dogs to sit and come, heel and stay. It wasn't rocket science. Yet people were always extremely grateful. And always, always, *amazed.*

Beth checked her watch. Keith—her ex—would be here soon. Though she had issues with the man—Lord knows she had serious issues—he had joint custody, simple as that, and she'd tried to make the best of it. She liked to tell herself that it was important for Ben to spend time with his dad. Boys needed to spend time with their dads, especially those coming up on their teenage years, and she had to admit that he wasn't a *bad* guy. Immature, yes, but not *bad*. He had a few beers now and then but wasn't an alcoholic; he didn't take drugs; he had never been abusive to either of them. He went to church every Sunday. He had a steady job and paid his child support on time. Or, rather, his family did. The money came from a trust, one of many that the family had established over the years. And for the most part, he kept his neverending string of girlfriends away on those weekends he spent with his son. Key words: "for the most part." Lately, he'd been better about that, but she was fairly sure it had less to do with a renewed commitment to parenting than the likelihood that he was between girlfriends right now. She wouldn't really have minded so much, except for the fact that his girlfriends were usually closer in age to Ben than they were to him and, as a general rule, had the IQs of salad bowls. She wasn't being spiteful; even Ben realized it. A couple of months back, Ben had to help one of them make a second batch of Kraft macaroni and cheese after the first attempt burned. The whole "add milk, butter, mix, and stir" sequence was apparently beyond her.

That wasn't what bothered Ben the most, however. The girlfriends were okay—they tended to treat him more like a younger brother than a son. Nor was he truly upset about the chores. He might have to rake the yard or clean the kitchen and take out the trash, but it wasn't as if her ex treated Ben like an indentured servant. And chores were good for him; Ben had weekend chores when he was with her, too. No, the problem was Keith's childish, relentless disappointment in Ben. Keith wanted an athlete; instead he got a son who wanted to play the violin. He wanted someone to hunt with; he got a son who would rather read. He wanted a son who could play catch or shoot baskets; he was saddled with a clumsy son with poor vision.

He never said as much to Ben or to her, but he didn't have to. It was all too apparent in the scornful way he watched Ben play soccer, in the way he refused to give Ben credit when he won his last chess tournament, in the way he continually pushed Ben to be someone he wasn't. It drove Beth crazy and broke her heart at the same time, but for Ben, it was worse. For years, he'd tried to please his dad, but over time, it had just exhausted the poor kid. Take learning to play catch. No harm in that, right? Ben might learn to enjoy it, he might even want to play Little League. Made perfect sense when her ex had suggested it, and Ben was gung ho in the beginning. But after a while, Ben came to hate the thought of it. If he caught three in a row, his dad would want him to try to catch four. When he did that, it had to be five. When he got even better, his dad wanted him to catch all of them. And then catch while he was running forward. Catch while he was running backward. Catch while he was sliding. Catch while he was diving. Catch the one his dad threw as hard as he could. And if he dropped one? You'd think the world was coming to an end. His dad wasn't the kind of guy who'd say, *Nice try, champ!* or, *Good effort!* No, he was the kind of guy who'd scream, *C'mon! Quit screwing up!*

Oh, she'd talked to him about it. Talked to him ad nauseam. It went in one ear and out the other, of course. Same old story. Despite—or perhaps because of—his immaturity, Keith was stubborn and opinionated about many things, and raising Ben was one of them. He wanted a certain kind of son, and by God, he was going to get him. Ben, predictably, began reacting in his own passive-aggressive way. He began to drop everything his dad threw, even simple lobs, while ignoring his father's growing frustration, until his father finally slammed his glove to the ground and stormed inside to sulk the rest of the afternoon. Ben pretended not to notice, taking a seat beneath a loblolly pine to read until she picked him up a few hours later.

She and her ex didn't battle just about Ben; they were fire and ice as well. As in, he was fire and she was ice. He was still attracted to her, which irritated her no end. Why on earth he could believe that she'd want anything to do with him was beyond her, but no matter what she said to him, it didn't seem to deter his overtures. Most of the time, she could barely remember the reasons she'd been attracted to him years ago. She could recite the reasons for marriage—she'd been young and stupid, foremost among them, and pregnant to boot—but nowadays, whenever he stared her up and down, she cringed inside. He wasn't her type. Frankly, he'd never been her type. If her entire life had been recorded on video, the marriage would be one of those events she would gladly record over. Except for Ben, of course.

She wished her younger brother, Drake, were here, and she felt the usual ache when she thought of him. Whenever he'd come by, Ben followed him around the way the dogs followed Nana. Together, they would wander off to catch butterflies or spend time in the tree house that Grandpa had built, which was accessible only by a rickety bridge that spanned one of the two creeks on the property. Unlike her ex, Drake accepted Ben, which in a lot of ways made him more of a father to Ben than her ex had ever been. Ben adored him, and she adored Drake for the quiet way he built confidence in her son. She remembered thanking him for it once, but he'd just shrugged. "I just like spending time with him," he'd said by way of explanation.

She knew she needed to check on Nana. Rising from her seat, she spotted the light on in the office, but she doubted that Nana was doing paperwork. More likely she was out in the pens behind the kennels, and she headed in that direction. Hopefully, Nana hadn't got it in her mind to try to take a group of dogs for a walk. There was no way she could keep her balance—or even hold them—if they tugged on the leashes, but it had always been one of her favorite things to do. She was of the opinion that most dogs didn't get enough exercise, and the property was great for remedying that. At nearly seventy acres, it boasted several open fields bordered by virgin hardwoods, crisscrossed by half a dozen trails and two small streams that flowed all the way to the South River. The property, bought for practically nothing fifty years ago, was worth quite a bit now. That's what the lawyer said, the one who'd come by to feel Nana out about the possibility of selling it.

She knew exactly who was behind all that. So did Nana, who pretended to be lobotomized while the lawyer spoke to her. She stared at him with wide, blank eyes, dropped grapes onto the floor one by one, and mumbled incomprehensibly. She and Beth giggled about it for hours afterward.

Glancing through the window of the kennel office, she saw no sign of Nana, but she could hear Nana's voice echoing from the pens.

"Stay. . . come. Good girl! Good come!"

Rounding the corner, Beth saw Nana praising a shih tzu as it trotted toward her. It reminded her of one of those wind-up toy dogs you could purchase from Wal-Mart.

"What are you doing, Nana? You're not supposed to be out here."

"Oh, hey, Beth." Unlike two months ago, now she hardly slurred her words anymore.

Beth put her hands on her hips. "You shouldn't be out here alone."

"I brought a cell phone. I figured I'd just call if I got into a problem."

"You don't have a cell phone."

"I have yours. I snuck it out of your purse this morning."

"Then who would you have called?"

She hadn't seemed to have considered that, and her brow furrowed as she glanced at the dog. "See what I have to put up with,

Precious? I told you the gal was sharper than a digging caterpillar."
She exhaled, letting out a sound like an owl.

Beth knew a change of subject was coming.

"Where's Ben?" she asked.

"Inside, getting ready. He's going to his dad's."

"I'll bet he's thrilled about that. You sure he's not hiding out in the tree house?"

"Go easy," Beth said. "He's still his dad."

"You *think*."

"I'm sure."

"Are you positive you didn't mess around with anyone else back then? Not even a single one-night stand with a waiter or trucker, or someone from school?" She sounded almost hopeful. She always sounded hopeful when she said it.

"I'm positive. And I've already told you that a million times."

She winked. "Yes, but Nana can always hope your memory improves."

"How long have you been out here, by the way?"

"What time is it?"

"Almost four o'clock."

"Then I've been out here three hours."

"In this heat?"

"I'm not broken, Beth. I had an incident."

"You had a stroke."

"But it wasn't a serious one."

"You can't move your arm."

"As long as I can eat soup, I don't need it anyway. Now let me go see my grandson. I want to say good-bye to him before he leaves." They started toward the kennel, Precious trailing behind them, panting quickly, her tail in the air. Cute dog.

"I think I want Chinese food tonight," Nana said. "Do you want Chinese?"

"I haven't thought about it."

"Well, think about it."

"Yeah, we can have Chinese. But I don't want anything too heavy. And not fried, either. It's too hot for that."

"You're no fun."

"But I'm healthy."

"Same thing. Hey, and since you're so healthy, would you mind putting Precious away? She's in number twelve. I heard a new joke I want to tell Ben."

"Where did you hear a joke?"

"The radio."

"Is it appropriate?"

"Of course it's appropriate. Who do you think I am?"

"I know exactly who you are. That's why I'm asking. What's the joke?"

"Two cannibals were eating a comedian, and one of them turns to the other and asks, 'Does this taste funny to you?'"

Beth chuckled. "He'll like that."

"Good. The poor kid needs something to cheer him up."

"He's fine."

"Yeah, sure he is. I didn't just fall off the milk cart, you know."

As they reached the kennel, Nana kept walking toward the house, her limp more pronounced than earlier this morning. She was improving, but there was still a long way to go.

4

Thibault

The Marine Corps is based on the number 3. It was one of the first things they taught you in basic training. Made things easy to understand. Three marines made a fire team, three fire teams made a squad, three squads made a platoon, three platoons made a company, three companies made a battalion, and three battalions made a regiment. On paper, anyway. By the time they invaded Iraq, their regiment had been combined with elements from other units, including the Light Armored Reconnaissance Battalion, Firing Battalions of the Eleventh Marines, the Second and Third Assault Amphibian Battalions, Company B from the First Combat Engineer Battalion, and the Combat Service Support Battalion 115. Massive. Prepared for anything. Nearly six thousand personnel in total.

As Thibault walked beneath a sky beginning to change colors with the onset of dusk, he thought back to that night, technically his first combat in hostile territory. His regiment, the First, Fifth, became the first unit to cross into Iraq with the intention of seizing the Rumaylah oil fields. Everyone remembered that Saddam Hussein had set most of the wells in Kuwait on fire as he'd retreated in the First Gulf War, and no one wanted the same thing to happen again. Long story short, the First, Fifth, among others, got there in time. Only seven wells were burning by the time the area was secured. From there Thibault's squad was ordered north to Baghdad to help to secure the capital city. The First, Fifth was the most decorated marine regiment in the corps and thus was chosen to lead the deepest assault into enemy territory in the history of the corps. His first tour in Iraq lasted a little more than four months.

Five years after the fact, most of the specifics about that first tour had blurred. He had done his job and eventually was sent back to Pendleton. He didn't talk about it. He tried not to think about it. Except for this: Ricky Martinez and Bill Kincaid, the other two men in Thibault's fire team, were part of a story he'd never forget.

Take any three people, stick them together, and they're going to have differences. No surprise there. And on the surface, they were different. Ricky grew up in a small apartment in Midland, Texas, and was a former baseball player and weight-lifting fanatic who'd played in the Minnesota Twins farm system before enlisting; Bill, who played the trumpet in his high school marching band, was from upstate New York and had been raised on a dairy farm with five sisters. Ricky liked blondes, Bill liked brunettes; Ricky chewed tobacco, and Bill smoked; Ricky liked rap music, Bill favored country-western. No big deal. They trained together, they ate together, they slept together. They debated sports and politics. They shot the breeze like brothers and played practical jokes on each other. Bill would wake with one eyebrow shaved off; Ricky would wake the next night with both of them gone. Thibault learned to wake at the slightest sound and somehow kept both eyebrows intact. They laughed about it for months. Drunk one night, they got matching tattoos, each proclaiming their fidelity to the corps.

After so much time together, they got to the point where they could anticipate what the others would do. Each of them in turn had saved Thibault's life, or at least kept him from serious harm.

Bill grabbed the back of Thibault's flak jacket just as Thibault was poised to move into the open; moments later, a sniper wounded two men nearby. The second time, a distracted Thibault was almost struck by a speeding Humvee driven by a fellow marine; that time, it was Ricky who grabbed his arm to stop him. Even in war, people die in auto accidents. Look at Patton.

After securing the oil fields, they had arrived at the outskirts of Baghdad with the rest of their company. The city had not fallen yet. They were part of a convoy, three men among hundreds, tightening their grip on the city. Aside from the roar of Allied vehicle engines, all was quiet as they entered the outlying neighborhoods. When gunfire was heard from a graveled road off the main thoroughfare, Thibault's squad was ordered to check it out.

They evaluated the scene. Two- and three-story buildings sandwiched together on either side of the potholed road. A lone dog eating garbage. The smoking ruins of a car a hundred meters away. They waited. Saw nothing. Waited some more. Heard nothing. Finally, Thibault, Ricky, and Bill were ordered to cross the street. They did so, moving quickly, reaching safety. From there, the squad proceeded up the street, into the unknown.

When the sound of gunfire rang out again that day, it wasn't a single shot. It was the death rattle of dozens and then hundreds of bullets from automatic weapons trapping them in a circle of gunfire. Thibault, Ricky, and Bill, along with the rest of the squad across the street, found themselves pinned in doorways with few places to hide.

The firefight didn't last long, people said later. It was long enough. The blizzard of fire cascaded from windows above them. Thibault and his squad instinctively raised their weapons and fired, then fired again. Across the street, two of their men were wounded, but reinforcements arrived quickly. A tank rolled in, fast-moving infantry in the rear. The air vibrated as the muzzle flashed and the upper stories of a building collapsed, dust and glass filling the air. Everywhere Thibault heard the sounds of screaming, saw civilians fleeing the buildings into the streets. The fusillade continued; the stray dog was shot and sent tumbling. Civilians fell forward as they were shot in the back, bleeding and crying out. A third marine was injured in the lower leg. Thibault, Ricky, and Bill were still unable to move, imprisoned by the steady fire chipping at the walls next to them, at their feet. Still, the three of them continued to fire. The air vibrated with a roar, and the upper floors of another building collapsed. The tank, rolling forward, was getting close now. All at once, enemy gunfire started coming from two directions, not just one. Bill glanced at him; he glanced at Ricky. They knew what they had to do. It was time to move; if they stayed, they would die. Thibault rose first.

In that instant, all went suddenly white, then turned black.

In Hampton, more than five years later, Thibault couldn't recall the specifics, other than the feeling that he'd been tossed into a washing machine. He was sent tumbling into the street with the explosion, his ears ringing. His friend Victor quickly reached his side; so did a naval corpsman. The tank continued to fire, and little by little, the street was brought under control.

He learned all this after the fact, just as he learned that the explosion had been caused by an RPG, a rocket-propelled grenade. Later, an officer would tell Thibault that it had most likely been meant for the tank; it missed the turret by inches. Instead, as if fated to find them, it flew toward Thibault, Ricky, and Bill.

Thibault was loaded into a Humvee and evacuated from the scene, unconscious. Miraculously, his wounds had been minor, and within three days he would be back with his squad. Ricky and Bill would not; each was later buried with full military honors. Ricky was a week away from his twenty-second birthday. Bill was twenty years old. They were neither the first casualties of the war nor the last. The war went on.

Thibault forced himself not to think about them much. It seemed callous, but in war the mind shuts down about things like that. It hurt to think about their deaths, to reflect on their absence, so he didn't. Nor did most of the squad. Instead, he did his job. He focused on the fact that he was still alive. He focused on keeping others safe.

But today he felt the pinpricks of memory, and loss, and he didn't bury them. They were with him as he walked the quiet streets of town, making for the outskirts on the far side. Following the directions he'd received from the front desk at the motel, he headed east on Route 54, walking on the grassy shoulder, staying well off the road. He'd learned in his travels never to trust drivers. Zeus trailed behind, panting heavily. He stopped and gave Zeus some water, the last in the bottle.

Businesses lined either side of the highway. A mattress shop, a place that did auto body repairs, a nursery, a Quick-N-Go that sold gas and stale food in plastic wrappers, and two ramshackle farmhouses that seemed out of place, as if the modern world had sprouted up around them. Which was exactly what had happened, he assumed. He wondered how long the owners would hold out or why anyone would want to live in a home that fronted a highway and was sandwiched between businesses.

Cars roared past in both directions. Clouds began to roll in, gray and puffy. He smelled rain before the first drop hit him, and within a few steps it was pouring. It lasted fifteen minutes, drenching him, but the heavy clouds kept moving toward the coast until only a haze remained. Zeus shook the water from his coat. Birdsong resumed from the trees while mist rose from the moist earth.

Eventually, he reached the fairgrounds. It was deserted. Nothing fancy, he thought, examining the layout. Just the basics. Parking on a dirt-gravel lot on the left; a couple of ancient barns on the far right; a wide grassy field for carnival rides separating the two, all lined with a chain-link fence.

He didn't need to jump the fence, nor did he need to look at the picture. He'd seen it a thousand times. He moved forward, orienting himself, and eventually he spotted the ticket booth.

Behind it was an arched opening where a banner could be strung. When he arrived at the arch, he turned toward the northern horizon, framing the ticket booth and centering the arch in his vision, just as it had appeared in the photograph. This was the angle, he thought; this was where the picture had been taken.

The structure of the marines was based on threes. Three men to a fire team, three fire teams to a squad, three squads to a platoon. He served three tours in Iraq. Checking his watch, he noted that he'd been in Hampton for three hours, and straight ahead, right where they should have been, were three evergreen trees clustered together.

Thibault walked back to the highway, knowing he was closer to finding her. He wasn't there yet, but he soon would be.

She'd been here. He knew that now.

What he needed now was a name. On his walk across the country, he'd had a lot of time to think, and he'd decided there were three ways to go about it. First, he could try to find a local veterans association and ask if any locals had served in Iraq. That might lead him to someone who might recognize her. Second, he could go to the local high school and see if it had copies of year-books from ten to fifteen years ago. He could look through the photographs one by one. Or third, he could show the photograph and ask around.

All had their drawbacks, none were guaranteed. As for the veterans association, he hadn't found one listed in the phone book. Strike one. Because it was still summer vacation, he doubted if the high school would be open; even if it was, it might be difficult to gain access to the library's yearbooks. Strike two—for now, anyway. Which meant that his best bet was to ask around and see if anyone recognized her.

Who to ask, though?

He knew from the almanac that nine thousand people lived in Hampton, North Carolina. Another thirteen thousand people lived in Hampton County. Way too many. The most efficient strategy was to limit his search to the likeliest pool of candidates. Again, he started with what he knew.

She appeared to be in her early twenties when the photograph had been taken, which meant she was in her late twenties now. Possibly early thirties. She was obviously attractive. Further, in a town this size, assuming an equal distribution among age brackets, that meant there were roughly 2,750 kids from newborns up to ten years of age, 2,750 from eleven to twenty, and 5,500 people in their twenties and thirties, her age bracket. *Roughly*. Of those, he assumed half were males and half were females. Females would tend to be more suspicious about his intentions, especially if they actually knew her. He was a stranger. Strangers were dangerous. He doubted they would reveal much.

Men might, depending on how he framed the question. In his experience, nearly all males noticed attractive females in their age bracket, especially if they were single men. How many men in her current age group were single? He guessed about thirty percent. Might be right, might be wrong, but he'd go with it. Say 900 or so. Of those, he figured eighty percent had been living here back then. Just a guess, but Hampton struck him as a town that people were more likely to emigrate from, as opposed to immigrate to. That brought the number down to 720. He could further cut that in half if he concentrated on single men aged twenty-five to thirty-five, instead of twenty to forty. That brought it down to 360. He figured a good chunk of those men either knew her or knew of her five years ago. Maybe they'd gone to high school with her or maybe not—he knew there was one in town—but they would know her if she was single. Of course, it was possible she wasn't single— women in small southern towns probably married young, after all—but he would work with this set of assumptions first. The words on the back of the photograph—"Keep Safe! E"—didn't strike him as romantic enough to have been given to a boyfriend or fiancé. No "Love you," no "I'll miss you." Just an initial. A friend.

Down from 22,000 to 360 in less than ten minutes. Not bad. And definitely good enough to get started. Assuming, of course, she lived here when the photograph had been taken. Assuming she hadn't been visiting.

He knew it was another big assumption. But he had to start someplace, and he knew she'd been here once. He would learn the truth one way or the other and move on from there.

Where did single men hang out? Single men who could be drawn into conversation? *I met her a couple of years ago and she told me to call her if I got back into town, but I lost her name and number.* . . .

Bars. Pool halls.

In a town this size, he doubted whether there were more than three or four places where locals hung out. Bars and pool halls had the advantage of alcohol, and it was Saturday night. They'd be filled. He figured he'd have his answer, one way or the other, within the next twelve hours.

He glanced at Zeus. "Seems like you're going to be on your own tonight. I could bring you, but I'd have to leave you outside and I don't know how long I'll be."

Zeus continued walking, his head down, tongue out. Tired and hot. Zeus didn't care.

"I'll put the air conditioner on, okay?"

5

Clayton

It was nine o'clock on Saturday night, and he was stuck at home babysitting. Great. Just great.

How else could a day like today end, though? First, one of the girls almost catches him taking pictures, then the department's camera gets stolen, and then Logan *Thigh-bolt* flattens his tires. Worse, he'd had to explain both the loss of the camera and the tires to his dad, Mr. County Sheriff. Predictably, his dad was spitting mad and somehow didn't buy the story he'd concocted. Instead he just kept peppering him with questions. By the end, Clayton had wanted to pop the old man. Dad might be a bigwig to a lot of the folks around here, but the man had no business talking to him like he was an idiot. But Clayton had kept to his story—he'd thought he'd seen someone, gone to investigate, and somehow run over a couple of nails. And the camera? Don't ask him. He had no idea if it had even been in the cruiser in the first place. Not great, he knew, but good enough.

"That looks more like a hole made by a buck-knife," said his dad, bending down, examining the tires.

"I told you it was nails."

"There's no construction out there."

"I don't know how it happened, either! I'm just telling you what happened."

"Where are they?"

"How the hell should I know? I pitched them in the woods."

The old man wasn't convinced, but Clayton knew enough to stick to his story. Always stick to the story. It was when you started backtracking that people got in trouble. Interrogation 101.

Eventually the old man left, and Clayton put on the spares and drove to the garage, where they patched the original tires. By then a couple of hours had passed, and he was late for an appointment with one Mr. Logan Thigh-bolt. Nobody, but nobody, messed with Keith Clayton, especially not some hippie drifter who thought he could put one over on him.

He spent the rest of the afternoon driving the streets of Arden, asking whether anyone had seen him. Dude like that was impossible to miss if only because of Cujo by his side. His search yielded zippo, which only infuriated him further, since he realized that it meant Thigh-bolt had lied to his face and Clayton hadn't picked up on it.

But he'd find the guy. Without a doubt he'd find the guy, if only because of the camera. Or, more accurately, the pictures. Especially the *other* pictures. Last thing he wanted was for Thigh-bolt to stroll into the sheriff's department and drop that baby on the counter—or even worse, head straight to the newspaper. Of the two, the department would be the lesser of two evils, since his dad could keep a lid on it. While his dad would blow a gasket and most likely put him on some crap detail for the next few weeks, he'd keep it quiet. His dad wasn't good for much, but he was good for things like that.

But the newspaper . . . now that was a different story. Sure, Gramps would pull some strings and do his best to keep it quiet there, too, but there was no way that sort of information could be kept in check. It was just too juicy, and the news would spread

like wildfire through this town, with or without an article. Clayton was already regarded as the black sheep of the family, and the
last thing he needed was another reason for Gramps to come
down on him. Gramps had a way of dwelling on the negative.
Even now, years later, Gramps was still bent that he and Beth had
divorced, not that it was even his business. And at family gather-
ings, he could usually be counted on to bring up the fact that
Clayton hadn't gone to college. With his grades, Clayton could
easily have handled it, but he simply couldn't imagine spending
another four years in the classroom, so he'd joined his father at
the sheriff's department. That was enough to placate Gramps. It
seemed like he'd spent half his life placating Gramps.

But he had no choice in the matter. Even though he didn't particularly like Gramps—Gramps was a devout Southern Baptist who
went to church every Sunday and thought that drinking and dancing were sins, which always struck Clayton as ridiculous—he knew
what Gramps expected of him, and let's just say that taking nudie
pictures of coeds was not on the "to do" list. Nor were some of the
other photos on the disk, especially of him and a few other ladies
in compromising positions. That sort of thing would definitely lead
to *serious disappointment,* and Gramps wasn't very patient with
those who disappointed him, even if they were family. *Especially* if
they were family. Claytons had lived in Hampton County since
1753; in many ways, they *were* Hampton County. Family members
included judges, lawyers, doctors, and landowners; even the mayor
had married into the family, but everyone knew Gramps was the
one who sat at the head of the table. Gramps ruled the place like
an old-fashioned Mafia don, and most people in town sang his
praises and went on and on about what a quality man he was.
Gramps liked to believe it was because he supported everything
from the library to the theater to the local elementary school, but
Clayton knew the real reason was that Gramps owned pretty much
every commercial building in the downtown area, as well as the
lumberyard, both marinas, three automobile dealerships, three stor-

age complexes, the only apartment complex in town, and vast tracts of farmland. All of it made for an immensely wealthy—and powerful—family, and since Clayton got most of his money from the family trusts, the last thing he needed was some stranger in town making trouble for him.

Thank God he'd had Ben in the short time he'd been with Beth. Gramps had this weird thing about lineage, and since Ben had been named after Gramps—a pretty slick idea, if he did say so himself—Gramps adored him. Most of the time, Clayton had the sense that Gramps liked Ben, his great-grandson, a lot more than he liked his grandson.

Oh, Clayton knew Ben was a good kid. It wasn't just Gramps—everyone said so. And he did love the kid, even if he was a pain in the ass sometimes. From his perch on the front porch, he looked through the window and saw that Ben had finished with the kitchen and was back on the couch. He knew he should join him inside, but he wasn't ready just yet. He didn't want to fly off the handle or say something he'd regret. He'd been working at being better about things like that; a couple of months back, Gramps had had a little talk with him about how important it was to be a *steady influence*. Peckerhead. What he should have done was talk to Ben about doing what his dad asked when he asked, Clayton thought. Would have done a lot more good. The kid had already pissed him off once tonight, but instead of exploding, he'd remembered Gramps and pressed his lips together before stalking outside.

Seemed like he was always getting pissed off at Ben these days. But it wasn't his fault; he honestly tried to get along with the kid! And they'd started out okay. Talked about school, had some burgers, tuned in to *SportsCenter* on ESPN. All good. But then, horror of horrors, he'd asked Ben to clean the kitchen. Like that was too much to ask, right? Clayton hadn't had the chance to get to it for the last few days, and he knew the kid would do a good job. So Ben promised he'd clean it, but instead of doing it, he'd just sat there. And sat. And the clock ticked by. And then he'd sat some more.

So Clayton had asked again—he was sure he'd said it nicely—and though he couldn't be certain, he was pretty sure that Ben had rolled his eyes as he'd finally trudged off. That was all it took. He hated when Ben rolled his eyes at him, and Ben knew he hated it. It was like the kid knew exactly which buttons to push, and he spent all his spare time trying to figure out new buttons to hit the next time he saw him. Hence, Clayton had found himself on the porch.

Behaviors like that were his mom's doing; of that, Clayton had no doubt. She was one hell of a good-looking lady, but she didn't know the first thing about turning a young boy into a man. He had nothing against the kid getting good grades, but he couldn't play soccer this year because he wanted to play the violin? What kind of crap was that? Violin? Might as well start dressing the boy in pink and teaching him to ride sidesaddle. Clayton did his best to keep that sort of pansy stuff in check, but the fact was, he had the kid only a day and a half every other weekend. Not his fault the kid swung a bat like a girl. Kid was too busy playing *chess*. And just so everyone was clear, there was no way on God's green earth that he'd be caught dead at a violin recital.

Violin recital. Good Lord. What was this world coming to?

His thoughts circled back to Thigh-bolt again, and though he wanted to believe the guy had simply left the county, he knew better. The guy was walking, and there was no way he could reach the far side of the county by nightfall. And what else? Something had been gnawing at him most of the day, and it wasn't until he'd come to cool off on the porch that he'd figured it out. If Thigh-bolt had been telling the truth about living in Colorado—and granted, he might not have been, but let's say he was—it meant he'd been traveling from west to east. And the next town east? Not Arden. That's for sure. That was southwest from where they'd met. Instead, heading east would have brought the guy to good old Hampton. Right here, his hometown. Which meant, of course, the guy might be less than fifteen minutes from where he was sitting now.

But where was Clayton? Out searching for the guy? No, he was babysitting.

He squinted through the window again at his son. He was reading on the couch, which was the only thing the kid ever seemed to want to do. Oh yeah, except for the violin. He shook his head, wondering if the kid had gotten any of his genes at all. Not likely. He was a mama's boy through and through. Beth's son.

Beth . . .

Yeah, the marriage didn't work. But there was still something between them. There always would be. She may have been preachy and opinionated, but he'd always watch out for her, not only because of Ben, but because she was surely the best-looking woman he'd ever slept with. Great-looking back then and somehow even better-looking now. Even better-looking than the coeds he'd seen today. Weird. Like she had reached an age that suited her perfectly and somehow stopped aging after that. He knew it wouldn't last. Gravity would take its toll, but still, he couldn't stop thinking about having a quick roll in the sack with her. One for old times' sake, and to help him . . . *unwind*.

He supposed he could call Angie. Or Kate, for that matter. One was twenty and worked in the pet store; the other was a year older and cleaned toilets at the Stratford Inn. They both had nice little figures and were always dynamite when it came time for a little bit of . . . *unwinding*. He knew Ben wouldn't care if he brought one of them over, but even so, he'd probably have to talk to them first. They'd been pretty angry at him the last time he'd seen either of them. He'd have to apologize and turn on the charm, and he wasn't sure he was up to listening to them smack their chewing gum and chatter away about what they'd seen on MTV or read in the *National Enquirer*. Sometimes they were too much work.

So that was out. Searching for Thigh-bolt tonight was out. Looking for Thigh-bolt tomorrow was out, too, since Gramps wanted everyone over for brunch after church. Still, Thigh-bolt was walking, and with the dog and the backpack, it meant catching a ride was unlikely. How far could he get by tomorrow afternoon? Twenty miles? Thirty at the most? No more than that, which meant he was still in the vicinity. He'd make some calls to a couple of other departments in the surrounding counties, ask them to keep an eye out. There weren't that many roads leading out of the county, and he figured that if he spent a few hours making phone calls to some of the businesses along those routes, someone would spot the guy. When that happened, he'd be on his way. Thigh-bolt never should have messed with Keith Clayton.

Lost in thought, Clayton barely heard the front door squeak open.

"Hey, Dad?"

"Yeah?"

"Someone's on the phone."

"Who is it?"

"Tony."

"Of course it is."

He rose from his seat, wondering what Tony wanted. Talk about a loser. Scrawny and pimpled, he was one of those hangers-on who sat near the deputies, trying to worm his way into pretending he was one of them. He was probably wondering where Clayton was and what he was doing later because he didn't want to be left out. Lame.

He finished his beer on the way in and tossed it in the can, listening to it rattle. He grabbed the receiver from the counter.

"Yeah?"

In the background, he could hear the distorted chords of a country-western song playing on a jukebox and the dull roar of loud conversation. He wondered where the loser was calling from.

"Hey, I'm at Decker's Pool Hall, and there's this strange dude here that I think you should know about."

His antenna went up. "Does he have a dog with him? Backpack? Kind of scruffy, like he's been out in the woods for a while?"

"No."

"You sure?"

"Yeah, I'm sure. He's shooting pool in the back. But listen. I wanted to tell you he's got a picture of your ex-wife."

Caught off guard, Clayton tried to sound nonchalant. "So?" he said.

"I just thought you'd want to know."

"Why would I give a holy crap about that?"

"I don't know."

"Of course you don't. Holler."

He hung up the phone, thinking the guy must have potato salad where his brains should be, and ran an appraising gaze over the kitchen. Clean as could be. Kid did a great job, as usual. He almost shouted that out from where he stood, but instead, as he caught sight of Ben, he couldn't help but notice again how small his son was. Granted, a big chunk of that might be genetics, early or late growth spurts, and all that, but another part came from general health. It was common sense. Eat right, exercise, get plenty of rest. The basics; things everyone's mother told their kids. And mothers were right. If you didn't eat enough, you couldn't grow. If you didn't exercise enough, your muscles stagnated. And when do you think a person grew? Night. When the body regenerated. When people dreamed.

He often wondered whether Ben got enough sleep at his mom's. Clayton knew Ben ate—he'd finished his burger and fries—and he knew the kid was active, so maybe lack of sleep was keeping him small. Kid didn't want to end up short, did he? Of course not. And besides, Clayton wanted a bit of alone time. Wanted to fantasize about what he was going to do to Thigh-bolt the next time he saw him.

He cleared his throat. "Hey, Ben. It's getting kind of late, don't you think?"

6

Thibault

On his way home from the pool hall, Thibault remembered his second tour in Iraq.

It went like this: Fallujah, spring 2004. The First, Fifth, among other units, was ordered in to pacify the escalating violence since the fall of Baghdad the year before. Civilians knew what to expect and began to flee the city, choking the highways. Maybe a third of the city evacuated within a day. Air strikes were called in, then the marines. They moved block by block, house by house, room by room, in some of the most intense fighting since the opening days of the invasion. In three days, they controlled a quarter of the city, but the growing number of civilian deaths prompted a cease-fire. A decision was made to abandon the operation, and most of the forces withdrew, including Thibault's company.

But not all of his company withdrew.

On the second day of operations, at the southern, industrial end of town, Thibault and his platoon were ordered to investigate a building rumored to hold a cache of weapons. The particular building hadn't been pinpointed however; it could be any one of a dozen dilapidated structures clustered near an abandoned gas station, forming a rough semicircle. Thibault and his platoon moved in, toward the buildings, giving the gas station a wide berth. Half went right, half went left. All was quiet, and then it wasn't. The gas station suddenly exploded. Flames leapt toward the sky, the explosion knocking half of the men to the ground, shattering eardrums. Thibault was dazed; his peripheral vision had gone black, and everything else was blurry. All at once, a hail of fire poured from the windows and rooftops above them and from behind the burned-out remains of automobiles in the streets.

Thibault found himself on the ground beside Victor. Two of the others in his platoon, Matt and Kevin—Mad Dog and K-Man, respectively—were with them, and the training of the corps kicked in. The brotherhood kicked in. Despite the onslaught, despite his fear, despite an almost certain death, Victor reached for his rifle and rose to one knee, zeroing in on the enemy. He fired, then fired again, his movements calm and focused, steady. Mad Dog reached for his rifle and did the same. One by one they rose; one by one fire teams were formed. *Fire. Cover. Move.* Except they couldn't move. There was noplace to go. One marine toppled, then another. Then a third and a fourth.

By the time reinforcements arrived, it was almost too late. Mad Dog had been shot in the femoral artery; despite having a tourniquet, he'd bled to death within minutes. Kevin was shot in the head and died instantly. Ten others were wounded. Only a few emerged unscathed: Thibault and Victor were among them.

In the pool hall, one of the young men he'd spoken with reminded him of Mad Dog. They could have been brothers—same height and weight, same hair, same manner of speaking—and there had been an instant there where he'd wondered whether they were brothers before telling himself that it simply wasn't possible.

He'd known the chance he was taking with his plan. In small towns, strangers are always suspect, and toward the end of the evening, he'd seen the skinny guy with bad skin make a call from the pay phone near the bathroom, eyeing Thibault nervously as he did so. He'd been jumpy before the call as well, and Thibault assumed the call had been either to the woman in the photograph or to someone close to her. Those suspicions were confirmed when Thibault had left. Predictably, the man had followed him to the door to see which way he was walking, which was why Thibault had headed in the opposite direction before doubling back.

When he'd arrived at the run-down pool hall, he'd bypassed the bar and made straight for the pool tables. He quickly identified the guys in the appropriate age group, most of whom seemed to be single. He asked to join in and put up with the requisite grumbling. Made nice, bought a few rounds of beers while losing a few games at pool, and sure enough, they began to loosen up. Casually, he asked about the social life in town. He missed the necessary shots. He congratulated them when they made a shot.

Eventually, they started asking about him. Where was he from? What was he doing here? He hemmed and hawed, mumbling something about a girl, and changed the subject. He fed their curiosity. He bought more beers, and when they asked again, he reluctantly shared his story: that he'd gone to the fair with a friend a few years back and met a girl. They'd hit it off. He went on and on about how great she was and how she'd told him to look her up if he ever came to town again. And he wanted to, but damned if he could remember her name.

You don't remember her name? they asked. *No*, he answered. *I've never been good with names. I got hit in the head with a baseball when I was a kid, and my memory doesn't work so good.* He shrugged, knowing they would laugh, and they did. *I got a photo, though*, he added, making it sound like an afterthought.

Do you have it with you? *Yeah. I think I do.*

He rummaged through his pockets and pulled out the photo. The men gathered around. A moment later, one of them began shaking his head. You're out of luck, he said. She's off-limits. *She's married?* No, but let's just say she doesn't date. Her ex wouldn't like it, and trust me, you don't want to mess with him.

Thibault swallowed. *Who is she?*

Beth Green, they said. She's a teacher at Hampton Elementary and lives with her grandma in the house at Sunshine Kennels.

Beth Green. Or, more accurately, Thibault thought, Elizabeth Green.

E.

It was while they were talking that Thibault realized one of the people he'd shown the picture to had slipped away. *I guess I'm out of luck, then,* Thibault said, taking back the photo.

He stayed for another half hour to cover his tracks. He made more small talk. He watched the stranger with the bad skin make the phone call and saw the disappointment in his reaction. Like a kid who got in trouble for tattling. Good. Still, Thibault had the feeling he'd see the stranger again. He bought more beers and lost more games, glancing occasionally at the door to see if anyone arrived. No one did. In time, he held up his hands and said he was out of money. He was going to hit the road. It had cost him a little more than a hundred dollars. They assured him he was welcome to join them anytime.

He barely heard them. Instead, all he could think was that he now had a name to go with the face, and that the next step was to meet her.

7

Beth

Sunday.

After church, it was supposed to be a day of rest, when she could recover and recharge for the coming week. The day she was supposed to spend with her family, cooking stew in the kitchen and taking relaxing walks along the river. Maybe even cuddle up with a good book while she sipped a glass of wine, or soak in a warm bubble bath.

What she didn't want to do was spend the day scooping dog poop off the grassy area where the dogs trained, or clean the kennels, or train twelve dogs one right after the next, or sit in a sweltering office waiting for people to come pick up the family pets that were relaxing in cool, air-conditioned kennels. Which, of course, was exactly what she'd been doing since she'd gotten back from church earlier that morning.

Two dogs had already been picked up, but four more were scheduled for pickup sometime today. Nana had been kind enough to lay out the files for her before she retreated to the house to watch the game. The Atlanta Braves were playing the Mets, and not only did Nana love the Atlanta Braves with a feverish passion that struck Beth as ridiculous, but she loved any and all memorabilia associated with the team. Which explained, of course, the Atlanta Braves coffee cups stacked near the snack counter, the Atlanta Braves pennants on the walls, the Atlanta Braves desk calendar, and the Atlanta Braves lamp near the window.

Even with the door open, the air in the office was stifling. It was one of those hot, humid summer days great for swimming in the river but unfit for anything else. Her shirt was soaked with perspiration, and because she was wearing shorts, her legs kept sticking to the vinyl chair she sat in. Every time she moved her legs, she was rewarded with a sort of sticky sound, like peeling tape from a cardboard box, which was just plain gross.

While Nana considered it imperative to keep the dogs cool, she'd never bothered to add cooling ducts that led to the office. "If you're hot, just prop the door to the kennels open," she'd always said, ignoring the fact that while she didn't mind the endless barking, most normal people did. And today there were a couple of little yappers in there: a pair of Jack Russell terriers that hadn't stopped barking since Beth had arrived. Beth assumed they'd barked nearly all night, since most of the other dogs seemed grumpy as well. Every minute or so, other dogs joined in an angry chorus, the sounds rising in pitch and intensity, as if every dog's sole desire was to voice its displeasure more loudly than the next. Which meant there wasn't a chance on earth that she was going to open the door to cool off the office.

She toyed with the idea of going up to the house to fetch another glass of ice water, but she had the funny feeling that as soon as she left the office, the owners who'd dropped off their cocker spaniel for obedience training would show up. They'd called half an hour ago, telling her that they were on their way—"We'll be there in ten minutes!"—and they were the kind of people who would be upset if their cocker spaniel had to sit in a kennel for a minute longer than she had to, especially after spending two weeks away from home.

But were they here yet? Of course not.

It would have been so much easier if Ben were around. She'd

seen him in church that morning with his father, and he'd looked as glum as she'd expected. As always, it hadn't been a lot of fun for him. He'd called before going to bed last night and told her that Keith had spent a good chunk of the evening sitting alone on the porch outside while Ben cleaned the kitchen. What, she wondered, was that about? Why couldn't he just enjoy the fact that his son was there? Or simply sit and talk with him? Ben was just about the easiest kid to get along with, and she wasn't saying that because she was biased. Well, okay, she admitted, maybe she was *a little* biased, but as a teacher, she'd spent time with lots of different kids and she knew what she was talking about. Ben was smart. Ben had a zany sense of humor. Ben was naturally kind. Ben was polite. Ben was great, and it made her crazy to realize that Keith was too dumb to see it.

She really wished she were inside the house doing . . . something. Anything. Even doing laundry was more exciting than sitting out here. Out here, she had way too much time to think. Not only about Ben, but about Nana, too. And about whether she would teach this year. And even the sad state of her love life, which never failed to depress her. It would be wonderful, she thought, to meet someone special, someone to laugh with, someone who would love Ben as much as she did. Or even to meet a man with whom she could go to dinner and a movie. A normal man, like someone who remembered to put his napkin in his lap in a restaurant and opened a door for her now and then. That wasn't so unreasonable, was it? She hadn't been lying to Melody when she'd said her choices in town were slim, and she'd be the first to admit that she was picky, but aside from the short time with Adam, she'd spent every other weekend at home this past year. Forty-nine out of fifty-two weekends. She wasn't *that* picky, that's for sure. The simple fact was that Adam had been the only one who'd asked her out, and for a reason she still didn't understand, he'd suddenly stopped calling. Which pretty much summed up the story of her dating life the last few years.

But no big deal, right? She'd survived without a relationship this long, and she'd soldier on. Besides, most of the time it didn't bother her. If it hadn't been such a miserably hot day, she doubted it would bother her now. Which meant she definitely had to cool off. Otherwise she'd probably start thinking about the past, and she definitely didn't want to go there. Fingering her empty glass, she decided to get that ice water. And while she was at it, a small towel to sit on.

As she rose from her seat, she peeked down the empty gravel drive, then she scribbled a note saying she'd be back in ten minutes and tacked it to the front door of the office. Outside, the sun pressed down hard, driving her toward the shade offered by the ancient magnolia and guiding her to the gravel path that led toward the house she'd grown up in. Built around 1920, it resembled a broad, low-country farmhouse, banded by a large porch and sporting carved molding in the eaves. The backyard, hidden from the kennel and office by towering hedges, was shaded by giant oaks and graced with a series of decks that made eating outside a pleasure. The place must have been magnificent long ago, but like so many rural homes around Hampton, time and the elements had conspired against it. These days the porch sagged, the floors squeaked, and when the wind was strong enough, papers would blow off the counters even when the windows were closed. Inside, it was pretty much the same story: great bones, but the place needed modern updates, especially in the kitchen and bathrooms. Nana knew it and mentioned doing something about it every now and then, but they were projects that always got put on the back burner. Besides, Beth had to admit that the place still had unique appeal. Not only the backyard—which was truly an oasis—but inside as well. For years, Nana had frequented antiques shops, and she favored anything French from the nineteenth century. She also spent good chunks of her weekends at garage sales, rummaging through old paintings. She had a knack for paintings in general and had developed some good friendships with a number of gallery owners throughout the South. The paintings hung on nearly every wall in the house. On a lark, Beth had once Googled a couple of the artists' names and learned that other works by those artists hung in the Metropolitan Museum of Art in New York City and the Huntington Library in San Marino, California. When she mentioned what she'd learned, Nana had winked and said, "It's like sipping champagne, ain't it?" Nana's nutty turns of phrase often disguised her razor sharp instincts.

After reaching the front porch and opening the door, Beth was hit by a blast of cool air so refreshing that she stood in the doorway, savoring the feeling.

"Close the door," Nana called over her shoulder. "You're letting the air out." She turned in her chair, giving Beth the once-over. "You look hot."

"I am hot."

"I take it that the office feels like a furnace today."

"Ya think?"

"I think you should have opened the door to the kennel like I told you. But that's just me. Well, come on in and cool off for a while."

Beth motioned to the set. "How're the Braves doing?"

"Like a bunch of carrots."

"Is that good or bad?"

"Can carrots play baseball?"

"I guess not."

"Then you have your answer."

Beth smiled as she walked to the kitchen. Nana always got a little edgy when the Braves were losing.

From inside the freezer she drew out an ice tray and cracked out a few cubes. After dropping them into a glass, she filled it and took a long, satisfying drink. Realizing she was hungry as well, she chose a banana from the fruit bowl and went back to the living room. She propped herself on the armrest of the couch, feeling the sweat evaporate in the cold draft, half watching Nana and half watching the game. Part of her wanted to ask how many touchdowns had been scored, but she knew Nana wouldn't appreciate the humor. Not if the Braves were playing like a bunch of carrots, anyway. Glancing at the clock, she exhaled, knowing she had to get back to the office.

"It was nice visiting with you, Nana."

"You too, sweetie. Try not to get too hot."

"I'll do my best."

Beth retraced her steps to the kennel office, noting with disappointment the absence of cars in the parking lot, which meant the owners still hadn't showed up. There was, however, a man walking up the drive, a German shepherd by his side. Dust spirals were rising in the dirt behind him, and the dog's head drooped, his tongue hanging out. She wondered why they were outside on a day like this. Even animals preferred to stay indoors. Thinking back, she realized it was the first time she could ever remember someone walking his dog to the kennel. Not only that, but whoever it was hadn't called for an appointment. People dropping off their pets always called for an appointment.

Figuring they'd reach the office at about the same time, she waved a greeting and was surprised when the man paused to stare at her. The dog did the same, his ears rising, and her first thought was that he looked a lot like Oliver, the German shepherd Nana had brought to the house when Beth was thirteen. He had the same black-and-tan markings, the same tilt of his head, the same intimidating stance in the presence of strangers. Not that she'd ever been afraid of Oliver. He'd been more Drake's dog during the day, but Oliver had always slept beside her bed at night, finding comfort in her presence.

Brought up short by memories of Drake and Oliver, she didn't realize at first that the man still hadn't moved. Nor had he said anything. Odd. Maybe he'd expected Nana. Because his face was in shadow, she couldn't tell one way or the other, but no matter. Once she reached the door, she took down the note and propped the door open, figuring he'd come to the office when he was ready. She walked around the counter and saw the vinyl chair, realizing she'd forgotten the towel. Figured.

Thinking she'd get the paperwork ready for the stranger to drop off his dog, she grabbed a sheet from the file cabinet and attached it to the clipboard. She rummaged through the desk for a pen and set both on the counter just as the stranger and his dog walked in. He smiled, and when their eyes met, it was one of the few times in her life that she felt at a complete loss for words.

It had less to do with the fact that he was staring than with the *way* he was staring. As crazy as it sounded, he was looking at her as though he *recognized* her. But she'd never seen him before; she was sure of that. She would have remembered him, if only because he reminded her of Drake in the way he seemed to dominate the room. Like Drake, he was probably close to six feet and lean, with wiry arms and broad shoulders. There was a rugged edge to his appearance, underscored by his sun-bleached jeans and T-shirt.

But that's where the similarities ended. While Drake's eyes were brown and rimmed with hazel, the stranger's were blue; where Drake had always kept his hair short, the stranger's hair was longer, almost wild looking. She noted that despite having walked here, he seemed to be sweating less than she was.

She felt suddenly self-conscious and turned away just as the stranger took a step toward the counter. From the corner of her eye, she watched him raise his palm slightly in the dog's direction. She'd seen Nana do that a thousand times, and the dog, attuned to every subtle move, stayed in place. The dog was already well trained, which probably meant he was here for boarding.

"Your dog is beautiful," she said, sliding the clipboard toward him. The sound of her own voice broke the awkward silence. "I had a German shepherd once. What's his name?"

"This is Zeus. And thank you."

"Hello, Zeus."

Zeus's head tilted to the side.

"I'm just going to need you to sign in," she said. "And if you have a copy of the vet's records, that would be great. Or the contact information."

"Excuse me?"

"The vet's records. You're here to board Zeus, right?"

"No," he said. He motioned over his shoulder. "Actually, I saw the sign in the window. I'm looking for work, and I was wondering if you still had anything available."

"Oh." She hadn't expected that and tried to reorient herself.

He shrugged. "I know I probably should have called first, but I was out this way anyway. I figured I'd just swing by in person to see if you had an application. If you want me to come back tomorrow, I will."

"No, it's not that. I'm just surprised. People usually don't come by on Sundays to apply for a job." Actually, they didn't come by on other days, either, but she left that part out. "I've got an application on file here somewhere," she said, turning toward the cabinet behind her. "Just give me a second to grab it." She pulled out the bottom drawer and began rummaging through the files. "What's your name?"

"Logan Thibault."

"Is that French?"

"On my father's side."

"I haven't seen you around here before."

"I'm new in town."

"Gotcha." She fished out the application. "Okay, here it is."

She set it in front of him on the counter along with a pen. As he printed his name, she noted a certain roughness to his skin, making her think that he spent a lot of time in the sun. At the second line of the form, he paused and looked up, their eyes meeting for the second time. She felt her neck flush slightly and tried to hide it by adjusting her shirt.

"I'm not sure what I should put for an address. Like I said, I just got to town and I'm staying at the Holiday Motor Court. I could also use my mom's mailing address in Colorado. Which would you prefer?"

"Colorado?"

"Yeah, I know. Kind of far from here."

"What brought you to Hampton?"

You, he thought. I came to find you. "It seems like a nice town, and I figured I'd give it a try."

"No family here?"

"None."

"Oh," she said. Handsome or not, his story didn't sit right, and she heard mental alarm bells starting to go off. There was something else, too, something gnawing at the back of her mind, and it took her a few seconds to realize what it was. When she did, she took a small step back from the counter, creating a bit more space between them. "If you just got to town, how did you know the kennel was hiring? I didn't run an ad in the paper this week."

"I saw the sign."

"When?" She squinted at him. "I saw you walking up, and there was no way you could have seen the sign until you got to the front of the office."

"I saw it earlier today. We were walking along the road, and Zeus heard dogs barking. He took off this way, and when I went to find him, I noticed the sign. No one was around, so I figured I'd come back later to see if that had changed."

The story was plausible, but she sensed that he was either lying or leaving something out. And if he had been here before, what did that mean? That he'd been scoping out the place?

He seemed to notice her unease and set the pen aside. From inside his pocket he pulled out his passport and flipped it open. When he slid it toward her, she glanced at the photo, then up at him. His name, she saw, was legitimate, though it didn't silence the alarm bells. No one passed through Hampton and decided to stay here on a whim. Charlotte, yes. Raleigh, of course. Greensboro, absolutely. But Hampton? Not a chance.

"I see," she said, suddenly wanting to end this conversation. "Just go ahead and put your mailing address on it. And your work experience. After that, all I need is a number where I can reach you and I'll be in touch."

His gaze was steady on hers. "But you're not going to call."

He was sharp, she thought. And direct. Which meant she would be, too. "No."

He nodded. "Okay. I probably wouldn't call me based on what you've heard so far, either. But before you jump to conclusions, can I add something else?"

"Go ahead."

Her tone made it plain that she didn't believe anything he said would matter.

"Yes, I'm temporarily staying at the motel, but I do intend to find a place to live around here. I will also find a job here." His gaze did not waver. "Now about me. I graduated from the University of Colorado in 2002 with a degree in anthropology. After that, I joined the marines, and I received an honorable discharge two years ago. I've never been arrested or charged with any crime, I've never taken drugs, and I've never been fired for incompetence. I'm willing to take a drug test, and if you think it necessary, you can have a background check run to confirm everything I said. Or if it's easier, you can call my former commanding officer, and he'll verify everything I've said. And even though the law doesn't require me to answer a question of this type, I'm not on medication of any kind. In other words, I'm not schizophrenic or bipolar or manic. I'm just a guy who needs a job. And I did see the sign earlier."

She hadn't known what she'd expected him to say, but he'd certainly caught her off guard.

"I see," she said again, focusing on the fact that he'd been in the military.

"Is it still a waste of time for me to fill out the application?"

"I haven't decided yet." She felt intuitively that he was telling the truth this time, but she was equally certain there was more to the story than he was revealing. She gnawed the inside of her cheek. She needed to hire someone. Which was more important—knowing what he was hiding or finding a new employee?

He stood before her erect and calm, and his posture spoke of easy confidence. Military bearing, she observed with a frown.

"Why do you want to work here?" The words sounded suspicious even to her. "With a degree, you could probably get a better job somewhere else in town."

He motioned toward Zeus. "I like dogs."

"It doesn't pay much."

"I don't need much."

"The days can be long."

"I figured they would be."

"Have you ever worked in a kennel before?"

"No."

"I see."

He smiled. "You say that a lot."

"Yes, I do," she said. *Note to self: Stop saying it.* "And you're sure you don't know anyone in town?"

"No."

"You just arrived in Hampton and decided to stay."

"Yes."

"Where's your car?"

"I don't have one."

"How did you get here?"

"I walked."

She blinked, uncomprehending. "Are you telling me that you walked all the way from Colorado?"

"Yes."

"You don't think that's odd?"

"I suppose it depends on the reason."

"What's your reason?"

"I like to walk."

"I see." She couldn't think of anything else to say. She reached for the pen, stalling. "I take it you're not married," she said.

"No."

"Kids?"

"None. It's just me and Zeus. But my mom still lives in Colorado."

She pushed a sweaty lock of hair back from her forehead, equal parts flustered and bemused. "I still don't get it. You walk across the country, you get to Hampton, you say you like the place, and now you want to work here?"

"Yes."

"There's nothing else you want to add?"

"No."

She opened her mouth to say something, then changed her mind. "Excuse me for a minute. I have to talk to someone."

Beth could handle a lot of things, but this was beyond her. As much as she tried, she couldn't quite grasp everything he'd told her. On some level, it made sense, but on the whole, it just seemed . . . off. If the guy was telling the truth, he was strange; if he was lying, he picked strange lies. Either way, it was weird. Which was why, of course, she wanted to talk to Nana. If anyone could figure him out, Nana could.

Unfortunately, as she approached the house, she realized the game wasn't over yet. She could hear the announcers debating whether it was right for the Mets to bring in a relief pitcher or something along those lines. When she opened the door, she was surprised to find Nana's seat empty.

"Nana?"

Nana poked her head out from the kitchen. "In here. I was just getting ready to pour myself a glass of lemonade. Would you like some? I can do it one-handed."

"Actually, I need to talk to you. Do you have a minute? I know the game is still on . . ."

She waved the thought away. "Oh, I'm done with that. Go ahead and turn it off. The Braves can't win, and the last thing I want to do is listen to their excuses. I hate excuses. There's no reason they should have lost, and they know it. What's going on?"

Beth walked into the kitchen and leaned against the counter as Nana poured the lemonade from the pitcher. "Are you hungry?" Nana inquired. "I can make you a quick sandwich."

"I just had a banana."

"That's not enough. You're as skinny as a golf club."

From your mouth to God's ears, Beth thought. "Maybe later. Someone came in to apply for the job. He's here now."

"You mean the cute one with the German shepherd? I figured that's what he was doing. How is he? Tell me that it's always been his dream to clean cages."

"You saw him?"

"Of course."

"How did you know he was applying for the job?"

"Why else would you want to talk to me?"

Beth shook her head. Nana was always a step ahead of her. "Anyway, I think you should talk to him. I don't quite know what to make of him."

"Does his hair have anything to do with it?"

"What?"

"His hair. It kind of makes him look like Tarzan, don't you think?"

"I really didn't notice."

"Sure you did, sweetie. You can't lie to me. What's the problem?"

Quickly, Beth gave her a rundown of the interview. When she was finished, Nana sat in silence.

"He walked from Colorado?"

"That's what he says."

"And you believe him?"

"That part?" She hesitated. "Yeah, I think he's telling the truth about that."

"That's a long walk."

"I know."

"How many miles is that?"

"I don't know. A lot."

"That's kind of strange, don't you think?"

"Yes," she said. "And there's something else, too."

"What?"

"He was a marine."

Nana sighed. "Why don't you wait here. I'll go talk to him."

For the next ten minutes, Beth watched them from behind the living room window curtains. Nana hadn't stayed in the office to conduct the interview; instead, she'd led them to the wooden bench in the shade of the magnolia tree. Zeus was dozing at their feet, his ear flicking every now and then, shooing away the occasional fly. Beth couldn't make out what either of them was saying, but occasionally she saw Nana frown, which seemed to suggest the interview wasn't going well. In the end, Logan Thibault and Zeus walked back up the gravel drive toward the main road, while Nana watched them with a concerned expression on her face.

Beth thought Nana would make her way back to the house, but instead she began walking toward the office. It was then that Beth noticed a blue Volvo station wagon rolling up the drive.

The cocker spaniel. She'd completely forgotten about the pickup, but it seemed obvious that Nana was going to handle it. Beth used the time to cool herself with a cold washcloth and drink another glass of ice water.

From the kitchen, she heard the front door squeak open as Nana came back inside.

"How'd it go?"

"It went fine."

"What did you think?"

"It was . . . interesting. He's intelligent and polite, but you're right. He's definitely hiding something."

"So where does that leave us? Should I put another ad in the paper?"

"Let's see how he works out first."

Beth wasn't sure she had heard Nana right. "Are you saying you're going to hire him?"

"No, I'm saying I did hire him. He starts Wednesday at eight."

"Why'd you do that?"

"I trust him." She gave a sad smile, as if she knew exactly what Beth was thinking. "Even if he was a marine."

8

Thibault

Thibault didn't want to return to Iraq, but once more, in February 2005, the First, Fifth was called up. This time, the regiment was sent to Ramadi, the capital of Al Anbar province and the southwest point of what was commonly referred to as "the triangle of death." Thibault was there for seven months.

Car bombs and IEDs—improvised explosive devices—were common. Simple devices but scary: usually a mortar shell with a fuse triggered by a cellular phone call. Still, the first time Thibault was riding in a Humvee that hit one, he knew the news could have been worse.

"I'm glad I heard the bomb," Victor had said afterward. By then, Victor and Thibault nearly always patrolled together. "It means I'm still alive."

"You and me both," Thibault had answered.

"But I'd rather not hit one again."

"You and me both."

But bombs weren't easy to avoid. On patrol the following day, they hit another one. A week after that, their Humvee was struck by a car bomb—but Thibault and Victor weren't unusual in that regard. Humvees were hit by one or the other on almost every patrol. Most of the marines in the platoon could honestly claim that they'd survived two or three bombs before they went back to Pendleton. A couple had survived four or five. Their sergeant had survived six. It was just that kind of place, and nearly everyone had heard the story of Tony Stevens, a marine from the Twenty-fourth MEU—Marine Expeditionary Unit—who'd survived nine bombs. One of the major newspapers had written an article about him entitled "The Luckiest Marine." His was a record no one wanted to break.

Thibault broke it. By the time he left Ramadi, he'd survived eleven explosions. But there was the one explosion he'd missed that continued to haunt him.

It would have been explosion number eight. Victor was with him. Same old story with a much worse ending. They were in a convoy of four Humvees, patrolling one of the city's major thoroughfares. An RPG struck the Humvee in front, with fortunately little damage, but enough to bring the convoy to a temporary halt. Rusted and decaying cars lined both sides of the road. Shots broke out. Thibault jumped from the second Humvee in the convoy line to get a better line of sight. Victor followed him. They reached cover and readied their weapons. Twenty seconds later, a car bomb went off, knocking them clear and destroying the Humvee they'd been in only moments before. Three marines were killed; Victor was knocked unconscious. Thibault hauled him back to the convoy, and after collecting the dead, the convoy returned to the safe zone.

It was around that time that Thibault began to hear whispers. He noticed that the other marines in his platoon began to act differently around him, as if they believed Thibault were somehow immune to the rules of war. That others might die, but he would not. Worse than that, his fellow marines seemed to suspect that while Thibault was especially lucky, those who patrolled with him were especially unlucky. It wasn't always overt, but he couldn't deny the change in his platoon members' attitude toward him. He was in Ramadi for two more months after those three marines died. The last few bombs he survived only intensified the whispers. Other marines began to avoid him. Only Victor seemed to treat him the same. Toward the end of their tour in Ramadi, while on duty guarding a gas station, he noticed Victor's hands shaking as he lit a cigarette. Above them, the night sky glittered with stars.

"You okay?" he asked.

"I'm ready to go home," Victor said. "I've done my part."

"You're not going to reup next year?"

He took a long drag from his cigarette. "My mother wants me home, and my brother has offered me a job. In roofing. Do you think I can build roofs?"

"Yeah, I think you can. You'll be a great roofer."

"My girl, Maria, is waiting for me. I've known her since I was fourteen."

"I know. You've told me about her."

"I'm going to marry her."

"You told me that, too."

"I want you to come to the wedding."

In the glow of Victor's cigarette, he saw the ghost of a smile. "I wouldn't miss it."

Victor took a long drag and they stood in silence, considering a future that seemed impossibly distant. "What about you?" Victor said, his words coming out with a puff of smoke. "You going to reup?"

Thibault shook his head. "No. I'm done."

"What are you going to do when you get out?"

"I don't know. Do nothing for a while, maybe go fishing in Minnesota. Someplace cool and green, where I can just sit in a boat and relax."

Victor sighed. "That sounds nice."

"You want to come?"

"Yes."

"Then I'll call you when I plan the trip," Thibault promised.

He could hear the smile in Victor's voice. "I'll be there." Victor cleared his throat. "Do you want to know something?"

"Only if you want to tell me."

"Do you remember the firefight? The one where Jackson and the others died when the Humvee blew up?"

Thibault picked up a small pebble and tossed it into the darkness. "Yeah."

"You saved my life."

"No, I didn't. I just hauled you back."

"Thibault, *I followed you*. When you jumped from the Humvee. I was going to stay, but when I saw you go, I knew I had no choice."

"What are you talking ab—?"

"The picture," Victor interrupted. "I know you carry it with you. I followed your luck and it saved me."

At first, Thibault didn't understand, but when he finally figured out what Victor was saying, he shook his head in disbelief. "It's just a picture, Victor."

"It's luck," Victor insisted, bringing his face close to Thibault's. "And you're the lucky one. And when you are finished with your tour, I think you should go find this woman in the picture. Your story with her is not finished."

"No—"

"It saved me."

"It didn't save the others. Too many others."

Everyone knew that the First, Fifth had suffered more casualties in Iraq than any other regiment in the Marine Corps.

"Because it protects you. And when I jumped from the Humvee, I believed it would save me, too, in the same way you believe it will always save you."

"No, I don't," Thibault began.

"Then why, my friend, do you still carry it with you?"

* * *

It was Friday, his third day working at the kennel, and though Thibault had shed most traces of his former life, he was always aware of the photograph in his pocket. Just as he always thought about everything Victor had said to him that day.

He was walking a mastiff on a shady trail, out of sight of the office but still on the property. The dog was enormous, at least the size of a Great Dane, and had a tendency to lick Thibault's hand every ten seconds. Friendly.

He'd already mastered the simple routines of the job: feeding and exercising the dogs, cleaning the cages, scheduling appointments. Not hard. He was fairly certain that Nana was considering allowing him to help train the dogs as well. The day before, she'd asked him to watch her work with one of the dogs, and it reminded him of his work with Zeus: clear, short, simple commands, visual cues, firm guidance with the leash, and plenty of praise. When she finished, she told him to walk beside her as she brought the dog back to the kennel.

"Do you think you could handle something like that?" she asked.

"Yes."

She peeked over her shoulder at Zeus, who was trailing behind them. "Is it the same way you trained Zeus?"

"Pretty much."

When Nana had interviewed him, Thibault had made two requests. First, he asked that he be allowed to bring Zeus to work with him. Thibault had explained that after spending nearly all their time together, Zeus wouldn't react well to long daily separations. Thankfully, Nana had understood. "I worked with shepherds for a long time, so I know what you're talking about," she'd said. "As long as he doesn't become a bother, it's fine with me."

Zeus wasn't a bother. Thibault learned early on not to bring Zeus into the kennels when he was feeding or cleaning, since Zeus's presence made some of the other dogs nervous. But other than that, he fit right in. Zeus followed along as Thibault exercised the dogs or cleaned the training yard, and he lay on the porch near the doorway when Thibault was doing paperwork. When clients came in, Zeus always went on alert, as he'd been trained to do. It was enough to make most clients stop in their tracks, but a quick, "It's okay," was enough to keep him still.

Thibault's second request to Nana was that he be allowed to start work on Wednesday so he'd have time to get settled. She'd agreed to that as well. On Sunday, on the way home after leaving the kennel, he'd picked up a newspaper and searched the classifieds for a place to rent. It wasn't hard to pare the list; there were only four homes listed, and he was immediately able to eliminate two of the larger ones since he didn't need that much room.

Ironically, the remaining two choices were on opposite ends of town. The first house he found was in an older subdivision just off the downtown area and within sight of the South River. Good condition. Nice neighborhood. But not for him. Houses were sandwiched too close together. The second house, though, would work out fine. It was located at the end of a dirt road about two miles from work, on a rural lot that bordered the national forest. Conveniently, he could cut through the forest to get to the kennel. It didn't shorten his commute much, but it would allow Zeus to roam. The place was one-story, southern rustic, and at least a hundred years old, but kept in relatively good repair. After rubbing the dirt from the windows, he peeked inside. It needed some work, but not the kind that would prevent him from moving in. The kitchen was definitely old-school, and there was a wood-burning stove in the corner, one that probably provided the house's only heat. The wide-plank pine flooring was scuffed and stained, and the cabinets had probably been around since the place was built, but these things seemed to add to the house's character rather than detract from it. Even better, it seemed to be furnished with the basics: couch and end tables, lamps, even a bed.

Thibault called the number on the sign, and a couple of hours later, he heard the owner drive up. They made the requisite small talk, and it turned out the guy had spent twenty years in the army, the last seven at Fort Bragg. The place had belonged to his father, he'd explained, who'd passed away two months earlier. That was good, Thibault knew; homes were like cars in that if they weren't used regularly, they began to decay at an accelerating rate. It meant this one was probably still okay. The deposit and rent seemed a bit high to him, but Thibault needed a place quickly. He paid two months' rent and the deposit in advance. The expression on the guy's face told him that the last thing he'd expected was to receive that much cash.

Thibault slept at the house Monday night, spreading his sleeping bag on top of the mattress; on Tuesday, he trekked into town to order a new mattress from a place that agreed to deliver it that evening, then picked up supplies as well. When he returned, his backpack was filled with sheets and towels and cleaning supplies. It took another two trips to town to stock the refrigerator and get some plates, glasses, and utensils, along with a fifty-pound bag of food for Zeus. By the end of the day, he wished for the first time since he'd left Colorado that he had a car. But he was settled in, and that was enough. He was ready to go to work.

Since starting at the kennel on Wednesday, he'd spent most of his time with Nana, learning the ins and outs of the place. He hadn't seen much of Beth, or Elizabeth, as he liked to think of her; in the mornings, she drove off dressed for work and didn't return until late afternoon. Nana mentioned something about teacher meetings, which made sense, since school would be starting up next week. Aside from an occasional greeting, the only time they'd actually spoken was when she'd pulled him aside on his first day and asked him to look after Nana. He knew what she meant. It was obvious that Nana had suffered a stroke. Their morning training sessions left her breathing harder than seemed warranted, and on her way back to the house, her limp was more pronounced. It made him nervous.

He liked Nana. She had a unique turn of phrase. It amused him, and he wondered how much of it was an act. Eccentric or not, she was intelligent—no doubt about that. He often got the sense she was evaluating him, even in the course of normal conversations. She had opinions about everything, and she wasn't afraid to share them. Nor did she hesitate to tell him about herself. In the past few days, he'd learned quite a bit about her. She'd told him about her husband and the kennel, the training she'd done in the past, some of the places she'd visited. She also asked about him, and he dutifully answered her questions about his family and upbringing. Strangely, however, she never asked about his military service or if he'd served in Iraq, which struck him as unusual. But he didn't volunteer the information, because he didn't really want to talk about it either.

The way Nana studiously avoided the topic—and the four-year hole in his life—suggested that she understood his reticence. And maybe even that his time in Iraq had something to do with the reason he was here.

Smart lady.

Officially, he was supposed to work from eight until five. Unofficially, he showed up at seven and usually worked till seven. He didn't like to leave knowing there was still more to do. Conveniently, it also gave Elizabeth the chance to see him when she got home from work. Proximity bred familiarity, and familiarity bred comfort. And whenever he saw her, he was reminded that he'd come here because of her.

After that, his reasons for being here were somewhat vague, even to him. Yes, he'd come, but why? What did he want from her? Would he ever tell her the truth? Where was all this leading? On his trek from Colorado, whenever he'd pondered these questions, he'd simply assumed that he'd know the answers if and when he found the woman in the picture. But now that he'd found her, he was no closer to the truth than he'd been when he'd left.

In the meantime, he'd learned some things about her. That she had a son, for instance. That was a bit of a surprise—he'd never considered the possibility. Ben was his name. Seemed like a nice kid, from what little he could tell. Nana mentioned that he played chess and read a lot, but that was about it. Thibault noticed that since he'd started work, Ben had been watching him from behind the curtains or peeking in Thibault's direction when he spent time with Nana. But Ben kept his distance. He wondered if that was his choice or his mother's.

Probably his mother's.

He knew he hadn't made a good first impression on her. The way he froze when he first saw her didn't help. He'd known she was attractive, but the faded photo didn't capture the warmth of her smile or the serious way she studied him, as if searching for hidden flaws.

Lost in thought, he reached the main training area behind the office. The mastiff was panting hard, and Thibault led him toward the kennel. He told Zeus to sit and stay, then put the mastiff back in his cage. He filled the water bowl, along with a few others that seemed low, and retrieved from the office the simple lunch he'd packed earlier. Then he headed for the creek.

He liked to eat there. The brackish water and shady oak with its low-slung branches draped with Spanish moss lent a prehistoric feeling to the place that he and Zeus both enjoyed. Through the trees and at the edge of his vision, he noted a tree house and wood-planked rope bridge that appeared to have been constructed with scraps, something thrown together by someone not completely sure what they were doing. As usual, Zeus stood in the water up to his haunches, cooling off before ducking his head underwater and barking. Crazy dog.

"What's he doing?" a voice asked.

Thibault turned and saw Ben standing at the edge of the clearing. "No idea." He shrugged. "Barking at fish, I guess."

He pushed up his glasses. "Does he do that a lot?"

"Every time he's out here."

"It's strange," the boy remarked.

"I know."

Zeus took note of Ben's presence, making sure no threat was evident, then stuck his head under the water and barked again. Ben stayed at the edge of the clearing. Unsure what to say next, Thibault took another bite of his sandwich.

"I saw you come out here yesterday," Ben said.

"Yeah?"

"I followed you."

"I guess you did."

"My tree house is over there," he said. He pointed. "It's my secret hideout."

"It's a good thing to have," Thibault said. He motioned to the branch beside him. "You want to sit down?"

"I can't get too close."

"No?"

"My mom says you're a stranger."

"It's a good idea to listen to your mom."

Ben seemed satisfied with Thibault's response but uncertain about what to do next. He turned from Thibault to Zeus, debating, before deciding to take a seat on a toppled tree near where he'd been standing, preserving the distance between them.

"Are you going to work here?" he asked.

"I am working here."

"No. I mean are you going to quit?"

"I don't plan to." He raised an eyebrow. "Why?"

"Because the last two guys quit. They didn't like cleaning up the poop."

"Not everyone does."

"Does it bother you?"

"Not really."

"I don't like the way it smells." Ben made a face.

"Most people don't. I just try to ignore it."

Ben pushed his glasses up on his nose again. "Where'd you get the name Zeus?"

Thibault couldn't hide a smile. He'd forgotten how curious kids could be. "That was his name when I got him."

"Why didn't you change it to something you wanted?"

"I don't know. Didn't think about it, I guess."

"We had a German shepherd. His name was Oliver."

"Yeah?"

"He died."

"I'm sorry."

"It's okay," Ben assured him. "He was old."

Thibault finished his sandwich, stuffed the plastic wrap back in the bag, and opened the bag of nuts he'd packed. He noticed Ben staring at him and gestured toward the bag.

"You want some almonds?"

Ben shook his head. "I'm not supposed to accept food from strangers."

"Okay. How old are you?"

"Ten. How old are you?"

"Twenty-eight."

"You look older."

"So do you."

Ben smiled at that. "My name's Ben."

"Nice to meet you, Ben. I'm Logan Thibault."

"Did you really walk here from Colorado?"

Thibault squinted at him. "Who told you that?"

"I heard Mom talking to Nana. They said that most normal people would have drove."

"They're right."

"Did your legs get tired?"

"At first they did. But after a while, I got used to all the walking.

So did Zeus. Actually, I think he liked the walk. There was always something new to see, and he got to chase a zillion squirrels."

Ben shuffled his feet back and forth, his expression serious. "Can Zeus fetch?"

"Like a champ. But only for a few throws. He gets bored after that. Why? Do you want to throw a stick for him?"

"Can I?"

Thibault cupped his mouth and called for Zeus to come; the dog came bounding out of the water, paused a few feet away, and shook the water from his coat. He focused on Thibault.

"Get a stick."

Zeus immediately put his nose to the ground, sifting through myriad fallen branches. In the end, he chose a small stick and trotted toward Thibault.

Thibault shook his head. "Bigger," he said, and Zeus stared at him with what resembled disappointment before turning away. He dropped the stick and resumed searching. "He gets excited when he plays, and if the stick is too small, he'll snap it in half," Thibault explained. "He does it every time."

Ben nodded, looking solemn.

Zeus returned with a larger stick and brought it to Thibault. Thibault broke off a few of the remaining twigs, making it a bit smoother, then gave it back to Zeus.

"Take it to Ben."

Zeus didn't understand the command and tilted his head, ears pricked. Thibault pointed toward Ben. "Ben," he said. "Stick."

Zeus trotted toward Ben, stick in his mouth, then dropped it at Ben's feet. He sniffed Ben, took a step closer, and allowed Ben to pet him.

"He knows my name?"

"Now he does."

"Forever?"

"Probably. Now that he's smelled you."

"How could he learn it so fast?"

"He just does. He's used to learning things quickly."

Zeus sidled closer and licked Ben's face, then retreated, his gaze flickering from Ben to the stick and back again.

Thibault pointed to the stick. "He wants you to throw it. That's his way of asking."

Ben grabbed the stick and seemed to debate his next move. "Can I throw it in the water?"

"He'd love that."

Ben heaved it into the slow-moving creek. Zeus bounded into the water and began to paddle. He retrieved the stick, stopped a few feet from Ben to shake off, then got close and dropped the stick again.

"I trained him to shake off before he gets too close. I don't like getting wet," Thibault said.

"That's cool."

Thibault smiled as Ben threw the stick again.

"What else can he do?" Ben asked over his shoulder.

"Lots of things. Like . . . he's great at playing hide-and-go-seek. If you hide, he'll find you."

"Can we do that sometime?"

"Anytime you want."

"Awesome. Is he an attack dog, too?"

"Yes. But mostly he's friendly."

Finishing the rest of his lunch, Thibault watched as Ben continued to throw the stick. On the last throw, while Zeus retrieved it, he didn't trot toward Ben. Instead, he walked off to the side and lay down. Holding one paw over the stick, he began to gnaw.

"That means he's done," Thibault said. "You've got a good arm, by the way. Do you play baseball?"

"Last year. But I don't know if I'll play this year. I want to learn how to play the violin."

"I played the violin as a kid," Thibault remarked.

"Really?" Ben's face registered surprise.

"Piano, too. Eight years."

Off to the side, Zeus raised his head from the stick, becoming alert. A moment later, Thibault heard the sound of someone coming up the path as Elizabeth's voice floated through the trees.

"Ben?"

"Over here, Mom!" Ben shouted.

Thibault raised his palm toward Zeus. "It's okay."

"There you are," she said, stepping into view. "What are you doing out here?"

Her friendly expression froze as soon as she spotted Thibault, and he could plainly read the question in her eyes: *Why is my son in the woods with a man I barely know?* Thibault felt no need to defend himself. He'd done nothing wrong. Instead, he nodded a greeting.

"Hey."

"Hi," she said, her tone cautious. By that time, Ben was already running toward her.

"You should see what his dog can do, Mom! He's supersmart. Even smarter than Oliver was."

"That's great." She put an arm around him. "You ready to come inside? I have lunch on the table."

"He knows me and everything. . . ."

"Who?"

"The dog. Zeus. He knows my name."

She turned her gaze to Thibault. "Does he?"

Thibault nodded. "Yeah."

"Well . . . good."

"Guess what? He played the violin."

"Zeus?"

"No, Mom. Mr. Thibault did. As a kid. He played the violin."

"Really?" She seemed startled by that.

Thibault nodded. "My mom was kind of a music fanatic. She wanted me to master Shostakovich, but I wasn't that gifted. I could play a decent Mendelssohn, though."

Her smile was forced. "I see."

Despite her apparent discomfort, Thibault laughed.

"What?" she asked, obviously remembering their earlier encounter as well.

"Nothing."

"What's wrong, Mom?"

"Nothing," she said. "It's just that you should have told me where you were going."

"I come out here all the time."

"I know," she said, "but next time, let me know, okay?"

So I can keep an eye on you, she didn't say. *So I know you're safe*. Again, Thibault understood the message, even if Ben didn't.

"I should probably head back to the office," he said, rising from the branch. He collected the remains of his lunch. "I want to check the mastiff's water. He was hot, and I'm sure he finished his bowl. See you later, Ben. You too." He turned. "Zeus! Let's go."

Zeus sprang from his spot and went to Thibault's side; a moment later, they stood at the head of the footpath.

"Bye, Mr. Thibault," Ben called.

Thibault turned around, walking backward. "Nice talking to you, Ben. And by the way, it's not Mr. Thibault. Just Thibault."

With that, he turned back around, feeling the weight of Elizabeth's gaze on him until he vanished from sight.

9

Clayton

That evening, Keith Clayton lay on the bed smoking a cigarette, kind of glad that Nikki was in the shower. He liked the way she looked after a shower, with her hair wet and wild. The image kept him from dwelling on the fact that he would rather she grab her things and go on home.

It was the fourth time in the last five days that she'd spent the night. She was a cashier at the Quick Stop where he bought his Doritos, and for the last month or so, he'd been wondering whether or not to ask her out. Her teeth weren't so great and her skin was kind of pockmarked, but her body was killer, which was more than enough, considering he needed a bit of stress reduction.

Seeing Beth last Sunday night while she was dropping Ben off had done it. Wearing shorts and a tank top, she'd stepped out onto the porch and waved at Ben, flashing this kind of Farrah Fawcett smile. Even if it was directed at Ben, it drove home the fact that she was getting better-looking with every passing year.

Had he known that would happen, he might not have consented to the divorce. As it was, he'd left the place thinking about how pretty she was and ended up in bed with Nikki a few hours later.

The thing was, he didn't want to get back together with Beth.

There wasn't a chance of that happening. She was way too pushy, for one thing, and she had a tendency to argue when he made a decision she didn't like. He'd learned those things a long time ago, and he was reminded of it every time he saw her. Right after the divorce, the last thing he'd wanted to do was think about her, and for a long while, he hadn't. He'd lived his life, had a great time with lots of different girls, and pretty much figured he'd never look back. Aside from the kid, of course. Still, sometime around when Ben turned three or four, he started to hear whispers about her beginning to date, and it bugged him. It was one thing for him to date . . . but it was an entirely different situation altogether if she dated. The last thing he wanted was for some other guy to step in and pretend he was Ben's daddy. Beyond that, he realized he didn't like the thought of some other man in bed with Beth. It just didn't sit right with him. He knew men and knew what they wanted, and Beth was pretty much naive about that stuff, if only because he'd been her first. Most likely he, Keith Clayton, was the *only* man she'd ever been with, and that was good, since it kept her priorities straight. She was raising their son, and even if Ben was a bit of a pansy, Beth was doing a good job with him. Besides, she was a good person, and the last thing she deserved was for some guy to break her heart. She'd always need him to watch out for her.

But the other night . . .

He wondered if she'd dressed in that skimpy outfit in anticipation of him coming over. Wouldn't that have been something? A couple of months back, she'd even invited him inside while Ben was gathering his things. Granted, it was raining buckets and Nana had scowled at him the whole time, but Beth had been downright pleasant and sort of set him to thinking that he might have underestimated her. She had needs; everyone had needs. And what would be the harm if he helped satisfy hers every now and then? It wasn't as if he'd never seen her naked before, and they did have a kid together. What did they call it these days? Friends with benefits? He could imagine enjoying something like that with Beth. As long as she didn't talk too much or saddle him with a bunch of expectations. Snubbing out his cigarette, he wondered how he might propose something like that to her.

Unlike him, he knew, she'd been alone for a long, long time. Guys came sniffing around from time to time, but he knew how to deal with them. He remembered the little talk he'd had with Adam a couple of months back. The one who wore a blazer over a T-shirt, like he was some stud from Hollywood. Stud or not, he was pasty white when Clayton had approached the window after pulling him over on his way home from his third date with Beth. Clayton knew they'd shared a bottle of wine at dinner—he'd watched them from across the street—and when Clayton gave him a sobriety test with the inhaler he'd rigged for just such instances, the guy's skin went from pasty to chalk white.

"Had one too many, huh?" Clayton asked, responding with the requisite doubtful expression when the guy swore up and down that he'd had only a single glass. When he slipped on the cuffs, he thought the guy was either going to faint or wet his pants, which almost made him laugh out loud.

But he didn't. Instead, he filled out the paperwork, slowly, before giving him the talk—the one he delivered to anyone Beth seemed interested in. That they'd been married once and had a kid together, and how important it was to understand that he had a duty to keep them safe. And that the last thing Beth needed in her life was someone to distract her from raising their son or to get involved with someone who might just be using her. Just because they were divorced didn't mean he'd stopped caring.

The guy got the message, of course. They all did. Not only because of Clayton's family and connections, but because Clayton offered to lose the inhaler and the paperwork if the guy promised to leave her alone for a while and remembered to keep their conversation to himself. Because if she found out about their little talk, that wouldn't be good. Might cause problems with the kid, you see? And he didn't take kindly to anyone who caused problems with his kid.

The next day, of course, he'd been sitting in his parked squad car when Adam got off work. The guy went white at the sight of Clayton fiddling with the inhaler. Clayton knew he'd gotten the message before driving off, and the next time he saw Adam, he was with some redheaded secretary who worked in the same accounting office he did. Which meant, of course, that Clayton had been right: The guy had never planned to see Beth for the long term. He was just some loser hoping for a quick roll in the sack.

Well, it wouldn't be with Beth.

Beth would throw a hissy fit if she found out what he'd been doing, but fortunately, he hadn't had to do it all that often. Just every now and then, and things were working out fine.

More than fine, actually. Even the whole coed picture-taking fiasco had turned out okay. Neither the camera nor the disk had surfaced at either the sheriff's department or the newspaper since last weekend. He hadn't had a chance to look for that hippie loser on Monday morning because of some papers that had to be served out in the county, but he found out the guy had been staying at the Holiday Motor Court. Unfortunately—or fortunately, he supposed—the guy had checked out, and he hadn't been seen since. Which most likely meant he was long gone by now.

All in all, things were good. Real good. He especially liked the brainstorm he'd had about Beth—the friends with benefits thing. Wouldn't that be something? He clasped his hands behind his head and lay back on the pillows just as Nikki stepped out of the bathroom wrapped in her towel, with steam trailing behind her. He smiled.

"Come here, Beth."

She froze. "My name is Nikki."

"I know that. But I want to call you Beth tonight."

"What are you talking about?"

His eyes flashed. "Just shut up and come here, would you?"

After a moment's hesitation, Nikki took a reluctant step forward.

10

Beth

Maybe she'd misjudged him, Beth admitted. At least as far as work went, anyway. In the last three weeks, Logan Thibault had been the perfect employee. Better than that, even. Not only hadn't he missed a day, but he arrived early so he could feed the dogs—something Nana had always done until her stroke—and stayed late to sweep the floors of the office. Once, she'd even seen him cleaning the windows with Windex and crumpled newspaper. The kennels were as clean as they'd ever been, the training yard was mowed every other afternoon, and he'd even started to reorganize the customer files. It got to the point that Beth felt guilty when she handed him his first paycheck. She knew that the paycheck was barely enough to live on. But when she'd handed the check to him, he'd simply smiled and said, "Thanks. This is great."

It was all she could do to muster a subdued, "You're welcome."

Other than that, they hadn't seen much of each other. They were in the third week of school, and Beth was still getting back into the flow of teaching again, which necessitated long hours in her small home office, updating lesson plans and correcting homework. Ben, on the other hand, raced out of the car as soon as he got home to play with Zeus. From what Beth observed from the window, Ben seemed to view the dog as his new best buddy, and the dog seemed to feel the same way. As soon as their car rolled up the drive, the dog would start nosing around for a stick, and he'd greet Ben with it when the car door swung open. Ben would scramble out, and as she walked up the porch steps, she'd hear Ben laughing as they raced across the yard. Logan—the name seemed to fit him better than Thibault, despite what he'd said at the creek—watched them as well, a slight smile playing across his face, before he turned back to whatever he was doing.

Despite herself, she liked his smile and the ease with which it surfaced when he was with Ben or Nana. She knew that sometimes war had a way of crawling into a soldier's psyche, making it hard to readapt to the civilian world, but he showed no sign of any post-traumatic stress disorder. He seemed almost normal—aside from walking across the country, that is—which suggested that he might never have been overseas. Nana swore that she hadn't asked him about it yet. Which was odd in and of itself, considering Nana, but that was another story. Still, he seemed to be fitting into their little family business better than she'd imagined possible. A couple of days earlier, just as Logan was finishing up work for the day, she'd heard Ben race through the house to his bedroom, only to clatter out the front door again. When she peeked out the window, she realized that Ben had retrieved his baseball from his room to play catch with Logan in the yard. She watched them throw the baseball back and forth, Zeus doing his best to chase down the missed balls before Ben could get to them.

If only her ex had been there to see how happily Ben played when he was not being pressured or criticized.

She wasn't surprised that Logan and Nana were getting along, but the frequency with which Nana brought him up after he'd left for the night, and the glowing nature of her comments, took her aback. "You'd like him," she'd say, or, "I wonder if he knew Drake," which was her way of hinting that Beth should make an effort to get to know him. Nana had even begun to allow him to train the dogs, which was something she'd *never* allowed another employee to do. Every now and then, she'd mention something interesting about his past—that he'd slept beside a family of armadillos in north Texas, for instance, or that he'd once dreamed of working for the Koobi Fora Research Project in Kenya, investigating the origin of man. When she mentioned such things, there was no denying her fascination with Logan and what made him tick.

Best of all, things around the kennel were beginning to calm down. After a long, hectic summer, their days had settled into a rhythm of sorts, which explained why Beth was eyeing Nana with apprehension over the dinner table at Nana's news.

"What do you mean you're going to visit your sister?"

Nana added a pat of butter to the bowl of shrimp and grits before her. "I haven't had a chance to visit my sister since the incident, and I want to see how she's doing. She's older than I am, you know. And now that you're teaching and Ben is at school, I can't think of a better time to go."

"Who's going to take care of the kennel?"

"Thibault. He's got it down to a science by now, even the training part of this. He said he'd be more than happy to work some additional hours. And he also said he'd drive me to Greensboro, so you don't have to worry about that, either. We've got it all worked out. He even volunteered to start straightening up the files for me." She speared a shrimp and chewed vigorously.

"Can he drive?" Beth inquired.

"He says he can."

"But he doesn't have a license."

"He said he'd get one at the DMV. That's why he left early. I called Frank, and he said he'd be glad to work him in for the driving test today."

"He doesn't have a car—"

"He's using my truck."

"How did he get there?"

"He drove."

"But he doesn't have a license!"

"I thought I already explained that." Nana looked at her as if she'd suddenly become slow-witted.

"What about the choir? You're just getting back into it."

"It's fine. I already told the music director I'd be visiting my sister, and she says there's no problem. In fact, she thinks it's a good idea. Of course, I've been with the choir a lot longer than she has, so she couldn't exactly say no."

Beth shook her head, trying to stay on subject. "When did you start planning all this? The visit, I mean?"

Nana took another bite and pretended to consider. "When she called and asked me, of course."

"When did she call you?" Beth pressed.

"This morning."

"This morning?" From the corner of her eye, Beth noticed Ben following the interchange like a spectator at a tennis match. She shot him a warning look before returning her attention to Nana. "Are you sure this is a good idea?"

"It's like candy on a battleship," Nana said with an air of finality.

"What does that mean?"

"It means," Nana said, "that I'm going to see my sister. She said she's bored and that she misses me. She asked me to come, and so I agreed to go. It's as simple as that."

"How long do you intend to be gone?" Beth suppressed a rising sense of panic.

"I'm guessing about a week."

"A week?"

Nana glanced at Ben. "I think your mom has caterpillars in her ears. She keeps repeating everything I say like she can't hear me."

Ben giggled and popped a shrimp into his mouth. Beth stared at them both. Sometimes, she thought, dinner with these two was no better than eating with the second graders in the cafeteria.

"What about your medicine?" she asked.

Nana added some more shrimp and grits to her bowl. "I'll bring it. I can take my pills there just as easy as I can take them here."

"What if something happens to you?"

"I'd probably be better off there, don't you think?"

"How can you say that?"

"Now that school has started, you and Ben are gone most of the day and I'm alone in the house. There's no way Thibault would even know if I was in trouble. But when I'm in Greensboro, I'll be with my sister. And believe it or not, she has a phone and everything. She stopped using smoke signals last year."

Ben giggled again but knew enough not to say anything. Instead, he grinned at the contents of his bowl.

"But you haven't left the kennel since Grandpa died—"

"Exactly," Nana cut her off.

"But . . ."

Nana reached across the table to pat Beth's hand. "Now, I know you're worried that you won't have my sparkling wit to keep you company for a while, but it'll give you a chance to get to know Thibault. He'll be here this weekend, too, to help you out with the kennel."

"This weekend? When are you leaving?"

"Tomorrow," she said.

"Tomorrow?" Beth's voice came out as a squeak.

Nana winked at Ben. "See what I mean? Caterpillars."

After cleaning up the dinner dishes, Beth wandered to the front porch for a few solitary minutes. She knew Nana's mind was made up, and she knew she'd overreacted. Stroke or not, Nana could take care of herself, and Aunt Mimi would be thrilled to see her. Aunt Mimi had trouble walking to the kitchen these days, and it might very well be the last chance Nana had to spend a week with her.

But the exchange troubled her. It wasn't the trip itself that bothered her, but what their little struggle at the dinner table signaled— the beginning of a new role for her in coming years, one she didn't feel altogether ready for. It was easy to play parent to Ben. Her role and responsibilities were clear-cut there. But playing parent to Nana? Nana had always been so full of life, so full of energy, that until a few months ago it had been inconceivable to Beth that Nana would ever slow down. And she was doing well, really well, especially considering the stroke. But what was going to happen the next time Nana wanted to do something that Beth honestly believed wasn't in her best interest? Something simple . . . like driving at night, for instance? Nana couldn't see as well as she used to, and what was going to happen in a few years when Nana insisted that she wanted to drive to the grocery store after work?

She knew that in the end, she'd handle these situations when the time came. But she dreaded it. It had been hard enough to keep Nana in check this summer, and that was when her physical problems were obvious even to Nana. What was going to happen when Nana didn't want to admit to them?

Her thoughts were interrupted by the sight of Nana's truck slowly rolling up the drive and coming to a stop near the back entrance to the kennel. Logan got out and went around to the bed of the truck. She watched him sling a fifty-pound bag of dog food over his shoulder and head inside. When he emerged, Zeus was trotting beside him, nosing at his hand; Beth figured that he must have kept Zeus inside the office while he'd been in town.

It took him a few more minutes to unload the rest of the dog food, and when he was done, he started toward the house. By then, dusk had begun to fall. The faint echo of thunder sounded in the distance, and Beth could hear the crickets beginning their evening song. She suspected the storm would hold off; with the exception of a couple of scattered showers, it had been miserably dry all summer. But the air, carried from the ocean, was scented with pine and salt, and she flashed on memories from a beach long ago. She could remember seeing spider crabs scuttling before beams from the flashlights that she and Drake and Grandpa were holding; her mom's face illuminated by the glow of the small bonfire her dad had started; the sight of Nana's marshmallow catching fire as they toasted them for s'mores. It was one of the few memories she had of her parents, and she wasn't even sure how much of it was real. Because she'd been so young, she suspected that Nana's memories had become fused with her own. Nana had told her the story of that night countless times, perhaps because it was the last time they'd all been together. Beth's parents had died in an auto accident only a few days later.

"Are you all right?"

Distracted by her memories, Beth hadn't noticed that Logan had reached the porch. In the fading light, his features seemed softer than she remembered.

"Yeah, I'm fine." She straightened up and smoothed her blouse. "I was just thinking."

"I have the keys to the truck," he said, his voice quiet. "I wanted to drop them off before I went home."

When he held them out, she knew she could simply thank him and say good night, but—maybe because she was still upset that Nana had made her decision to leave without talking to her about it first, or maybe because she wanted to make her own decision about Logan—she took the keys and deliberately held his gaze. "Thanks," she said. "Long day for you, huh?"

If he was surprised by her invitation to talk, he didn't show it. "It wasn't too bad. And I got a lot done."

"Like regaining the ability to drive legally?"

He offered a lazy smile. "Among other things."

"Did the brakes give you any problems?"

"Not once I got used to the grinding."

Beth grinned at the thought. "I'll bet the examiner loved that."

"I'm sure he did. I could tell by the wincing."

She laughed, and for a moment, neither of them said anything. On the horizon, lightning flashed. It took some time before the thunder sounded, and she knew the storm was still a few miles off.

In the silence, she noticed Logan was looking at her with that peculiar déjà vu expression again. He seemed to realize it and quickly turned away. Beth followed his gaze and saw that Zeus had wandered toward the trees. The dog stood at attention, staring at Logan as if to ask, *Do you want to go for a walk?* Emphasizing his point, Zeus barked and Logan shook his head.

"Hold your horses," he called out. He turned back toward Beth. "He's been cooped up for a while and he wants to wander."

"Isn't he doing that now?"

"No, I mean he wants me to wander with him. He won't let me out of his sight."

"Ever?"

"He can't help it. He's a shepherd and he thinks I'm his flock."

Beth raised his eyebrow. "Small flock."

"Yeah, but it's growing. He's really taken to Ben and Nana."

"Not me?" She pretended to look wounded.

Logan shrugged. "You haven't thrown a stick for him."

"That's all it takes?"

"He's a cheap date."

She laughed again. Somehow she hadn't expected him to have a sense of humor. Surprising her, he motioned over his shoulder. "Would you like to walk with us? For Zeus, it's almost as good as throwing a stick."

"Oh, it is, huh?" she parried, stalling.

"I don't make the rules. I just know what they are. And I'd hate for you to feel left out."

She hesitated briefly before accepting that he was just trying to be friendly. She glanced over her shoulder. "I should probably let Nana and Ben know I'm going."

"You can, but we won't be gone long. Zeus just wants to go to the creek and splash around for a few minutes before we go home. Otherwise, he gets hot." He rocked on his heels, hands in his pockets. "You ready?"

"Yeah, let's go."

They stepped off the porch and headed down the gravel path. Zeus trotted ahead of them, checking every now and then to make sure they were following. They walked side by side, but with enough distance to ensure they didn't touch accidentally.

"Nana told me you're a teacher?" Logan inquired.

Beth nodded. "Second grade."

"How's your class this year?"

"It seems like a good group of kids. So far, anyway. And I've already had seven mothers sign up to volunteer, which is always a good sign."

Moving past the kennel, they approached the small trail that led to the creek. The sun had dipped below the trees, casting the trail in shadow. As they walked, thunder boomed again.

"How long have you been teaching?"

"Three years."

"Do you enjoy it?"

"Most of the time. I work with a lot of great people, so that makes it easier."

"But?"

She didn't seem to understand his question. He pushed his hands into his pockets and went on.

"There's always a 'but' when it comes to jobs. Like, I love my job and my colleagues are first-rate, but . . . a couple of them like to dress up like superheroes on the weekend and I can't help but wonder if they're nuts."

She laughed. "No, they really are great. And I do love teaching. It's just that every now and then there's a student who comes from a challenging family background, and you know there's nothing you can do for them. It's enough to break your heart sometimes." She walked a few steps in silence. "How about you, though? Do you like working here?"

"Yeah, I do." He sounded sincere.

"But?"

He shook his head. "No buts."

"That's not fair. I told you."

"Yes, but you weren't talking to the boss's granddaughter. And speaking of my boss, do you have any idea what time we'll be leaving tomorrow?"

"She didn't tell you?"

"No. I figured I'd ask when I dropped off the keys."

"She didn't say, but I'm sure she'll want you to train and exercise the dogs before you leave so the dogs won't get antsy."

They'd come within sight of the creek, and Zeus plunged ahead into the water, splashing and barking. Logan and Beth watched him frolic before Logan motioned toward the low branch. Beth took a seat and he joined her, carefully preserving the space between them.

"How far is Greensboro from here?" he asked.

"Five hours, there and back. It's mainly on the interstate."

"Do you have any idea when she'll be coming home?"

Beth shrugged. "She told me a week."

"Oh . . ." Logan seemed to digest this.

All worked out, my foot, Beth thought. Logan was more in the dark than she was. "I'm getting the impression Nana didn't tell you much about this."

"Just that she was going and I was driving, so I'd better get my license. Oh, and that I'd be working this weekend."

"That figures. Listen, about that . . . I can handle things this weekend if you have things to do—"

"It's no problem," Logan said. "I don't have anything planned. And there are some things I haven't had a chance to get to yet. Just some little things that need to be fixed."

"Like installing an air conditioner in the kennel office?"

"I was thinking more along the lines of painting the door trim and seeing what I can do to get the office window to open."

"The one that's painted shut? Good luck. My grandpa tried to fix it for years. He once worked a whole day on it with a razor blade and ended up wearing Band-Aids for a week. It still wouldn't open."

"You're not filling me with confidence here," Logan said.

"Just trying to warn you. And it's funny because it was my grandpa who painted it shut in the first place, and he had a whole storage shed full of just about every tool you could imagine. He was one of those guys who thought he could fix anything, but it never quite worked out as well as he'd planned. He was more of a visionary than a nuts-and-bolts kind of guy. Have you seen Ben's tree house and the bridge?"

"From a distance," Logan admitted.

"A case in point. It took Grandpa most of one summer to build it, and whenever Ben goes there now, I cringe. How it's lasted this long without blowing over I have no idea. It scares me, but Ben loves to go there, especially when he's upset or nervous about something. He calls it his hideout. He goes there a lot." When she paused, he could see her concern, but it lasted only an instant before she came back to him. "Anyway, Grandpa was a prize. All heart and soul, and he gave us the most idyllic childhood you could imagine."

"Us?"

"My brother and me." She gazed toward the tree, the leaves silver in the moonlight. "Did Nana tell you what happened to my parents?"

He nodded. "Briefly. I'm sorry."

She waited, wondering if he'd add anything else, but he didn't. "What was it like?" she asked. "Walking across the country?"

Logan took his time answering. "It was . . . peaceful. Just being able to go where I wanted, when I wanted, with no rush to get there."

"You make it sound therapeutic."

"It was, I suppose." A sad smile flickered across his face, then was gone. "In a way."

As he said it, the fading light reflected in his eyes, making them seem as if they were changing color incrementally. "Did you find what you were looking for?" she asked, her expression serious.

Logan paused. "Yeah, actually I did."

"And?"

"I don't know yet."

She evaluated his answer, unsure what to make of it. "Now don't take this the wrong way, but for some reason, I don't see you staying in one place for very long."

"Is that because I walked from Colorado?"

"That has a lot to do with it."

He laughed, and for the first time, Beth was conscious of how long it had been since she'd had a conversation like this. It felt easy and unforced. With Adam, the conversation had been stiff, as though both had been trying too hard. She still wasn't sure how she felt about Logan, but it seemed right that they were finally on friendly terms. She cleared her throat. "Now, about tomorrow. I'm thinking that maybe the two of you should take my car, and I'll use the truck to go to school. I'm a little worried about the truck's brakes."

"I have to admit I wondered about that, too. But I'm pretty sure I can fix it. Not by tomorrow, but on the weekend."

"You can repair cars, too?"

"Yes. But brakes aren't hard. They need some new pads, but I think the rotors are probably okay."

"Is there anything you can't do?" Beth asked, only half feigning amazement.

"Yes."

She laughed. "That's good. But okay, I'll talk to Nana and I'm sure she'll be fine with using my car. I don't trust those brakes at highway speed. And I'll make sure to check on the dogs when I finish up at school, okay? I'm sure Nana didn't mention that to you either. But I will."

He nodded just as Zeus padded out. He shook off, then moved closer to sniff at Beth before licking her hands.

"He likes me."

"He's probably just tasting you."

"Funny," she said. It was the type of thing Drake would have said, and she was struck by the sudden desire to be alone once again. She stood. "I should probably be heading back. I'm sure they're wondering where I am."

Logan noticed the clouds had continued to thicken. "Yeah, me too. I want to get home before it starts pouring. The storm seems to be getting closer."

"Do you want a ride?"

"Thank you, but no, that's okay. I like to walk."

"Gee, I never would have known," she said with a faint smile. They retraced their steps to the house, and when they reached the gravel drive, Beth pulled a hand out of her jeans pocket and gave a small wave.

"Thanks for the walk, Logan."

She expected him to correct her the way he had with Ben—to tell her again he was called Thibault—but he didn't. Instead, he raised his chin slightly and grinned.

"You too, Elizabeth."

She knew the storm wouldn't last long, though they desperately needed the rain. It had been a hot, dry summer, and it seemed like the heat would never break. As she sat listening to the last drops of rain falling on the tin roof, she found herself thinking about her brother.

Before Drake left, he'd told her that the sound of rain on their roof was the sound he would miss most of all. She wondered if he often dreamed of these North Carolina summer storms in the dry land where he ended up. The thought made her feel hollow and sad all over again.

Nana was in her room packing for her trip, as excited as she'd been in years. Ben, on the other hand, was becoming more and more subdued, which meant he was thinking about the fact that he'd have to spend a big chunk of the weekend with his father. Which also meant she'd have a weekend alone at home, her first solo weekend in a long, long time.

Except for Logan.

She could understand why both Nana and Ben had been drawn to him. He possessed a quiet confidence that seemed rare these days. It was only after she got back to the house that she realized she'd learned little about him that he hadn't already told her during their initial interview. She wondered whether he'd always been so private or if it stemmed from his time in Iraq.

He'd been there, she'd decided. No, he hadn't said as much, but she'd seen something in his expression when she'd mentioned her parents—his simple response hinted at a familiarity with tragedy and an acceptance of it as an unavoidable aspect of life.

She didn't know whether that made her feel better or worse about him. Like Drake, he was a marine. But Logan was here, and Drake was gone, and for that reason as well as more complicated ones, she wasn't sure that she could ever look at Logan with fairness in her heart.

Gazing up at the stars that had emerged between the storm clouds, she felt the loss of Drake like a newly reopened wound. After their parents had died, they had been inseparable, even sleeping in the same bed for a year. He was only a year younger than her, and she distinctly remembered walking to school with him on the first day of kindergarten. To stop his tears, she had promised that he'd make lots of friends and that she'd wait by the swing set to walk him home. Unlike many siblings, they had never been rivals. She was his biggest cheerleader, and he was her unwavering supporter. Throughout high school, she went to every football, basketball, and baseball game he played and tutored him when he needed it. For his part, he was the only one who remained unfazed by her dizzying teenage mood swings. The only disagreement they'd ever had concerned Keith, but unlike Nana, Drake kept his feelings largely to himself. But she knew how he felt, and when she and Keith separated, it was Drake she turned to for support as she tried to find her footing as a newly single mother. And it was Drake, she knew, who kept Keith from pounding on her door late at night in the months immediately afterward. Drake had been the one person she'd ever known that Keith was afraid to cross.

By that point, he'd matured. Not only had he been an excellent athlete in virtually every sport, but he'd taken up boxing when he was twelve. By eighteen, he'd won the Golden Gloves in North Carolina three times, and he sparred regularly with troops stationed at Fort Bragg and Camp Lejeune. It was the hours he spent with them that first made Drake consider enlisting.

He'd never been a great student, and he lasted only a year at a community college before deciding it wasn't for him. She'd been the only one he'd talked to about enlisting. She had been proud of his decision to serve his country, her heart bursting with love and admiration the first time she saw him outfitted in his dress blues. Though she had been scared when he was posted to Kuwait and, later, Iraq, she couldn't help but believe that he was going to make it. But Drake Green never did make it home.

She could barely recall the days immediately after she'd learned that her brother had died, and she didn't like to think of them now. His death had left her with an emptiness that she knew would never fill completely. But time had lessened the pain. In the immediacy of his loss, she never would have believed it possible, but she couldn't deny that when she thought of Drake these days, it was usually the happier times she remembered. Even when she visited the cemetery to talk to him, she no longer experienced the agony those visits once aroused. Nowadays, her sadness felt less visceral than her anger.

But it felt real right now, in the wake of the realization that she—like Nana and Ben—was drawn to Thibault, too, if only because she felt an ease with him that she hadn't known with anyone since losing Drake.

And there was this: Only Drake had ever called her by her given name. Neither her parents nor Nana, nor Grandpa, nor any of her friends growing up had ever called her anything but Beth. Keith hadn't, either; to be honest, she wasn't sure he even knew her real name. Only Drake had called her Elizabeth, and only when they were alone. It was their secret, a secret meant for just the two of them, and she'd never been able to imagine how it would sound coming from someone else.

But, somehow, Logan made it sound just right.

11

Thibault

In the fall of 2007, a year after getting out of the Marine Corps, Thibault arranged to meet Victor in Minnesota, a place neither of them had ever been. For both of them, it couldn't have come at a better time. Victor had been married for six months, and Thibault had stood beside him as best man. That had been the only time they'd seen each other since they'd been discharged. When Thibault had called to suggest the trip, he'd suspected that time alone was exactly what Victor needed.

On the first day, as they sat in a small rowboat on the lake, it was Victor who broke the silence.

"Have you been having nightmares?" his friend asked.

Thibault shook his head. "No. Have you?"

"Yes," Victor said.

The air was typically crisp for autumn, and a light morning mist floated just above the water. But the sky was cloudless, and Thibault knew the temperature would rise, making for a gorgeous afternoon.

"The same as before?" Thibault asked.

"Worse," he said. He reeled in his line and cast again. "I see dead people." He gave a wry half-smile, fatigue written into the lines of his face. "Like in that movie with Bruce Willis? *The Sixth Sense?*"

Thibault nodded.

"Kind of like that." He paused, somber now. "In my dreams, I relive everything we went through, except there are changes. In most of them, I get shot, and I scream for help, but no one comes, and I realize everyone else has been shot as well. And I can feel myself dying little by little." He rubbed his eyes before going on. "As hard as that is, it's worse when I see them during the day—the ones who died, I mean. I'll be at the store, and I'll see them all, standing there blocking the aisle. Or they're on the ground bleeding as medics work on them. But they never make a sound. All they do is stare at me, like it's my fault they were wounded, or my fault that they're dying. And then I blink and take a deep breath and they're gone." He stopped. "It makes me think I'm going crazy."

"Have you talked to anyone about it?" Thibault asked.

"No one. Except for my wife, I mean, but when I say those things to her, she gets frightened and starts to cry. So I don't talk to her about it anymore."

Thibault said nothing.

"She's pregnant, you know," Victor went on.

Thibault smiled, grasping at this ray of hope. "Congratulations."

"Thank you. It's a boy. I'm going to name him Logan."

Thibault sat up straight and nodded at Victor. "I'm honored."

"It frightens me sometimes—the thought of having a son. I'm worried I won't be a good father." He stared out over the water.

"You'll be a great dad," Thibault assured him.

"Maybe."

Thibault waited.

"I have no patience anymore. So many things make me angry. Little things, things that shouldn't mean anything, but for some reason they do. And even though I try to push the anger back down, it sometimes comes out anyway. It hasn't caused me any problems yet, but I wonder how long I can keep pushing it down before it gets away from me." He adjusted the line with his fishing rod. "This happens to you, too?"

"Sometimes," Thibault admitted.

"But not too often?"

"No."

"I didn't think so. I forgot that things are different for you. Because of the picture, I mean."

Thibault shook his head. "That's not true. It hasn't been easy for me, either. I can't walk down the street without looking over my shoulder or scanning the windows above to make sure no one has a gun pointed at me. And half the time, it's like I don't re-member how to have an ordinary conversation with people. I can't relate to most of their concerns. Who works where and how much they earn, or what's on television, or who's dating who. I feel like asking, Who cares?"

"You never were any good at making small talk," Victor snorted.

"Thanks."

"But as for looking over your shoulder, that's normal. I do that, too."

"Yeah?"

"But so far, no guns."

Thibault laughed under his breath. "Good thing, huh?" Then, because he wanted to change the subject, he asked, "How do you like roofing?"

"It's hot in the summer."

"Like Iraq?"

"No. Nothing is hot like Iraq. But hot enough." He smiled. "I got a promotion. I'm a crew leader now."

"Good for you. How's Maria?"

"Getting bigger, but she's happy. And she is my life. I am so lucky to have married her." He shook his head in wonder.

"I'm glad."

"There is nothing like love. You should try it."

Thibault shrugged. "Maybe one day."

Elizabeth.

He'd seen something cross her face when he'd called her Elizabeth, some emotion he couldn't identify. The name captured her essence far more than plain and simple "Beth." There was an elegance to it that matched the graceful way she moved, and though he hadn't planned on calling her that, the syllables had rolled off his tongue as if he'd had no choice.

On his walk back home, he found himself replaying their conversation and recalling how natural it felt to sit beside her. She was more relaxed than he'd imagined, but he could sense that, like Nana, she wasn't sure what to think of him. Later, as he lay in bed at night staring at the ceiling, he wondered what she thought of him.

On Friday morning, Thibault made sure everything was taken care of before driving Nana to Greensboro in Elizabeth's car. Zeus rode in the backseat with his head out the window for most of the trip, his ears blown back, intrigued by the ever changing smells and scenery. Thibault hadn't expected Nana to allow Zeus to ride along, but she'd waved the dog into the car. "Beth won't care. And besides, my case will fit in the trunk."

The drive back to Hampton seemed to go faster, and when he pulled in he was pleased to see Ben near the house, tossing a ball into the air. Zeus bounded toward him expectantly, and Ben sent the ball flying. Zeus zoomed after it, his ears back, tongue hanging out. As Thibault approached, he saw Elizabeth walk out onto the front porch and realized with sudden certainty that she was one of the most beautiful women he'd ever seen. Dressed in a summer blouse and shorts that revealed her shapely legs, she gave a friendly wave when she spotted them, and it was all he could do not to stare.

"Hey, Thibault!" Ben called from the yard. He was chasing after

Zeus, who pranced with the ball in his mouth, proud of his ability to stay just a couple of steps ahead of Ben no matter how fast the boy ran.

"Hey, Ben! How was school?"

"Boring!" he shouted. "How was work?"

"Exciting!"

Ben kept running. "Yeah, right!"

Since Ben had started school, they'd shared pretty much the same exchange every day. Thibault shook his head in amusement just as Elizabeth stepped down from the porch.

"Hi, Logan."

"Hello, Elizabeth."

She leaned against the railing, a slight smile on her face. "How was the drive?"

"Not too bad."

"Must have been strange, though."

"How so?"

"When was the last time you drove for five hours?"

He scratched at the back of his neck. "I don't know. It's been a long time."

"Nana said you were kind of fidgety as you drove, like you couldn't get comfortable." She motioned over her shoulder. "I just hung up the phone with her. She's already called twice."

"Bored?"

"No, the first time she called to talk to Ben. To see how school went."

"And?"

"He told her it was boring."

"At least he's consistent."

"Sure, but I wish he would say something different. Like, 'I learned a lot and have so much fun doing it.'" She smiled. "Every mother's dream, right?"

"I'll take your word for it."

"Are you thirsty?" she asked. "Nana left some lemonade in a pitcher. She made it before she left this morning."

"I'd love some. But I should probably check on the dogs' water first."

"Already done." She turned and went to the door. She held it open for him. "Come on in. I'll be just a minute, okay?"

He went up the steps, paused to wipe his feet, and stepped inside. Taking in the room, he noted the antique furniture and original paintings that hung on the wall. Like a country parlor, he thought, which wasn't what he had pictured.

"Your home is lovely," he called out.

"Thank you." Her head poked out from the kitchen. "Haven't you seen it before?"

"No."

"I just assumed you had. Feel free to take a look around."

She vanished from view, and Thibault wandered around the room, noting the collection of Hummels displayed on the shelves of the dining room hutch. He smiled. He'd always liked those things.

On the mantel, he spotted a collection of photographs and moved to study them. Two or three were of Ben, including one in which he was missing a couple of his front teeth. Beside them was a nice shot of Elizabeth in a cap and gown, standing beside her grandparents, and a portrait of Nana and her husband. In the corner, he noted a portrait of a young marine in dress blues, standing at ease.

The young marine who'd lost the photo in Iraq?

"That's Drake," she said from behind him. "My brother."

Thibault turned. "Younger or older?"

"A year younger."

She handed him the glass of lemonade without further comment, and Thibault sensed that the subject was closed. She took a step toward the front door.

"Let's go sit on the porch. I've been inside all day, and besides, I want to keep an eye on Ben. He has a tendency to wander."

Elizabeth took a seat on the steps out front. The sun drilled down through the clouds, but the shade from the porch stretched to cover them. Elizabeth tucked a strand of hair behind her ear. "Sorry. This is the best I can do. I've been trying to talk Nana into getting a porch swing, but she says it's too country."

In the distance, Ben and Zeus were running through the grass, Ben laughing as he tried to grab for the stick in Zeus's mouth. Elizabeth smiled. "I'm glad to see him getting his energy out. He had his first violin lesson today, so he didn't have a chance after school."

"Did he enjoy it?"

"He liked it. Or at least he said he did." She turned toward him. "Did you like it when you were a kid?"

"Most of the time. Until I got older, anyway."

"Let me guess. Then you got interested in girls and sports?"

"Don't forget cars."

"Typical," she groaned. "But normal. I'm just excited because it was his choice. He's always been interested in music, and his teacher is a gem. She's got all the patience in the world."

"That's good. And it'll be good for him."

She pretended to scrutinize him. "I don't know why, but I see you as more of an electric guitar player than someone who played the violin."

"Because I walked from Colorado?"

"Don't forget your hair."

"I had a buzz cut for years."

"And then your clippers went on strike, right?"

"Something like that."

She smiled and reached for her glass. In the silence that followed, Thibault took in the view. Across the yard, a flock of starlings broke from the trees, moving in unison before settling again on the opposite side. Puffy clouds drifted past, changing shape as they moved in the afternoon breeze, and he could sense Elizabeth watching him.

"You don't feel the need to talk all the time, do you," she said.

He smiled. "No."

"Most people don't know how to appreciate silence. They can't help talking."

"I talk. I just want to have something to say first."

"You're going to have a tough time in Hampton. Most people around here either talk about their family, their neighbors, the weather, or the championship prospects of the high school football team."

"Yeah?"

"It gets boring."

He nodded. "I can see that." He took another drink, finishing his glass. "So how does the football team look this year?"

She laughed. "Exactly." She reached for his glass. "Would you like more?"

"No, I'm fine. Thank you. Very refreshing."

She set his glass beside hers. "Homemade. Nana squeezed the lemons herself."

He nodded. "I noticed she has a forearm like Popeye."

She circled the rim of her glass with her finger, secretly admitting to herself that she liked his wit. "So I guess it'll be just you and me this weekend."

"What about Ben?"

"He's going to see his father tomorrow. He goes every other weekend."

"Yeah?"

She sighed. "But he doesn't want to go. He never wants to go."

Thibault nodded, studying Ben from a distance.

"Nothing to say?" she prodded.

"I'm not sure what I should say."

"But if you would have said something . . ."

"I would have said that Ben probably has a good reason."

"And I would have said you're right."

"You two don't get along?" Thibault asked carefully.

"Actually, we get along okay. Not great, mind you. But okay. It's Ben and his dad who don't get along. My ex has problems with Ben," she said. "I think he wanted a different kind of kid."

"Why do you let Ben go, then?" His gaze focused on her with surprising intensity.

"Because I don't have a choice."

"There's always a choice."

"Not in this case there isn't." She leaned off to the side, plucking a marigold from beside the stairs. "The dad has joint custody, and if I tried to fight him on it, let's just say the courts would probably rule in his favor. If anything, Ben would probably have to go even more than he does now."

"That doesn't sound fair."

"It isn't. But for now, there's not much else I can do but tell Ben to try to make the best of it."

"I get the sense there's a lot more to the story."

She laughed. "You have no idea."

"Want to talk about it?"

"Not really."

Whatever urge Thibault might have had to press further was contained by the sight of Ben walking toward the porch. He was drenched in sweat, his face red. His glasses were slightly crooked. Zeus trailed behind, panting hard.

"Hey, Mom!"

"Hi, sweetie. Did you have a good time?"

Zeus lapped at Thibault's hand before collapsing at his feet.

"Zeus is great! Did you see us playing keep-away?"

"Of course," she said, drawing Ben close. She ran a hand through his hair. "You look hot. You should drink some water."

"I will. Are Thibault and Zeus staying for dinner?"

"We haven't talked about it."

Ben pushed his glasses up on his nose, oblivious to the fact that they were cockeyed. "We're having tacos," he announced to Thibault. "They're awesome. Mom makes her own salsa and everything."

"I'm sure they are," Thibault said, his tone neutral.

"We'll talk about it, okay?" She brushed the grass from his shirt. "Now go on. Get some water. And don't forget to wash up."

"I want to play hide-and-go-seek with Zeus," Ben whined. "Thibault said I could."

"Like I said, we'll talk about it," Elizabeth said.

"Can Zeus come inside with me? He's thirsty, too."

"Let's leave him out here, okay? We'll get him some water. What happened to your glasses?"

Ignoring Ben's protests, she slid them off. "It'll only take a second." She bent the frame, examined her handiwork, and bent them once more before handing them back to him. "Try them now."

Ben's eyes darted toward Thibault as he put them on; Thibault pretended not to notice. Instead, he petted Zeus as the dog lay quietly next to him. Elizabeth leaned back to get a better view.

"Perfect," she said.

"Okay," Ben conceded. He headed up the steps, pulled open the screen door, and let it close with a loud bang. When he was gone, Elizabeth turned to Thibault.

"I embarrassed him."

"That's what mothers do."

"Thanks," she said, not hiding the sarcasm. "Now what's this about Zeus and hide-and-go-seek?"

"Oh, I told him about it when we were down at the creek. He was asking what Zeus could do and I mentioned it. But we don't have to do it tonight."

"No, that's fine," she said, reaching for her glass of lemonade. She rattled the ice cubes, debating, before finally turning toward him. "Would you like to stay for dinner?"

He met her eyes. "Yeah," he said, "I'd like that very much."

"It's only tacos," she qualified.

"I heard. And thank you. Tacos sound like a treat." He smiled and stood. "But for now, let me get this guy some water. And he's probably hungry, too. Would you mind if I got him some food from the kennel?"

"Of course not. There's plenty. Someone just unloaded a bunch of bags yesterday."

"Who could that have been?"

"I don't know. Some long-haired drifter, I think."

"I thought he was a college-educated veteran."

"Same thing." Picking up the glasses, she rose as well. "I'm going to make sure Ben washed up. He tends to forget to do that. See you in a few minutes."

At the kennel, Thibault filled Zeus's bowls with water and food, then took a seat on one of the empty cages, waiting. Zeus took his time, drinking a bit, then nibbling at a few bites of his food, peering occasionally over at Thibault as if to ask, *Why are you watching me?* Thibault said nothing; he knew that any comment would slow Zeus down even more.

Instead, he checked the other kennels even though Elizabeth had said she'd already done so, making sure none of the other dogs were low on water. They weren't. Nor did they stir much. Good. He turned out the lights in the office and locked the door before returning to the house. Zeus trailed behind him, his nose to the ground.

At the door, he motioned for Zeus to lie down and stay, then pulled open the screen door.

"Hello?"

"Come on in. I'm in the kitchen."

Thibault stepped inside and made his way to the kitchen. Elizabeth had put on an apron and was standing at the stove, browning ground beef. On the counter beside her was an open bottle of Michelob Light.

"Where's Ben?" Thibault asked.

"He's in the shower. He should be down in a couple of minutes." She added some packaged taco seasoning and water to the beef, then rinsed her hands. After drying them on the front of her apron, she reached for her beer. "Would you like one? I always have a beer on taco night."

"I'd love one."

She pulled a beer from the refrigerator and handed it to him. "It's light. It's all I have."

"Thank you."

He leaned against the counter and took in the kitchen. In some ways, it reminded him of the one in the house he'd rented. Cabinets original with the house, stainless-steel sink, older appliances, and a small dining room set pushed beneath a window, but all in slightly better condition, with women's touches here and there. Flowers in a vase, a bowl of fruit, window treatments. Homey.

From the refrigerator, Elizabeth pulled out some lettuce and tomatoes, along with a block of cheddar cheese, and put them on the counter. She followed that with green peppers and onions, moved the whole lot to the butcher block, then pulled out a knife and cheese grater from a counter drawer. She started slicing and dicing the onion, her movements quick and fluid.

"Need a hand?"

She shot him a skeptical look. "Don't tell me that in addition to training dogs, fixing cars, and being a musician, you're an expert chef."

"I wouldn't go that far. But I know my way around the kitchen. I make dinner every night."

"Oh yeah? What did you have last night?"

"Turkey sandwich on wheat. With a pickle."

"And the night before?"

"Turkey sandwich on wheat. No pickle."

She giggled. "What was the last hot meal you cooked?"

He pretended to rack his brains. "Uh . . . beans and franks. On Monday."

She feigned amazement. "I stand corrected. How are you at grating cheese?"

"In that, I would consider myself an expert."

"Okay," she said. "There's a bowl in the cupboard over there, beneath the blender. And you don't need to do the whole block. Ben usually has two tacos, and I have only one. Anything more would be for you."

Thibault set his beer on the counter and retrieved the bowl from the cupboard. Then he moved to the sink to wash his hands and unwrap the block of cheese. He snuck glances at Elizabeth as he worked. Finished with the onion, she'd already moved on to the green pepper. The tomato came next. The knife danced steadily, the movements precise.

"You do that so quickly."

She answered without breaking the rhythm of her movements. "There was a while there when I dreamed of opening my own restaurant."

"When was that?"

"When I was fifteen. For my birthday, I even asked for the Ginsu knife."

"You mean the one that used to be advertised on late-night television? Where the guy on the commercial uses it to cut through a tin can?"

She nodded. "That's the one."

"Did you get it?"

"It's the knife I'm using now."

He smiled. "I've never known anyone who actually admitted to buying one."

"Now you do," she said. She stole a quick look at him. "I had this dream about opening this great place in Charleston or Savannah and having my own cookbooks and television show. Crazy, I know. But anyway, I spent the summer practicing my dicing. I'd dice everything I could, as fast as I could, until I was as fast as the guy on the commercial. There were Tupperware bowls filled with zucchini and carrots and squash that I'd picked from the garden. It drove Nana crazy, since it meant we had to have summer stew just about every single day."

"What's summer stew?"

"Anything mixed together that can be served over noodles or rice."

He smiled as he shifted a pile of grated cheese to the side. "Then what happened?"

"Summer ended, and we ran out of vegetables."

"Ah," he said, wondering how someone could look so pretty in an apron.

"Okay," she said, pulling another pot from under the stove, "let me whip up the salsa."

She poured in a large can of tomato sauce, then added the onions and peppers and a dash of Tabasco, along with salt and pepper. She stirred them together and set the heat on medium.

"Your own recipe?"

"Nana's. Ben doesn't like things too spicy, so this is what she came up with."

Finished with the cheese, Thibault rewrapped it. "What else?"

"Not much. I just have to shred some lettuce and that's it. Oh, and heat up the shells in the oven. I'll let the meat and the salsa simmer for a bit."

"How about I do the shells?"

She handed him a cookie sheet and turned on the oven. "Just spread the shells out a little. Three for us, and however many you want for you. But don't put them in yet. We still have a few minutes. Ben likes the shells fresh out of the oven."

Thibault did as she requested, and she finished with the lettuce at about the same time. She put three plates on the counter. Picking up her beer again, she motioned toward the door. "Come out back. I want to show you something."

Thibault followed her out, then stopped short as he took in the view from the covered deck. Enclosed by a hedge lay a series of cobblestone paths that wove among several circular brick plant-ers, each with its own dogwood tree; in the center of the yard, serving as a focal point, was a three-tiered fountain that fed a large koi pond.

"Wow," he murmured. "This is gorgeous."

"And you never knew it was here, right? It is pretty spectacular, but you should see it in the spring. Every year, Nana and I plant a few thousand tulips, daffodils, and lilies, and they start blooming right after the azaleas and dogwoods. From March through July, this garden is one of the most beautiful places on earth. And over there? Behind that lower hedge?" She pointed toward the right. "That's the home of our illustrious vegetable and herb garden."

"Nana never mentioned she gardened."

"She wouldn't. It was something she and Grandpa shared, kind of like their little secret. Because the kennel is right there, they wanted to make this a kind of oasis where they could escape the business, the dogs, the owners . . . even their employees. Of course, Drake and I, and then Ben and I, pitched in, but for the most part, it was theirs. It was the one project at which Grandpa really excelled. After he died, Nana decided to keep it up in his memory."

"It's incredible," he said.

"It is, isn't it? It wasn't so great when we were kids. Unless we were planting bulbs, we weren't allowed to play back here. All our birthday parties were on the lawn out front that separates the house from the kennel. Which meant that for two days before-hand, we'd have to scoop up all the poop so no one would acci-dentally step in it."

"I can see how that would be a party stopper—

"Hey!" a voice rang out from the kitchen. "Where are you guys?"

Elizabeth turned at the sound of Ben's voice. "Out here, sweetie. I'm showing Mr. Thibault the backyard."

Ben stepped outside, dressed in a black T-shirt and camouflage pants. "Where's Zeus? I'm ready for him to find me."

"Let's eat first. We'll do that after dinner."

"Mom . . ."

"It'll be better when it's dark anyway," Thibault interjected. "That way you can really hide. It'll be more fun for Zeus, too."

"What do you want to do until then?"

"Your Nana said you played chess."

Ben looked skeptical. "You know how to play chess?"

"Maybe not as good as you, but I know how to play."

"Okay." He scratched at his arm. "Hey, where did you say Zeus was?"

"On the porch out front."

"Can I go play with him?"

"You'll have to set the table first," Elizabeth instructed him. "And you'll only have a couple of minutes. Dinner's almost ready."

"Okay," he said, turning around. "Thanks."

As he raced off, she leaned around Thibault and cupped her mouth with her hands. "Don't forget the table!"

Ben skidded to a halt. He opened a drawer and grabbed three forks, then threw them onto the table like a dealer in Vegas, followed by the plates Elizabeth had set aside earlier. In all, it took him less than ten seconds—and the table showed it—before he vanished from view. When he was gone, Elizabeth shook her head. "Until Zeus got here, Ben used to be a quiet, easygoing child after school. He used to read and study, and now all he wants to do is chase your dog."

Thibault made a guilty face. "Sorry."

"Don't be. Believe me, I like a little . . . calmness as much as the next mother, but it's nice to see him so excited."

"Why don't you get him his own dog?"

"I will. In time. Once I see how things go with Nana." She took a sip of beer and nodded toward the house. "Let's go check on dinner. I think the oven's probably ready."

Back inside, Elizabeth slipped the cookie sheet into the oven and stirred the meat and salsa before ladling both into bowls. As she brought them to the table along with a stack of paper napkins, Thibault straightened the silverware and plates and grabbed the cheese, lettuce, and tomatoes. When Elizabeth set her beer on the table, Thibault was struck again by her natural beauty.

"Do you want to call Ben, or should I?"

He forced himself to turn away. "I'll call Ben," he said.

Ben was sitting on the front porch, stroking a panting Zeus from his forehead to his tail in one long stroke.

"You tired him out," Thibault observed.

"I run pretty fast," Ben agreed.

"You ready to eat? Dinner's on the table."

Ben got up, and Zeus raised his head. "Stay here," Thibault said. Zeus's ears flattened as if he were being punished. But he laid his head back down as Ben and Thibault entered the house.

Elizabeth was already seated at the table. As soon as Ben and Thibault sat down, Ben immediately started loading his taco with the seasoned ground beef.

"I want to hear more about your walk across the country," Elizabeth said.

"Yeah, me too," Ben said, spooning on salsa.

Thibault reached for his napkin and spread it on his lap. "What would you like to know?"

She flourished her napkin. "Why don't you start at the beginning?"

For a moment, Thibault considered the truth: that it began with a photograph in the Kuwaiti desert. But he couldn't tell them about that. Instead, he started by describing a cold March morning, when he'd slung his backpack over his arm and started down the shoulder of the road. He told them about the things he saw—for Ben's sake, he made sure to describe all the wildlife he'd

encountered—and talked about some of the more colorful people
he'd encountered. Elizabeth seemed to realize that he wasn't ac-
customed to talking so much about himself, so she prompted him
by asking him questions whenever he seemed to be running out
of things to say. From there, she asked him a bit more about college and was amused when Ben learned that the man sitting at
the table *actually dug up real-life skeletons*. Ben asked a few questions of his own: Do you have any brothers or sisters? *No.* Did you
play sports? *Yeah, but I was average, not great.* What's your favorite
football team? *The Denver Broncos, of course.* As Ben and Thibault chatted, Elizabeth followed their exchange with amusement
and interest.

As the evening wore on, the sunlight slanting through the
window shifted and waned, dimming the kitchen. They finished
eating, and after excusing himself, Ben rejoined Zeus on the porch.
Thibault helped Elizabeth clean up the table, wrapping the left-
overs and stacking plates and silverware in the dishwasher. Breaking her own rule, Elizabeth opened a second beer and offered
another to Thibault before they escaped the heat of the kitchen
and went outside.

On the porch, the air felt noticeably cooler, and a breeze made
the leaves on the trees dance. Ben and Zeus were playing again,
and Ben's laughter hung suspended in the air. Elizabeth leaned
on the railing, watching her son, and Thibault had to force himself not to stare in her direction. Neither of them felt the need to
speak, and Thibault took a long, slow pull of his beer, wondering
where on earth all of this was going.

12

Beth

As night fell, Beth stood on the back deck, watching Logan concentrate on the chess board in front of him, thinking, *I like him*. The thought, when it struck her, felt at once surprising and natural.

Ben and Logan were on their second game of chess, and Logan was taking his time on his next move. Ben had handily won the first game, and she could read the surprise in Logan's expression. He took it well, even asking Ben what he'd done wrong. They'd reset the board to an earlier position, and Ben showed Logan the series of errors he had made, first with his rook and queen and then, finally, with his knight.

"Well, I'll be," Logan had said. He'd smiled at Ben. "Good job."

She didn't want to even imagine how Keith would have reacted had he lost. In fact, she didn't have to imagine it. They'd played once a couple of years ago, and when Ben won, Keith had literally flipped the board over before storming out of the room. A few minutes later, while Ben was still gathering the pieces from behind the furniture, Keith came back into the room. Instead of apologizing, he declared that chess was a waste of time and that Ben would be better off doing something important, like studying for his classes at school or going to the batting cage, since "he hit about as well as a blind man."

She really wanted to strangle the man sometimes.

With Logan, though, things were different. Beth could see that Logan was in trouble again. She couldn't tell by looking at the board—the intricacies that separated the good from the great players were beyond her—but whenever Ben studied his opponent rather than his pieces, she knew the end was coming, even if Logan didn't seem to realize it.

What she loved most about the scene was that despite the concentration the game required, Logan and Ben still managed to . . . *talk*. About school and Ben's teachers and what Zeus had been like when he was a puppy, and because Logan seemed genuinely interested, Ben revealed a few things that surprised her—that one of the other boys in his class had taken his lunch a couple of times and that Ben had a crush on a girl named Cici. Logan didn't deliver advice; instead he asked Ben what he thought he should do. Based on her experience with men, most assumed that when you talked to them about a problem or dilemma, they were expected to offer an opinion, even when all you wanted was for them to *listen*.

Logan's natural reticence actually seemed to give Ben room to express himself. It was clear that Logan was comfortable with who he was. He wasn't trying to impress Ben or impress her by showing her how well he could get along with Ben.

Though she'd dated infrequently over the years, she'd found that most suitors either pretended Ben didn't exist and said only a few words to him or went overboard in the way they talked to him, trying to prove how wonderful they were by being overly friendly with her son. From an early age, Ben had seen through both types almost immediately. So had she, and that was usually enough for her to end things. Well, when *they* weren't ending the relationship with *her*, that is.

It was obvious that Ben liked spending time with Logan, and even better, she got the sense that Logan liked spending time with

Ben. In the silence, Logan continued to stare at the board, his finger resting momentarily on his knight before moving it to his pawn. Ben's eyebrows rose ever so slightly. She didn't know whether Ben thought the move Logan was considering was a good one or a bad one, but Logan went ahead and moved the pawn forward.

Ben made his next move almost immediately, something she recognized as a bad sign for Logan. A few minutes later, Logan seemed to realize that no matter what move he made, there was no way for his king to escape. He shook his head.

"You got me."

"Yeah," Ben confirmed, "I did."

"I thought I was playing better."

"You were," Ben said.

"Until?"

"Until you made your second move."

Logan laughed. "Chess humor?"

"We've got lots of jokes like that," Ben said, obviously proud. He motioned to the yard. "Is it dark enough?"

"Yeah, I think so. You ready to play, Zeus?"

Zeus's ears pricked up and he cocked his head. When Logan and Ben stood, Zeus scrambled to his feet.

"You coming, Mom?"

Beth rose from her chair. "I'm right behind you."

They wended their way in the darkness to the front of the house. Beth paused by the front steps. "Maybe I should get a flashlight."

"That's cheating!" Ben complained.

"Not for the dog. For you. So you don't get lost."

"He won't get lost," Logan assured her. "Zeus will find him."

"Easy to say when it's not your son."

"I'll be fine," Ben added.

She looked from Ben to Logan before shaking her head. She wasn't entirely comfortable, but Logan didn't seem worried at all. "Okay," she said, sighing. "I want one for me, then. Is that okay?"

"Okay," Ben agreed. "What do I do?"

"Hide," Logan said. "And I'll send Zeus to find you."

"Anywhere I want?"

"Why don't you hide out that way?" Logan said, pointing toward a wooded area west of the creek, on the opposite side of the driveway from the kennel. "I don't want you accidentally slipping into the creek. And besides, your scent will be fresh out that way. Remember, you two were playing out this way before dinner. Now once he finds you, just follow him out, okay? That way you won't get lost."

Ben peered toward the woods. "Okay. How do I know he won't watch?"

"I'll put him inside and count to a hundred before I let him out."

"And you won't let him peek?"

"Promise." Logan focused his attention on Zeus. "Come," he said. He went to the door and opened it before pausing. "Is it okay if I let him in?"

Beth nodded. "It's fine."

Logan motioned for Zeus to go in and lie down, then closed the door. "Okay, you're ready."

Ben started to jog toward the woods as Logan began to count out loud. In midstride, Ben called over his shoulder, "Count slower!" His figure gradually merged into the darkness, and even before reaching the woods, he'd vanished from sight.

Beth crossed her arms. "I must say that I don't have a good feeling about this."

"Why not?"

"My son hiding in the woods at night? Gee, I wonder."

"He'll be fine. Zeus will find him in two or three minutes. At the most."

"You have an inordinate amount of faith in your dog."

Logan smiled, and for a moment they stood on the porch, taking in the evening. The air, warm and humid but no longer hot, smelled like the land itself: a mixture of oak and pine and earth, an odor that never failed to remind Beth that even though the world was constantly changing, this particular place always seemed to stay the same.

She was aware that Logan had been observing her all night, trying hard not to stare, and she knew she'd been doing the same with him. She realized she liked the way Logan's intent made her feel. She was pleased he found her attractive but liked that his attraction didn't possess any of the urgency or naked desire she often felt when men stared at her. Instead, he seemed content simply to stand beside her, and for whatever reason, it was exactly what she needed.

"I'm glad you stayed for dinner," she offered, not knowing what else to say. "Ben's having a great time."

"I'm glad, too."

"You were so good with him in there. Playing chess, I mean."

"It's not hard."

"You wouldn't think so, right?"

He hesitated. "Are we talking about your ex again?"

"Am I that obvious?" She leaned against a post. "You're right, though. I am talking about my ex. The putz."

He leaned against the post on the opposite side of the stairs, facing her. "And?"

"And I just wish things could be different."

He hesitated, and she knew he was wondering whether or not to say anything more. In the end, he said nothing.

"You wouldn't like him," she volunteered. "In fact, I don't think he'd like you, either."

"No?"

"No. And consider yourself lucky. You're not missing anything."

He looked at her steadily, not saying anything. Remembering the way she had shut him down earlier, she supposed. She brushed away a few strands of hair that had fallen into her eyes, wondering whether to go on. "Do you want to hear about it?"

"Only if you want to tell me," he offered.

She felt her thoughts drifting from the present to the past and sighed. "It's the oldest story in the book . . . I was a nerdy high school senior, he was a couple of years older than me, but we'd gone to the same church for as long as I can remember, so I knew exactly who he was. We started going out a few months before I graduated. His family is well-off, and he'd always dated the most popular girls, and I guess I just got caught up in the fantasy of it all. I overlooked some obvious problems, made excuses for others, and the next thing you know, I found out I was pregnant. All of a sudden, my life just . . . changed, you know? I wasn't going to go to college that fall, I had no idea how to even be a mother, let alone a single mother; I couldn't imagine how I was going to pull it all off. The last thing in the world I expected was for him to propose. But for whatever reason, he did, and I said yes, and even though I wanted to believe that it was all going to work out and did my best to convince Nana that I knew what I was doing, I think both of us knew it was a mistake before the ink was dry on the marriage certificate. We had virtually nothing in common. Anyway, we argued pretty much constantly, and ended up separating soon after Ben was born. And then, I was really lost."

Logan brought his hands together. "But it didn't stop you."

"Stop me from what?"

"From eventually going to college and becoming a teacher. And figuring out how to be a single mother." He grinned. "And somehow pulling it off."

She gave him a grateful smile. "With Nana's help."

"Whatever it takes." He crossed one leg over the other, seeming to study her before he smirked. "Nerdy, huh?"

"In high school? Oh yeah. I was definitely nerdy."

"I find that hard to believe."

"Believe what you want."

"So how did college work?"

"With Ben, you mean? It wasn't easy. But I already had some AP credits, which gave me a bit of a head start, and then I took classes at the community college while Ben was still in diapers. I took classes only two or three days a week while Nana took care of Ben, and I'd come home and study when I wasn't being Mom. Same thing when I transferred to UNC Wilmington, which was close enough to go to school and make it back here at night. It took me six years to get my degree and certificate, but I didn't want to take advantage of Nana, and I didn't want to give my ex any reason to get full custody. And back then, he might have tried for it, just because he could."

"He sounds like a charmer."

She grimaced. "You have no idea."

"You want me to beat him up?"

She laughed. "That's funny. There might have been a time when I would have taken you up on that, but not anymore. He's just . . . immature. He thinks every woman he meets is crazy for him, gets angry at little things, and blames other people when things go wrong. Thirty-one going on sixteen, if you know what I mean." From the side, she could sense Logan watching her. "But enough about him. Tell me something about you."

"Like what?"

"Anything. I don't know. Why did you major in anthropology?"

He considered the question. "Personality, I guess."

"What does that mean?"

"I knew I didn't want to major in anything practical like business or engineering, and toward the end of my freshman year, I started talking to other liberal arts majors. The most interesting ones I met were anthropology majors. I wanted to be interesting."

"You're kidding."

"I'm not. That's why I took the first introductory classes, at least. After that, I realized that anthropology is a great blend of history and supposition and mystery, all of which appealed to me. I was hooked."

"How about frat parties?"

"Not my thing."

"Football games?"

"No."

"Did you ever think you missed out on what college was supposed to be?"

"No."

"Me neither," she agreed. "Not once I had Ben, anyway."

He nodded, then gestured toward the woods. "Umm . . . do you think we should have Zeus find Ben now?"

"Oh, my gosh!" she cried, her tone slightly panicked. "Yes. He can find him, right? How long has it been?"

"Not long. Five minutes, maybe. Let me get Zeus. And don't worry. It won't take long."

Logan went to the door and opened it. Zeus trotted out, tail wagging, then wandered down the stairs. He immediately lifted a leg by the side of the porch, then trotted back up the stairs to Logan.

"Where's Ben?" Logan asked.

Zeus's ears rose. Logan pointed in the direction Ben had gone. "Find Ben."

Zeus turned and started trotting in wide arcs, nose to the ground. Within seconds, he'd picked up the trail and he vanished into the darkness.

"Should we follow him?" Beth asked.

"Do you want to?"

"Yes."

"Then let's go."

They'd barely reached the first of the trees when she heard Zeus emit a playful bark. Right after that, Ben's voice sounded in a squeal of delight. When she turned toward Logan, he shrugged.

"You weren't lying, were you?" she asked. "What was that? Two minutes?"

"It wasn't hard for him. I knew Ben wouldn't be too far away."

"What's the longest he's ever tracked something?"

"He followed a deer trail for, I don't know, eight miles or so? Something like that, anyway. He could have gone on, too, but it ended at someone's fence. That was in Tennessee."

"Why did you track the deer?"

"Practice. He's a smart dog. He likes to learn, and he likes to use his skills." At that moment, Zeus came padding out from the trees, Ben a step behind him. "Which is why this is just as much fun for him as it is for Ben."

"That was amazing!" Ben called out. "He just walked right up to me. I wasn't making a sound!"

"You want to do it again?" Logan asked.

"Can I?" Ben pleaded.

"If it's okay with your mom."

Ben turned to his mother, and she raised her hands. "Go ahead."

"Okay, put him inside again. And I'm really going to hide this time," Ben declared.

"You got it," Logan said.

The second time Ben hid, Zeus found him in a tree. The third time, with Ben retracing his steps in an attempt to throw him off, Zeus found him a quarter mile away, in his tree house by the creek. Beth wasn't thrilled with this final choice; the unstable bridge and platform always seemed far more dangerous at night, but by then, Ben was getting tired and ready to call it quits anyway.

Logan followed them back to the house. After saying good night to an exhausted Ben, he turned to Beth and cleared his throat. "I want to thank you for a great evening, but I should probably be heading home," he said.

Despite the fact that it was close to ten o'clock, part of her didn't want him to go just yet.

"Do you need a ride?" she offered. "Ben will be asleep in a couple of minutes, and I'd be glad to bring you home."

"I appreciate the offer, but we'll be fine. I like to walk."

"I know. I don't know much about you, but I do know that." She smiled. "I'll see you tomorrow, right?"

"I'll be here at seven."

"I can feed the dogs if you'd rather come in a bit later."

"It's no problem. And besides, I'd like to see Ben before he leaves. And I'm sure Zeus will, too. Poor guy probably won't know what to do without Ben chasing him."

"All right, then . . ." She hugged her arms, suddenly disappointed at the thought of Logan's departure.

"Would it be okay if I borrowed the truck tomorrow? I need to run into town to get a few things to fix the brakes. If not, I can walk."

She smiled. "Yeah, I know. But it's not a problem. I have to drop Ben off and run some errands, but if I don't see you, I'll just put the keys under the mat on the driver's side."

"Fine," he said. He looked directly at her. "Good night, Elizabeth."

"Good night, Logan."

Once he was gone, Beth checked on Ben and gave him another kiss on the cheek before going to her room. She replayed the evening as she undressed, musing on the mystery of Logan Thibault.

He was different from any man she'd ever met, she thought, and then immediately chided herself for being so obvious. *Of course he was different*, she told herself. *He was new to her. She'd never spent much time with him before.* Even so, she reasoned she was mature enough to recognize the truth when she saw it.

Logan *was* different. Lord knows Keith wasn't anything like him. Nor, in fact, was anyone else she'd dated since the divorce. Most of those men had been fairly easy to read; no matter how polite and charming or rough and unrefined they might be, everything they did seemed like transparent efforts at getting her into bed. "Man crap," as Nana described it. And Nana, she knew, wasn't wrong.

But with Logan . . . well, that was the thing. She had no idea what he wanted from her. She knew he found her attractive, and he seemed to enjoy her company. But after that, she had absolutely no idea what his intentions might be, since he seemed to enjoy Ben's company as well. In a way, she thought, he treated her like a number of the married men she knew: *You're pretty and you're interesting, but I'm already taken.*

It occurred to her, though, that maybe he was taken. Maybe he had a girlfriend back in Colorado, or maybe he'd just broken up with the love of his life and was still getting over it. Thinking back, she realized that even though he'd described the things he'd seen and done on his journey across the country, she still had no idea why he'd gone on the walk in the first place or why he'd decided to end his trek in Hampton. His history wasn't so much mysterious as hidden, which was strange. If she'd learned one thing about men, it was that they liked to talk about themselves: their jobs, their hobbies, past accomplishments, their motivations. Logan did none of those things. Puzzling.

She shook her head, thinking she was probably reading too much into it. It wasn't as if they'd gone out on a date, after all. It was more like a friendly get-together—tacos, chess, and conversation. A family event.

She put on pajamas and picked up a magazine from her bedside table. She absently flipped through the pages before turning out the light. But when she closed her eyes, she kept visualizing the way the corners of his mouth would turn up slightly whenever she said something he found humorous or the way his eyebrows knit together when he concentrated on a task. For a long time, she tossed and turned, unable to sleep, wondering if maybe, just maybe, Logan was awake and thinking of her, too.

13

Thibault

Thibault watched as Victor cast his line into the cool Minnesota water. It was a cloudless Saturday morning. The air was still, the lake mirroring the pristine skies. They had set out on the lake early, wanting to fish before it became crowded with Jet Skis and speedboats. It was their last day of vacation; tomorrow, both were scheduled to fly out. For their final evening, they planned to eat at a local steak house they'd heard was the best in town.

"I think you'll be able to find this woman," Victor announced without preamble.

Thibault was reeling in his own line. "Who?"

"The woman in the photo who brings you luck."

Thibault squinted at his friend. "What are you talking about?"

"When you look for her. I think you'll be able to find her."

Thibault inspected his hook carefully and cast again. "I'm not going to look for her."

"So you say now. But you will."

Thibault shook his head. "No, I won't. And even if I wanted to, there's no way I could."

"You'll find a way." Victor sounded smug in his certainty.

Thibault stared at his friend. "Why are we even talking about this?"

"Because," Victor pronounced, "it's not over yet."

"Believe me, it's over."

"I know you think so. But it isn't."

Thibault had learned long ago that once Victor started on a topic, he would continue to expound on it until he was satisfied he'd made his point. Because it wasn't the way Thibault wanted to spend their last day, he figured he might as well get it over with once and for all.

"Okay," he said, sighing. "Why isn't it over?"

Victor shrugged. "Because there is no balance."

"No balance," Thibault repeated, his tone flat.

"Yes," Victor said. "Exactly. You see?"

"No."

Victor groaned at Thibault's denseness. "Say someone comes to put a roof on your house. The man works hard, and at the end, he is paid. Only then is it over. But in this case, with the photograph, it is as if the roof has been put on, but the owner has not paid. Until payment is made, everything is out of balance."

"Are you saying that I owe this woman something?" Thibault's voice was skeptical.

"Yes. The photo kept you safe and brought you luck. But until payment is made, it is not over."

Thibault reached for a soda in the cooler. He handed one to Victor. "You do realize you sound insane."

Victor accepted the can with a nod. "To some, maybe. But eventually, you will look for her. There is a greater purpose to all this. It is your destiny."

"My destiny."

"Yes."

"What does that mean?"

"I don't know. But you will know it when you get there."

Thibault stayed quiet, wishing Victor had never brought up the subject. In the silence, Victor studied his friend.

"Maybe," he speculated, "you're meant to be together."

"I'm not in love with her, Victor."

"No?"

"No," he said.

"And yet," Victor observed, "you think about her often."

To this, Thibault said nothing, for there was nothing he could say.

On Saturday morning, Thibault arrived early and went straight to work at the kennels, feeding, cleaning, and training as usual. While he worked, Ben played with Zeus until Elizabeth called him inside to get ready to go. She waved from her spot on the porch, but even from a distance, he could see she was distracted.

She had gone back inside by the time he took the dogs out; he usually walked them in groups of three, with Zeus trailing behind him. Away from the house, he would let the dogs off the leash, but they tended to follow behind him no matter what direction he headed. He liked to vary the route he took; the variety kept the dogs from wandering too far away. Like people, dogs got bored if they did the same thing every day. Usually, the walks lasted about thirty minutes per group. After the third group, he noticed that Elizabeth's car was gone, and he assumed she'd gone to drop Ben off at his father's.

He didn't like Ben's father, mostly because Ben and Elizabeth didn't. The guy sounded like a piece of work, but it wasn't his place to do much more than listen when she talked about him. He didn't know enough to offer any advice, and even if he did, she wasn't asking for any. In any event, it wasn't his business.

But what was his business, then? Why was he here? Despite himself, his thoughts drifted back to his conversation with Victor, and he knew he was here because of what Victor had said to him that morning at the lake. And, of course, because of what happened later.

He forced the memory away. He wasn't going to go there. Not again.

Calling to the dogs, Thibault turned and made for the kennels. After putting the dogs away, he went to explore the storage shed. When he turned on the light in the shed, he stared at the walls and shelves in amazement. Elizabeth's grandfather didn't have just a few tools—the place resembled a cluttered hardware store. He wandered inside, scanning the racks and sorting through the Snap-on tool cabinets and piles of items on the workbench. He eventually picked out a socket wrench set, a couple of adjustable and Allen wrenches, and a jack and carried them out to the truck. As Elizabeth had promised, the keys were under the mat. Thibault drove down the driveway, heading for the auto supply store he vaguely remembered seeing near downtown.

The parts were in stock—replacement pads, C-clamp, and some high-temp grease—and he was back at the house in less than half an hour. He put the jack in place and raised the car, then removed the first wheel. He retracted the piston with the C-clamp, removed the old pad, checked the rotors for damage, and reinstalled a new pad before replacing the wheel and repeating the process with the other wheels.

He was finishing the third brake pad when he heard Elizabeth pull up, rolling to a stop next to the old truck. He glanced over his shoulder just as she got out, realizing she'd been gone for hours.

"How's it going?" she asked.

"Just about done."

"Really?" She sounded amazed.

"It's just brake pads. It's not a big deal."

"I'm sure that's the same thing a surgeon would say. It's just an appendix."

"You want to learn?" Thibault asked, staring up at her figure silhouetted against the sky.

"How long does it take?"

"Not long." He shrugged. "Ten minutes?"

"Really?" she repeated. "Okay. Just let me get the groceries inside."

"Need help?"

"No, it's just a couple of bags."

He slipped the third wheel back on and finished tightening the lug nuts before moving to the final wheel. He loosened the nuts just as Elizabeth reached his side. When she squatted beside him, he could smell a hint of the coconut lotion she'd applied earlier that morning.

"First, you take the wheel off . . . ," he began, and methodically walked her through the process, making sure she understood each step. When he lowered the jack and started to collect the tools, she shook her head.

"That seemed almost too easy. I think even I could do it."

"Probably."

"Then why do they charge so much?"

"I don't know."

"I'm in the wrong line of work," she said, rising and gathering her hair into a loose ponytail. "But thank you for taking care of it. I've wanted those fixed for a while now."

"No problem."

"Are you hungry? I picked up some fresh turkey for sandwiches. And some pickles."

"That sounds delicious," he said.

They had lunch on the back porch, overlooking the garden. Elizabeth still seemed distracted, but they chatted a little about what it was like to grow up in a small southern town, where everyone knew everything about everybody else. Some of the stories were amusing, but Thibault admitted that he preferred a more anonymous existence.

"Why am I not surprised?" she asked.

Afterward, Thibault went back to work while Elizabeth spent the afternoon cleaning the house. Unlike her grandfather, Thibault was able to pry open the office window that had been painted shut, though it turned out to be more difficult than fixing the brakes. Nor was it easy to open or close afterward, no matter how much sanding he did to smooth it. Then, he painted the trim.

After that, it was a normal workday. By the time he finished up his duties at the kennel, it was coming up on five, and though he could have easily left for the day, he didn't. Instead, he began work on the files again, wanting to get a head start on what he knew would be a long day tomorrow. He settled in for the next couple of hours, making what he thought was headway—who could tell, though?—and didn't hear Elizabeth approach. Instead, he noticed Zeus get to his feet and start toward the door.

"I'm surprised you're still here," she said from the doorway. "I saw the light on and thought you'd forgotten to turn it off."

"I wouldn't forget."

She pointed to the stacks of files on the desk. "I can't tell you how glad I am that you're doing that. Nana tried to talk me into organizing the files this summer, but I was extremely adept at put-ting her off."

"Lucky me," he drawled.

"No, lucky me. I almost feel guilty about it."

"I'd almost believe you, except for that smirk. Have you heard from Ben or Nana?"

"Both," she said. "Nana's great, Ben is miserable. Not that he said as much. I could hear it in his voice."

"I'm sorry," he said, meaning it.

She offered a tense shrug before reaching for the door handle. She rotated it in both directions, seemingly interested in the mechanism. Finally, she let out a sigh. "Do you want to help me make some ice cream?"

"Excuse me?" He set down the file he'd been labeling.

"I love homemade ice cream. There's nothing better when it's hot, but it's no fun to make if you can't share it with someone."

"I don't know if I've ever had homemade ice cream. . . ."

"Then you don't know what you're missing. You in?"

Her childlike enthusiasm was contagious. "Yeah, okay," he agreed. "That sounds fun."

"Let me run to the store and get what we need. I'll be back in a few minutes."

"Wouldn't it be easier just to buy some ice cream?"

Her eyes shone with delight. "But it's not the same. You'll see. I'll be back in a few minutes, okay?"

She was as good as her word. Thibault just had time to straighten up the desk and check on the dogs one last time before he heard her coming up the drive on her way back from the store. He met her as she was getting out of the car.

"Would you mind bringing in the bag of crushed ice?" she asked. "It's in the backseat."

He followed her into the kitchen with the bag of ice, and she motioned to the freezer as she set a quart of half-and-half on the counter.

"Can you get the ice-cream maker? It's in the pantry. Top shelf on the left."

Thibault emerged from the pantry with a crank-handled ice-cream maker that looked to be at least fifty years old. "Is this the one?"

"Yeah, that's it."

"Does it still work?" he wondered aloud.

"Perfectly. Amazing, isn't it? Nana got that as a gift for her wedding, but we still use it all the time. It makes delicious ice cream."

He brought it over to the counter and stood beside her. "What can I do?"

"If you agree to crank, I'll do the mixing."

"Fair enough," he said.

She dug out an electric mixer and a bowl, along with a measuring cup. From the spice cabinet, she chose sugar, flour, and vanilla extract. She added three cups of sugar and a cup of flour to the bowl and mixed it by hand, then put the bowl on the mixer. Next, she beat in three eggs, all the half-and-half, and three teaspoons of vanilla extract before turning on the mixer. Finally, she splashed in a bit of milk and poured the entire mixture into the cream can, put the can in the ice-cream maker, and surrounded it with crushed ice and rock salt.

"We're ready," she announced, handing it to him. She picked up the rest of the ice and the rock salt. "To the porch we go. You have to make it on the porch, or it isn't the same."

"Ah," he said.

She took a seat beside him on the porch steps, sitting fractionally closer than she had the day before. Wedging the can between his feet, Thibault began to rotate the crank, surprised at how easily it turned.

"Thanks for doing this," she said. "I really need the ice cream. It's been one of those days."

"Yeah?"

She turned toward him, a sly smile playing on her lips. "You're very good at that."

"What?"

"Saying, 'Yeah?' when someone makes a comment. It's just enough to make someone keep talking without being too personal or prying."

"Yeah?"

She giggled. "Yeah," she mimicked. "But most people would have said something like, 'What happened?' Or, 'Why?'"

"All right. What happened? Why was it one of those days?"

She gave a disgusted snort. "Oh, it's just that Ben was really grumpy this morning while he was packing, and I ended up snapping at him to hurry up because he was taking so long. His dad usually doesn't like it when he's late, but today? Well, today, it was as if he'd forgotten that Ben was even coming. I must have knocked on the door for a couple of minutes before he eventually opened it, and I could tell he'd just gotten out of bed. Had I known he was sleeping in, I wouldn't have been so hard on Ben, and I still feel guilty about it. And, of course, as I'm pulling away,

I see Ben already hauling out the garbage because dear old Dad was too lazy to do it. And then, of course, I spent the whole day cleaning, which wasn't so bad the first couple of hours. But by the end, I really needed ice cream."

"Doesn't sound like a relaxing Saturday."

"It wasn't," she muttered, and he could tell she was debating whether to say more. There was something more, something else bothering her, and she drew a long breath before sighing. "It's my brother's birthday today," she said, the faintest tremor in her voice. "That's where I went today, after dropping Ben off. I brought flowers to the cemetery."

Thibault felt a thickness in his throat as he remembered the photograph on the mantel. Though he'd suspected that her brother had been killed, it was the first time that either Nana or Elizabeth had confirmed it. He immediately understood why she hadn't wanted to be alone tonight.

"I'm sorry," he said, meaning it.

"So am I," she said. "You would have liked him. Everyone liked him."

"I'm sure."

She twisted her hands in her lap. "It slipped Nana's mind. Of course, she remembered this afternoon and called to tell me how sorry she was that she couldn't be here. She was practically in tears, but I told her it was okay. That it wasn't a big deal."

"It is a big deal. He was your brother and you miss him."

A wistful smile flickered across her face, then faded away. "You remind me of him," she offered, her voice soft. "Not so much in your appearance, but in your mannerisms. I noticed that the first time you walked in the office to apply for the job. It's like you two were stamped out of the same mold. I guess it's a marine thing, huh?"

"Maybe," he said. "I've met all types."

"I'll bet." She paused, drawing her knees to her chest and wrapping her arms around them. "Did you like it? Being in the marines?"

"Sometimes."

"But not all the time?"

"No."

"Drake loved it. Loved everything about it, in fact." Though she seemed mesmerized by the movement of the crank, Thibault could tell she was lost in her memories. "I remember when the invasion began. With Camp Lejeune less than an hour away, it was big news. I was scared for him, especially when I heard talk about chemical weapons and suicide stands, but do you want to know what he was worried about? Before the invasion, I mean?"

"What?"

"A picture. A dumb old photograph. Can you believe that?"

The unexpected words made Thibault's heart suddenly hammer in his chest, but he forced himself to appear calm.

"He took this picture of me when we first arrived at the fair that year," she said, going on. "It was the last weekend we spent together before he joined, and after we made the usual rounds, we just kind of wandered off to be alone. I remember sitting with him near this giant pine tree and talking for hours as we watched the Ferris wheel. It was one of the big ones, all lit up, and we could hear kids oohing and aahing as it went round and round under this perfect summer sky. We talked about our mom and dad, and we wondered what they would have been like or whether they'd have gray hair or whether we would have stayed in Hampton or moved away, and I remember looking up at the sky. All of a sudden, this shooting star went by, and all I could think was that they were listening to us somehow."

She paused, lost in the memory, before going on. "He had the picture laminated and kept it with him all through basic training. After he got to Iraq, he e-mailed me and told me that he'd lost it, and asked if I could send him another one. It seemed kind of crazy to me, but I wasn't there, and I didn't know what he was going through, so I said I'd send another one. But I didn't get around to sending it right away. Don't ask me why. It was like I had some sort of mental block against doing it. I mean, I'd put the disk into my purse, but every time I was near the drugstore, I'd just forget to get the photograph developed. And before I knew it, the invasion had started. I finally got around to sending it, but the letter was eventually returned to me unopened. Drake died in the first week of the invasion."

She stared at him over the tops of her knees. "Five days. That was how long he lasted. And I never got him the one thing he wanted from me. You know how that makes me feel?"

Thibault felt sick to his stomach. "I don't know what to say."

"There's nothing you can say," she said. "It's just one of those terrible, impossibly sad things. And now . . . today, I kept thinking that he's just slipping away. Nana didn't remember, Ben didn't remember. At least with Ben, I can sort of understand it. He wasn't even five when Drake was killed, and you know how memories are at that age. Only a little bit sticks. But Drake was so good with him because he actually enjoyed being around him." She shrugged. "Kind of like you."

Thibault wished she hadn't said it. He didn't belong here. . . .

"I didn't want to hire you," she continued, oblivious to Thibault's turmoil. "Did you know that?"

"Yes."

"But not because you walked here from Colorado. That was part of it, but it was mainly because you'd been in the marines."

He nodded, and in the silence she reached for the ice-cream maker. "It probably needs some more ice," she said. She opened the lid, added more ice, and then handed it back to him.

"Why are you here?" she finally asked.

Though he knew what she really meant, he pretended he didn't. "Because you asked me to stay."

"I mean, why are you here in Hampton? And I want the truth this time."

He grasped for the right explanation. "It seemed like a nice place, and so far, it has been."

He could tell by her expression that she knew there was more, and she waited. When he didn't add anything else, she frowned. "It has something to do with your time in Iraq, doesn't it?"

His silence gave him away.

"How long were you there?" she asked.

He shifted in his seat, not wanting to talk about it but knowing he had no choice. "Which time?"

"How many times did you go?"

"Three."

"Did you see a lot of combat?"

"Yes."

"But you made it out."

"Yes."

Her lips tightened, and she suddenly looked on the verge of tears. "Why you and not my brother?"

He turned the crank four times before answering with what he knew was a lie. "I don't know."

When Elizabeth got up to get bowls and spoons for the ice cream, Thibault fought the urge to call Zeus and simply leave, right then, before he changed his mind, and go back home to Colorado.

He couldn't stop thinking about the photograph in his pocket, the photograph that Drake had lost. Thibault had found it, Drake had died, and now he was here, in the home where Drake had been raised, spending time with the sister he'd left behind.

On the surface, it was all so improbable, but as he fought the sudden dryness in his mouth, he concentrated on those things he knew to be true. The photograph was simply that: a picture of Elizabeth that her brother had taken. There were no such things as lucky charms. Thibault had survived his time in Iraq, but so had the vast majority of marines who'd been posted there. So, in fact, had most of his platoon, including Victor. But some marines had died, Drake among them, and though it was tragic, it had nothing to do with the photograph. It was war. As for him, he was here because he'd made a decision to search for the woman in the picture. It had nothing to do with destiny or magic.

But he'd searched because of Victor. . . .

He blinked and reminded himself that he didn't believe anything Victor had told him.

What Victor believed was just superstition. It couldn't be true. At least not all of it.

Zeus seemed to sense his struggle and lifted his head to stare. With his ears raised, he gave a soft whine and wandered up the stairs to lick Thibault's hand. Thibault raised Zeus's head, and the dog nuzzled his face.

"What am I doing here?" Thibault whispered. "Why did I come?"

As he waited for an answer that would never come, he heard the screen door slam behind him.

"Are you talking to yourself or to your dog?" Elizabeth asked.

"Both," he said.

She sat next to him and handed him his spoon. "What were you saying?"

"Nothing important," he said. He motioned for Zeus to lie down, and the dog squished himself onto the step in an attempt to remain close to both of them.

Elizabeth opened the ice-cream maker and scooped some ice cream into each of the bowls. "I hope you like it," she said, handing him a bowl.

She dipped her spoon in and had a taste before turning toward him, her expression earnest. "I want to apologize," she said.

"For what?"

"For what I said before . . . When I asked why you made it and my brother didn't."

"It's a fair question." He nodded, uncomfortable under her scrutiny.

"No, it isn't," she said. "And it was wrong to ask you. So I'm sorry."

"It's okay," he said.

She ate another spoonful, hesitating before going on. "Do you remember when I told you that I didn't want to hire you because you were in the marines?"

He nodded.

"It's not what you probably think. It wasn't because you reminded me of Drake. It's because of the way Drake died." She tapped her spoon against the bowl. "Drake was killed by friendly fire."

Thibault turned away as she went on.

"Of course, I didn't know that at first. We kept getting the runaround. 'The investigation is continuing' or 'We're looking into the matter,' things like that. It took months to find out how he was killed, and even then, we never really learned who was responsible."

She groped for the right words. "It just . . . didn't seem right, you know? I mean, I know it was an accident, I know whoever did it didn't mean to kill him, but if something like that happened here in the States, someone would be charged with manslaughter. But if it happens in Iraq, no one wants the truth to come out. And it never will."

"Why are you telling me this?" Thibault said, his voice quiet.

"Because," she said, "that's the real reason I didn't want to hire you. After I found out what happened, it seemed like every time I saw a marine, I'd be asking myself, Was he the one who killed Drake? Or is he covering up for someone who killed him? I knew it wasn't fair, I knew it was wrong, but I couldn't help it. And after a while, the anger I felt just sort of became part of me, like it was the only way I knew how to handle the grief. I didn't like who I'd become, but I was stuck in this horrible cycle of questions and blame. And then, out of the blue, you walked into the office and applied for a job. And Nana, even though she knew exactly how I was feeling—maybe because of the way I was feeling—decided to hire you."

She set her bowl aside. "That's why I didn't have much to say to you the first couple of weeks. I didn't know what I could say. I figured I wouldn't have to say anything, since more than likely you'd quit within a few days like everyone else. But you didn't. Instead, you work hard and stay late, you're wonderful to Nana and my son . . . and all of a sudden, you're not so much a marine as you are just a man." She paused as if lost in thought, then finally nudged him with her knee. "And not only that, you're a man who allows emotional women to ramble on without telling them to stop."

He nudged her back to show her it was okay. "It's Drake's birthday."

"Yes, it is." She raised her bowl. "To my little brother, Drake," she said.

Thibault tapped his bowl against hers. "To Drake," he echoed.

Zeus whined and stared up at them anxiously. Despite the tension, she reached out and ruffled his fur. "You don't need a toast. This is Drake's moment."

He tilted his head in puzzlement, and she laughed.

"Blah, blah, blah. He doesn't understand a word I'm saying."

"True, but he can tell you were upset. That's why he stayed close."

"He's really amazing. I don't think I've ever seen a dog so intuitive and well trained. Nana said the same thing, and believe me, that's saying a lot."

"Thanks," he said. "Good bloodlines."

"Okay," she said. "Your turn to talk. You pretty much know everything there is to know about me."

"What do you want to know?"

She picked up her bowl and spooned more ice cream into her mouth before asking, "Have you ever been in love?"

When he raised his eyebrows at the nonchalant way she'd said it, she waved him off. "Don't even think I'm being too personal. Not after everything I've told you. 'Fess up."

"Once," he admitted.

"Recently?"

"No. Years ago. When I was in college."

"What was she like?"

He seemed to search for the right word. "Earthy," he offered.

She said nothing, but her expression told him she wanted more.

"Okay," he continued. "She was a women's studies major, and she favored Birkenstocks and peasant skirts. She despised makeup. She wrote opinions for the student newspaper and championed the causes of pretty much every sociological group in the world except white males and the rich. Oh, and she was a vegetarian, too."

She studied him. "For some reason, I can't see you with someone like that."

"Neither could I. And neither could she. Not in the long run, anyway. But for a while, it was surprisingly easy to overlook our obvious differences. And we did."

"How long did it last?"

"A little more than a year."

"Do you ever hear from her anymore?"

He shook his head. "Never."

"And that's it?"

"Aside from a couple of high school crushes, that's it. But bear in mind that the last five years haven't exactly been conducive to starting new relationships."

"No, I don't suppose so."

Zeus got up and stared down the drive, his ears twitching. Alert. It took a moment, but Thibault heard the faint sound of a car engine, and in the distance, a broad, dispersed light flashed in the trees before it began to narrow. Someone pulling up the drive. Elizabeth frowned in confusion before a sedan slowly rounded the corner and came toward the house. Even though the lights from the porch didn't illuminate the drive, Thibault recognized the car and sat up straighter. It was either the sheriff or one of his deputies.

Elizabeth recognized it as well. "This can't be good," she muttered.

"What do you think they want?"

She stood from her spot on the porch. "It's not a they. It's a him. My ex-husband." She started down the steps and motioned toward him. "Just wait here. I'll handle this."

Thibault motioned for Zeus to sit and stay as the car pulled to a stop beside Elizabeth's car at the far end of the house. Through the bushes, he saw the passenger door open and watched as Ben got out, dragging his backpack behind him. He started toward his mother, keeping his head down. When the driver's-side door opened, Deputy Keith Clayton stepped out.

Zeus let out a low growl, alert and ready, waiting for Thibault's command to go after the guy. Elizabeth glanced at Zeus in surprise until Ben stepped into the light. Thibault noticed the absence of Ben's glasses and the black-and-blue bruises around Ben's eye at the same moment Elizabeth did.

"What happened!" she cried, hurrying toward her son. She squatted to get a better look. "What did you do?"

"It's nothing," Clayton responded, approaching them. "It's just a bruise."

Ben turned away, not wanting her to see.

"What about his glasses?" Elizabeth said, still trying to make sense of it. "Did you hit him?"

"No, I didn't hit him. Christ! I wouldn't hit him. Who do you think I am?"

Elizabeth didn't seem to hear him and focused her attention on her son. "Are you all right? Oh, that looks bad! What happened, sweetie? Are your glasses broken?"

She knew he wouldn't say anything until after Clayton left. Tilting his face up to hers, she could see the vessels had burst in his eye, leaving it bloody.

"How hard did you throw it?" she demanded, her expression horrified.

"Not too hard. And it's just a bruise. His eye is fine, and we managed to tape his glasses back together."

"It's more than a bruise!" Elizabeth's voice rose, barely controlled.

"Stop acting like this is my fault!" Clayton barked.

"It is your fault!"

"He's the one who missed it! We were just playing catch. It was an accident, for God's sake! Wasn't it, Ben? We were having fun, right?"

Ben stared at the ground. "Yeah," he mumbled.

"Tell her what happened. Tell her it wasn't my fault. Go ahead."

Ben shifted from one foot to the other. "We were playing catch. I missed the ball and it hit me in the eye." He held up his glasses, crudely taped at the bridge and the top of one lens with duct tape. "Dad fixed my glasses."

Clayton held up his palms. "See? No big deal. Happens all the time. It's part of the game."

"When did this happen?" Elizabeth demanded.

"A few hours ago."

"And you didn't call me?"

"No. I took him to the emergency room."

"The emergency room?"

"Where else was I supposed to take him? I knew I couldn't bring him back here without having him checked out, so I did. I did what any responsible parent would do, just like you did when he fell off the swing and broke his arm. And if you remember, I didn't get all crazy on you, just like I don't get crazy about you letting him play in the tree house. The thing is a death trap."

She seemed too shocked to speak, and he shook his head in disgust. "Anyway, he wanted to go home."

"Okay," she said, still struggling with her words. A muscle clenched and unclenched in her jaw. She waved Clayton off. "Whatever. Just go. I'll take it from here."

With her arm around Ben, she started to lead him away, and it was in that instant that Clayton spotted Thibault sitting on the porch, staring directly at him. Clayton's eyes widened before they flashed in anger. He started for the porch.

"What are you doing here?" he demanded.

Thibault simply stared at him without moving. Zeus's growls grew more ominous.

"What's he doing here, Beth?"

"Just go, Keith. We'll talk about this tomorrow." She turned away.

"Don't walk away from me," he spat, reaching for her arm. "I'm just asking you a question."

At that moment, Zeus snarled and his rear legs began to quiver. For the first time, Clayton seemed to notice the dog, his teeth bared, the fur on his back standing straight up.

"If I were you, I'd let go of her arm," Thibault said. His voice was flat and calm, more a suggestion than an order. "Right now."

Clayton, eyeing the dog, let go immediately. As Elizabeth and Ben hurried to the porch, Clayton glared at Thibault. Zeus took a single step forward, continuing to snarl.

"I think you'd better go," Thibault said, his voice quiet.

Clayton debated for an instant, then took a step backward and turned away. Thibault heard him cursing under his breath as he stalked back to the car, opened the door, and slammed it shut behind him.

Thibault reached out to pet Zeus. "Good boy," he whispered.

Clayton backed out of his spot, made a sloppy three-point turn, and took off up the drive, spewing gravel. His taillights receded from view, and only then did the fur on Zeus's back finally lower. His tail wagged as Ben approached.

"Hi, Zeus," Ben said.

Zeus glanced at Thibault for permission. "It's okay," Thibault said, releasing him. Zeus pranced toward Ben as if to say, *I'm so happy you're home!* He nosed at Ben, who started to pet him.

"You missed me, huh?" Ben said, sounding pleased. "I missed you, too. . . ."

"Come on, sweetie," Elizabeth urged, moving him forward again. "Let's go inside and put some ice on your eye. And I want to see it in the light."

As they opened the screen door, Thibault stood.

"Hey, Thibault," Ben said, waving.

"Hi, Ben."

"Can I play with Zeus tomorrow?"

"If it's okay with your mom, it's okay with me." Thibault could tell by looking at Elizabeth that she wanted to be alone with her son. "I should probably go," he said, rising from his spot. "It's getting late, and I've got an early morning."

"Thanks," she said. "I appreciate it. And sorry for all this."

"There's nothing to be sorry for."

He walked a ways down the drive, then turned toward the house. He could just make out movement behind the curtains of the living room window.

Staring at the shadows of the two figures in the window, he felt for the first time that he was finally beginning to understand the reason he'd come.

14

Clayton

Of all the places in all the world, he had to find the guy at Beth's place. What were the odds on that? Pretty damn small, that's for sure.

He hated that guy. No, scratch that. He wanted to destroy the guy. Not only because of the whole *stealing-the-camera-and-flattening-his-tires* thing, though that was definitely worthy of a little time locked in the jail alongside a couple of violent methamphetamine addicts. And it wasn't because Thigh-bolt had him over a barrel with the camera disk. It was because the guy, the same guy who'd played him once, had made him look like a quivering jellyfish in front of Beth.

If I were you, I'd let go of her arm had been bad enough. But after that? Oh, that's where the guy went seriously wrong. *Right now. . . . I think you'd better go. . . .* All spoken in that serious, steady, *don't-piss-me-off* tone of voice that Clayton himself used on criminals. And he'd actually done it, slinking away like some stray dog with his tail between his legs, which made the whole thing worse.

Normally, he wouldn't have put up with that for a second, even with Beth and Ben around. No one gave him orders and got away with it, and he would have made it perfectly clear that the guy had just made the biggest mistake of his life. But he couldn't! That was the thing. He couldn't. Not with Cujo around, eyeballing his crotch like it was an appetizer at the Sunday buffet. In the dark, the thing actually looked like a rabid wolf, and all he could do was remember the stories Kenny Moore told him about Panther.

What the hell was he doing with Beth, anyway? How did that come about? It was like some sort of evil cosmic plan to ruin what had been for the most part a pretty crappy day—starting with mopey, moody Ben showing up at noon and complaining straight off about having to take out the garbage.

He was a patient guy, but he was tired of the kid's attitude. Real tired of it, which was why he hadn't let Ben stop at just the garbage. He'd had the kid clean the kitchen and the bathrooms, too, thinking it would show him how the real world worked, where having a halfway decent attitude actually mattered. Power of positive thinking and all that. And besides, everyone knew that while mamas did the spoiling, dads were supposed to teach kids that nothing in life was free, right? And the kid did real well with the cleaning, like he always did, so for Clayton the whole thing was over and done with. It was time for a break, so he took Ben outside to play catch. What kid wouldn't want to play catch with his dad on a beautiful Saturday afternoon?

Ben. That's who.

I'm tired. It's really hot, Dad. Do we have to? One stupid complaint after the other until they finally get outside, and then the kid shuts up tighter than a clam and won't say a thing. Worse, no matter how many times Clayton told him to watch the damn ball, the kid kept missing it because he wasn't even trying. Doing it on purpose, no doubt. But would he run to the ball after he missed it? Of course not. Not his kid. His kid is too busy sulking about the unfairness of it all while playing catch like a blind man.

In the end, it pissed him off. He was trying to have a good time with his son, but his son was working against him, and yeah, okay, maybe he did throw the ball a little hard that last time. But what happened next wasn't his fault. If the kid had been paying attention, the ball wouldn't have ricocheted off his glove and Ben wouldn't have ended up screaming like a baby, like he was dying or something. Like he was the only kid in the history of the world to get a shiner playing ball.

But all that was beside the point. The kid got hurt. It wasn't serious, and the bruises would be gone in a couple of weeks. In a year, Ben would either forget it completely or brag to his friends about the time he got a shiner playing ball.

Beth, on the other hand, would never forget. She'd carry that grudge around inside her for a long, long time, even if it had been more Ben's fault than his. She didn't understand the simple fact that all boys remembered their sports injuries with pride.

He'd known Beth would overreact tonight, but he didn't necessarily blame her for it. That's what mothers did, and Clayton had been prepared for that. He thought he'd handled the whole thing pretty well, right up until the end, when he'd seen the guy with the dog sitting on the porch like he owned the place.

Logan Thigh-bolt.

He remembered the name right off, of course. He'd searched for the guy for a few days without luck and had pretty much put it behind him when he figured the guy had left town. No way some dude and his dog couldn't be noticed, right? Which was why he'd eventually stopped asking folks whether they'd seen him.

Stupid.

But what to do now? What was he going to do about this . . . new turn of events?

He'd deal with Logan Thigh-bolt, that much was certain, and he wasn't about to be caught off guard again. Which meant that before he did anything, he needed information. Where the guy lived, where the guy worked, where he liked to hang out. Where he could find the guy alone.

Harder than it sounded, especially with the dog. He had the

funny feeling Thigh-bolt and the dog were seldom, if ever, separated. But he'd figure out what to do about that, too.

Obviously, he needed to know what was going on with Beth and Thigh-bolt. He hadn't heard about her seeing anyone since Adam the dork. It was hard to believe that Beth could be seeing Thigh-bolt, considering the fact that he *always* heard what Beth was up to. Frankly, he couldn't imagine what she'd see in someone like Thigh-bolt in the first place. She'd gone to college; the last thing she wanted in her life was some drifter who rolled into town. The guy didn't even have a car.

But Thigh-bolt had been with her on a Saturday night, and that obviously counted for something. Somewhere, something didn't make sense. He pondered it, wondering if the guy worked there. . . . Either way, he'd figure it out, and when he did, he'd deal with it, and Mr. Logan Thigh-bolt would find himself hating the day he'd ever showed up in Clayton's town.

15

Beth

Sunday was the hottest day of the summer yet, with high humidity and temperatures in the triple digits. Lakes had begun to go dry in the Piedmont, the citizens of Raleigh were rationing their water, and in the eastern part of the state, crops had begun to wither under the never-ending heat. In the past three weeks, the forests had become a tinderbox, waiting to be ignited by a carelessly tossed cigarette or bolt of lightning, both of which seemed inevitable. The only question was when and where exactly the fire would start.

Unless they were in their kennels, the dogs were miserable, and even Logan had been feeling the effects of the heat. He shortened the training sessions by five minutes each, and when he walked the dogs, his destination was always the creek, where they could wade into the water and cool off. Zeus had been in and out of the water at least a dozen times, and though Ben tried to start a game of fetch as soon as he got back from church, Zeus showed only halfhearted interest. Instead, Ben set up a floor fan on the front porch of the house, angling the breeze toward Zeus, and sat beside the dog while he read *The Murder of Roger Ackroyd*, one of the few books by Agatha Christie that he had yet to finish. He stopped briefly to visit with Logan in a desultory fashion before going back to his book.

It was the kind of lazy Sunday afternoon Beth typically enjoyed, except that every time she saw the bruise on Ben's face and his crudely repaired glasses, she felt a flash of anger at what Keith had done. She'd have to take Ben to the optician on Monday to get his glasses repaired. Despite what he'd said, Keith had thrown the ball way too hard, and she wondered what kind of a father would do that to a ten-year-old.

The Keith Clayton kind, obviously.

It was one thing to have made a mistake by marrying him, it was another thing to have that mistake endlessly compounded for the rest of her life. Ben's relationship with his father seemed to be getting worse, not better. Granted, Ben needed an adult male figure in his life, and Keith was his father, but . . .

She shook her head. Part of her wanted to take Ben and simply move away. Relocate to another part of the country and start over. It was easy to fantasize that if she simply had the guts to do it, her troubles would be over. But that wasn't reality. She had the guts; it was everything else that made the scenario impossible. Even if Nana was healthy enough to handle things on her own—and she wasn't—Keith would find her no matter where she went. Gramps would insist on it, and the courts, including Judge Clayton, would intervene. Most likely, in her absence, Keith would be awarded sole custody. Keith's uncle would make sure of it; that had been the implied threat since the divorce, a threat she had to take seriously in this county. Maybe she would have a shot on appeal, but how long would that take? Twelve months? Eighteen months? She wasn't going to risk losing Ben for even that long. And the last thing she wanted was for Ben to have to spend more time with Keith.

The truth was, Keith didn't want full custody any more than she wanted him to have it, and over the years, they'd worked out an unspoken solution: Keith would have Ben as infrequently as possible, but enough to keep Gramps happy. It wasn't fair for either of them to use Ben like a pawn, but what else could she do? She didn't want to risk losing him. Keith would do what he had to do to keep the money flowing, and Gramps wanted Ben around.

People liked to imagine they were free to choose their own lives, but Beth had learned that choice was sometimes illusory. At least in Hampton, anyway, where the Claytons pretty much ran everything. Gramps was always polite when they bumped into him at the church, and though he'd wanted to buy Nana's land for years, he hadn't made things difficult for them. *So far*. But in the world of black and white, there was no question that the Clayton family, Gramps included, were masters of the gray, and they used their power when it suited them. Each and every one of them had grown up with the idea that they were special—anointed, even— which was why she'd been surprised at how easily Keith had left her house last night.

She was glad that Logan and Zeus had been there. Logan had handled the situation perfectly, and she appreciated the fact that he hadn't hung around afterward. He'd known she wanted to be alone with Ben and had accepted that as easily as he'd dismissed Keith.

In all things, Logan was calm and steadfast, she reflected. When she talked about Drake, he didn't turn the conversation to himself or how it made him feel, nor did he offer advice. It was one of the reasons she trusted him and had ended up telling him so much about herself. She'd been a little out of sorts because of Drake's birthday, but in truth, she had known exactly what she was doing. She'd been the one to ask him to stay in the first place, and she supposed that deep down, she'd wanted to share those parts of herself with him.

"Hey, Mom?"

Beth turned toward Ben. His eye still looked terrible, but she pretended she didn't notice. "What's up, sweetie?"

"Do we have any garbage bags? And straws?"

"Of course we do. Why?"

"Thibault said he'd show me how to make a kite and that we could fly it when it was done."

"That sounds like fun."

"He said he used to make them when he was a kid and that they fly great."

She smiled. "Is that all you need? Garbage bags and straws?"

"I already found the fishing line. And the duct tape. They were in Grandpa's garage."

From across the yard, she saw Logan heading toward them. Ben noticed him at the same time.

"Hey, Thibault!" he shouted. "Are you ready to build the kite?"

"I was coming to ask if you were ready," Logan called back.

"Almost. I just have to get the straws and the garbage bags."

Logan waved in acknowledgment. As he drew nearer, Beth noted the shape of his shoulders, the tight cinch of his waist. It wasn't the first time she'd noticed his body, but today it felt almost as if she were . . . staring. She turned away, laying a hand on Ben's shoulder, feeling suddenly ridiculous. "The garbage bags are under the sink, and the straws are in the pantry by the cookies. Do you want to get them or should I?"

"I'll get them," he said. Then, to Logan: "I'll be back in a second."

Logan reached the steps just as Ben disappeared inside.

"Making a kite?" she asked, both surprised and impressed.

"He said he was bored."

"Do you really know how?"

"It's not as hard as it sounds. You want to help us?"

"No," she said. Up close, she noticed the way his sweat made the T-shirt cling to his chest, and she quickly averted her gaze. "I'll let you two do that. It's more of a guy project. But I'll bring the lemonade. And afterwards, if you're hungry, you're welcome to stay. Nothing fancy—Ben was in the mood for some hot dogs and macaroni and cheese."

Logan nodded. "I'd like that."

Ben came back out the door, bags in one hand and straws in the other. His face, despite the bruises and cockeyed glasses, was animated.

"Got 'em!" he said. "You ready?"

Logan continued to hold Beth's gaze longer than necessary, and Beth felt her neck flush before she turned away. Logan smiled at Ben.

"Whenever you are."

Beth found herself studying Logan as he worked on the kite with Ben. They were sitting at the picnic table near the large oak tree with Zeus at their feet, and the wind would occasionally carry the sound of their voices—Logan telling Ben what to do next or Ben asking if something had been done correctly. It was clear they were enjoying their little project; Ben was chattering away, making the occasional mistake, which Logan would then patiently correct with extra tape.

How long had it been since she'd blushed when a man stared at her? She wondered how much of her newfound self-consciousness had to do with the fact that Nana was away. For the last couple of nights, it had almost felt like she was really on her own for the first time in her life. After all, she'd moved from Nana's home to Keith's and back to Nana's and had been there ever since. And although she enjoyed Nana's company and liked the stability, it wasn't exactly how she'd imagined her adult life would turn out. She'd once dreamed of having her own place, but the timing had never seemed right. After Keith, she'd needed Nana's help with Ben; when Ben was old enough, both her brother and her grandfather had died, and Beth had needed Nana's support as much as Nana needed Beth's. And then? Just when she was thinking she was finally ready to find a home of her own, Nana had a stroke, and there wasn't a chance she was going to leave the woman who'd raised her.

But in this moment, she had an unexpected picture of what her life would have been like under a different set of circumstances. Now, as the starlings above her moved from tree to tree, she sat on the porch of an otherwise empty house, witnessing the kind of scene that made her believe that all could be right with the world. Even from a distance, she could see Ben concentrating while Logan showed him how to put the final touches on the kite. Every now and then, Logan would lean forward and offer direction, his demeanor patient and steady, but he let Ben have most of the fun. That he seemed to be simply working on the project, rectifying Ben's mistakes without frustration or anger, made her feel a burst of gratitude and affection toward him. She was still marveling at the novelty of it all when she saw them move to the center of the yard. Logan held the kite above his head, and Ben unwound the fishing line. As Ben started to run, Logan followed, allowing the kite to catch the wind before letting go. Logan stopped and gazed skyward as the kite began to soar above them, and when he clapped his hands at Ben's obvious joy, she was struck by the simple truth that sometimes the most ordinary things could be made extraordinary, simply by doing them with the right people.

Nana called that night to say that she needed to be picked up the following Friday, and in her absence, Logan joined Beth and Ben for dinner every night. Most of the time, Ben was the one who pleaded with Logan to stay, but by Wednesday, it had become obvious to Beth that Logan was not only pleased to spend time with them, but more than happy to let Ben continue to orchestrate things. Perhaps, she found herself wondering occasionally, Logan was as inexperienced at intimacy as she was.

After dinner, they usually went for a walk. Ben and Zeus would race ahead on the path that led to the creek, while she and Logan followed; once, they headed toward town to visit the banks of the South River, where they sat beneath the bridge that spanned it. Sometimes they talked around the edges of things—whether anything interesting had happened at work or Logan's progress in reorganizing the files; at other times it seemed he was content to walk beside her without saying much. Because Logan was so comfortable with silence, she felt surprisingly comfortable as well.

But something was happening between them, and she knew it. She was drawn to him. At school, with her class of second graders milling around her, she'd occasionally find herself wondering what he was doing at that very minute. She gradually acknowledged that she looked forward to coming home because it meant that she would see him.

On Thursday evening, they all piled into Nana's truck and drove into town for pizza. Zeus rode in the truck bed, head hanging over the side and his ears blown back. Odd as it seemed, Beth had the strange feeling that this was almost a date, albeit one with a ten-year-old chaperone.

Luigi's Pizza was located on one of the quiet cross streets downtown, sandwiched between an antiques store and a law firm. With scuffed brick floors, picnic tables, and paneled walls, the place had a cozy familiarity, partly because Luigi hadn't updated the décor since Beth was a little girl. In the rear of the restaurant, the video games Luigi offered dated from the early 1980s: Ms. Pac-Man, Millipede, and Asteroids. The games were as popular now as they'd been back then, probably owing to the lack of any video arcades in town.

Beth loved this place. Luigi and his wife, Maria, both in their sixties, not only worked seven days a week, but lived in an apartment above the restaurant. With no children of their own, they were surrogate parents to pretty much every teenager in town, and they embraced everyone with a kind of unconditional acceptance that kept the place packed.

Tonight, it was crowded with the usual mix of people: families with children, a couple of men who were dressed like they'd just finished work at the law office next door, a few elderly couples, and clusters of teenagers here and there. Maria beamed when she saw Beth and Ben enter. She was short and round, with dark hair and a genuinely warm smile. She walked toward them, reaching for menus on the way.

"Hello, Beth. Hello, Ben." As she passed the kitchen, she

ducked her head in for an instant. "Luigi! Come out here. Beth and Ben are here!"

It was something she did every time Beth visited, and though Beth was sure she welcomed everyone with equal warmth, it still made her feel special.

Luigi bustled out of the kitchen. As usual, the apron he wore was coated in flour and was stretched tight across his ample girth. Since he still made the pizzas and the restaurant was always busy, he didn't have time to do much more than wave. "It's good to see you!" he cried. "Thank you for coming!"

Maria laid an affectionate hand on Ben's shoulder. "You're getting so tall, Ben! You're a young man now. And you're as lovely as springtime, Beth."

"Thanks, Maria," Beth said. "How are you?"

"The same. Always busy. And you? You're still teaching, yes?"

"Still teaching," she confirmed. A moment later, Maria's expression turned serious, and Beth could predict her next question. In small towns, nothing was secret.

"And how is Nana?"

"Getting better. She's up and around now."

"Yes, I heard she's visiting her sister."

"How did you know that?" Beth couldn't hide her surprise.

"Who knows." She shrugged. "People talk, I hear." For the first time, Maria seemed to notice Logan. "And who is this?"

"This is my friend Logan Thibault," Beth said, willing herself not to blush.

"You are new? I haven't seen you before." Maria's eyes swept him up and down in frank curiosity.

"I just moved to town."

"Well, you're with two of my favorite customers." She waved them forward. "Come. I'll get you a place in one of the booths."

Maria led the way and set the menus on the table as they slid into their seats. "Sweet teas all around?"

"That would be great, Maria," Beth agreed. As soon as Maria

hurried toward the kitchen, she faced Logan. "She makes the best sweet tea around. I hope you don't mind."

"Sounds good to me."

"Can I have some quarters?" Ben asked. "I want to play some video games."

"I figured you would," Beth said, reaching into her handbag. "I grabbed some from the change jar before we left. Have fun," she said. "And don't leave with any strangers."

"I'm ten years old," he said, sounding exasperated. "Not five."

She watched Ben head toward the games, amused at his response. Sometimes he sounded as if he were in high school.

"This place has lots of character," Logan commented.

"The food is fantastic, too. They do Chicago-style deep-dish pizzas that are out of this world. What do you like on your pizza?"

He scratched his chin. "Mmm . . . lots of garlic, extra anchovies."

Her nose wrinkled. "Really?"

"Just kidding. Get whatever you order normally. I'm not particular."

"Ben likes pepperoni."

"Then make it pepperoni."

She eyed him playfully. "Did anyone ever tell you that you're pretty easygoing?"

"Not lately," he said. "But then again, I didn't have many people to talk to while I was walking."

"Did you get lonely?"

"Not with Zeus. He's a good listener."

"But he can't contribute to the conversation."

"No. But he didn't whine about the walk, either. Most people would have."

"I wouldn't have whined." Beth tossed a length of hair over her shoulder.

Logan said nothing.

"I'm serious," she protested. "I easily could have walked across the country."

Logan said nothing.

"Okay, you're right. I might have whined once or twice."

He laughed before surveying the restaurant. "How many people do you know in here?"

Glancing around, she considered it. "I've seen most of them around town over the years, but those I actually know? Maybe thirty people."

He estimated it to be well more than half the patrons. "What's that like?"

"You mean where everyone knows everything? I guess it depends on how many big mistakes you make, since that's what most people end up talking about. Affairs, lost jobs, drug or alcohol abuse, auto accidents. But if you're like me, on the other hand, someone as pure as the wind-driven snow, it's not so hard."

He grinned. "It must be nice being you."

"Oh, it is. Trust me. Let's just say you're lucky to be sitting at my table."

"Of that," he said, "I have no doubt."

Maria dropped off the drinks. As she was leaving, she raised her eyebrows just enough to let Beth know she liked Logan's appearance and expected to find out later what, if anything, was going on between them.

Beth took a gulp of her tea, as did Logan.

"What do you think?"

"It's definitely sweet," Logan said. "But it's tasty."

Beth nodded before wiping the condensation from the outside of her glass with a paper napkin. She crumpled it and set it aside. "How long are you going to stay in Hampton?" she asked.

"What do you mean?"

"You're not from here, you have a college degree, you're working in a job that most people would hate, and getting paid very little for it. I think my question is fair."

"I don't plan on quitting," he said.

"That's not what I asked. I asked how long you were going to stay in Hampton. Honestly."

Her voice brooked no evasions, and it was easy for Logan to imagine her bringing order to an unruly classroom. "Honestly? I don't know. And I say that because I've learned over the past five years never to take anything for granted."

"That may be true, but again, it doesn't really answer the question."

He seemed to register the disappointment in her voice and struggled with his response. "How about this?" he finally said. "So far, I like it here. I like my job, I think Nana's terrific, I enjoy spending time with Ben, and right now, I have no intention of leaving Hampton any time in the foreseeable future. Does that answer your question?"

She felt a jolt of anticipation at his words and the way his gaze roamed over her face as he spoke. She leaned forward as well. "I noticed you left out something important in that list of things you like."

"I did?"

"Yeah. Me." She studied his face for a reaction, her lips upturned in a teasing grin.

"Maybe I forgot," he said, responding with the faintest of smiles.

"I don't think so."

"I'm shy?"

"Try again."

He shook his head. "I'm out of suggestions."

She winked at him. "I'll give you a chance to think about it and maybe come up with something. Then we can talk about it again later."

"Fair enough. When?"

She wrapped her hands around her glass, feeling strangely nervous at what she was about to say next. "Are you free on Saturday night?"

If he was surprised by the question, she couldn't tell.

"Saturday night it is." He lifted his glass of iced tea and took a long drink, never taking his eyes off her.

Neither one noticed Ben walk back to the table.

"Did you order the pizza yet?"

Lying in bed that night, Beth stared at the ceiling and asked herself, *What on earth was I thinking?*

There were so many reasons to avoid what she had done. She didn't really know much about him or his past. He was still hiding the reason he'd come to Hampton, which meant not only that he didn't trust her, but that she didn't completely trust him either. Not only that, but he worked at the kennel—for Nana and within sight of her home. What would happen if it didn't work out? What if he had . . . *expectations* she wasn't willing to meet? Would he show up on Monday? Would Nana be on her own? Would she have to quit her job as a teacher and go back to helping Nana with the kennel?

There were lots of potential problems with all of this, and the more she thought about it, the more she was convinced she had made a terrible mistake. And yet . . . she was tired of being alone. She loved Ben and she loved Nana, but spending time with Logan over the past few days had reminded her of what she was missing. She liked the walks they took after dinner, she liked the way he looked at her, and she especially liked the way he was with Ben.

Moreover, she found it ridiculously easy to imagine a life with Logan. She knew she hadn't really known him long enough to make that kind of judgment, but she couldn't deny her intuition.

Could he be the One?

She wouldn't go that far. They hadn't even been on a date yet. It was easy to idealize someone you barely knew.

Sitting up, she plumped her pillow a few times and then lay back down. Well, they'd go out once and see what happened next. She had hopes, she couldn't deny that, but that's where it ended. She liked him but certainly didn't love him. Not yet, anyway.

16

Thibault

On Saturday evening Thibault waited on the couch, wondering if he was doing the right thing.

In another place and time, he wouldn't have thought twice about it. He was attracted to Elizabeth, certainly. He liked her openness and intelligence, and together with her playful sense of humor, and of course her looks, he couldn't imagine how she'd remained single as long as she had.

But it wasn't another place and time, and nothing was normal about any of this. He'd carried her picture for more than five years. He'd searched the country for her. He'd come to Hampton and taken a job that kept him close to her. He'd befriended her grandmother, her son, and then her. Now, they were minutes away from their first date.

He'd come for a reason. He'd accepted that as soon as he'd left Colorado. He'd accepted that Victor had been right. He still wasn't sure, however, that meeting her—becoming close to her— was it. Nor was he sure that it wasn't.

The only thing he knew for sure was that he'd been looking forward to their evening together. The day before, he'd thought about it consistently on the drive to pick up Nana. For the first half hour on the way back to Hampton, Nana had chattered on about everything from politics to her sister's health before turning toward him with a knowing smirk.

"So you're going to go out with the boss's granddaughter, huh?"

Thibault shifted on the seat. "She told you."

"Of course she told me. But even if she hadn't, I knew it was coming. Two young, attractive, and lonely single people? I knew it would happen as soon as I hired you."

Thibault said nothing, and when Nana spoke again, her voice was tinged with melancholy.

"She's as sweet as sugared watermelon," she said. "I worry about her sometimes."

"I know," Thibault said.

That had been the extent of their conversation, but it told him that he had Nana's blessing, something he knew was important given Nana's place in Elizabeth's life.

Now, with evening beginning to settle in, he could see Elizabeth's car coming up the drive, the front end bouncing slightly in the potholes. She hadn't told him anything about where they were going, other than to dress casually. He stepped out onto the porch as she pulled to a stop in front of the house. Zeus followed him, his curiosity alerted. When Elizabeth got out and stepped into the dim light of the porch, all he could do was stare.

Like him, she was wearing jeans, but the creamy blouse she wore accentuated the sun-browned tint of her skin. Her honey-colored hair swept the neckline of her sleeveless blouse, and he noted that she was wearing a trace of mascara. She looked both familiar and tantalizingly foreign.

Zeus padded down the steps, tail wagging and whining, and went to her side.

"Hey, Zeus. Did you miss me? It's only been a day." She stroked his back, and Zeus whined plaintively before licking at her hands. "Now *that* was a greeting," she said, looking up at him. "How are you? Am I late?"

He tried to sound nonchalant. "I'm fine," he said. "And you're right on time. I'm glad you made it."

"Did you think I wouldn't?"

"This place is kind of hard to find."

"Not if you've lived here your whole life." She motioned toward the house. "So this is home?"

"This is it."

"It's nice," she said, taking it in.

"Is it what you expected?"

"Pretty much. Solid. Efficient. Kind of hidden."

He acknowledged her double entendre with a smile, then turned to Zeus and commanded him to stay on the porch.

He walked down the steps to join her.

"Will he be okay outside?"

"He'll be fine. He won't move."

"But we'll be gone for hours."

"I know."

"Amazing."

"It seems that way. But dogs don't have much sense of time. In a minute, he won't remember anything other than the fact that he's supposed to stay. But he won't know why."

"How did you learn so much about dogs and training?" Elizabeth asked, curious.

"Mainly books."

"You read?"

He sounded amused. "Yes. Surprised?"

"I am. It's hard to tote books when you're walking across the country."

"Not if you don't keep them when you finish."

They reached the car, and when Thibault started toward the driver's side to open the door for her, she shook her head. "I might have asked you out, but I'm going to make you drive."

"And here I thought I was going out with a liberated woman," he protested.

"I am a liberated woman. But you'll drive. And pick up the check."

He laughed as he walked her back around to the other side. Once he was settled behind the wheel, she peeked toward the porch. Zeus seemed confused about what was happening, and she heard him whining again.

"He sounds sad."

"He probably is. We're seldom apart."

"Mean man," she scolded him.

He smiled at her playful tone as he slipped the car into reverse. "Should I head downtown?"

"Nope," she said. "We're getting out of town tonight. Just go to the main highway and head toward the coast. We're not going to the beach, but there's a good place on the way. I'll let you know when we're getting close to the next turn."

Thibault did as she said, driving quiet roads in the deepening twilight. They reached the highway in a few minutes, and as the car picked up speed, the trees on either side began to blur. Shadows stretched across the road, darkening the car's interior.

"So tell me about Zeus," she said.

"What do you want to know?"

"Whatever you want to tell me. Something I wouldn't know."

He could have said, *I bought him because a woman in a photograph owned a German shepherd,* but he didn't. Instead he said, "I bought Zeus in Germany. I flew out there and picked him from the litter myself."

"Really?"

He nodded. "The shepherd in Germany is like the bald eagle in America. It's a symbol of national pride, and breeders take their work very seriously. I wanted a dog with strong, working bloodlines, and if that's what you want, you'll usually find the best dogs in Germany. Zeus comes from a long line of Schutzhund competitors and champions."

"What's that?'"

"In Schutzhund, the dogs are tested not only in obedience, but in tracking and protection. And the competition is intense. Usually it lasts two days, and as a rule, the winners tend to be the most intelligent and trainable dogs of all. And since Zeus comes from a long line of competitors and champions, he's been bred for both those things."

"And you did all the training," she said, sounding impressed.

"Since he was six months old. When we walked from Colorado, I worked with him every day."

"He's an incredible animal. You could always give him to Ben, you know. He'd probably love it."

Thibault said nothing.

She noticed his expression and slid closer to him. "I was kidding. I wouldn't take your dog from you."

Thibault felt the continuing warmth of her body radiate down his side.

"If you don't mind my asking, how did Ben react when you told him you were going out with me tonight?" he asked.

"He was fine with it. He and Nana were already planning to watch videos. They'd talked on the phone about having a movie night earlier in the week. Made a date and everything."

"Do they do that a lot?"

"They used to do it all the time, but this is the first time since she had her stroke. I know Ben was really excited about it. Nana makes popcorn and usually lets him stay up extra late."

"Unlike his mom, of course."

"Of course." She smiled. "What did you end up doing today?"

"Catching up around the house. Cleaning, laundry, shopping, that kind of thing."

She raised an eyebrow. "I'm impressed. You're a real domestic animal. Can you bounce a quarter on your bedspread after you make it?"

"Of course."

"You'll have to teach Ben how to do that."

"If you'd like."

Outside, the first stars were beginning to emerge, and the car's headlights swept the curves of the road.

"Where exactly are we going?" Thibault asked.

"Do you like crabs?"

"Love 'em."

"That's a good start. How about shag dancing?"

"I don't even know what that is."

"Well, let's just say you're going to have to learn quick."

Forty minutes later, Thibault pulled to a stop in front of a place that looked to have once been a warehouse. Elizabeth had directed him to the industrial section of downtown Wilmington, and they had parked in front of a three-story structure with aged wide-plank siding. There was little to differentiate it from the neighboring buildings other than the nearly hundred cars parked in the lot and a small wooden walkway that led around the building, stringed with inexpensive strands of white Christmas tree lights.

"What's this place called?"

"Shagging for Crabs."

"Original. But I'm having a hard time visualizing this as a major tourist attraction."

"It's not—it's strictly for locals. One of my friends from college told me about it, and I've always wanted to go."

"You've never been here?"

"No," she said. "But I've heard it's a lot of fun."

With that, she headed up the creaking walkway. Straight ahead, the river sparkled, as if lit from below. The sound of music from inside grew steadily louder. When they opened the door, the music broke over them like a wave, and the smell of crabs and butter filled the air. Thibault paused to take it all in.

The massive building's interior was crude and unadorned. The front half was jammed with dozens of picnic tables covered with red-and-white plastic tablecloths that appeared stapled to the wood. Tables were packed and rowdy, and Thibault saw waitresses unloading buckets of crabs onto tables everywhere. Small pitchers of melted butter sat in the center, with smaller bowls in front of diners. Everyone wore plastic bibs, cracking crabs from the communal buckets and eating with their fingers. Beer seemed to be the drink of choice.

Directly ahead of them, on the side that bordered the river, was a long bar—if it could be called that. It seemed to be nothing more than discarded driftwood stacked atop wooden barrels. People milled around three deep. On the opposite side of the building was what seemed to be the kitchen. What caught his eye mostly was the stage located at the far end of the building, where Thibault saw a band playing "My Girl" by the Temptations. At least a hundred people were dancing in front of the stage, following the prescribed steps of a dance he wasn't familiar with.

"Wow," he shouted over the din.

A thin, fortyish woman with red hair and an apron approached them. "Hey there," she drawled. "Food or dancing?"

"Both," Elizabeth answered.

"First names?"

They glanced at each other. "Elizabeth . . . ," he said.

"And Logan," she finished.

The woman jotted down their names on a pad of paper. "Now, last question. Fun or family?"

Elizabeth looked lost. "Excuse me?"

The woman snapped her gum. "You haven't been here before, have you?"

"No."

"It's like this. You're going to have to share a table. That's how it works here. Everyone shares. Now, you can either request fun, which means you want a table with a lot of energy, or you can ask for family, which is usually a little quieter. Now, I can't guarantee how your table is, of course. I just ask the question. So, what'll it be? Family or fun?"

Elizabeth and Thibault faced each other again and came to the same conclusion.

"Fun," they said in unison.

They ended up at a table with six students from UNC Wilmington. The waitress introduced them as Matt, Sarah, Tim, Allison, Megan, and Steve, and the students each raised their bottles in turn and announced in unison: "Hey, Elizabeth! Hey, Logan! We have crabs!"

Thibault stifled a laugh at the play on words—crab was slang for something undescribable picked up during sexual encounters, which was obviously the point—but was flummoxed when he saw them staring at him expectantly.

The waitress whispered, "You're supposed to say, 'We want crabs, especially if we can get them with you.'"

This time he did laugh, along with Elizabeth, before saying the words, playing along with the ritual everyone observed here.

They sat opposite each other. Elizabeth ended up sitting next to Steve, who didn't hide the fact that he found her extremely attractive, while Thibault sat next to Megan, who showed no interest in him whatsoever because she was far more interested in Matt.

A plump, harried waitress rushed by, barely pausing to call out, "More crabs?"

"You can give me crabs anytime," the students replied in chorus. All around them, Thibault heard the same response over and over. The alternative response, which he also heard, was, "I can't believe you gave me crabs!" which seemed to signify that no more were needed. It reminded him of *The Rocky Horror Picture Show*, where regulars knew all the official responses and newcomers learned them on the fly.

The food was first-rate. The menu featured only a single item, prepared a single way, and every bucket came with extra napkins and bibs. Crab pieces were tossed into the center of the table—a

tradition—and every now and then, teenagers in aprons came by
to scoop them up.

As promised, the students were boisterous. A running string of
jokes, plenty of harmless interest in Elizabeth, and two beers each,
which added to the raucous spirit. After dinner, Thibault and
Elizabeth went to the restroom to wash up. When she came back
out, she looped her arm through his.

"You ready to shag?" she asked suggestively.

"I'm not sure. How do you do it?"

"Learning to shag dance is like learning to be from the South. It's
learning to relax while you hear the ocean and feel the music."

"I take it you've done it before."

"Once or twice," she said with false modesty.

"And you're going to teach me?"

"I'll be your partner. But the lesson starts at nine."

"The lesson?"

"Every Saturday night. That's why it's so crowded. They offer
a lesson for beginners while the regulars take a break, and we'll
do what they tell us. It starts at nine."

"What time is it?"

She glanced at her watch. "It's time for you to learn to shag."

Elizabeth was a much better dancer than she'd suggested, which
thankfully made him better on the dance floor, too. But the best
part of dancing with her was the almost electrical charge he felt
whenever they touched and the smell of her when he twirled her
out of his arms, a mixture of heat and perfume. Her hair grew wild
in the humid air, and her skin glowed with perspiration, making
her seem natural and untamed. Every now and then, she'd gaze at
him as she spun away, her lips parted in a knowing smile, as if she
knew exactly the effect she was having on him.

When the band decided to take a break, his first instinct was
to leave the floor with the rest of the crowd, but Elizabeth stopped
him when the recorded strains of "Unforgettable" by Nat King

Cole began to waft through the speakers. She looked up at him then, and he knew what he had to do.

Without speaking, he slipped one arm behind her back and reached for her hand, then tucked it into position. He held her gaze as he pulled her close, and ever so slowly, they began to move to the music, turning in slow circles.

Thibault was barely conscious of other couples joining the dance floor around them. As the music played in the background, Elizabeth leaned into him so close that he could feel each of her slow, languid breaths. He closed his eyes as she put her head on his shoulder, and in that instant, nothing else mattered. Not the song, not the place, not the other couples around him. Only this, only her. He gave himself over to the feel of her body as it pressed against him, and they moved slowly in small circles on the sawdust-strewn floor, lost in a world that felt as though it had been created for just the two of them.

As they drove home on darkened roads, Thibault held her hand and felt her thumb tracking slowly over his skin in the quiet of the car.

When he pulled into his driveway a little before eleven, Zeus was still lying on the porch and raised his head as Thibault turned off the ignition. He turned to face her.

"I had a wonderful time tonight," he murmured. He expected her to say the same, but she surprised him with her response.

"Aren't you going to invite me in?" she suggested.

"Yes," he said simply.

Zeus sat up as Thibault opened Elizabeth's door and stood as Elizabeth got out. His tail started to wag.

"Hey, Zeus," Elizabeth called out.

"Come," Thibault commanded, and the dog bounded from the porch and ran toward them. He circled them both, his cries sounding like squeaks. His mouth hung half-open in a grin as he preened for their attention.

"He missed us," she said, bending lower. "Didn't you, big boy?" As she bent lower, Zeus licked her face. Straightening up, she wrinkled her nose before wiping her face. "That was gross."

"Not for him," Thibault said. He motioned toward the house. "You ready? I have to warn you not to expect too much."

"Do you have a beer in the fridge?"

"Yes."

"Then don't worry about it."

They made their way up the steps of the house. Thibault opened the door and flipped the switch: A single floor lamp cast a dim glow over an easy chair near the window. In the center of the room stood a coffee table decorated only with a pair of candles; a medium-size couch faced it. Both the couch and the easy chair were covered in matching navy blue slipcovers, and behind them, a bookshelf housed a small collection of books. An empty magazine rack along with another floor lamp completed the minimalist furnishings.

Still, it was clean. Thibault had made sure of that earlier in the day. The pine floors had been mopped, the windows washed, the room dusted. He disliked clutter and despised dirt. The endless dust in Iraq had only reinforced his neatnik tendencies.

Elizabeth took in the scene before walking into the living room. "I like it," she said. "Where did you get the furniture?"

"It came with the place," he said.

"Which explains the slipcovers."

"Exactly."

"No television?"

"No."

"No radio?"

"No."

"What do you do when you're here?"

"Sleep."

"And?"

"Read."

"Novels?"

"No," he said, then changed his mind. "Actually, a couple. But mostly biographies and histories."

"No anthropology texts?"

"I have a book by Richard Leakey," he said. "But I don't like a lot of the heavy postmodernist anthropology books that seem to dominate the field these days, and in any case those kinds of books aren't easy to come by in Hampton."

She circled the furniture, running her finger along the slipcovers. "What did he write about?"

"Who? Leakey?"

She smiled. "Yeah. Leakey."

He pursed his lips, organizing his thoughts. "Traditional anthropology is primarily interested in five areas: when man first began to evolve, when he started to walk upright, why there were so many hominid species, why and how those species evolved, and what all of that means for the evolutionary history of modern man. Leakey's book mainly talked about the last four, with a special emphasis on how toolmaking and weapons influenced the evolution of *Homo sapiens*."

She couldn't hide her amusement, but he could tell she was impressed.

"How about that beer?" she asked.

"I'll be back in a minute," he said. "Make yourself comfortable."

He returned with two bottles and a box of matches. Elizabeth was seated in the middle of the couch; he handed her one of the bottles and took a seat beside her, dropping the matches on the table.

She immediately picked up the matches and struck one, watching as the small flame flickered to life. In a fluid motion, she held it to the wicks, lighting both candles, then extinguished the match.

"I hope you don't mind. I love the smell of candles."

"Not at all."

He rose from the couch to turn off the lamp, the room now dimly lit by the warm glow of the candles. He sat closer to her when he returned to the couch, watching as she stared at the flame, her face half in shadow. He took a sip of his beer, wondering what she was thinking.

"Do you know how long it's been since I've been alone in a candlelit room with a man?" she said, turning her face to his.

"No," he said.

"It's a trick question. The answer is never." She seemed amazed by the idea herself. "Isn't that odd? I've been married, I have a child, I've dated, and never once has this happened before." She hesitated. "And if you want to know the truth, this is the first time I've been alone with a man at his place since my divorce." Her expression was almost sheepish.

"Tell me something," she said, her face inches from his. "Would you have asked me inside if I hadn't invited myself?" she asked. "Answer honestly. I'll know if you're lying."

He rotated the bottle in his hands. "I'm not sure."

"Why not?" she pressed. "What is it about me—"

"It has nothing to do with you," he interrupted. "It has more to do with Nana and what she might think."

"Because she's your boss?"

"Because she's your grandmother. Because I respect her. But mostly, because I respect you. I had a wonderful time tonight. In the past five years, I can't think of a better time I've had with anybody."

"And you still wouldn't have invited me in." Elizabeth seemed baffled.

"I didn't say that. I said I'm not sure."

"Which means no."

"Which means I was trying to figure out a way of asking you in without offending you, but you beat me to the punch. But if what you're really asking is whether I wanted to invite you in, the answer is, yes, I did."

He touched his knee to hers. "Where's all this coming from?"

"Let's just say I haven't had a lot of luck in the dating world."

He knew enough to stay silent, but when he lifted his arm, he felt her lean into him. "It didn't bother me at first," she finally said. "I mean, I was so busy with Ben and school, I didn't pay much attention to it. But later, when it kept happening, I began to wonder. I began to wonder about me. And I'd ask myself all these crazy questions. Was I doing something wrong? Was I not paying enough attention? Did I smell funny?" She tried to smile, but she couldn't fully mask the undercurrent of sadness and doubt. "Like I said, crazy stuff. Because every now and then, I'd meet a guy and think that we were getting along great, and suddenly I'd stop hearing from him. Not only did he stop calling, but if I happened to bump into him sometime later, he always acted like I had the plague. I didn't understand it. I still don't. And it bothered me. It hurt me. With time, it got harder and harder to keep blaming the guys, and I eventually came to the conclusion that there was something wrong with me. That maybe I was simply meant to live my life alone."

"There's nothing wrong with you," he said, giving her arm a reassuring squeeze.

"Give me a chance. I'm sure you'll find something."

Thibault could hear the wound beneath the jest. "No," he said. "I don't think I will."

"You're sweet."

"I'm honest."

She smiled as she took a sip from her beer. "Most of the time."

"You don't think I'm honest?"

She shrugged. "Like I said. Most of the time."

"What's that supposed to mean?"

She put the bottle of beer on the table and gathered her thoughts. "I think you're a terrific guy. You're smart, you work hard, you're kind, and you're great with Ben. I know that, or at least I think I do, because that's what I see. But it's what you don't say that makes me wonder about you. I tell myself that I know you, and then when I think about it, I realize that I don't. What were you like in college? I don't know. What happened after that? I don't know. I know you went to Iraq and I know that you walked here from Colorado, but I don't know why. When I ask, you just say that 'Hampton seems like a nice place.' You're an intelligent college graduate, but you're content to work for minimum wage. When I ask why, you say that you like dogs." She ran a hand through her hair. "The thing is, I get the sense that you're telling me the truth. You're just not telling all of it. And the part you're leaving out is the part that would help me understand who you are."

Listening to her, Thibault tried not to think about everything else he hadn't told her. He knew he couldn't tell her everything; he would never tell her everything. There was no way she would understand, and yet . . . he wanted her to know who he really was. More than anything, he realized that he wanted her to ac- cept him.

"I don't talk about Iraq because I don't like to remember my time there." he said

She shook her head. "You don't have to tell me if you'd rather not. . . ."

"I want to," he said, his voice quiet. "I know you read the papers, so you probably have this image in your mind of what it's like. But it's not like what you imagine, and there's not really any way I could make it real to you. It's something you had to have experienced yourself. I mean, most of the time it wasn't nearly as bad as you probably think it was. A lot of the time—most of the time—it was okay. Easier for me than for others, since I didn't have a wife or kids. I had friends, I had routines. Most of the time, I went through the motions. But some of the time, it was bad. Really bad. Bad enough to make me want to forget I'd ever been there at all."

She was quiet before drawing a long breath. "And you're here in Hampton because of what happened in Iraq?"

He picked at the label on his bottle of beer, slowing peeling away the corner and scratching the glass with his fingernail. "In a way," he said.

She sensed his hesitation and laid a hand on his forearm. Its warmth seemed to release something inside him.

"Victor was my best friend in Iraq," Thibault began. "He was with me through all three tours. Our unit suffered a lot of casualties, and by the end, I was ready to put my time there behind me. And I succeeded, for the most part, but for Victor, it wasn't so easy. He couldn't stop thinking about it. After we were out, we went our separate ways, trying to get on with life. He went home to California, I went back to Colorado, but we still needed each other, you know? Talked on the phone, sent e-mails in which both of us pretended we were doing just fine with the fact that while we'd spent the last four years trying every day to avoid being killed, people back home were acting as if the world was ending if they lost a parking spot or got the wrong latte at Starbucks. Anyway, we ended up reuniting for a fishing trip in Minnesota—"

He broke off, not wanting to remember what happened but knowing he had to. He took a long pull on his beer and set the bottle on the table.

"This was last fall, and I . . . I was just so happy to see him again. We didn't talk about our time in Iraq, but we didn't have to. Just spending a few days with someone else who knew what we'd been through was enough for the both of us. Victor, by then, was doing okay. Not great, but okay. He was married with a kid on the way, and I remember thinking that even though he was still having nightmares and the occasional flashback, he was going to be all right."

He looked at her with an emotion she couldn't name.

"On our last day, we went fishing early in the morning. It was just the two of us in this little rowboat, and when we rowed out, the lake was as still as glass, like we were the first people ever to disturb the water. I remember watching a hawk fly over the lake while its mirror image glided directly beneath it, thinking I'd never seen anything more beautiful." He shook his head at the memory. "We planned on finishing up before the lake got too crowded; then we were going to head into town later and have some beers and steaks. A little celebration to end our trip. But time just sort of got away from us and we ended up staying on the lake too long."

He started to knead his forehead, trying to keep his composure. "I'd seen the boat earlier. I don't know why I noticed that one among all the others. Maybe my time in Iraq had something to do with it, but I remembered thinking to myself to keep an eye out for them. It was strange, though. It wasn't as if they were doing anything different than any of the other boaters out there. Just some teenagers having fun: waterskiing, tubing. There were six of them on the boat—three boys and three girls—and you could tell they were out there for a last hurrah on the water while it was still warm enough to do so."

When he continued, his voice was hoarse. "I heard it coming," he said, "and I knew we were in trouble even before I saw it. There's a particular sound that an engine makes when it turns in your direction at full speed. It's like the noise begins to trail behind the engine by a millisecond that the brain can pick up only subconsciously, and I knew we were in trouble. I barely had time to turn my head before I saw the bow coming at us at thirty miles an hour." He pressed his fingertips together. "By then, Victor had realized what was happening, and I can still remember his expression—it was this horrible mixture of fear and surprise—the exact same thing I'd seen on faces of my friends in Iraq right before they died."

He exhaled slowly. "The boat sliced right through ours. It hit Victor head-on and killed him instantly. One minute we were talking about how happy he was that he'd married his wife, and in the next instant, my best friend—the best friend I'd ever had—was dead."

Elizabeth put her hand on his knee and squeezed it. Her face had grown pale. "I'm so sorry. . . ."

He didn't seem to hear her.

"It's just not fair, you know? To live through three tours in Iraq, to survive some of the things we had . . . only to be killed on a fishing trip? It didn't make sense. After that, I don't know, I was pretty messed up. Not physically. But mentally, it's like I went down a deep hole for a long time. I just gave up. I couldn't eat, I couldn't sleep more than a few hours a night, and there were times when I couldn't stop crying. Victor had confessed to me that he was haunted by visions of dead soldiers, and after his death, I became haunted, too. All of a sudden, the war was front and center again. Every time I tried to go to sleep, I'd see Victor or scenes from the firefights we'd lived through and I'd start shaking all over. The only thing that kept me from going completely crazy was Zeus."

He stopped to look at Elizabeth. Despite his memories, he was struck by the beauty of her face and the dark gold curtain of her hair.

Her face registered her compassion. "I don't know what to say."

"I don't either." He shrugged. "I still don't."

"You know it wasn't your fault, right?"

"Yeah," he muttered. "But that's not where the story ends." He put his hand on hers, knowing he'd come too far with his story to stop.

"Victor liked to talk about destiny," he finally said. "He was a big believer in all sorts of things like that, and on our last day together, he said that I would know my destiny when I found it. I couldn't get that thought out of my mind even while I was struggling. I kept hearing him say it over and over, and little by little, I slowly came to the realization that while I wasn't sure where to find it, I knew I wouldn't find it in Colorado. Eventually, I packed my backpack and just started to walk. My mom thought I'd lost my mind. But with every step I took down the road, I began to feel like I was becoming whole again. Like the journey was what

I needed to heal. And by the time I got to Hampton, I knew I didn't need to walk any further. This was the place I was meant to go."

"So you stayed."

"Yeah."

"And your destiny?"

He didn't respond. He'd told her as much of the truth as he could, and he didn't want to lie to her. He stared at her hand beneath his, and all at once, everything about this felt wrong. He knew he should end it before it went any further. Get up from the couch and walk her back to the car. Say good night and leave Hampton before the sun came up tomorrow. But he couldn't say the words; he couldn't make himself get up from the couch. Something else had taken hold of him, and he turned toward her with dawning amazement. He'd walked halfway across the country in search of a woman he knew only in a photograph and ended up slowly but surely falling in love with this real, vulnerable, beautiful woman who made him feel alive in a way he hadn't been since the war. He didn't fully understand it, but he'd never been more certain of anything in his life.

What he saw in her expression was enough to tell him that she was feeling exactly the same way, and he gently pulled her toward him. As his face drew near to hers, he could feel her heated breaths as he brushed his lips against hers once and then twice before finally meeting them for good.

Burying his hands in her hair, he kissed her with everything he had, everything he wanted to be. He heard a soft murmur of contentment as he slid his arms around her. He opened his mouth slightly and felt her tongue against his, and all at once, he knew that she was right for him, what was happening was the right thing for both of them. He kissed her cheek and her neck, nibbling softly, then kissed her lips again. They stood from the couch, still entwined, and he led her quietly to the bedroom.

They took their time making love. Thibault moved above her,

wanting it to last forever, while whispering his love for her. He felt her body quiver with pleasure again and again. Afterward, she remained curled beneath his arm, her body coiled in contentment. They talked and laughed and nuzzled, and after making love a second time, he lay beside her, staring into her eyes before running a gentle finger along her cheek. He felt the words rise up inside him, words he had never imagined himself saying to anyone.

"I love you, Elizabeth," he whispered, knowing they were true in every way.

She reached for his fingers before kissing them one by one.

"I love you, too, Logan."

17

Clayton

Keith Clayton stared at Beth as she left the house, knowing exactly what had happened inside. The more he thought about it, the more he wanted to follow her and give her a little talking-to as soon as she got back home. Explain the situation in a way she'd understand, so she would realize that this sort of thing just wasn't acceptable. Like with a slap or two, not enough to hurt, but enough for her to know he meant business. Not that it would do any good. And not that he'd really do it. He'd never slapped Beth. He wasn't that kind of guy.

What in the royal hell was going on? Could any of this possibly get any worse?

First, it turns out the guy works at the kennel. Next, they spend a few days having dinner at her place, trading the kinds of drippy stares you saw in crappy Hollywood movies. And then—and here was the kicker—they go out to that dance joint for losers, and afterward, even though he couldn't see past the drapes, he had no doubt that she started putting out like a harlot. Probably on the couch. Probably because she'd had too much to drink.

He remembered those days. Give the woman a few glasses of wine and keep filling it when she wasn't looking, or spike her beers with a bit of vodka, listen for when her words started to slur, and then end up having some seriously great sex right there in the living room. Booze was great for that. Get her sloppy drunk, and the woman not only couldn't say no, but became a tiger in the sack. As he'd staked out the house, he'd had no trouble imagining what her body looked like as she took her clothes off. If he hadn't been so damn angry, it might have excited him, knowing she was in there, getting it on, getting all hot and sweaty. But the point was this: She wasn't exactly acting like a mother, was she?

He knew how it went. Once she started having sex with guys she dated, it would become normal and accepted. Once it became normal and accepted, she'd do the same on other dates. Simple as that. One guy would lead to two, which would lead to four or five or ten or twenty, and the last thing he wanted was for her to start leading a parade of guys through Ben's life who'd wink at him on their way out the door as if to say, *Your mom sure is one hot lady*.

He wasn't going to let that happen. Beth was dumb in the way most women were dumb, which was why he'd been watching out for her all these years. And it had worked out just fine, until Thigh-bolt rolled into town.

The guy was a walking nightmare. Like his sole intent was to ruin Clayton's life.

Well, that wasn't going to happen, either, was it?

He'd learned quite a bit about Thigh-bolt in the last week. Not only that he worked at the kennel—what were the odds on that, by the way?—but that he lived in a ramshackle dump near the forest. And after making a few official-sounding calls to law enforcement in Colorado, professional courtesy did the rest. He learned that Thigh-bolt had graduated from the University of Colorado. And that he'd been a marine, served in Iraq, and received a couple of commendations. But most interesting, that a couple of guys in his platoon spoke about him as though he'd made some sort of deal with the devil to stay alive.

He wondered what Beth would think of that.

He didn't believe it. He'd met enough marines to know most of them were as smart as rocks. But something fishy was definitely going on with the guy if his fellow marines didn't quite trust him.

And why walk across the country and stop here? The guy knew no one in town, and from the sound of things, he'd never been here before. Something fishy about that, too. More than that, he couldn't escape the feeling that the answer was staring him in the face, but he couldn't figure it out. He would. He always did.

Clayton continued to stare at the house, thinking it was time he finally dealt with the guy. Not now, though. Not tonight. Not with the dog around. Next week, maybe. When Thigh-bolt was at work.

See, that was the difference between him and other people. Most people lived their lives like criminals: act first, worry about the consequences later. Not Keith Clayton. He thought things through beforehand. He planned. He anticipated. Which was the main reason he'd done nothing so far, even when he'd seen the two of them pull up tonight, even though he knew what was going on in the house, even as he'd watched Beth walk back outside, her face flushed and hair all wild. In the end, he knew, this was about power, and right now, Thigh-bolt had the power. Because of the disk. The disk with photos that might cut off the flow of money to Clayton.

But power was nothing if it wasn't used. And Thigh-bolt hadn't used it. Which meant that Thigh-bolt either didn't realize what he had, or had gotten rid of the disk, or was the kind of guy who generally minded his own business.

Or maybe all three.

Clayton had to make sure. First things first, so to speak. Which meant he had to look for the disk. If the guy still had it, he'd find it and destroy it. Power would shift back to Clayton, and Thigh-bolt would get what was coming to him. And if Thigh-bolt had gotten rid of the disk soon after finding it? Even better. He'd handle Thigh-bolt, and things would start getting back to normal with him and Beth. That was the most important thing.

Damn, she'd looked good walking out of that house. There was something hot and sexy about seeing her and knowing what she'd done, even if it had been with Thigh-bolt. It had been a long time since she'd had a man, and she seemed . . . different. More than that, he knew that after tonight, she'd surely be ready for more.

That friends with benefits thing was looking better all the time.

18

Beth

I take it you had a good time," Nana drawled.

It was Sunday morning, and Beth had just stumbled down to the kitchen table. Ben was still sleeping upstairs.

"We did," she said, yawning.

"And?"

"And . . . nothing."

"You got in kind of late, considering you did nothing."

"It wasn't that late. See? I'm up bright and early." She poked her head into the refrigerator, then closed the door without removing anything. "That would be impossible if I got in too late. And why are you so curious?"

"I just want to know if I'll still have an employee on Monday." Nana poured herself a cup of coffee and collapsed into a chair at the table.

"I don't see why you wouldn't."

"So it went well?"

This time, Beth let the question hang for a moment as she remembered the evening. Stirring her coffee, she felt happier than she had in a long time. "Yeah," she offered. "It went well."

* * *

During the next few days, Beth spent as much time with Logan as she could, without making it seem too obvious to Ben. She wasn't sure why that felt important. It did seem consistent with the kind of advice family counselors would offer about the realities of dating when children were involved. But deep down, she knew that wasn't the entire reason. There was just something exciting about maintaining the pretense that nothing had changed between them; it gave the relationship an illicit feeling, almost like an affair.

It didn't fool Nana, of course. Every now and then while Beth and Logan were engaged in keeping up their elaborate facade, Nana would mutter something nonsensical like "camels in the Sahara" or "it's like hair and slippers." Later, with Logan, Beth would try to make sense of her mutterings. The first seemed to imply they were meant to be together; the second took a little longer to figure out, and she was stumped until Logan shrugged and suggested, "Maybe it has something to do with 'Rapunzel' and 'Cinderella'?"

Fairy tales. But good ones, with happily-ever-after endings. Nana being sweet without revealing herself as a softie.

Those stolen moments when they were alone had an almost dreamlike intensity. Beth was hyperattuned to his every movement and gesture, tantalized by the quiet way he'd take her hand as they trailed behind Ben on their evening walks, then release it as soon as Ben rounded into view again. Logan had a sixth sense about how far away Ben had wandered—a skill developed, she guessed, in the military—and she was grateful that her desire to fly under the radar for now didn't bother him in the slightest.

To her relief, Logan continued to treat Ben exactly as he had before. On Monday, he showed up with a small bow-and-arrow set he'd picked up at the sporting goods store. He and Ben spent an hour shooting at targets, time that was mainly used searching for wayward shots that ended up in prickly holly bushes or snagged in tree branches, leaving them both with scratches up to their elbows.

After dinner, they ended up playing chess in the living room while she and Nana cleaned up the kitchen. As she dried the dishes, she concluded that if for no other reason, she could love Logan forever simply because of the way he treated her son.

Despite maintaining a low profile, they still found excuses to be alone together. On Tuesday, when she got home from school, she noticed that with Nana's permission, he'd installed a porch swing so "we don't have to sit on the steps." While Ben was at his music lesson, she reveled in the slow, steady motion of the swing as she sat beside him. On Wednesday, she rode with him to town to pick up another load of dog food. Everyday activities, but simply being alone with him was enough. Sometimes when they were in the truck together, he'd put his arm around her and she'd lean into him, savoring how good it felt.

She thought about him while she worked, imagining what he was doing or wondering what he and Nana were talking about. She pictured the way his shirt would tack against his skin with perspiration or his forearms would flex as he trained the dogs. On Thursday morning, as Logan and Zeus walked up the drive to begin work, she turned from the window in the kitchen. Nana was at the table, slowly working her way into her rubber boots, a challenge made more difficult by the weakness in her arm. Beth cleared her throat.

"Is it okay if Logan takes the day off?" she asked.

Nana didn't bother to hide the smirk on her face. "Why?"

"I want to get away with him today. Just the two of us."

"What about school?"

She was already dressed, her own lunch packed. "I'm thinking about calling in sick."

"Ah," Nana said.

"I love him, Nana," she blurted.

Nana shook her head, but her eyes glittered. "I was wondering when you'd just come right out and say it, instead of making me come up with those silly riddles."

"Sorry."

Nana stood and stomped a couple of times, making sure the boots were snug. A thin layer of dirt collected on the floor. "I suppose I could handle things today. Probably be good for me. I've been watching too much television anyway."

Beth tucked a strand of hair behind her ear. "Thank you."

"My pleasure. Just don't make a habit of it. He's the best employee we've ever had."

They spent the afternoon wrapped in each other's arms, making love over and over, and when it was finally time for her to return home—she wanted to be around when Ben got home from school—she was certain that Logan loved her as much as she loved him and that he, too, was beginning to imagine spending the rest of their lives together.

The only thing that marred her perfect happiness was the sense she had that something was bothering him. It wasn't her—she was sure of that. Nor was it the state of their relationship; the way he acted when they were together made that obvious. It was something else, something she couldn't put her finger on, but in thinking back, she realized she'd first noticed it on Tuesday afternoon, just after she'd gotten home with Ben.

Ben, as usual, had darted from the car to play with Zeus, anxious to burn off energy before his music lesson. As she stood visiting with Nana in the kennel office, she spied Logan standing in the yard, his hands in his pockets, seemingly lost in concentration. Even in the truck, as he'd slipped his arm around her, she could tell he'd remained preoccupied. And tonight after his game of chess with Ben, he'd wandered out onto the porch alone.

Beth joined him a few minutes later and took a seat beside him on the swing.

"Is something bothering you?" she finally asked.

He didn't answer right away. "I'm not sure," he said.

"Are you upset with me?"

He shook his head and smiled. "Not at all."

"What's going on?"

He hesitated. "I'm not sure," he said again.

She stared at him from beneath her lashes. "Do you want to talk about it?"

"Yeah," he said. "But not yet."

On Saturday, with Ben at his father's, they drove to Sunset Beach near Wilmington.

By that point, the summer crowds had disappeared, and aside from a few people strolling the beach, they had the place to themselves. The ocean, fed by the Gulf, was still warm enough to enjoy, and they waded knee-deep in the surf as Logan lobbed a tennis ball beyond the breakers. Zeus was having the time of his life, paddling furiously and occasionally barking as if trying to intimidate the ball into staying in one place.

She'd packed a picnic along with some towels, and when Zeus grew tired, they retreated farther up the beach and settled down for lunch. Methodically, she pulled out the makings for sandwiches and cut up fresh fruit. As they ate, a shrimp trawler rode the horizon, and for a long time, Logan focused on it with the preoccupied gaze she'd noticed on and off for most of the week.

"You're getting that look again," she finally said.

"What look?"

"Spill it," she said, ignoring his question. "What's bothering you? And no vague answers this time."

"I'm fine," he said, turning to meet her gaze. "I know I've seemed a little off for the last few days, but I'm just trying to figure something out."

"What, exactly?"

"Why we're going out."

Her heart skipped a beat. It wasn't what she'd expected to hear, and she could feel her expression freeze.

"That came out wrong," he said, shaking his head quickly. "I didn't mean it the way you think. I was thinking more about why this opportunity even existed. It doesn't make sense."

She frowned. "I'm still not following you."

Zeus, who'd been lying beside them, lifted his head to watch a flock of seagulls that landed nearby. Beyond them, at the water's edge, were pipers darting about for tiny sand crabs. Logan studied them before going on. When he spoke, his voice was steady, like a professor elaborating on a subject he taught.

"If you look at this from my perspective, this is what I see: an intelligent, charming, beautiful woman, not yet thirty, witty, and passionate. Also, when she wishes, extremely seductive." He gave her a knowing smile before continuing. "In other words, a catch, by pretty much anyone's definition." He paused. "Stop me if I'm making you uncomfortable."

She reached over and tapped his knee. "You're doing just fine," she said. "Go on."

He ran a restless hand through his hair. "That's what I've been trying to understand. I've been thinking about it the last few days."

She tried without success to follow his train of thought. This time instead of tapping his knee, she squeezed it. "You need to learn to be more clear. I'm still not following you."

For the first time since she'd known him, she saw a flash of impatience cross his features. Almost immediately it was gone, and she sensed somehow that it was directed more at himself than at her.

"I'm saying that it doesn't make sense that you haven't had a relationship since your ex." He paused, as if searching for the right phrase. "Yes, you have a son, and for some men, that might make a relationship with you a nonstarter. But then, you don't generally hide the fact that you're a mother, and I assume most people in this small town know your situation. Am I right?"

She hesitated. "Yes."

"And the men who asked you out. They all knew you had a son in advance?"

"Yes."

He fixed her with a speculative expression. "Then where are they?"

Zeus rotated his head into her lap, and she began to stroke him behind the ears, feeling her defensiveness rise.

"What does it matter?" she asked. "And to be honest, I'm not sure I'm all that thrilled with these kinds of questions. What happened in the past is my business, and I can't undo it, and I'll be damned if you're going to sit here and question me about who I dated and when I dated them and what happened on those dates. I am who I am, and I'd think you of all people would understand that, Mr. *I-walked-from-Colorado-but-don't-ask-me-why*."

He was quiet, and she knew he was reflecting on what she'd said. When he spoke again, his voice brimmed with unexpected tenderness.

"I'm not saying this to make you angry. I'm saying this because I think you're the most remarkable woman I've ever met." Again, he paused before going on, making sure his words had penetrated. "The thing is, I'm pretty sure that almost every man would feel the same way I do. And since you have gone out with other men, especially in this small town where there are only so many available women in your age group, I'm sure they would have recognized the terrific person that you are. Okay, maybe some of them weren't your cup of tea, so you ended it. But what about the others? The ones you liked? There had to have been someone, somewhere along the line with whom you seemed to click."

He scooped up a handful of sand and slowly spread his fingers, allowing the grains to slip through his fingers. "That's what I've been thinking about. Because it's just not plausible that you wouldn't have clicked with someone, and yet you told me yourself that you haven't had a lot of luck in the dating world."

He wiped his hand on the towel. "Am I wrong so far?"

She stared at him, wondering how he knew so much. "No," she said.

"And you've wondered about it, haven't you?"

"Sometimes," she confessed. "But don't you think you're reading way too much into this? Even if I were as perfect as you say, you have to remember that times have changed. There are probably thousands, if not tens of thousands, of women that you could describe in the same way."

"Perhaps." He shrugged.

"But you're not convinced."

"No." His clear blue eyes held her in their unwavering scrutiny.

"What? You think there's some sort of conspiracy?"

Instead of answering directly, he reached for another handful of sand. "What can you tell me about your ex?" he asked.

"Why does that matter?"

"I'm curious as to how he feels about you dating."

"I'm sure he doesn't care in the slightest. And I can't imagine why you think that even matters."

He released the sand all at once. "Because," he said, his voice low. He turned toward her. "I'm pretty sure he was the one who broke into my house the other day."

19

Thibault

Late Saturday evening, after Elizabeth had left, Thibault found Victor sitting in his living room, still dressed in the shorts and cabana-style shirt he'd been wearing on the day he died.

The sight of him stopped Thibault in his tracks. All he could do was stare. It wasn't possible, nor was it really happening. Thibault knew that Victor was gone, buried in a small plot near Bakersfield. He knew Zeus would have reacted had anyone real been in the house, but Zeus simply wandered to his water bowl.

In the silence, Victor smiled. "There is more," he said, his voice a hoarse promise.

When Thibault blinked, Victor was gone, and it was obvious he'd never been there at all.

It was the third time Thibault had seen Victor since he had passed away. The first time had been at the funeral, when Thibault had rounded a corner near the back of the church and seen Victor staring at him from the end of the hallway. "It's not your fault," Victor had said before dissolving away. Thibault's throat had closed up, forcing him to rush to catch his breath.

The second appearance occurred three weeks before he set out on his walk. That time, it had happened in the grocery store, as

Thibault was rummaging through his wallet, trying to figure out how much beer he could purchase. He'd been drinking heavily in those days, and as he counted the bills, he saw an image from the corner of his eye. Victor shook his head but said nothing. He didn't have to. Thibault knew that he was being told that it was time to end the drinking.

Now, this.

Thibault didn't believe in ghosts, and he knew that the image of Victor hadn't been real. There was no specter haunting him, no visits from beyond, no restless spirit with a message to deliver. Victor was a figment of his imagination, and Thibault knew that his subconscious had conjured up the image. After all, Victor had been the one person Thibault had always listened to.

He knew the boating accident had been just that: an accident. The kids who'd been driving the boat had been traumatized, and their horror at what had happened was genuine. As for the drinking, he'd known deep down that the booze was doing more harm than good. Somehow, though, it was easier to listen to Victor.

The last thing he'd expected was to see his friend once more.

He considered Victor's words—*there is more*—and wondered whether they related to his conversation with Elizabeth. Somehow he didn't think so, but he couldn't figure it out, and it nagged at him. He suspected that the harder he pressed himself for an answer, the less likely it was that the answer would come. The subconscious was funny like that.

He wandered to the small kitchen to pour himself a glass of milk, put some food in the bowl for Zeus, and went to his room. Lying in bed, he brooded on the things he'd told Elizabeth.

He'd thought long and hard about saying anything at all. He wasn't even certain what he'd hoped to accomplish by doing so, other than to open her eyes to the possibility that Keith Clayton might just be controlling her life in ways she couldn't imagine.

Which was exactly what the man was doing. Thibault had become sure of it when he'd first noticed the break-in. Of course, it could have been anyone—someone wanting to make a quick buck grabbing items that could be sold in pawnshops—but the way it had been done suggested otherwise. It was too neat. Nothing had been strewn about. Nothing was even out of place. Nearly everything had, however, been *adjusted*.

The blanket on the bed was the first giveaway. There was a tiny ridge in the blanket, caused by someone who didn't know how to tuck in the covers military fashion—something few, if anyone, would have noticed. He noticed. The clothes in his drawers showed similar disturbances: a rumple here, a sleeve folded the wrong way there. Not only had someone entered the home while he'd been at work, but he'd searched the house thoroughly.

But why? Thibault had nothing of value to steal. A quick peek through the windows beforehand made it plain there was nothing valuable in the place. Not only was the living room devoid of electronics, but the second bedroom stood completely empty, and the room where he slept contained only a bed, end table, and lamp. Aside from dishes and utensils and an ancient electric can opener on the counter, the kitchen was empty, too. The pantry contained dog food, a loaf of bread, and a jar of peanut butter. But someone had taken the time to search the house anyway from top to bottom, including under his mattress. Someone had diligently gone through his drawers and cleaned up afterward.

No outrage at finding nothing of value. No evident frustration that the break-in had been a waste. Instead, the burglar had attempted to cover his tracks.

Whoever had broken in had come to the house not to steal, but to look for something. Something specific. It hadn't taken long to figure out what it was and who had been responsible.

Keith Clayton wanted his camera. Or, more likely, he wanted the disk. Probably because the photographs on the disk could get him in trouble. No great leap of logic, considering what Clayton had been doing the first time they'd bumped into each other.

All right, so Clayton wanted to cover his tracks. But there

was still more to this than met the eye. And it had to do with Elizabeth.

It *didn't* make sense that she hadn't had any relationships in the past ten years. But it did jibe with something he'd heard while standing around the pool table, showing her picture to the group of locals. What had one of them said? It had taken a while to recall the exact words, and he wished he had paid more attention to the comment. He'd been so focused on learning Elizabeth's name, he'd ignored it at the time—a mistake. In hindsight, there was something menacing about the comment's implication.

. . . let's just say she doesn't date. Her ex wouldn't like it, and trust me, you don't want to mess with him.

He reviewed what he knew about Keith Clayton. Part of a powerful family. A bully. Quick to anger. In a position to abuse his power. Someone who thought he deserved whatever he wanted whenever he wanted it?

Thibault couldn't be certain about the last one, but it all fit the picture.

Clayton didn't want Elizabeth to see other men. Elizabeth hadn't had any meaningful relationships in years. Elizabeth occasionally wondered why but hadn't even considered the possible connection between her ex-husband and failed relationships. To Thibault, it seemed entirely plausible that Clayton was manipulating people and events and—at least in one way—still controlling her life. For Clayton to know that Elizabeth was dating someone in the past meant that Clayton had been watching over her for years. Just as he was watching over her now.

It wasn't hard to imagine how Clayton had ended her previous relationships, but so far, he'd kept his distance when it came to Thibault and Elizabeth. So far, Thibault hadn't seen him spying from afar, hadn't noticed anything out of the ordinary. Instead, Clayton had broken into his house in search of the disk when he knew Thibault would be at work.

Getting his ducks in a row?

Probably. But the question was, to what end? To run Thibault out of town, at the very least. Still, Thibault couldn't shake the feeling that this wouldn't be the end. As Victor had said, *there is more*.

He'd wanted to share with Elizabeth what he knew about her ex, but he couldn't come right out and tell her about the comment he'd overheard at the pool hall. That would mean telling her about the photograph, and he couldn't do that yet. Instead, he wanted to point her in the right direction, hoping she would begin to make the connections herself. Together, once they both knew the extent to which Clayton was willing to sabotage her relationships, they would be able to handle whatever he chose to do. They loved each other. They would know what to expect. It would all work out.

Was this the reason he'd come? To fall in love with Elizabeth and make a life together? Was this his destiny?

For some reason, it didn't feel right. Victor's words seemed to confirm that. There was another reason that he'd come here. Falling in love with Elizabeth may have been part of it. But that wasn't all. Something else was coming.

There is more.

Thibault slept the rest of the night without waking, just as he had since arriving in North Carolina. A military thing—or, more accurately, a combat thing, something he'd learned out of necessity. Tired soldiers made mistakes. His father had said that. Every officer he'd ever known had said that. His wartime experience confirmed the truth of their statements. He'd learned to sleep when it was time to sleep, no matter how chaotic things were, trusting he'd be better for it the following day.

Aside from the brief period after Victor's death, sleep had never been a problem. He liked sleep, and he liked the way his thoughts seemed to coalesce while he was dreaming. On Sunday, when he woke, he found himself visualizing a wheel with spokes extending from the center. He wasn't sure why, but a few minutes later, when he was walking Zeus outside, he was suddenly struck by the notion that Elizabeth wasn't the center of the wheel, as he'd unconsciously assumed. Instead, he realized, everything that had happened since he'd arrived in Hampton seemed to revolve around Keith Clayton.

Clayton, after all, had been the first person he'd met in town. He'd taken Clayton's camera. Clayton and Elizabeth had been married. Clayton was Ben's father. Clayton had sabotaged Elizabeth's relationships. Clayton had seen them spending an evening together on the night he'd brought Ben home with the black eye; in other words, he'd been the first to know about them. Clayton had broken into his house. Clayton—not Elizabeth—was the reason he'd come to Hampton.

In the distance, thunder sounded, low and ominous. There was a storm on the way, and the heaviness in the air portended a big one.

Aside from what Elizabeth had told him about Clayton, he realized he knew very little about Elizabeth's former husband. As the first drops began to fall, Thibault went back inside. Later, he would visit the library. He had a little research ahead of him if he hoped to get a better feel for Hampton and the role the Claytons played in it.

20

Beth

D oesn't surprise me," Nana snorted. "I wouldn't put anything past your late husband."

"He's not dead, Nana."

Nana sighed. "Hope springs eternal."

Beth took a sip of her coffee. It was Sunday, and they had just returned from church. For the first time since Nana's stroke, Nana had had a small solo in one of the musical numbers, and Beth hadn't wanted her to be distracted. She knew how much the choir meant to her.

"You're not helping me," Beth said.

"What's to help?"

"I was just saying . . ."

Nana leaned across the table. "I know what you're saying. You've already told me, remember? And if you're asking whether I think Keith actually broke into Thibault's house, I'm simply saying that it wouldn't surprise me. I've never liked that man."

"Gee, really?"

"There's no reason to get fresh about it."

"I'm not getting fresh."

Nana didn't seem to hear her. "You look tired. Do you want more coffee? Or how about some cinnamon toast?"

Beth shook her head. "I'm not hungry."

"Even so, you still have to eat. It's not healthy to skip meals, and I know you've already skipped breakfast." She got up from the table. "I'm making toast."

Beth knew there was no point in arguing. Once Nana made up her mind about something, there was no way to dissuade her.

"What about the other part? About whether Keith had something to do with . . ." She trailed off.

Nana shrugged as she put two pieces of bread in the toaster. "About running other men off? Nothing that man did would surprise me. And it kind of explains things, doesn't it?"

"But it doesn't make sense. I can name at least half a dozen women he's gone out with, and it's not like he's even hinted that he wants to get back together. Why would he care whether or not I date?"

"Because he's no better than a spoiled child," Nana declared. She put a couple of dabs of butter into a saucepan and turned on the burner. A small blue flame *whoosh*ed to life. "You were his toy, and even though he's got new toys, it doesn't mean he wants anyone to play with his old toys."

Beth shifted in her seat. "I'm not sure I like that analogy."

"It doesn't matter if you like it. All that matters is whether it's true."

"And you think it is?"

"That's not what I said. What I said was that it wouldn't surprise me. And don't tell me you're surprised, either. I've seen the way he still looks you up and down. It gives me the willies, and it's all I can do to keep from clobbering him with the pooper-scooper."

Beth smiled, but it lasted only an instant. When the toast popped up, Nana grabbed the pieces and put them on a plate. She dribbled melted butter over the top, then added sugar and cinnamon. She brought over the plate and set it in front of Beth.

"Here. Eat something. You're skeletal these days."

"I weigh the same as I always have."

"Which isn't enough. It's never been enough. If you're not careful, you'll blow away in the storm." She nodded toward the window as she took her seat again. "It's going to be a big one. Which is good. We need the rain. I hope we don't have any howlers in the kennel."

Howlers were dogs that were afraid of storms, and they made life miserable for the other dogs. Beth recognized the conversation's shift as an opportunity to change the subject. Nana usually offered a way out, but as Beth took a bite of her toast, she realized there was something else she wanted to discuss.

"I think they've met before," she finally said.

"Who? Thibault and the loser?"

Beth raised her hands. "Please don't call him that. I know you don't like him, but he's still Ben's father and I don't want you to get into the habit of calling him that when Ben can hear you. I know he's not here right now . . ."

Nana gave a rueful smile. "You're right," she said. "I'm sorry. I won't say it again. But what were you telling me?"

"Do you remember when I told you about the night Keith brought Ben back home with the black eye? You were at your sister's . . ." She saw Nana nod. "Last night, I got to thinking about it. I didn't pick up on it then, but when Keith saw Logan, he didn't ask who Logan was. Instead, it was like a switch went on and he got angry right away. He said something like, 'What are you doing here?'"

"So?" Nana's expression was blank.

"It was the *way* he said it. He wasn't so much surprised that some man was at the house as much as he was surprised that Logan in particular was at the house. Like Logan was the last person he'd expected to see."

"What does Thibault say?"

"He hasn't said anything. But it makes sense, doesn't it? That they've crossed paths before? Since he thinks Keith broke into his house?"

"Maybe," Nana said, then shook her head. "I don't know. Did Thibault say what he thought your ex might be looking for?"

"No," she said, "he didn't. Other than to say that there wasn't much to find."

"Which is a way of answering the question without really answering it."

"Mmm," Beth agreed. She took another bite of toast, thinking there was no way she could finish all of it.

Nana leaned forward. "And that worries you, too?"

"A little," Beth said, giving a small nod.

"Because you feel like he's keeping something from you?"

When Beth didn't answer, Nana reached across the table and took her hand. "I think you're worrying about the wrong things here. Maybe your ex broke into Thibault's house, and maybe he didn't. Maybe they have come across each other before, or maybe not. But neither of those things is as important as whether or not your ex has been working behind the scenes against you. If I were you, that's what I'd be concerned about because that's the part that mainly affects you." She paused, letting her words sink in. "I say that because I've seen you and Thibault together, and it's obvious how much he cares for you. And I think the reason he told you his suspicions was because he doesn't want the same thing to happen to him that's happened to the other men you've dated."

"So you think Logan is right?"

"Yes," Nana said. "Don't you?"

It took a long time for Beth to respond. "I think so, too."

It was one thing to think it; it was another thing to be sure. After their conversation, Beth changed into her jeans, threw on her raincoat, and drove into town. The rain had started in earnest a couple of hours earlier, a gusty downpour powered by a tropical storm that had come up through Georgia by way of South Carolina. The news was predicting six to eight inches of rain in the next twenty-four hours, with more to come. Two more storms in

the Gulf of Mexico had come ashore in recent days and were expected to eventually roll through the area as well, bringing even
more rain. The hot, dry summer was officially coming to an end.

Beth could barely see through the windshield even with the
wipers at full speed. The gutters were beginning to flood, and as she
drove toward town she saw jagged eddies of water making their way
to the river. So far, the river hadn't risen yet, but it would: Nearly
every tributary within fifty miles fed it, and she suspected the river
would reach the flood stage before long. The town could handle
flooding; storms like these were a part of life in this region of the
country, and most of the businesses were far enough away from the
river to avoid most of the effects of all but the most exceptional of
storms. The road that led to the kennel—because it ran parallel to
the river—was another story. In heavy storms, especially during
hurricanes, the river would sometimes stretch across it, making
passage dangerous. It wouldn't be a problem today, but later in the
week, she suspected things might get a lot worse.

In the car, she continued to mull over her conversation with
Nana. Yesterday morning, things had seemed so much simpler, but
now she couldn't shake the questions going through her mind. Not
only about Keith, but about Logan. If it was true that Logan and
Keith had met before, why hadn't Logan said anything? And what
had Keith been looking for in Logan's house? As a sheriff, Keith
had access to all sorts of personal information, so it couldn't be
something along those lines. What was it, then? For the life of her,
she couldn't figure it out.

And Keith . . .

What if Nana and Logan were right? And assuming they were
right—because after giving the matter some thought, she felt instinctively that it was all true—how could she have not seen it?

It was hard to admit that she could have misjudged him. She'd
been dealing with the man for over ten years now, and though she'd
never regarded him as a beacon of goodness, the idea of him sabo-
taging her personal life was something she'd never considered.

Who would do something like that? And why? The way Nana described it—that he thought of her as a toy he didn't want to share—had a ring of truth that made her neck tense as she drove.

What surprised her most was that in this small town, where secrets were nearly impossible to keep, she'd never even suspected it. It made her wonder about her friends and neighbors, but mostly it made her wonder about the men who'd asked her out in the first place. Why wouldn't they simply have told Keith to mind his own business?

Because, she reminded herself, he was a Clayton. And those men didn't argue for the same reason she didn't press Keith when it came to Ben. Sometimes it was easier just to get along.

She really hated that family.

Of course, she was getting ahead of herself here. Just because Logan and Nana suspected that Keith was up to something didn't necessarily make it true, she reminded herself. Which was why she was making this trip.

She took a left at the major intersection, heading toward an older neighborhood, one dominated by Craftsman-style homes and large, spacious porches. The streets were lined with massive trees, most at least a hundred years old, and she remembered that as a kid, it had always been her favorite neighborhood. It was a tradition among the families there to lavishly decorate the exterior of the homes on holidays, giving the place a picturesque, cheery feel.

His house was in the middle of the street, and she could just make out his car parked beneath the carport. Another car was parked behind it, and though it meant he had company, she didn't feel like coming back later. After pulling to a stop in front of the house, she put up the hood on her raincoat and stepped out into the storm.

She splashed through shallow puddles that had accumulated on the walkway and climbed the steps to the porch. Through the windows, she could see a lamp blazing in the corner of the living room; a television nearby was broadcasting the latest race from NASCAR. The visitor must have insisted on it; there wasn't a chance that the owner of the house had tuned it in. The man hated NASCAR, she knew.

She rang the doorbell and took a small step back. When his face appeared in the doorway, it took only an instant for him to recognize her. In his expression, she saw a mixture of surprise and curiosity, along with a trace of something else she hadn't expected: fear.

His gaze traveled quickly up the road in both directions before coming to rest on her.

"Beth," he said. "What are you doing here?"

"Hi, Adam." She smiled. "I was wondering if you had just a couple of minutes. I'd really like to talk to you."

"I've got company," he said in a low voice. "It's not a good time."

As if on cue, she heard a woman's voice call out from somewhere behind him, "Who is it?"

"Please?" Beth said.

He seemed to be calculating whether or not to close the door in her face before he sighed. "A friend," he called out. He turned. "Give me a minute, okay?"

A woman appeared over his shoulder, holding a beer and wearing jeans and a T-shirt that were a little too snug. Beth recognized her as a secretary in Adam's office. Noelle, or something like that.

"What does she want?" Noelle asked. It was obvious by her tone that the recognition was reciprocal.

"I don't know," Adam said. "She just dropped by, okay?"

"But I want to see the race," she pouted, draping an arm possessively around his waist.

"I know," he said. "I won't be long." He hesitated when he saw Noelle's expression. "I promise," he reassured her.

Beth wondered whether the whine she'd noticed in his tone had always been there, and if so, why she hadn't noticed it before. Either he'd tried to hide it or she'd been willing to ignore it. She suspected the latter, and the thought left her feeling a bit deflated.

Adam stepped outside and closed the door behind him. As he faced her, she couldn't tell whether he was frightened or angry. Or both.

"What is so important?" he asked. He sounded like an adolescent.

"Nothing important," she countered. "I just came by to ask you a question."

"About what?"

Beth willed him to look at her. "I want to know the reason you never called after our dinner date."

"What?" He shifted from one foot to the other, reminding her of a skittish horse. "You've got to be kidding."

"I'm not."

"I just didn't, okay? It didn't work out. I'm sorry. Is that what you're here for? An apology?"

It came out like a whine, and she found herself wondering why she'd ever gone out with him.

"No, I'm not here for an apology."

"Then what? Look, I've got company." He jerked a thumb over his shoulder. "I've got to go."

As the question hung in the air, he glanced up and down the street again, and she realized what was going on.

"You're afraid of him, aren't you," she said.

Though he tried to hide it, she knew she'd hit a nerve. "Who? What are you talking about?"

"Keith Clayton. My ex."

He opened his mouth to say something, but nothing came out. Instead, he swallowed again in an attempt to deny it. "I don't know what you're talking about."

She took a step closer. "What did he do? Did he threaten you? Scare you?"

"No! I don't want to talk about this," he said. He turned for the door and reached for the knob. She grabbed his arm to stop him, pushing her face close to his. His muscles tensed before relaxing.

"He did, didn't he?" she pressed.

"I can't talk about this." He hesitated. "He . . ."

Though she'd suspected that both Logan and Nana were right, though her own intuition had prompted her to come here in the first place, she felt something crumple inside when Adam confirmed it.

"What did he do?"

"I can't tell you. You should understand that more than anyone. You know how he is. He'll . . ."

He trailed off, as if suddenly realizing that he'd said too much.

"He'll what?"

He shook his head. "Nothing. He's not going to do anything." He stood straighter. "It didn't work out between us. Just leave it at that."

He opened the door. He paused, drawing a deep breath, and she wondered if he was about to change his mind.

"Please don't come back," he said.

Beth sat on her front porch in the swing, staring at the sheets of rain coming down, her clothes still wet. For the most part, Nana left her alone with her thoughts, intruding only to hand her a cup of hot tea and a warm, homemade peanut-butter cookie, but she'd been uncharacteristically silent when she'd done so.

Beth sipped the tea before realizing she didn't want it. She wasn't cold; despite the relentless downpour, the air was warm and she could see fingers of mist crawling along the property. In the distance, the driveway seemed to vanish into the grayish blur.

Her ex would be here soon. Keith Clayton. Every now and then, she'd whisper the name, making it sound like a profanity.

She couldn't believe it. No, scratch that. She could—and did—believe it. Even though she'd wanted to slap Adam for being such a wimp about the situation, she knew she couldn't really blame him. He was a nice guy, but he wasn't, nor had he ever been, the kind of guy who would have been picked first for a pickup basketball or baseball game. There wasn't a chance that he would have stood up to her ex.

She only wished Adam had revealed how Keith had done it. It was easy to imagine; she had no doubt Adam rented his office from the Clayton family. Almost every business downtown did. Did he play the rent card? Or the "we can make life difficult for you" card? Or did he play the law enforcement card? How far had the man been willing to go?

Since she'd been sitting outside, she'd tried to figure out exactly how many times it had happened. There weren't that many, maybe five or six, she thought, that had ended in much the same sudden, inexplicable way it had ended with Adam. That was counting Frank, which was what? Seven years ago? Had he been following her, *spying* on her, that long? The realization made her sick to her stomach.

And Adam . . .

What was it about the men she picked that made each of them roll over and play dead the moment Keith intervened? Yes, they were a powerful family, and yes, he was a sheriff, but whatever happened to being a man? Telling him to mind his own business? And why didn't they at least come to her and tell her? Instead, they'd slunk off with their tails between their legs. Between them and Keith, she hadn't had the best of luck with men. How did that saying go? Fool me once, shame on you. Fool me twice, shame on me? Was it her fault for picking such disappointing men?

Maybe, she admitted. Still, that wasn't the issue. The issue was that Keith had been working behind the scenes to keep things exactly the way he wanted. As if he owned her.

The thought made her stomach roil again, and she wished that Logan were here. Not because Keith would be here soon to drop off Ben. She didn't need him for that. She wasn't afraid of Keith. She'd never been afraid of him because she knew that deep down he was a bully, and bullies were quick to back down when anyone stood up to them. It was the same reason Nana wasn't afraid of Keith. Drake, too, had sensed that, and she knew he'd always made Keith nervous.

No, she wanted Logan here because he was good at listening, and she knew he wouldn't interrupt her rant, or try to solve her problem, or get bored if she said, "I can't believe he actually did that," a hundred times. He would let her vent.

Then again, she thought, the last thing she wanted was to talk the anger out of her system. It was much better to let it simmer. She needed the anger when she confronted Keith—it would keep her sharp—but at the same time, she didn't want to lose control. If she started screaming, Keith would simply deny it all before storming off. What she wanted, however, was for Keith to stay out of her private life—especially now that Logan was in the picture—without making Ben's weekends with his father any worse than they already were.

No, it was better that Logan wasn't here. Keith might overreact if he saw Logan again, even provoke Logan to action somehow, which could be a problem. If Logan so much as touched her ex, he'd find himself in jail for a long, long time. She had to talk to Logan about that later to make sure he understood how the deck was stacked in Hampton. But for now, she had to handle her little problem.

In the distance, headlights appeared and the car seemed first to liquefy, then solidify as it approached the house. She saw Nana peek through the curtains, then pull back. Beth rose from the swing and stepped toward the edge of the porch as the passenger door swung open. Ben scrambled out holding his backpack and stepped into a puddle, soaking his shoes. He didn't seem to notice as he trotted toward the steps and up to the porch.

"Hey, Mom," he said. They hugged before he looked up at her. "Can we have spaghetti for dinner?"

"Sure, sweetie. How was your weekend?"

He shrugged. "You know."

"Yeah," she said. "I know. Why don't you go inside and change? I think Nana baked some cookies. And take off your shoes, okay?"

"Are you coming?"

"In a few minutes. I want to talk to your dad first."

"Why?"

"Don't worry. It's not about you."

He tried to read her expression, and she put her hand on his shoulder. "Go on. Nana's waiting."

Ben went inside as Keith rolled down his window a couple of inches. "We had a great time this weekend! Don't let him tell you any different."

His tone was full of an airy confidence. Probably, she thought, because Logan wasn't around.

She took another step forward. "Do you have a minute?"

He stared at her through the crack before he slipped the car into park and shut off the engine. He pushed open the door, stepped out, and ran toward the steps. Once on the porch, he shook his head, sending a few drops of water flying before grinning at her. He probably thought he looked sexy.

"What's up?" he asked. "Like I said, Ben and I had a great time this weekend."

"Did you make him clean your kitchen again?"

The grin faded. "What do you want, Beth?"

"Don't get sore. I just asked a question."

He continued to stare at her, trying to read her. "I don't tell you what to do with Ben when he's with you, and I expect the same courtesy. Now what did you want to talk about?"

"A few things, actually." Despite the disgust she felt, she forced a smile and motioned to the porch swing. "Would you like to sit down?"

He seemed surprised. "Sure," he said. "But I can't stay long. I've got plans this evening."

Of course you do, she thought. Either that, or you want me to think that you do. The kind of reminder that had been typical since their divorce.

They took a seat on the swing. After sitting, he jiggled it back and forth before leaning back and spreading his arms. "This is nice. Did you do this?"

She tried to keep as much distance between them on the swing as she could. "Logan put it up."

"Logan?"

"Logan Thibault. He works for Nana at the kennel now. Remember? You met him."

He scratched his chin. "The guy that was here the other night?"

As if you don't know. "Yes, that's him."

"And he's okay with cleaning cages and scooping up crap?" he asked.

She ignored the obvious dig. "Uh-huh."

He exhaled as he shook his head. "Better him than me." He turned toward her with a shrug. "So what's up?"

She considered her words carefully. "This is hard for me to say . . ." She trailed off, knowing it would make him more interested.

"What is it?"

She sat up straighter. "I was talking to one of my friends the other day, and she said something that just didn't sit right with me."

"What did she say?" Keith leaned toward her, alert.

"Well, before I tell you, I just want to say that it was one of those rumor mill things. A friend of a friend of a friend heard something, and it eventually got passed on to me. It's about you."

His expression was curious. "You have my attention."

"What she said was . . ." She hesitated. "She said that in the past, you've followed me on my dates. And that you told some of them that you didn't want them to date me."

She made a point not to look directly at him, but from the corner of her eye, she saw his expression freeze. Not only shocked. Guilty. She pressed her lips together to keep from blowing up.

His face relaxed. "I can't believe it." He drummed his fingers on his leg. "Who told you that?"

"It's not important." She waved off the comment. "You don't know her."

"I'm curious," he pressed.

"It's not important," she said again. "It's not true, is it?"

"Of course not. How could you even think something like that?"

Liar! she screamed inside, willing herself not to say anything. In the silence, he shook his head.

"Sounds to me like you need to start picking better friends. And to be honest, I'm a little hurt that we're even having this conversation."

She forced herself to smile. "I told her it wasn't true."

"But you wanted to make sure by asking me in person."

She heard a tinge of anger in his voice and reminded herself to be careful.

"You were coming over," she said, trying to sound casual. "And besides, we've known each other long enough that we can talk like adults." She looked at him wide-eyed, the victim of an innocent mistake. "Did it bother you that I asked?"

"No, but still, to even think it . . ." Keith threw up his hands.

"I didn't. But I wanted to tell you because I figured you might want to know what other people might be saying behind your back. I don't like them talking about Ben's father that way, and I said that to her."

Her words had the effect she wanted: He puffed up with self-righteous pride.

"Thanks for defending me."

"Nothing to defend. You know how gossip is. It's the toxic waste of small towns." She shook her head. "So how's everything else? Work going well?"

"Same as always. How's your class this year?"

"It's a pretty good group of kids. So far, anyway."

"Good," he said. He motioned toward the yard. "Some storm, huh? I could barely see the road."

"I was thinking the same thing when you drove up. It's crazy. It was gorgeous at the beach yesterday."

"You were at the beach?"

She nodded. "Logan and I went. We've been seeing each other for a while now."

"Huh," he said. "Sounds like it's getting serious."

She offered a sidelong glance. "Don't tell me that woman was right about you."

"No, of course not."

She worked up a playful smile. "*I know*. I was just teasing. And no, we're not serious yet, but he's a great guy."

He brought his hands together. "How does Nana feel about that?"

"Why does that matter?"

He shifted in his seat. "I'm just saying that situations like this can be complicated."

"What are you talking about?"

"He works here. And you know how the courts are these days. You're opening yourself up to a major sexual harassment lawsuit."

"He wouldn't do that—"

Keith spoke with patience, as if lecturing someone much younger. "Trust me. That's what everyone says. But think about it. He has no ties to the community, and if he's working for Nana, I doubt he has much money. No offense. But remember, your family owns a lot of land." He shrugged. "I'm just saying that if I were you, I'd be very careful."

He sounded persuasive and, despite her knowledge to the contrary, caring. A friend who was generally concerned for her well-being. The man should be an actor, she thought.

"Nana owns the land and the house. Not me."

"You know how lawyers can be."

I know exactly, she thought. I remember what your lawyer did at the custody hearing. "I don't think it'll be a problem. But I'll talk to Nana about it," Beth conceded.

"That's probably a good idea." He sounded smug.

"I'm just glad I was right about you."

"What do you mean?"

"You know—not having a problem with me dating someone like Logan. Aside from the sexual harassment concern. I really like him."

He uncrossed his legs. "I wouldn't say I have no problem with it."

"But you just said—"

"I said I don't care who you date, and I don't. But I do care who comes into my son's life because I care about my son."

"As you should. But what does that have to do with anything?" Beth protested.

"Think about it, Beth . . . you don't see the things that I have to see. In your work, I mean. But I see terrible things all the time, so of course I'd be concerned about anyone who spends a lot of time with Ben. I'd want to know if he was violent or if he was some sort of pervert—"

"He's not," Beth interrupted. She felt her color rising despite herself. "We ran a background check on him."

"They can be faked. It's not hard to come up with a new identity. How do you even know his real name's Logan? It's not like you can ask anyone around here. Have you talked to anyone from his past? Or his family?"

"No . . ."

"There you go. I'm just telling you to be careful." He shrugged. "And I'm not saying that just because of Ben. It's for you, too. There are some bad people in the world, and the reason they're not in jail is because they've learned how to hide it."

"You make it sound like he's some sort of criminal!"

"I'm not trying to. He could be the nicest, most responsible guy in the world. I'm just saying that you don't know who he really is. And until you do, it's better to be safe than sorry. You read the papers and watch the news. I'm not telling you something you don't already know. I just don't want anything to happen to Ben. And I don't want to see you get hurt."

Beth opened her mouth to say something, but for the first time since sitting down with her ex, she could think of nothing to say.

21

Clayton

Clayton sat behind the wheel of the car, feeling pretty damn pleased with himself.

He'd had to do some quick thinking, but it went far better than he'd thought it would, especially considering the way the conversation had begun. Someone had ratted him out, and as he drove, he tried to figure out who it might have been. Generally, there was no such thing as a secret in small towns, but this one was as close as you could get. The only ones who knew were the few men he'd had the little talk with and, of course, himself.

He figured it could have been one of them, but somehow he doubted it. They were worms, each and every one of them, and each and every one of them had moved on. There was no reason for them to have said anything. Even Adam the dork had found a new girlfriend, which made it unlikely he'd start talking now either.

Then again, it might simply have been a rumor. It was possible that someone had suspicions about what he'd been up to, just by connecting the dots. Beautiful woman getting dumped over and over for no apparent reason . . . and, thinking back, he might have mentioned something to Moore or even Tony about Beth that someone might have overheard—but he'd never been dumb or drunk enough to be specific. He knew the problems that could cause with his dad, especially since usually he'd had to rely on law enforcement threats. But someone had said something to Beth.

He didn't put much stock in the fact that Beth had said a female friend had told her. She could easily have changed that little detail to throw him off. It could have been a man or a woman; what he was more certain about was the fact that she'd learned the detail recently. Knowing her as he did, he knew there wasn't a chance she could have kept something like that bottled up for long.

That's where things got confusing. He'd picked up Ben on Saturday morning; she'd said nothing then. By her own admission, she'd been at the beach on Saturday with Thigh-bolt. On Sunday, he'd seen her in church, but she was home by late afternoon.

So who had told her? And when?

It could have been Nana, he thought. The woman had always been a thorn in his side. Gramps's, too. For the last four or five years, he'd been trying to get Nana to sell the land so he could develop it. Not only did it have a beautiful riverfront, but the creeks were valuable, too. People who moved down from the North loved waterfront property. Gramps generally took her rejections in stride; for whatever reason, he liked Nana. Probably because they went to the same church, something that didn't seem to matter when it came to Nana's opinion of her former son-in-law, who went to the same church as well.

Still, this seemed like the kind of trouble Thigh-bolt would start. But how on earth would he know? They'd seen each other only twice, and there wasn't a chance that Thigh-bolt could have deduced the truth from those two meetings. But what about the break-in? Clayton thought about it before rejecting his idea. He'd been in and out in twenty minutes, and he hadn't even had to jimmy the lock, since the guy hadn't bothered to lock the front door. And nothing had been missing, so why would Thigh-bolt even have suspected someone had been inside in the first place?

And even if he'd guessed that someone had been in the house, why would he draw the connection to Clayton?

He couldn't answer those questions to his satisfaction, but the theory that Thigh-bolt had had something to do with this little wrinkle seemed to fit. He'd had nothing but problems since Thigh-bolt had arrived. So he figured Thigh-bolt was high on his list of folks who probably should have minded their own business. Which gave him one more reason to finally fix the guy.

He wasn't going to get too caught up with that now, though. He was still feeling pretty good about how he'd salvaged the conversation with Beth. It could have been a fiasco. The last thing on earth he'd expected when she'd called him over was for her to ask him about his involvement in her previous relationships. But he'd handled it well. Not only was he able to muster a plausible denial, but he'd also made her think twice about Thigh-bolt. He could tell by her expression that he'd brought up a number of issues she hadn't considered about Thigh-bolt . . . and best of all, he'd convinced her that it was all in Ben's best interest. Who knows? Maybe *she'd* end up dumping *him*, and Thigh-bolt would leave town. Wouldn't that be something? Yet another of Beth's relationship problems would be solved, and Thigh-bolt would be out of the picture.

He drove slowly, savoring the taste of victory. He wondered whether he should head out for a celebratory beer but decided against it. It wasn't as if he could talk about what happened. Talking was what might have gotten him into trouble in the first place.

After turning onto his street, he cruised past a number of large, well-maintained homes, each sitting on half an acre. He lived at the end of the cul-de-sac; his neighbors were a doctor and lawyer. He hadn't done too badly, if he did say so himself.

It was only when he turned in the driveway that he noticed someone standing on the sidewalk in front of the house. When he slowed, he saw the dog poised beside him and he slammed on the brakes, blinking in disbelief. He jammed the car into park. Despite the rain, he stepped out of the car and headed directly for Thigh-bolt.

When Zeus snarled and began to creep forward, Clayton stopped short. Thigh-bolt raised a hand and the dog froze.

"What the hell are you doing here?" he shouted, making his voice heard over the rain.

"Waiting for you," Thigh-bolt replied. "I think it's time we had a talk."

"Why the hell would I want to talk to you?" he spat out.

"I think you know."

Clayton didn't like the sound of that, but he wasn't about to be intimidated by the guy. Not now. Not ever.

"What I know is that you're loitering. In this county, that's a crime."

"You won't arrest me."

Part of him considered doing just that. "Don't be so sure."

Thigh-bolt continued to stare at him as if daring him to prove it. Clayton wanted to wipe that expression off Thigh-bolt's face with his fist. But ever present Cujo was there.

"What do you want?"

"Like I said, it's time for us to talk." His tone was even and steady.

"I've got nothing to say to you," Clayton fumed. He shook his head. "I'm going inside. If you're still out here when I reach the porch, I'll have you arrested for threatening a deputy with a lethal weapon."

He turned and started up the walk, toward the door.

"You didn't find the disk," Thigh-bolt called out.

Clayton stopped and turned around. "What?"

"The disk," Thigh-bolt repeated. "That's what you were look-ing for when you broke into my house. When you went through my drawers, looked under the mattress, checked the cabinets."

"I didn't break into your house." He squinted at Thigh-bolt.

"Yes," he said, "you did. Last Monday, when I was at work."

"Prove it," he barked.

"I already have all the proof I need. The motion detector I had set up in the fireplace turned on the video recorder. It was hidden in the fireplace. I figured you might try to find the disk one day and you'd never think to look there."

Clayton felt his stomach lurch as he tried to figure out whether Thigh-bolt was bluffing. Maybe he was or maybe he wasn't; he couldn't tell.

"You're lying."

"Then walk away. I'll be happy to walk the videotape over to the newspaper and sheriff's department right now."

"What do you want?"

"I told you, I thought it was time we had a little talk."

"About what?"

"About what a dirt-bag you are." He let the words roll out lazily. "Taking dirty pictures of coeds? What would your grandfather think of that? I wonder what would happen if he somehow found out about it, or what the newspaper might say. Or what your dad—who I believe is the county sheriff—would think about his son breaking into my house."

Clayton felt his stomach give another nasty twist. There was no way the guy could know these things . . . but he did. "What do you want?" Despite his best effort, he knew his tone had risen a notch when he said it.

Thigh-bolt continued to stand before him, his gaze steady. Clayton swore the man never so much as blinked.

"I want you to be a better person," he said.

"I don't know what you're talking about."

"Three things. Let's start with this: Stay out of Elizabeth's business."

Clayton blinked. "Who's Elizabeth?"

"Your ex-wife."

"You mean Beth?"

"You've been running her dates off ever since you've been divorced. You know it and I know it. And now she knows it, too. It's not going to happen again. Ever. Are we clear?"

Clayton didn't respond.

"Number two—stay out of my business. That means my house, my job, my life. Got it?"

Clayton stayed silent.

"And number three. This is very important." He raised a palm outward, as if taking an imaginary oath. "If you take your anger at me out on Ben, you'll have to answer to me."

Clayton felt the hairs on the back of his neck rise. "Is that a threat?"

"No," Thigh-bolt said, "it's the truth. Do those three things, and you'll have no trouble from me. No one will know what you've done."

Clayton clenched his jaw.

In the silence, Thigh-bolt moved toward him. Zeus stayed in place, his frustration evident at being forced to stay behind. Thigh-bolt stepped closer until they were face-to-face. His voice remained as calm as it had been all along.

"Know this: You've never met someone like me before. You don't want me as an enemy."

With that, Thigh-bolt turned away and started down the sidewalk. Zeus continued to stare at Clayton until he heard the command to come. Then he trotted toward Thigh-bolt, leaving Clayton standing in the rain, wondering how everything that had been so perfect could have suddenly gone so wrong.

22

Thibault

I think I want to be an astronaut," Ben said.

Thibault was playing chess with him on the back porch and trying to figure out his next move. He had yet to win a game, and though he wasn't absolutely sure, the fact that Ben had started talking struck him as a bad sign. They'd been playing a lot of chess lately; there hadn't been a day without steady, heavy rain since October began nine days earlier. Already, the eastern part of the state was flooding, with additional rivers rising daily.

"Sounds good."

"Either that or a fireman."

Thibault nodded. "I've known a couple of firemen."

"Or a doctor."

"Hmm," Thibault said. He began reaching for his bishop.

"I wouldn't do that," Ben said.

Thibault looked up.

"I know what you're thinking you should do," Ben added. "It won't work."

"What should I do?"

"Not that."

Thibault drew his hand back. It was one thing to lose, it was another thing to lose continually. Worse, he didn't seem to be closing the gap. If anything, Ben was getting better faster than he was. The previous game had lasted all of twenty-one moves.

"Would you like to see my tree house?" Ben said. "It's really cool. It's got the big platform that hangs out over the creek, and this shaky bridge."

"I'd love to see it."

"Not now. Some other time, I mean."

"Sounds great," Thibault said. He reached for his rook.

"I wouldn't move that one either."

Thibault arched his brow as Ben leaned back.

"I'm just telling you," he added.

"What should I do?"

He shrugged, looking and sounding like the ten-year-old he was. "Whatever you want."

"Except move the bishop and the rook?"

Ben pointed to another piece. "And your other bishop. Knowing you, that's what you'll try next, since you're trying to set up your knight. But it won't work either, since I'll sacrifice the bishop for mine, and move my queen in to take the pawn over there. That freezes your queen, and after I castle my king, I'll move my knight there. Two moves after that, I'll have you in checkmate."

Thibault brought his hand to his chin. "Do I have any chance in this game?"

"No."

"How many moves do I have left?"

"Anywhere from three to seven."

"Then maybe we should start over."

Ben pushed his glasses up on his nose. "Maybe."

"You could have told me earlier."

"You seemed so serious about the game. I didn't want to bother you."

The next game was no better. If anything, it was worse because Elizabeth had decided to join them and their conversation proceeded in much the same way. He could see Elizabeth trying to stifle her giggles.

Over the last week and a half, they'd settled into a routine. After work, with overpowering rain coming down continuously, he'd come up to the house to play a few games of chess with Ben and stay for dinner, where the four of them would sit at the table, chatting amiably. After that, Ben would go upstairs to shower and Nana would send them outside to sit on the porch while she stayed in the kitchen to clean up, saying things like, "Cleaning to me is like being naked to a monkey."

Thibault knew she wanted to give them time alone before he left. It still amazed him that she was able to stop being the boss as soon as his workday was done and shift so easily to the role of grandmother of the woman he was dating. He didn't think there were many people who would be able to pull that off.

It was getting late, though, and Thibault knew it was time to leave. Nana was talking on the phone, Elizabeth had gone inside to tuck Ben into bed, and as Thibault sat on the porch, he could feel the exhaustion in his shoulders. He hadn't been sleeping much since his confrontation with Clayton. That night, unsure how Clayton would respond, he'd gone back to his house and made it appear as though he planned to spend a normal evening at home. Instead, once he turned out the lights, he'd climbed out the window in his bedroom at the rear of the house and trotted into the woods, Zeus by his side. Despite the rain, he'd stayed out most of the night, watching for Clayton. The next night, he'd watched Elizabeth's; on the third night, he'd alternated between his house and hers. The endless rain didn't bother him or Zeus in the slightest; he'd rigged a couple of camouflaged lean-tos that kept them dry. The hard part for him was working after sleeping only the last few hours before dawn. Since then, he'd been alternating nights, but it still wasn't enough sleep for him to catch up.

He wouldn't stop, though. The man was unpredictable, and he looked for signs of Clayton's presence when he was at work and when he ran errands in town. In the evening, he took different routes home, cutting through wooded areas at a run and then watching the road to make sure Clayton wasn't following. He wasn't afraid of the man, but he wasn't stupid, either. Clayton was not only a member of the First Family of Hampton County, but also in law enforcement, and it was the latter that most concerned him. How hard would it be to plant something—drugs, stolen items, even a gun that had been used in a crime—in Thibault's home? Or claim that Thibault had them in his possession and arrange to have that evidence discovered? Not hard. Thibault was certain that any jury in the county would side with testimony provided by law enforcement over a stranger's, no matter how flimsy the evidence might be or what genuine alibi he had. Add to that the deep pockets and influence of the Claytons, and it wouldn't be hard to line up witnesses fingering Thibault for any number of crimes.

The scary part was that he could imagine Clayton doing any of those things, which was why he'd gone to see Clayton and told him about both the disk and the videotape in the first place. Though he had neither—he'd cracked and tossed the disk soon after taking the camera, and the motion-activated recorder had been an inspired invention—bluffing seemed to be the only option he had to buy him enough time to figure out his next step. The animosity Clayton felt for him was dangerous and unpredictable. If he'd been willing to break into Thibault's house, if he'd manipulated Elizabeth's personal life, the man would probably do whatever he thought necessary to get rid of Thibault.

The other threats—about the newspaper and the sheriff, the hint about informing the grandfather—simply reinforced the bluff. He knew that Clayton was searching for the disk because he believed Thibault could use it against him. It was either because of his job or because of his family, and a few hours researching the illustrious family history in the library on Sunday afternoon had been enough to convince Thibault that it was probably a bit of both.

But the problem with bluffs was that they worked until they didn't. How long would it be until Clayton called it? A few more weeks? A month? More than that? And what would Clayton do? Who could tell? Right now, Clayton thought Thibault had the upper hand, and Thibault had no doubt that was only enraging Clayton even further. In time, the anger would get the better of him and Clayon would react, to either him, Elizabeth, or Ben. When Thibault didn't follow through in the aftermath and produce the disk, Clayton would be free to act as he pleased.

Thibault still wasn't sure what to do about that. He couldn't imagine leaving Elizabeth . . . or Ben and Nana, for that matter. The longer he stayed in Hampton, the more it felt to him like this was the place he belonged, and that meant he had to not only watch out for Clayton, but avoid the man as much as possible. He supposed his hope was that after enough time, Clayton would simply accept the matter and let it rest. Unlikely, he knew, but for now, it was all he had.

"You look distracted again," Elizabeth said, opening the screen door behind him.

Thibault shook his head. "Just tired from the week. I thought the heat was hard, but at least I could dodge some of that. There's no avoiding the rain."

She took a seat beside him on the porch swing. "You don't like being drenched?"

"Let's just say it's not the same as being on vacation."

"I'm sorry."

"It's okay. And I'm not complaining. I really don't mind it most of the time, and it's better me getting wet than Nana. And tomorrow's Friday, right?"

She smiled. "Tonight I'm driving you home. No arguments this time."

"Okay," he said.

Elizabeth peeked in the window before turning her attention to Thibault again. "You weren't lying when you said you could play the piano, right?"

"I can play."

"When was the last time you played?"

He shrugged, thinking about it. "Two or three years ago."

"In Iraq?"

He nodded. "One of my commanding officers was having a birthday. He loved Willie Smith, who was one of the great jazz pianists of the 1940s and 1950s. When word got out that I knew how to play, I got roped into doing a performance."

"In Iraq," she said again, not hiding her disbelief.

"Even marines need a break."

She tucked a strand of hair behind her ear. "I take it you can read music."

"Of course," he said. "Why? Do you want me to teach Ben?"

She didn't seem to hear him. "How about church? Do you ever go?"

For the first time, he looked at her.

"I'm getting the sense there's more to this conversation than simply the two of us getting to know each other better."

"When I was inside, I heard Nana talking on the phone. You know how much Nana loves the choir, right? And that she just started to sing solos again?"

He considered his response, suspicious of where this was going and not bothering to hide it. "Yes."

"Her solo this Sunday is even longer. She's so excited about it."

"Aren't you?"

"Kind of." She sighed, a pained expression on her face. "It turns out that Abigail fell yesterday and broke her wrist. That's what Nana has been talking about on the phone."

"Who's Abigail?"

"The pianist with the church. She accompanies the choir every Sunday." Elizabeth started to move the swing back and forth, staring out into the storm. "Anyway, Nana said she'd find someone to fill in. In fact, she promised."

"Oh?" he said.

"She also said that she already had someone in mind."

"I see."

Elizabeth shrugged. "I just thought you'd want to know. I'm pretty sure Nana will want to talk to you in a few minutes, but I didn't want her to blindside you. I figured it would be better if I did it."

"I appreciate that."

For a long moment, Thibault said nothing. In the silence, Elizabeth put a hand on his knee.

"What do you think?"

"I'm getting the sense I don't really have a choice."

"Of course you have a choice. Nana won't force you to do it."

"Even though she promised?"

"She'd probably understand. Eventually." She placed a hand over her heart. "Once her broken heart healed, I'm sure she'd even forgive you."

"Ah," he said.

"And most likely it wouldn't make her health any worse, either. What with the stroke and all and the disappointment she'd feel. I'm sure she wouldn't end up bedridden or anything."

Thibault cracked a smile. "Don't you think you're overdoing it?"

Elizabeth's eyes sparkled with mischief. "Maybe. But the question is, will you do it?"

"I suppose."

"Good. And you know you're going to have to practice tomorrow."

"Okay."

"It might be a long rehearsal. Friday rehearsals are always long. They really love their music, you know."

"Great," he said, and sighed.

"Look at it this way: You won't have to work in the rain all day."

"Great," he said again.

She kissed him on the cheek. "You're a good man. I'll be silently cheering for you in the pews."

"Thanks."

"Oh, and when Nana comes out, don't let her know I told you."

"I won't."

"And try to be more excited. Honored, even. Like you couldn't imagine that you'd ever be offered such a wonderful opportunity."

"I can't just say yes?"

"No. Nana will want you to be thrilled. Like I said, it means a lot to her."

"Ah," he said again. He took her hand in his. "You do realize you simply could have asked me. I didn't need the whole guilt-inducing story."

"I know," she said. "But it was a lot more fun to ask the other way."

As if on cue, Nana stepped outside. She flashed a quick smile at both of them before wandering to the railing and turning toward him.

"Do you ever play the piano anymore?" Nana asked.

It was all Thibault could do not to laugh.

Thibault met with the music director the following afternoon, and despite her initial dismay at his jeans, T-shirt, and long hair, it didn't take long for her to realize that Thibault not only could play, but was obviously an accomplished musician. Once he'd warmed up, he made very few errors, though it helped that the chosen musical pieces weren't terribly challenging. After rehearsal, when the pastor showed up, he was walked through the service so he'd know exactly what to expect.

Nana, meanwhile, alternately beamed at Thibault and chattered away with her friends, explaining that Thibault worked at the kennel and was spending time with Beth. Thibault could feel the gazes of the women sweep over him with more than a little interest and, for the most part, approval.

On their way out the door, Nana looped her arm through his. "You were better than a duck on a stick," she said.

"Thanks," he said, mystified.

"Are you up for a little drive?"

"Where?"

"Wilmington. If we go now, I think I can have you back in time to take Beth to dinner. I'll watch Ben."

"What am I going to buy?"

"A sport jacket and chinos. A dressier shirt. I don't mind you in jeans, but if you're going to play the piano at the service on Sunday, you're going to need to dress up."

"Ah," he said, recognizing at once that he had no choice in the matter.

That evening, while dining at Cantina, the only Mexican restaurant downtown, Elizabeth stared over her margarita at Thibault.

"You know you're in like Flynn now," she said.

"With Nana?"

"She couldn't stop talking about how good you were, and how polite you were to her friends, and how respectful you sounded when the pastor showed up."

"You make it sound like she expected me to be a troglodyte."

She laughed. "Maybe she did. I heard you were covered in mud before you went."

"I showered and changed."

"I know. She told me that, too."

"What didn't she tell you?"

"That the other women in the choir were swooning."

"She said that?"

"No. She didn't have to, but I could see it in her face. They were. It's not every day a young and handsome stranger comes into their church and dazzles them on the piano. How could they not swoon?"

"I think you're probably overstating things."

"I think," she said, dabbing her finger on the rim of her glass and tasting the salt, "that you still have a lot to learn about living in a small southern town. This is big news. Abigail has played for fifteen years."

"I'm not going to take her spot. This is temporary."

"Even better. It'll give people a chance to pick sides. They'll talk about it for years."

"This is what people do here?"

"Absolutely," she said. "And by the way, there's no faster way to get accepted around here."

"I don't need to be accepted by anyone but you."

"Always the sweet talker." She smiled. "Okay, how about this? It'll drive Keith crazy."

"Why?"

"Because he's a member of the church. In fact, Ben will be with him when he sees you. It'll kill him to see how much everyone appreciates the way you pitched in to help."

"I'm not sure I want him any angrier. I'm already worried about what he's going to do."

"He can't do anything. I know what he's been up to."

"I wouldn't be so sure," Thibault cautioned.

"Why do you say that?"

Thibault noted the crowded tables surrounding them. She seemed to read his mind and slid out from her side of the booth to sit beside him. "You know something you're not telling me," she whispered. "What is it?"

Thibault took a sip of his beer. When he put the bottle back on the table, he described his encounters with her ex. As he told the story, her expression changed from disgusted to amused, finally settling into something resembling concern.

"You should have told me earlier," she said, frowning.

"I didn't get concerned until he broke into my house."

"And you really think he's capable of setting you up?"

"You know him better than I do."

She realized she wasn't hungry anymore. "I thought I did."

Because Ben was with his father—a situation that felt somewhat surreal to both of them considering the circumstances—Thibault and Elizabeth went to Raleigh on Saturday, which made it easy to avoid dwelling on what Keith Clayton might or might not do. In the afternoon, they had lunch at a sidewalk café downtown and visited the Museum of Natural History; on Saturday evening, they made their way to Chapel Hill. North Carolina was playing Clemson, and the game was being broadcast on ESPN. Though the game was in South Carolina, the bars downtown were packed, full of students watching it on giant flat-screen televisions. As Thibault heard them cheering and booing, as if the future of the world hung on the outcome of the game, he found himself thinking about the kids their age serving in Iraq and wondered what they would make of these college students.

They didn't stay long. After an hour, Elizabeth was ready to leave. On their way back to the car, as they walked with their arms around each other, she leaned her head against his shoulder.

"That was fun," she said. "But it was so loud in there."

"You just say that because you're getting old."

She squeezed his waist, liking the fact that there was nothing but skin and muscle there. "Watch it, bub, or you might not get lucky tonight."

"Bub?" he repeated.

"It's a term of endearment. I say it to all the guys I date."

"All of them?"

"Yep. Strangers, too. Like if they give me their seat on the bus, I might say, 'Thanks, bub.'"

"I guess I should feel special."

"And don't you forget it."

They walked among the throngs of students on Franklin Street, peeking in windows and soaking up the energy. It made sense to Thibault that she'd wanted to come here. This was an experience she'd missed because of Ben. Yet what impressed him most was that although she was obviously enjoying herself, she didn't seem wistful or bitter about what she'd missed. If anything, she acted more like an observant anthropologist, intent on studying new-found cultures. When he said as much, she rolled her eyes.

"Don't ruin the evening. Trust me, I'm not thinking that deep. I just wanted to get out of town and have some fun."

They went to Thibault's and stayed up late, talking and kissing and making love well into the night. When Thibault woke in the morning, he found Elizabeth lying beside him, studying his face.

"What are you doing?" he murmured, his voice thick with sleep.

"Watching you," she said.

"Why?"

"I wanted to."

He smiled as he ran a finger over her arm, feeling a surge of gratitude for her presence in his life. "You're pretty awesome, Elizabeth."

"I know."

"That's it? You're just going to say, 'I know'?" he demanded in mock outrage.

"Don't get needy on me. I hate needy guys."

"And I'm not sure I like women who hide their feelings."

She smiled, leaning in to kiss him. "I had a great time yesterday."

"I did, too."

"I mean it. These last few weeks, being with you, have been the best weeks of my life. And yesterday, just being with you . . . you have no idea what that was like. Just being . . . a woman. Not a mother, not a teacher, not a granddaughter. Just me. It's been a long time since that has happened."

"We've gone out before."

"I know. But it's different now."

She was talking about the future, he knew, a future that had acquired a clarity and purpose it never had before. Staring at her, he knew exactly what she meant.

"So what's next?" he asked, his tone serious.

She kissed him again, her breath on his lips warm and moist. "Next is getting up. You have to be at the church in a couple of hours." She swatted him on the hip.

"That's a lot of time."

"Maybe for you. But I'm here and my clothes are at home. You've got to get up and start getting ready, so I have time to get ready."

"This church stuff is tough."

"Sure," she said. "But it's not like you have an option. And by the way?" She reached for his hand before going on. "You're pretty awesome, too, Logan."

23

Beth

I really like him, Nana," said Beth.

Standing in the bathroom, she was doing her best with the curling iron, though she suspected that in the rain, all would be for naught. After a brief respite the day before, the first of the two tropical storms that were expected had entered the area.

"I think it's time you start being honest with me. You don't just like him. You think he's the One."

"I'm not that obvious," Beth said, not wanting to believe it.

"Yes, you are. You might as well be sitting on the front porch picking petals off a daisy."

Beth grinned. "Believe it or not, I actually understood that metaphor."

Nana waved her off. "Accidents happen. The point is, I know you like him. The question is, does he like you?"

"Yes, Nana."

"Have you asked what that means?"

"I know what it means."

"Just making sure," she said. She glanced in the mirror and adjusted her hair. "Because I like him, too."

* * *

She drove with Nana toward Logan's house, worried that her wipers couldn't keep up with the rain. Seemingly endless storms had swelled the river; though the water didn't quite reach the street, it was almost lapping at its edges. A few more days of this, she thought, and roads would begin closing. Businesses closest to the river would soon be stacking sandbags to prevent water from ruining low-lying merchandise.

"I wonder if anyone is going to make it to the church today," Beth remarked. "I can barely see beyond my window."

"A little rain won't keep people away from the Lord," Nana intoned.

"It's more than a little rain. Have you seen the river?"

"I saw it. It's definitely angry."

"If it gets any higher, we might not be able to make it into town."

"It'll all work out," she declared.

Beth glanced across at her. "You're in a good mood today."

"Aren't you? Since you stayed out all night?"

"Nana," Beth protested.

"I'm not judging. Just mentioning. You're an adult and it's your life."

Beth had long grown used to her grandmother's pronouncements. "I appreciate that."

"So it's going well? Even with your ex trying to cause trouble?"

"I think so."

"Do you think he's a keeper?"

"I think it's a little early to even consider something like that. We're still getting to know each other."

Nana leaned forward and wiped at the condensation on the window. Though the moisture disappeared momentarily, fingerprint smudges remained. "I knew right away that your grandfather was the One."

"He told me that the two of you dated for six months before he proposed."

"We did. But that doesn't mean I wouldn't have said yes earlier. I knew within a few days that he was the one for me. I know how crazy that sounds. But being with him was like toast and butter from the very beginning."

Her smile was gentle, her eyes half-closed, as she remembered. "I was sitting with him in the park. It must have been the second or third time we'd ever been alone, and we were talking about birds when a young boy, obviously from out in the county, wandered up to listen. His face was dirty, he didn't have shoes, and his clothes, as ragged as they were, didn't even fit him. Your grandfather winked at him before going on, as if to tell the boy he was welcome to stay, and the boy kind of smiled. It touched me to think that he didn't pass judgment based on the way the boy looked." She paused. "Your grandfather kept on talking. He must have known the name of every kind of bird in this part of the state. He'd tell us whether they migrated and where they nested, and the sound of their calls. After a while, this young boy sat right down and just stared as your grandfather made everything sound . . . well, *enchanting*. And it wasn't just the young boy. I felt it, too. Your grandfather had this soothing, lullabylike voice, and while he talked, I got the sense that he was the kind of person who couldn't hold anger for more than a few minutes, because it just wasn't in him. It could never grow into resentment or bitterness, and I knew then that he was the kind of man who would be married forever. And I decided then and there that I should be the one to marry him."

Despite her familiarity with Nana's stories, Beth was moved.

"That's a wonderful story."

"He was a wonderful man. And when a man is that special, you know it sooner than you think possible. You recognize it instinctively, and you're certain that no matter what happens, there will never be another one like him."

By that point, Beth had reached Logan's graveled drive, and as she turned in and approached the house, bouncing and splashing through the mud, she caught sight of him standing on the porch, dressed in what seemed to be a new sport jacket and a pair of freshly pressed chinos.

When he waved, she couldn't suppress an ear-to-ear smile.

The service began and ended with music. Nana's solo was greeted with hearty applause, and the pastor singled out both Logan and Nana, thanking Logan for filling in at the last minute and Nana for demonstrating the wonder of God's grace in the face of a challenge.

The sermon was informative, interesting, and delivered with the humble recognition that God's mysterious works aren't always understood; Beth felt that their gifted pastor was one of the reasons membership in the church continued to grow.

From her seat in the upper balcony, she could easily see both Nana and Logan. Whenever Ben was with his father for the weekend, she liked to sit in the same spot, so Ben would know where to find her. Usually, he caught her eye two or three times during the service; today, he turned around constantly, sharing his awe at the fact that he was friends with someone so accomplished.

But Beth kept her distance from her ex. Not because of what she'd recently learned about him—though that was reason enough—but because it made things easier on Ben. Despite Keith's lascivious impulses, in church he behaved as though he viewed her presence as a dangerously disruptive force that might somehow upset his clan. Gramps sat in the center of the first row, with the family fanning out on either side and in the row behind him. From her spot, she could see him read along with the Bible passages, take notes, and listen intently to everything the pastor said. He sang every word to every hymn. Out of the entire family, Beth liked him the best—he'd always been fair with her and unfailingly polite, unlike most of the others. After church, if they happened to bump into each other, he always remarked that she was looking well and thanked her for the admirable job she was doing with Ben.

There was honesty in the way he spoke to her, but there was a line in the sand as well: She understood that she wasn't to rock the boat. He knew she was a far better parent than Keith and that Ben was turning into a fine young man because of her, but that knowledge didn't override the fact that Ben was, and always would be, a Clayton.

Still, she liked him—despite everything, despite Keith, despite the line in the sand. Ben liked him, too, and half the time she got the sense that Gramps demanded Keith show up with Ben to spare Ben from having to be alone with his father for the entire weekend.

All of those realities were far from her mind as she watched Logan play the piano. She hadn't known what to expect. How many people took lessons? How many people claimed to be able to play well? It didn't take long to realize Logan was exceptionally skilled, far above the level she'd expected. His fingers moved effortlessly and fluidly over the keys; he didn't even seem to read the music in front of him. Instead, as Nana sang, he focused his attention on her while keeping perfect rhythm and pace, more interested in her performance than his own.

As he continued to play, she couldn't help thinking about the story that Nana had recounted in the car. Tuning out the service, she found herself recalling easy conversations with Logan, the feel of his solid embrace, his natural way with Ben. Admittedly, there was a lot she still didn't know about him, but she did know this: He completed her in a way that she'd never thought possible. Knowledge isn't everything, she told herself, and she knew then that, in Nana's words, he was the toast to her butter.

After the service, Beth stood in the background, amused by the thought that Logan was being treated like a rock star. Okay, a rock star with fans who collected Social Security checks, but as far as she could tell, he seemed both flattered and flustered by the unexpected attention.

She caught him looking at her, silently pleading for her to rescue him. Instead, she simply shrugged and smiled. She didn't want to intrude. When the pastor came up to thank him a second time for filling in, he suggested that Logan might want to consider playing even after Abigail's wrist was healed. "I'm sure we'd be able to work something out," the pastor urged.

She was most surprised when Gramps, with Ben at his side, made his way over to Logan as well. Like Moses parting the Red Sea, Gramps didn't have to wait amid the throng to offer his compliments. In the distance, Beth saw Keith, his expression a mixture of anger and disgust.

"Fine job, young man," Gramps said, offering his hand. "You play as if you've been blessed."

She could see from Logan's expression that he recognized the man, though she had no idea how. He shook Gramps's hand.

"Thank you, sir."

"He works at the kennel with Nana," Ben piped up. "And I think him and Mom are dating."

At that, a stillness fell over the throng of admirers, punctuated by a few uncomfortable coughs.

Gramps stared at Logan, though she couldn't read his reaction. "Is that right?" he said.

"Yes, sir," Logan answered.

Gramps said nothing.

"He was in the marines, too," Ben offered, oblivious to the social currents eddying around him. When Gramps seemed surprised, Logan nodded.

"I served with the First, Fifth out of Pendleton, sir."

After a pregnant pause, Gramps nodded. "Then thank you for your service to our country as well. You did a marvelous job today."

"Thank you, sir," he said again.

* * *

"You were so polite," Beth observed when they were back home. She'd said nothing about what had gone on until Nana was out of earshot. Outside, the lawn was beginning to resemble a lake, and still the rain continued to fall. They'd picked up Zeus on the way back, and he lay nestled at their feet.

"Why wouldn't I be?"

She made a face. "You know why."

"He's not your ex." He shrugged. "I doubt he has any idea what your ex is doing. Why? Do you think I should have clocked him?"

"Absolutely not."

"I didn't think so. But I did happen to see your ex while I was talking to the grandfather. He looked as though he'd just swallowed a worm."

"You noticed that, too? I thought it was kind of funny."

"He's not going to be happy."

"Then he can join the club," she said. "After what he did, he deserves to eat a worm."

Logan nodded, and she snuggled up to him. He lifted his arm and pulled her close.

"You looked mighty handsome up there while you were playing."

"Yeah?"

"I know I shouldn't have been thinking that since I was at church, but I couldn't help it. You should wear a sport jacket more often."

"I don't have the kind of job that requires one."

"Maybe you have the kind of girlfriend who does."

He pretended to be puzzled. "I have a girlfriend?"

She nudged him playfully before looking up at him. She kissed him on the cheek. "Thanks for coming to Hampton. And deciding to stay."

He smiled. "I didn't have a choice."

* * *

Two hours later, right before dinner, Beth saw Keith's car plow through puddles on his way up the drive. Ben scrambled out of the car. Keith already had the car in reverse and was pulling away before Ben reached the porch steps.

"Hey, Mom! Hey, Thibault!"

Logan waved as Beth stood up. "Hey, sweetie," Beth said. She gave him a hug. "Did you have a good time?"

"I didn't have to clean the kitchen. Or take out the trash."

"Good," she said.

"And you know what?"

"What?"

Ben shook the water from his raincoat. "I think I want to learn how to play the piano."

Beth smiled, thinking, Why am I not surprised.

"Hey, Thibault?"

Logan raised his chin. "Yeah?"

"Do you want to see my tree house?"

Beth cut in. "Honey . . . with the storm and all, I'm not sure that's a good idea."

"It's fine. Grandpa built it. And I was there just a couple of days ago."

"The water's probably higher."

"Please? We won't stay long. And Thibault will be with me the whole time."

Against her better judgment, Beth agreed.

24

Clayton

Clayton didn't want to believe it, but there was Gramps actually complimenting Thigh-bolt after church. Shaking his hand, acting like he was some sort of hero while Ben stared up at Thigh-bolt with big puppy-dog eyes.

It was all he could do to make it through brunch without cracking open a beer, and since dropping Ben at his mother's, he'd already gone through four. He was pretty sure he'd finish off the twelve-pack before turning in. In the past two weeks, he'd had a lot of beer. He knew he was overdoing it, but it was the only thing that kept him from dwelling on the latest run-in with Thigh-bolt.

Behind him, the phone rang. Again. Fourth time in the last couple of hours, but he wasn't in the mood to answer it.

Okay, he admitted it. He had underestimated the guy. Thigh-bolt had been one step ahead of him from the very beginning. He used to think Ben knew how to press his buttons; this guy dropped bombs. No, Clayton thought suddenly, he didn't drop bombs. He directed cruise missiles with pinpoint accuracy, all geared toward the destruction of Clayton's life. Even worse, Clayton hadn't seen it coming. Not once.

It was beyond frustrating, especially since the situation seemed to be getting worse. Now, Thigh-bolt was *telling* him what to do.

Ordering him around, like he was some flunkie on payroll, and for the life of him, Clayton couldn't figure a way out. He wanted to believe that Thigh-bolt had been bluffing about videotaping the break-in. He had to be bluffing—no one was that smart. He had to be. But what if he wasn't?

Clayton went to the refrigerator and opened another beer, knowing he couldn't risk it. Who knew what the guy was planning next? He took a long pull, praying for the numbing effect to kick in soon.

This should have been easier to handle. He was a deputy sheriff, and the guy was new in town. Clayton should have had the power all along, but instead he found himself sitting in a messy kitchen because he hadn't wanted to ask Ben to clean it for fear the kid would tell Thigh-bolt, which just might spell the end of Clayton's life as he knew it.

What did the guy have against him? That's what Clayton wanted to know. Clayton wasn't the one causing problems, Thigh-bolt was the one making things difficult—and to rub salt in the wound, the guy was sleeping with Beth as well.

He took another drink, wondering how his life could have turned to crap so quickly. Sunk in misery, he barely registered the sound of someone knocking at the front door. He pushed back from the table and stumbled through the living room. When he opened the door, he saw Tony standing on the porch, looking like a drowned rat. As if everything else weren't bad enough, the worm was here.

Tony took a slight step back. "Whoa, dude. You okay? You smell like you've been drinking."

"What do you want, Tony?" He wasn't in the mood for this.

"I've been trying to call you, but you didn't pick up."

"Get to the point."

"I haven't seen you around much lately."

"I've been busy. And I'm busy now, so go away." He started to close the door, and Tony raised his hand.

"Wait! I have something to tell you," he whined. "It's important."

"What is it?"

"Do you remember when I called you? I don't know, it must have been a couple of months ago?"

"No."

"You remember. I called you from Decker's about this guy showing Beth's picture around?"

"And?"

"That's what I wanted to tell you." He pushed a clump of greasy hair out of his eyes. "I saw him again today. And I saw him talking to Beth."

"What are you talking about?"

"After church. He was talking to Beth and your grandfather. He was the dude on the piano today."

Despite the buzz, Clayton felt his head begin to clear. It came back to him vaguely at first, then sharper. That was the weekend Thigh-bolt had taken the camera and disk.

"You sure?"

"Yeah, I'm sure. I'd remember that dude anywhere."

"He had Beth's picture?"

"I already told you that. I saw it. I just thought it was weird, you know? And then I see them together today? I thought you'd want to know."

Clayton processed Tony's news. "I want you to tell me everything you can remember about the picture."

Tony the worm had a surprisingly good memory, and it didn't take long for Clayton to get the full story. That the picture was a few years old and had been taken at the fair. That Thigh-bolt didn't know her name. That Thigh-bolt was looking for her.

After Tony left, Clayton continued to ponder what he'd learned.

No way had Thigh-bolt been here five years ago and forgotten her name. So where did he get the picture? Had he walked across the country to find her? And if so, what did that mean?

That he'd stalked her?

He wasn't sure yet, but something wasn't right. And Beth, naive as usual, had allowed him not only into her bed, but into Ben's life as well.

He frowned. He didn't like it. He didn't like it at all, and he was pretty sure Beth wouldn't like it, either.

25

Thibault

So that's it, huh?"

Despite the canopy offered by the trees, Thibault was drenched by the time he and Ben reached the tree house. Water poured from the raincoat he was wearing, and his new pants were soaked below the knees. Inside his boots, his socks squished unpleasantly. Ben, on the other hand, was bundled from head to toe in a hooded rain suit; on his feet, he wore Nana's rubber boots. Aside from his face, Thibault doubted he even noticed the rain.

"This is how we reach it. It's awesome, isn't it?" Ben motioned to an oak tree on the near side of the creek. A series of nailed two-by-fours climbed the side of the trunk. "All we have to do is climb the tree ladder here so we can cross the bridge."

Thibault noticed with apprehension that the creek had already swollen to twice its normal size, and the water was moving fast.

Turning his attention to the small bridge, he saw that it was composed of three parts: A fraying rope bridge led from the oak tree on the near side toward a central landing station in the center of the creek that was supported by a four listing pillars; this landing was connected by another rope bridge section to the platform on the tree house. Thibault noticed the debris deposited around the pillars by the rushing waters. Though he hadn't previously inspected the bridge, he suspected that the relentless storms and rapid flow of water had weakened the landing's support. Before he could say anything, Ben had already scaled the tree ladder to the bridge.

Ben grinned at him from above. "C'mon! What are you waiting for?"

Thibault raised his arm to shield his face from the rain, feeling a sudden sense of dread. "I'm not sure this is a good idea—"

"Chicken!" Ben taunted. He started across, the bridge swaying from side to side as he ran.

"Wait!" Thibault shouted to no effect. By then, Ben had already reached the central landing.

Thibault climbed the tree ladder and stepped cautiously onto the rope bridge. The waterlogged boards sagged under his weight. As soon as Ben saw him coming, he scrambled up the last section to the tree house. Thibault's breath caught in his throat as Ben hopped up on the tree house's platform. It bowed under Ben's weight but held steady. Ben turned around, his grin wide.

"Come on back!" Thibault shouted. "I don't think the bridge will hold me."

"It'll hold. My grandpa built it!"

"Please, Ben?"

"Chicken!" Ben taunted again.

It was obvious that Ben considered the whole thing a game. Thibault took another look at the bridge, concluding that if he moved slowly, it might be safe. Ben had run—lots of torque and impact pressure. Would it hold the weight of Thibault's body?

With his first step, the boards, drenched and ancient, sagged under his weight. Dry rot, no doubt. Thibault's mind flashed on the photograph in his pocket. The creek swirled and spun, a torrent beneath his feet.

No time to lose. He walked slowly and reached the central landing, then started up the last suspended section of the rope bridge. Noting the rickety platform, he doubted it would support their combined weight simultaneously. In his pocket, the photograph felt as if it were on fire.

"I'll meet you inside," Thibault said, trying to sound offhand. "You don't have to wait in the rain for an old man like me."

Thankfully, Ben laughed and ducked into the tree house. Thibault breathed a sigh of relief as he made the shaky rise to the platform. He took a large, quick step to avoid the platform and stumbled into the tree house.

"This is where I keep my Pokémon cards," Ben said, ignoring his entrance and motioning to the tin boxes in the corner. "I've got a Charizard card. And a Mewtwo."

Thibault wiped the rain from his face as he collected himself and sat on the floor. "That's great," he said, puddles from his rain gear collecting around him.

He took in the tiny room. Toys lay heaped in the corners, and a cutout window exposed much of the interior to the elements, soaking the unsanded planks. The only piece of furniture was a single beanbag chair in the corner.

"This is my hideout," Ben said, collapsing into the chair.

"Yeah?"

"I come here when I get mad. Like when kids at school are mean."

Thibault leaned back against the wall, shaking the water from his sleeves. "What do they do?"

"Stuff. You know." He shrugged. "Teasing me about how I play basketball or kick ball or why I have to wear glasses."

"That must be hard."

"It doesn't bother me."

Ben didn't seem to notice his obvious contradiction, and Thibault went on. "What do you like most about being here?"

"The quiet," said Ben. "When I'm here, no one asks me questions or asks me to do stuff. I can sit here and think."

Thibault nodded. "Makes sense." Through the window, he could see the rising wind beginning to drive the rain sideways. The storm was getting worse.

"What do you think about?" he asked.

Ben shrugged. "Like growing up and stuff. Getting older." He paused. "I wish I was bigger."

"Why?"

"There's this kid in my class who always picks on me. He's mean. Yesterday, he pushed me down in the cafeteria."

The tree house rocked in a gust of wind. Again, the photo seemed to burn, and Thibault absently found his hand wandering to his pocket. He didn't understand the compulsion, but before he realized what he was doing, he pulled out the photo.

Outside, the wind continued to howl and he could hear branches slapping against the structure. With every passing minute, he knew, the rain was engorging the creek. All at once, an image arose of the tree house platform collapsing, with Ben trapped in the raging water beneath it.

"I want to give you something," Thibault said, the words out before he'd even consciously thought them. "I think it'll take care of your problem."

"What is it?"

Thibault swallowed. "It's a picture of your mom."

Ben took the photo and looked at it, his expression curious. "What do I do with it?"

Thibault leaned forward and tapped the corner of the photo. "Just carry it with you. My friend Victor called it a lucky charm. He said it's what kept me safe in Iraq."

"For real?"

That was the question, wasn't it? After a long moment, Thibault nodded. "I promise."

"Cool."

"Will you do me a favor?" Thibault asked.

"What?"

"Will you keep this between the two of us? And promise to keep it with you?"

Ben considered it. "Can I fold it?"

"I don't think it matters."

Ben thought about it. "Sure," he finally said, folding it over and slipping it into his pocket. "Thanks."

It was the first time in over five years that the photo had ever been farther from him than the distance to the shower or the sink, and the sense of loss disoriented him. Somehow, Thibault hadn't expected to feel its absence so acutely. As he watched Ben cross the bridge and he caught sight of the raging creek, the feeling only intensified. When Ben waved to him from the other side of the creek and began to descend the tree ladder, Thibault reluctantly stepped onto the platform, before moving onto the bridge as fast as he could.

He felt exposed as he crossed the bridge step by step, ignoring the certainty that the bridge would plunge into the creek, ignoring the fact that he no longer carried the photo. When he reached the oak tree on the other side, he breathed a shaky sigh of relief. Still, as he climbed down, he felt a nagging premonition that whatever he had come here for still wasn't over—and was, in fact, only beginning.

26

Beth

On Wednesday, Beth stared out her classroom window at lunchtime. She had never seen anything like it—hurricanes and nor'easters had nothing on the series of storms that had recently pounded Hampton County as well as every county from Raleigh to the coast. The problem was that unlike most tropical storms, these weren't passing quickly out to sea. Instead, they had lingered day after thunderous day, bringing nearly every river in the eastern part of the state to flood levels. Small towns along the Pamlico, Neuse, and Cape Fear rivers were already knee-deep in water, and Hampton was getting close. Another day or two of rain would mean that most of the businesses downtown would be reachable only by canoe.

The county had already decided to close the schools for the rest of the week, since the school buses could no longer make their routes and only a little more than half the teachers had been able to make it in. Ben, of course, was thrilled by the idea of staying home and playing in the puddles with Zeus, but Beth was a little more leery. Both the newspapers and the local news had reported that while the South River had already risen to dangerous levels, it was going to get far worse before it got better as the creeks and tributaries fed the rise. The two creeks that surrounded the kennel, usually a quarter mile away, could now be seen from the windows of the house, and Logan was even keeping Zeus away because of the debris washed out with the deluge.

Being trapped indoors was hard on the kids, which was one of the reasons she'd stayed in her classroom. After lunch, they'd return to their classrooms, where in theory they'd happily color or draw or read quietly in lieu of playing kick ball or basketball or tag outside. In reality, kids needed to get their energy out, and she knew it. For years, she'd been asking that on days like this, they simply fold up the cafeteria lunch tables and allow the kids to run or play for twenty minutes, so they could concentrate when they returned to class after lunch. Not a chance, she was told, because of regulatory issues, liability issues, janitorial union issues, and health and safety issues. When asked what that meant, she was given a long explanation, but to her, it all came down to French fries. As in, *We shouldn't allow kids to slip on French fries*, or, *If they do slip on French fries, the school district will get sued*, or, *The janitors would have to renegotiate their contract if they didn't clean the French fries from the cafeteria at the time they were scheduled to do so*, and finally, *If someone slipped on a French fry that had fallen on the floor, the children might be exposed to harmful pathogens*.

Welcome to the world of lawyers, she thought. Lawyers, after all, didn't have to teach the kids after keeping them cooped up inside the classroom all day with no recess.

Usually, she would have retreated to the teacher's lounge for lunch, but with so little time to set up the classroom for activities, she'd decided to stay and get things ready. In the corner, she was setting up a beanbag-tossing game—stored in the closet for just such emergencies—when she noted movement from the doorway. She turned that way, and it took her an instant to register who it was. The shoulders of his uniform were wet, and a few water droplets dripped from the belt where he stored his gun. In his hand was a manila file.

"Hi, Beth," he said. His voice was quiet. "Do you have a minute?"

She stood. "What is it, Keith?"

"I came to apologize," he said. He clasped his hands in front of him, the picture of contrition. "I know you don't have a lot of time, but I wanted to talk to you when you were alone. I took a chance that you'd be here, but if it's not a good time, maybe we could set up another time that's better for you."

She glanced at the clock. "I've got five minutes," she said.

Keith stepped into the classroom and started to close the door. Midway, he paused, seeking her permission. She nodded, wanting to get whatever he had to say over with. He moved toward her, stopping at a respectful distance.

"Like I said, I came here to tell you I was sorry."

"About what?"

"About the rumors you heard," he said. "I wasn't completely truthful with you."

She crossed her arms. "In other words, you lied," she stated.

"Yes."

"You lied to my face."

"Yes."

"About what?"

"You asked if I ever ran off some of the guys you've dated in the past. I don't think I did, but I didn't tell you that I did talk to some of them."

"You *talked* to them."

"Yes."

She did her best to keep her anger in check. "And . . . what? You're sorry you did it, or sorry you lied?"

"Both. I'm sorry I did it, I'm sorry I lied. I shouldn't have done those things." He paused. "I know we haven't had the greatest relationship since the divorce, and I also know that you think marrying me was a mistake. You're right about that. We weren't meant to be married, and I accept that. But between the two of us—and I'll be honest, you've had a lot more to do with this than me—we have a great son. You might not think I'm the best father in the world, but I've never once regretted having Ben, or having Ben live with you most of the time. He's a great kid, and you've done a great job with him."

She wasn't sure what to say. In the silence, he went on.

"But I still worry, and I always have. Like I told you, I worry about who comes into Ben's life, whether it be friends, or acquaintances, or even people that you might introduce to him. I know that's not fair and that you probably consider it an intrusion into your personal life, but that's the way I am. And to be honest, I don't know if I'm ever going to change."

"So you're saying that you'll keep following me forever?"

"No," he said quickly. "I won't do it again. I was just explaining why I did it before. And trust me—I didn't threaten those guys or try to intimidate them. I *talked* to them. I explained that Ben meant a lot to me and that being his father was the most important thing in my life. You may not always agree with the way I parent him, but if you think back a couple of years, it wasn't always like this. He used to enjoy coming over to my place. Now he doesn't. But I haven't changed. He's changed. Not in a bad way—growing up is normal, and that's all he's been doing. And maybe I need to realize and accept the fact that he's getting older."

She said nothing. As Keith watched her, he drew a long breath. "I also told those men that I didn't want you to get hurt. I know that might sound like I was being possessive, but I wasn't. I said it like a brother would have said it. Like Drake would have said it. As in, if you like her, if you respect her, just make sure you treat her that way. That's all I said to them." He shrugged. "I don't know. Maybe some of them took it the wrong way because I'm a deputy or because of my last name, but I can't help those things. Believe me, the last thing I want is for you to be unhappy. It might not have worked out between us, but you're the mother of my son and you always will be."

Keith's gaze fell as he shuffled his feet. "You have every reason to be angry with me. I was wrong."

"Yes, you were." Beth remained where she stood, arms crossed.

"Like I said, I'm sorry and it's never going to happen again."

She didn't respond right away. "Okay," she finally said. "I'm going to hold you to that."

He flashed a quick, almost defeated smile. "Fair enough."

"Is that it?" She bent to retrieve three beanbags from the closet floor.

"Actually, I also wanted to talk to you about Logan Thibault. There's something you should know about him."

She held up her hands to stop him. "Don't even go there."

He wasn't dissuaded. Instead, he took a step forward, kneading the brim of his hat. "I'm not going to talk to him unless you want me to talk to him. I want to make that clear. Believe me, Beth. This is serious. I wouldn't be here if it wasn't. I'm here because I care about you."

His chutzpah nearly took her breath away. "Do you honestly expect me to believe you have my best interests at heart after admitting that you've been spying on me for years? And that you were responsible for ruining any chance I had of finding a relationship?"

"This has nothing to do with those things."

"Let me guess . . . you think he's using drugs, right?"

"I have no idea. But I should warn you that he hasn't been honest with you."

"You have no idea whether he's been honest with me. Now get out. I don't want to talk to you, I don't want to hear what you have to say—"

"Then ask him yourself," Clayton interrupted. "Ask him whether he came to Hampton to find you."

"I'm done," she declared, moving toward the door. "And if you so much as touch me on the way out, I'm going to scream for help."

She walked past him, and as she was about to cross the threshold, Keith sighed audibly.

"Ask him about the photograph," he said.

His comment brought her to a halt. "What?"

Keith's expression was as serious as she'd ever seen it. "The photograph he got from Drake."

27

Clayton

Clayton knew by her expression that he had her attention but wasn't sure she understood the implications.

"He has a photograph of you," he went on, "and when he first got to town, he flashed it around Decker's Pool Hall. Tony was there that night and he saw it. Actually, he called me right away because he thought the guy's story sounded weird, but I didn't think much of it. Last weekend, though, Tony came by to tell me that he recognized Thibault when he was playing the piano at church."

Beth could only stare at him.

"I don't know if Drake gave it to him, or if he took it from Drake. But I figure that's the only thing that makes sense. Both Drake and Thibault were in the marines, and according to Tony, the picture was an older one, taken a few years ago."

He hesitated. "I know that what I told you about the way I behaved might make it seem like I'm trying to run him off, but I'm not going to talk to him. I do think that you should, however, and I'm not saying this because I'm your ex-husband. I'm saying this as a deputy sheriff."

Beth wanted to walk away but couldn't seem to find the will to move.

"Think about it. He had a picture of you, and based only on

that, he walked across the country to find you. I don't know why, but I can make a pretty good guess. He was obsessed with you even though you'd never met, like someone who gets obsessed with movie stars. And what did he do? He hunted you down, but seeing you from afar—or simply meeting you—wasn't enough. Instead, he had to become part of your life. That's what dangerous stalkers do, Beth."

His tone was calm and professional, which only intensified the dread she'd begun to feel.

"By your expression, I know that all of this is news to you. You're wondering if I'm telling the truth or if I'm lying, and my track record isn't perfect. But, please, for Ben's sake—for your own sake—ask him about it. I can be there if you want me to be there, or I could even send another deputy if you'd prefer that. Or you can call someone else—your friend Melody. I just want you to understand how serious this is. How . . . creepy and weird this is. This is scary stuff, and I can't impress on you enough how important it is that you take it seriously, too."

His mouth was set in a straight line as he set the file on a child's desk beside him. "This is some general information on Logan Thibault. I didn't have time to dig too deep, and I can get in big trouble for even letting you see this, but since I don't know what else he hasn't told you . . ." He trailed off before looking up at her again.

"Think about what I told you. And be careful, okay?"

28

Beth

She could barely see through the windshield, but this time it had less to do with the rain than her inability to concentrate. After Keith had left, she kept blinking in confusion as she stared at the file, trying to make sense of the things her ex had told her.

Logan had Drake's photograph . . . Logan had become obsessed with her . . . Logan had decided to seek her out . . . Logan had hunted her down.

She found it hard to breathe, and it had been all she could do to go to the office and tell the principal that she had to go home. The principal had taken one look at her face and agreed, offering to cover her class the rest of the afternoon. Nana would pick up Ben after school, Beth informed him.

On the drive home, her mind flashed from one image to the next, a kaleidoscope of sight and sound and smell. She tried to convince herself that Keith was lying, grasping for a way to rationalize his news. It was possible, especially considering the way he'd lied in the past, and yet . . .

Keith had been serious. More professional than personal, and he'd told her something she could easily check. He knew she would ask Logan about it . . . he *wanted* her to ask Logan . . . which meant . . .

She squeezed the wheel, possessed by a feverish need to talk to Logan. He would clear this up. He had to be able to clear this up.

Water from the river now stretched across the road, but in her preoccupied state, she didn't realize it until she plowed into the water. She jerked forward as the car almost came to a stop. The river flowed around her, and she thought the water would stall the engine, but the car continued to roll forward into ever deeper water, before finally emerging in a shallower patch.

By the time Beth reached the house, she wasn't even sure what to feel, other than confused. One instant she felt angry and betrayed and manipulated; in the next, she was able to convince herself that it couldn't be true, that Keith had lied to her again.

As she came up the drive, she found herself scanning the rain-swept grounds for Logan.

Up ahead, through low-hanging mist, she could see lights on in the house. She considered going in to talk to Nana, longing for Nana's clarity and common sense to straighten everything out. But when she saw the lights on in the office and noted the propped-open door, she felt something catch in her throat. She turned the wheel in the direction of the office, telling herself that Logan didn't have the picture, that the whole thing had been a mistake. She bounced through muddy puddles, the rain coming so hard now that the wipers couldn't keep up. On the office porch, she saw Zeus lying near the door, his head raised.

She pulled to a stop out front and ran for the porch, rain stinging her face. Zeus approached her, nosing at her hand. She ignored him as she walked inside, expecting to find Logan at the desk.

He wasn't there. The door that led from the office to the kennel stood open. She steeled herself, pausing in the middle of the office, as shadows moved in the darkened corridor. She waited as Logan emerged into the light.

"Hey, Elizabeth," he said. "I didn't expect to see you . . ." He trailed off. "What happened?"

Staring at him, she felt her emotions threaten to boil over. Her mouth suddenly felt papery dry, and she didn't know how to start or what to say. Logan said nothing, sensing her volatile state.

She closed her eyes, feeling on the verge of tears, then drew a careful breath. "Why did you come to Hampton?" she finally asked. "I want the truth this time."

He didn't move. "I told you the truth," he said.

"Did you tell me everything?"

He hesitated for a fraction of a second before answering. "I've never lied to you," he said, his voice quiet.

"That's not what I asked!" she snapped. "I asked if you've been hiding anything!"

He appraised her carefully. "Where's this coming from?"

"That doesn't matter!" This time, she heard the anger in her tone. "I just want to know why you came to Hampton!"

"I told you—"

"Do you have a picture of me?"

Logan said nothing.

"Answer the question!" She took a step toward him, biting out the words. "Do you have a picture of me?"

She wasn't sure how she expected him to react, but other than a soft exhale, he didn't flinch.

"Yes," he said.

"The one I gave Drake?"

"Yes," he said again.

With his answer, she felt her whole world begin to topple like a row of dominoes. All at once, everything made sense—the way he'd stared at her when they first met, the reason he was willing to work for such a low wage, why he'd befriended Nana and Ben, and all his talk about destiny. . . .

He had the photo. He'd come to Hampton to find her. He'd tracked her down like prey.

All at once, it was difficult to breathe.

"Oh, my God."

"It's not what you think. . . ."

He stretched his hand toward her, and she absently watched it draw closer before she finally realized what was happening. With a start, she reeled back, desperate to put more space between them. All of it had been a lie. . . .

"Don't touch me!"

"Elizabeth . . ."

"My name is Beth!"

She stared at him as if he were a stranger until he lowered his arm.

His voice was a whisper when he tried again. "I can explain—"

"Explain what?" she demanded. "That you stole the picture from my brother? That you walked across the country to find me? That you fell in love with an image . . ."

"It wasn't like that," he said, shaking his head.

She didn't hear him. All she could do was stare at him, wondering if anything he'd said was true.

"You stalked me . . . ," she said, almost as if talking to herself. "You *lied* to me. You *used* me."

"You don't understand . . ."

"Understand? You want me to *understand?*"

"I didn't steal the photo," he said. His voice remained steady and even. "I found the photo in Kuwait, and I posted it on a bulletin board where I thought it would be claimed. But no one ever claimed it."

"And so . . . you took it back?" She shook her head in disbelief. "Why? Because you had some sick and twisted idea about me?"

"No," he said, his voice rising for the first time. The sound startled her, slowing her thoughts, if only for an instant. "I came here because I owed you."

"You owed me?" She blinked. "What does that even mean?"

"The photo . . . it saved me."

Though she heard him plainly, she couldn't comprehend the words. She waited for more, and in the steady silence that followed, she realized she found them . . . *chilling* somehow. The hairs on her arms prickled, and she took another step back. "Who are you?" she hissed. "What do you want from me?"

"I don't want anything. And you know who I am."

"No, I don't! I don't know anything about you!"

"Let me explain . . ."

"Then explain why if this was all so pure and true that you didn't tell me about the photograph when you first came here!" she shouted, her voice echoing in the room. In her mind's eye, she saw Drake and all the details of the night the photo was taken. She pointed a finger at him. "Why didn't you say, 'I found this in Iraq and I figured you might want it back'? Why didn't you tell me when we were talking about Drake?"

"I don't know. . . ."

"It wasn't your photo to keep! Don't you get that? It wasn't meant for you! It was for my brother, not for you! It was his and you had no right to keep it from me!"

Logan's voice was almost a whisper. "I didn't mean to hurt you."

Her eyes bored into him, piercing him with the force of her rage.

"This whole thing is a sham, isn't it? You found this photo and came up with some . . . twisted fantasy in which you could play the starring role. You played me from the moment we met! You took your time to find out what you could do to make it seem like you were the perfect guy for me. And you thought that because you were obsessed with me, you could trick me into falling in love with you."

She saw Logan flinch at her words, and she went on.

"You planned all this from the very beginning! It's sick and it's wrong and I can't believe I fell for it."

He rocked back slightly on his heels, stunned by her words.

"I admit that I wanted to meet you," he said, "but you're wrong about the reason. I didn't come here to trick you into falling in love with me. I know it sounds crazy, but I came to believe that the photograph kept me safe from harm and that . . . I owed you somehow, even if I didn't know what that meant or what would come of it. But I didn't plan anything after I got here. I took the job, and then I fell in love with you."

Her expression didn't soften as he spoke. Instead, she slowly began to shake her head.

"Can you even hear what you're saying?"

"I knew you wouldn't believe it. That's why I didn't tell you—"

"Don't try to justify your lies! You got caught up in some sick fantasy and you won't even admit it."

"Stop calling it that!" he shouted back. "You're the one who's not listening. You're not even trying to understand what I'm saying!"

"Why should I try to understand? You've been lying to me since the beginning. You've been using me since the beginning."

"I haven't used you," he said, forcing his back straight, regaining his composure. "And I didn't lie about the photo. I just didn't tell you about it because I didn't know how to tell you in a way that wouldn't make you think I was crazy."

She raised her hands. "Don't even think of blaming this on me. You're the one who lied! You're the one who kept secrets! I told you everything! I gave my heart to you! I let my son become attached to you!" she shouted. As she went on, her voice broke and she could feel the tears beginning to form. "I went to bed with you because I thought you were someone I could trust. But now I know that I can't. Can you imagine how that makes me feel? To know this whole thing was some sort of charade?"

His voice was soft. "Please, Elizabeth . . . Beth . . . just listen."

"I don't want to listen! I've already been lied to enough."

"Don't be like this."

"You want me to listen?" she screamed. "Listen to what? That you obsessed over a picture and came to find me because you believe it kept you safe? That's insane, and the most disturbing thing is, you don't even recognize that your explanation only makes you sound psychotic!"

He stared at her, and she saw his jaw clench shut.

She felt a shudder run through her. She was done with this. Done with him. "I want it back," she gritted out. "I want the photo that I gave to Drake."

When he didn't respond, she reached over to the window ledge and grabbed a small flower pot. She threw it at him, shouting, "Where is it? I want it!"

Logan ducked as the pot whizzed overhead and crashed into the wall behind him. For the first time, Zeus barked in confusion.

"It's not yours!" she shouted.

Logan stood straight again. "I don't have it."

"Where is it?" she demanded

Logan paused before answering. "I gave it to Ben," he admitted.

Her eyes narrowed. "Get out."

Logan paused before finally moving toward the door. Beth stepped away, keeping her distance from him. Zeus swiveled his gaze from Logan to Beth and back again before padding slowly after Logan.

At the door, Logan stopped and turned toward her.

"I swear on my life I didn't come here to fall in love with you, or try to make you fall in love with me. But I did."

She stared at him. "I told you to go and I meant it."

With that, he turned and strode out into the storm.

29

Thibault

Despite the rain, Thibault couldn't imagine going back to his house. He wanted to be outside; it didn't feel right to be warm and dry. He wanted to purge himself of what he had done, of all the lies he had told.

She'd been right: He hadn't been honest with her. Despite the hurt he felt at some of the things she'd said and her unwillingness to listen, she had been justified in feeling betrayed. But how to explain? He didn't fully understand why he'd come, even when he tried to put it into words. He could see why she interpreted his actions as those of an obsessed madman. And, yes, he was obsessed, just not in the way she imagined.

He should have told her about the photograph as soon as he'd arrived, and he struggled to remember why he hadn't done so. Odds were, she would have been surprised and asked a few questions, but it would have ended at that. He suspected that Nana would have hired him anyway, and then none of this would have happened.

More than anything, he wanted to turn around and go back to her. He wanted to explain, to tell his whole story from the beginning.

He wouldn't, though. She needed time alone—or at least time

away from him. Time to recover and maybe, just maybe, under-stand that the Thibault she'd come to care for was the only Thibault there was. He wondered whether time alone would bring forgiveness.

Thibault sank in the mud; he noted as a car passed slowly that the water reached its axles. Up ahead, he saw the river stretching across the road. He decided to cut through the woods. Perhaps this would be the last time he would make this walk. Perhaps it was time to return to Colorado.

Thibault moved forward. The autumn foliage, still hanging on, provided partial cover from the rain, and as he walked deeper into the woods, he felt the distance between them grow with each step he took.

30

Beth

Freshly showered, Beth was standing in her bedroom in an oversize T-shirt when Nana peeked her head in.

"Do you want to talk about it?" Nana said. She jerked her thumb toward the window. "The school called to tell me you were on your way home. The principal seemed a little worried about you, and later I saw you pull up to the office. I figured the two of you were having a spat."

"It's more than a spat, Nana," Beth said, her tone weary.

"That I gathered from the fact that he left. And that you stayed on the porch so long afterwards."

Beth nodded.

"Was it about Ben? He didn't hurt him, did he? Or you?"

"No, nothing like that," Beth said.

"Good. Because that's the one thing that can't be fixed."

"I'm not sure this can, either."

Nana stared out the window before heaving a great sigh. "I take it I'll have to feed the dogs tonight, huh?"

Beth shot her a look of annoyance. "Thanks for being so understanding."

"Kitty cats and maple trees," she said with a wave of her hand.

Beth thought about it before finally grunting in frustration. "What does that mean?"

"It means nothing, but for a second there, you were too exasperated to feel sorry for yourself."

"You don't understand. . . ."

"Try me," she said.

Beth looked up. "He stalked me, Nana. For five years, and then he trekked across the country to search for me. He was obsessed."

Nana was uncharacteristically silent. "Why don't you start from the beginning," she suggested, taking a seat on Beth's bed.

Beth wasn't sure she wanted to talk about it, but she figured it was better to get it over with. She began by recounting Keith's visit to her classroom, and over the next twenty minutes, she told Nana about her abrupt departure from school, her agonizing uncertainty, and ended with her confrontation with Logan. When she finished, Nana folded her hands together in her lap.

"So Thibault admitted he had the picture? And—in your words—babbled about it being a lucky charm and claimed that he came here because he felt that he owed you something?"

Beth nodded. "Pretty much."

"What did he mean by it being a lucky charm?"

"I don't know."

"You didn't ask?"

"I didn't care, Nana. The whole thing is . . . creepy and weird. Who would do something like that?"

Nana's eyebrows knit together. "I'll admit it sounds strange, but I think I would have wanted to know why he believed it was a lucky charm."

"Why does that matter?"

"Because you weren't there," she emphasized. "You didn't go through the things he did. Maybe he was telling the truth."

Beth winced. "The picture isn't a lucky charm. That's crazy."

"Maybe," Nana responded, "but I've been around long enough to know that strange things happen in war. Soldiers come to believe all sorts of things, and if they think something keeps them safe, what's the harm?"

Beth exhaled. "It's one thing to believe it. It's entirely different to become obsessed with a photograph and stalk the subject."

Nana put a hand on Beth's knee. "Everyone acts crazy at times."

"Not like this," Beth insisted. "There's something scary about this."

Nana was quiet before letting out a sigh. "You might be right." She shrugged.

Beth studied Nana's face, suddenly overcome with exhaustion. "Will you do me a favor?"

"What is it?"

"Will you call the principal and ask him to bring Ben home after school? I don't want you driving in this weather, but I'm not really up to doing it myself."

31

Clayton

Clayton tried and failed to negotiate the lake that had formed in front of Beth's house, his boots disappearing into the mud. He stifled the urge to issue a string of profanities. He could see the windows open near the front door, and he knew that Nana would hear him. Despite her age, the woman had the hearing of an owl, and the last thing he wanted to do was make a poor impression. The woman already disliked him enough.

He climbed the steps and knocked on the door. He thought he heard someone moving inside, saw Beth's face in the window, and finally watched as the door swung open.

"Keith? What are you doing here?"

"I was worried," he said. "I wanted to make sure everything was okay."

"It's fine," she said.

"Is he still here? Do you want me to talk to him?"

"No. He's gone. I don't know where he is."

Clayton shuffled his feet, trying to look contrite. "I'm sorry about this, and I hate that I had to be the one to tell you. I know you really liked him."

Beth nodded, her lips pursed.

"I also wanted to tell you not to be so hard on yourself. Like I mentioned earlier, people like that . . . they've learned to hide it. They're sociopaths, and there's no way you could have known."

Beth crossed her arms. "I don't want to talk about it."

Clayton held up his hands, knowing he'd pushed too hard, knowing he had to backtrack. "I figured. And you're right. It's not my place, especially given the crappy way I've treated you in the past." He tucked his thumb into his belt and forced a smile. "I just wanted to make sure you were doing okay."

"I'm fine. And thanks."

Clayton turned to leave, then stopped. "I want you to know that from what Ben said, Thibault seemed like a nice guy."

She looked up in surprise.

"I just wanted to tell you that, because had it been different—had anything happened to Ben—Thibault would have regretted the day he was born. I would die before I let anything happen to our son. And I know you feel the same way. That's why you're such a great mom. In a life where I've made a ton of mistakes, one of the best things I've done is to let you raise him."

She nodded, trying to stop the tears, and turned away. When she swiped at her eyes, Clayton took a step toward her.

"Hey," he said, his voice soft. "I know you don't want to hear this now, but trust me, you did the right thing. And in time, you're going to find someone, and I'm sure he's going to be the best guy ever. You deserve that."

Her breath hiccuped, and Clayton reached out for her. Instinctively, she leaned into him. "It's okay," he whispered, and for a long moment, they stood on the porch, their bodies close together as he held her.

Clayton didn't stay long. There was no need, he thought: He'd accomplished what he'd set out to do. Beth now saw him as the kind, caring, and compassionate friend, someone who'd atoned for his sins. The hug was just the icing on the cake—nothing he'd planned, but a nice conclusion to their encounter.

He wouldn't press her. That would be a mistake. She needed some time to get over Thigh-bolt. Even if he was a sociopath, even if the guy left town, feelings aren't turned on and off like a switch. But they would pass as surely as the rain would continue to fall. Next step: to make sure that Thigh-bolt was on his way back to Colorado.

And then? Be the nice guy. Maybe invite Beth over while he and Ben were doing something, ask her to stay for a barbecue. Keep it casual at first, so she didn't suspect anything, and then suggest doing something with Ben on another night of the week. It was essential that he keep the whole thing far from Nana's prying eyes, which meant staying away from here. Though he knew Beth wouldn't be thinking straight for at least a few weeks, Nana would be, and the last thing he wanted was for Nana to get in Beth's ear about what he was likely up to.

After that, as they got used to each other again, maybe they'd have a few beers together while Ben was sacked out, sort of a spur-of-the-moment thing. Maybe spike her beer with a bit of vodka so she couldn't drive home. Then offer to let her sleep in the bed while he took the couch. Be the perfect gentleman, but keep the beer flowing. Talk about the old times—the good ones—and let her cry about Thigh-bolt. Let the emotions flow and slip a comforting arm around her.

He smiled as he started the car, pretty sure he knew what would happen after that.

32

Beth

Beth didn't sleep well and woke up exhausted.

The storm had hit in full fury last night, bringing heavy winds and massive amounts of rain, dwarfing the previous deluge. The day before, she couldn't have imagined the water getting any deeper, but when she looked out the window, the office looked like an isolated island in the midst of the ocean. Last night, she'd pulled her car onto a spit of higher land near the magnolia tree; good thing, she realized now. It, too, was its own little island, while the water nearly reached the high floorboards of Nana's truck. The truck had always managed well in floods, but it was a good thing that the brakes had been fixed. Otherwise they would have been stranded.

Last night, she'd taken it into town to buy a gallon of milk and a few other basic necessities, but the trip had been pointless. Everything was closed, and the only other vehicles that she'd seen on the road were utility trucks and SUVs driven by the sheriff's department. Half the town was without power, but so far their house was unaffected. If there was one bright spot, it was that TV and radio reports predicted the last of the storms would roll through today; tomorrow, hopefully, the water would begin to recede.

She sat in the porch swing outside while Nana and Ben were

playing gin rummy at the kitchen table. It was the one game in which they were equally matched, and it kept Ben from getting bored. Later, she figured she'd let him splash around in the front yard while she went to check on the dogs. She'd probably give up any attempt to keep him dry and simply let him wear his swimsuit; when she'd gone out earlier in the morning to feed the dogs, her raincoat had been useless.

Listening to the sound of the rain drumming steadily on the roof, she found her thoughts drifting to Drake. She wished for the thousandth time that she could talk to him and wondered what he would have said about the photograph. Had he, too, believed in its power? Drake had never been particularly superstitious, but her heart lurched every time she recalled his inexplicable panic at the loss of the photo.

Nana was right. She didn't know what Drake had experienced over there, and she didn't know what Logan had, either. As informed as she tried to be, none of it felt real to her. She wondered about the stress they felt, thousands of miles from home, wearing flak jackets, living among people who spoke a foreign language, trying to stay alive. Was it impossible to believe that anyone would latch on to something he believed would keep him safe?

No, she decided. It was no different from carrying a St. Christopher medal or a rabbit's foot. It didn't matter that there was nothing logical about it—logic didn't matter. Nor did an absolute belief in magic powers. If it made someone feel safer, it simply did.

But tracking her down? Stalking her?

That's where her understanding broke down. As skeptical as she was about Keith's intentions—or even his attempt to appear genuinely concerned for her well-being —she had to admit that the situation made her feel acutely vulnerable.

What had Logan said? Something about owing her? For his life, she assumed, but how?

She shook her head, drained by the thoughts chasing endlessly through her mind. She looked up when she heard the door creak open.

"Hey, Mom?"

"Yeah, sweetie."

Ben came over and took a seat beside her. "Where's Thibault? I haven't seen him yet."

"He's not coming in," she said.

"Because of the storm?"

She hadn't told him yet, nor was she ready to. "He had some things to do," she improvised.

"Okay," Ben said. He looked out into the yard. "You can't even see the grass anymore."

"I know. But the rain's supposed to stop soon."

"Has it ever been like this before? When you were little?"

"A couple of times. But always with a hurricane."

He nodded before pushing his glasses up. She ran a hand through his hair.

"I heard Logan gave you something."

"I'm not supposed to talk about it," he said, his voice serious. "It's a secret."

"You can tell your mom. I'm good at keeping secrets."

"Nice try," he teased. "I'm not falling for that one."

She smiled and leaned back, pushing the swing into motion with her feet. "That's okay. I already know about the picture."

Ben looked over at her, wondering how much she knew.

"You know," she went on, "for protection?"

His shoulders slumped. "He told you?"

"Of course."

"Oh," he said, his disappointment evident. "He told me to keep it between the two of us."

"Do you have it? I'd like to see it if you do."

Ben hesitated before reaching into his pocket. He pulled out a folded snapshot and handed it over. Beth opened the photo and stared, feeling a surge of memories overtake her: her last weekend with Drake and the conversation they'd had, the sight of the Ferris wheel, the shooting star.

"Did he say anything else when he gave it to you?" she asked, handing the photo back to him. "Aside from it being a secret, I mean?"

"He said his friend Victor called it a lucky charm, and that it kept him safe in Iraq."

She felt her pulse pick up tempo, and she brought her face close to Ben's.

"Did you say Victor called it a lucky charm?"

"Uh-huh." Ben nodded. "That's what he said."

"Are you sure?"

"Of course I'm sure."

Beth stared at her son, feeling at war with herself.

33

Thibault

Thibault loaded his backpack with the few provisions he had in the house. The wind was gusting and the rain still coming down hard, but he'd walked through worse weather before. Still, he couldn't seem to summon the energy he needed to walk out the door.

It had been one thing to walk here; it was different to walk away. He was different. He'd left Colorado feeling more alone than he'd ever felt before; here, his life seemed full and complete. Or it had until yesterday.

Zeus was finally settled in the corner. He'd spent most of the day pacing, restless because Thibault hadn't taken him for his walk. Every time Thibault got up to get a glass of water, Zeus scrambled to his feet, anxious to know if it was time to go.

It was midafternoon, but the cloudy, rainy sky made it darker. The storm continued to lash the house, but he sensed it was in its dying stages; like a recently caught fish flopping on the dock, it wasn't going to go quietly.

He spent most of the day trying not to think about what had happened or how it all could have been avoided: that was a fool's game. He had messed it up, simple as that, and the past couldn't be undone. He'd always tried to live his life without dwelling on things that couldn't be undone, but this was different. He wasn't sure he'd ever get over it.

At the same time, he couldn't shake the feeling that it wasn't yet over, that something remained unfinished. Was it simply closure that he was missing? No, it was more than that; his wartime experience had taught him to trust his instincts, even though he'd never been sure where they'd come from. Inasmuch as he knew he should leave Hampton, if only to get as far away from Keith Clayton as possible—he was under no illusions that Clayton would forgive and forget—he couldn't bring himself to walk out the door.

Clayton was the center of the wheel. Clayton—and Ben and Elizabeth—was the reason he had come. He just couldn't figure out why or what he was supposed to do.

In the corner, Zeus rose to his feet and headed toward the window. Thibault turned toward him just as he heard a knock at the door. Instinctively he tensed, but when Zeus peeked through the glass, his tail started to wag.

When Thibault opened the door, he saw Elizabeth standing before him. He froze. For a moment, they simply stared at each other.

"Hi, Logan," she fnally said.

"Hello, Elizabeth."

A tentative smile, so quick as to be almost nonexistent, flashed across her features. He wondered whether he'd imagined it.

"May I come in?"

Thibault stepped aside, studying her as she removed her slicker, her blond hair spilling out of the hood. She held it out uncertainly until Thibault took it from her. He hung it on the front-door knob before facing her.

"I'm glad you came," he said.

She nodded. Zeus nosed her hand, and she stroked him behind the ears before turning her attention to Thibault again.

"Can we talk?" she said.

"If you'd like." He motioned to the couch, and Elizabeth took a seat on one end. He took a seat on the other.

"Why did you give the photo to Ben?" she asked without preamble.

Thibault studied the far wall, trying to figure out how to explain himself without making things even worse. Where to begin?

"Tell me in ten words or less," she suggested, sensing his reticence. "Then we'll go from there."

Thibault massaged his forehead with one hand before sighing, his eyes moving toward her. "Because I thought it would keep him safe."

"Safe?"

"Out at the tree house. The storm has weakened the whole structure, including the bridge. He shouldn't go there again. It's on the verge of collapse."

Her gaze was intense and unblinking. "Why didn't you keep it?"

"Because I felt like he needed it more than me."

"Because it would keep him safe."

Thibault nodded. "Yes."

She fiddled with the couch cover before turning toward him again. "So you honestly believe what you said? About the photo being a lucky charm?"

Zeus walked toward him and lay at his feet. "Maybe," Thibault said.

She leaned forward. "Why don't you tell me the whole story?"

Thibault gazed at the floor, resting his elbows on his knees, and began, hesitantly, to tell her the whole saga of the photograph. He started with the poker games in Kuwait, then moved on to the RPG that knocked him unconscious and the firefight in Fallujah. He detailed the car bombs and the IEDs he'd survived in Ramadi, including the one in which Victor claimed that the photograph had saved both their lives. He talked about the reaction of his fellow marines and the legacy of their distrust.

He paused before meeting her eyes.

"But even after all that, I still didn't believe it. But Victor did. He always had. He believed in that kind of stuff, and I humored him because it was important to him. But I never believed it, at least not consciously." He clasped his hands together, his voice becoming softer. "On our last weekend together, Victor told me that I owed a debt to the woman in the photo because the photo had kept me safe—that otherwise, there was no balance. It was my destiny to find her, he said. A few minutes later, Victor was dead, but I escaped unharmed. Even then, I didn't believe it. But then, I began to see his ghost."

In a halting voice, he told her about those encounters, reluctant to meet her gaze for fear of seeing utter disbelief there. In the end, he shook his head and sighed. "After that, the rest is just like I told you. I was messed up, so I took off. Yes, I went to find you, but not because I'd been obsessed with you. Not because I loved you or wanted you to love me. I did it because Victor said it was my destiny, and I kept seeing his ghost. I didn't know what to expect when I got here. And then, somewhere along the way, it became a challenge—whether I could find you, how long it would take me. When I finally arrived at the kennel and saw the 'Help Wanted' sign, I guess I thought that would be a way to repay the debt. Applying for the job felt like the right thing to do. Just like when Ben and I were in the tree house; giving the photo to him felt like the right thing to do. But I'm not sure I could explain those things even if I tried."

"You gave Ben the photo to keep him safe," Elizabeth repeated.

"As crazy as it sounds? Yes."

She digested this in silence. Then: "Why didn't you tell me from the beginning?"

"I should have," he said. "The only thing I can think is that I carried the photo with me for five years, and I didn't want to give it up until I understood its purpose."

"Do you think you understand it now?"

He leaned over to pet Zeus before answering. He looked directly at her. "I'm not sure. What I can say is that what happened between us, everything that happened, didn't start when I found the photo. It started when I walked into the kennel. That was when you first became real to me, and the more I got to know you, the more real *I* felt. Happier and alive in a way I hadn't felt in a long, long time. Like you and I were meant to be."

"Your destiny?" She lifted an eyebrow.

"No . . . not like that. It has nothing to do with the photo, or the journey here, or anything Victor said. It's just that I've never met anyone like you before, and I'm certain I never will again. I love you, Elizabeth . . . and more than that, I *like* you. I enjoy spending time with you."

She scrutinized him, her expression unreadable. When she spoke, her voice was matter-of-fact. "You realize that it's still a crazy story that makes you sound like an obsessive nut job."

"I know," Thibault agreed. "Believe me, I feel like a freak even to myself."

"What if I told you to leave Hampton and never contact me again?" Elizabeth probed.

"Then I'd leave, and you'd never hear from me again."

The comment hung in the air, pregnant with meaning. She shifted on the couch, turning away in apparent disgust before swiveling her face back toward him.

"You wouldn't even *call?* After all we've been through?" she sniffed. "I can't believe that."

Relief swept through him when he realized she was teasing. He exhaled, unaware that he had been holding his breath, and grinned.

"If that's what it took for you to believe I'm not a psycho."

"I think that's pathetic. A guy should at least call."

He scooted imperceptibly closer on the couch. "I'll keep that in mind."

"You do realize that you're not going to be able to tell this story if you intend to live around here."

He slid even closer, noticeably this time. "I can live with that."

"And if you expect a raise just because you're dating the boss's granddaughter, you can forget that, too."

"I'll make do."

"I don't know how. You don't even have a car."

By then he had sidled up next to her, and she'd turned back to him, her hair just brushing his shoulder. He leaned in and kissed her neck. "I'll figure something out," he whispered, before pressing his lips to hers.

They kissed on the couch for a long time. When he finally carried her to the bedroom, they made love, their bodies together as one. Their exchange was passionate and angry and forgiving, as raw and tender as their emotions. Afterward, Thibault lay on his side, gazing at Elizabeth. He brushed her cheek with his finger, and she kissed it.

"I guess you can stay," she whispered.

34

Clayton

Clayton stared at the house in disbelief, his knuckles white on the steering wheel. He blinked repeatedly to clear his vision, but he still saw the same things: Beth's car in the driveway, the couple kissing on the couch, Thigh-bolt leading her to the bedroom.

Beth and Thigh-bolt together. With every passing minute, he felt stronger waves of anger cresting and crashing inside him. His perfect plans, all of them, up in smoke. And Thigh-bolt would forever have him over a barrel.

He pressed his lips together in a tight line. He was tempted to storm in on them, but then there was the damn dog. *Again*. It had been hard enough already, following them through his binoculars from his car without being noticed.

Thigh-bolt. The dog. *Beth* . . .

He banged the steering wheel. How could this have happened? Hadn't Beth heard what he'd said? Didn't she understand how much danger she was in? Didn't she care about Ben?

No way was that psycho going to be part of his son's life.

Not a chance.

Not on his life.

He should have expected this. He should have known how stupid Beth would be. She might be pushing thirty, but she had the intelligence of a child. He should have known that she'd see in Thigh-bolt whatever she wanted to see and ignore the obvious.

It would come to an end, though. Sooner rather than later. He'd make her see the light, no matter what it took.

35

Thibault

After kissing Elizabeth good-bye at the door, Thibault collapsed on the sofa, feeling both drained and relieved. He reveled in the knowledge that Elizabeth had forgiven him. That she'd tried to understand and make sense of the convoluted journey he'd taken to get here seemed nothing short of miraculous. She accepted him, warts and all—something he'd never thought possible.

Before she left, she'd invited him for dinner, and though he'd readily agreed, he planned to rest up before he went. He somehow doubted that he'd have the energy for conversation otherwise.

Before his nap, he knew he needed to take Zeus out, at least for a little while. He went to the back porch and retrieved his rain suit. Zeus followed him outside, watching him with interest.

"Yeah, we're going out," he said. "Just let me get dressed first."

Zeus barked and leapt with excitement, like a prancing deer. He raced to the door and back to Thibault again.

"I'm going as fast as I can. Relax."

Zeus continued to circle and prance around him.

"Relax," he said again. Zeus fixed him with a beseeching gaze before reluctantly sitting.

Thibault donned the rain suit and a pair of boots, then pushed open the screen door. Zeus bounded out into the rain, immediately sinking into the muddy ground. Unlike Nana's place, his property occupied a slight rise; the water collected a quarter mile away. Up ahead, Zeus veered toward the forest, then back to the open area again, then circled around to the graveled driveway, running and bounding in sheer joy. Thibault smiled, thinking, I know exactly how you feel.

They spent a few minutes outside, wandering in the storm. The sky had turned charcoal, heavy with rain-burdened clouds. The wind had picked up again, and Thibault could feel the water stinging his face as it blew sideways. It didn't matter; for the first time in years, he felt truly free.

At the base of the driveway, he noted that Elizabeth's tire tracks had nearly washed away. In a few more minutes, the rain would smooth them away completely. Something snagged his attention, though, and he tried to make sense of what he was seeing. His first thought was that the tires that had left the tracks seemed too wide.

He walked over for a closer look, reasoning that the set of tracks she'd left going out had probably overlapped the set coming in. It was only when he stood at the edge of the drive that he realized he'd been mistaken. There were two sets of tracks, both leading in and out. Two vehicles. At first, it didn't make sense.

His mind began to click quickly as the puzzle pieces slid into place. Someone else had been here. That didn't make sense, unless . . .

He glanced toward the path that led through the forest to the kennel. At that moment, the wind and rain unleashed in full fury, and he squinted before his breath caught in his throat. All at once he took off at a run, making sure to pace himself. His mind raced as he ran, calculating how long it would take to get there. He hoped he would make it in time.

36

Beth

As fate would have it, Nana was in the kennel office when Keith stormed into the house and closed the door behind him, acting as if he owned the place. Even from the kitchen, Beth could see the veins on his neck protruding. His hands balled into fists when his eyes locked on hers.

When he marched through the living room, Beth felt something give way inside her; fear filled its place. Never once had she seen him like this, and she backed away, following the angles of the cabinets. Keith surprised her by stopping at the entrance to the kitchen. He smiled, but his expression was off somehow, a grotesque and demented caricature of what it was supposed to be.

"Sorry for barging in like this," he said with exaggerated courtesy, "but we need to talk."

"What are you doing here? You can't just walk in here—"

"Cooking dinner, huh?" he said. "I remember when you used to cook dinner for me."

"Get out, Keith," she said, her voice hoarse.

"I'm not going anywhere," he said, looking at her as if she didn't know what she was talking about. He motioned toward the chair. "Why don't you sit down?"

"I don't want to sit down," she whispered, hating how frightened she sounded. "I want you to leave."

"That's not going to happen," he said. He smiled again, but it was no better than his first attempt. There was a vacancy in his gaze she'd never seen before. She felt her heartbeat speed up.

"Would you get me a beer, please?" he asked. "It's been a long day at the office, if you know what I mean."

She swallowed, afraid to look away. "I don't have any more."

He nodded, glancing around the kitchen before fixing his gaze on her again. He pointed. "I see one right there, by the stove. There's got to be another one somewhere. You mind if I check the fridge?" He didn't wait for an answer. He walked to the fridge and opened it before reaching for the bottom shelf. He came out with a bottle. "Found one," he crowed. He looked at her as he opened it. "Guess you were mistaken, huh?" He took a long pull and winked.

She forced herself to stay calm. "What do you want, Keith?"

"Oh, you know. Just wanted to catch up. See if there's anything I should know."

"Know about what?" she asked, her stomach clenching.

"About Thigh-bolt," he said.

She ignored the mangling of the name. "I don't know what you're talking about."

He took another drink, swishing the beer in his mouth as he nodded. He swallowed, the sound loud. "Driving over here, that's what I thought you might say," he said, sounding almost conversational. "But I know you better than you think I do." He gestured at her with his beer bottle. "There was a time there when I wasn't sure I knew you at all, but that's changed in the past few years. Raising a son together really bonds a couple, don't you think?"

She didn't respond.

"That's why I'm here, you know. Because of Ben. Because I want the best for him, and right now, I'm not sure you're thinking all that clearly about things."

He stepped toward her and took another long pull of his beer. The bottle was already nearly empty. He wiped his mouth with the back of his hand before going on. "See, I've been thinking that you and I haven't always had the best relationship. That's not good for Ben. He needs to know that we still get along. That we're still close friends. Don't you think that's an important lesson to teach him? That even if your parents get divorced, they can still be friends?"

She didn't like the sound of his rambling monologue, but she was afraid to cut him off. This was a different Keith Clayton . . . a dangerous one.

"I think it's important," he continued. He took another step toward her. "In fact, I can't think of anything more important."

"Just stay back," she said.

"I don't think so," he scolded her. "You haven't been thinking all that clearly in the last couple of days."

As he neared, she slid farther down the bank of counters, trying to keep him in front of her.

"Don't come any closer. I'm warning you."

He kept closing the distance, staring at her with those vacant eyes. "See what I mean? You're acting like you think I'm going to hurt you. I'd never, ever hurt you. You should know that about me."

"You're crazy."

"No, I'm not. A little angry, maybe, but not crazy." When he smiled again, the vacancy in his eyes vanished and her stomach did a flip-flop. He went on. "Do you know that even after all you've put me through, I still think you're beautiful?"

She didn't like where this was going. Not at all. By then, she'd reached the corner, with noplace left to go. "Just leave, okay? Ben's upstairs and Nana will be back in a minute—"

"All I want is a kiss. Is that such a big deal?"

She wasn't sure she'd heard him right. "A kiss?" she parroted.

"For now," he said. "That's all. Just for old times' sake. Then I'll go. I'll walk right out of here. I promise."

"I'm not going to kiss you," she said, stunned.

By then, he was standing before her. "You will," he said. "And you'll do more, later. But for now, a kiss is fine."

She arched her back, trying to keep away. "Please, Keith. I don't want this. I don't want to kiss you."

"You'll get over it," he said. When he leaned in, she turned away. He took hold of her upper arms. As he moved his lips toward her ear, Beth could feel her heart begin to hammer.

"You're hurting me!" she gasped.

"Here's the thing, Beth," he whispered. She could feel the warmth of his breath on her neck. "If you don't want to kiss me, that's fine. I'll accept that. But I've decided that I want to be a little more than friends."

"Get out!" she hissed, and with a laugh, Keith let her go.

"Sure," he said. He took a step back. "No problem. I'll leave. But I should let you know what's going to happen if we don't work something out."

"Just leave!" she shouted.

"I think we should go on a . . . date every now and then. And I'm not going to take no for an answer."

The way he said "date" made her skin crawl. Beth couldn't believe what she was hearing.

"After all, I warned you about Thigh-bolt," he added, "but where were you today? At his place." He shook his head. "That was a big mistake. You see, it's pretty easy for me to make a case that he stalked you and that he's obsessive. Both of those things make him dangerous, but you're obviously ignoring it. And that makes it dangerous for Ben to be forced to live with you."

His expression was neutral. Beth was paralyzed by his words.

"I'd hate to have to go to the courts and tell them what you're doing, but I will. And I'm sure they'll grant me full custody this time."

"You wouldn't," she whispered.

"I will. *Unless*." His obvious enjoyment as he spoke made it that much more horrifying. He paused, letting it sink in, before speaking like a professor again. "Let me make sure you understand. First, you tell Thigh-bolt that you never want to see him again. Then you tell him to leave town. And after that, we'll go out. For old times' sake. It's either that, or Ben's going to live with me."

"I'm not going to live with you!" a small voice shouted from the kitchen doorway.

Beth looked past Keith to see Ben, his expression horrified. Ben started to back away. "I'm not going to do it!"

Ben turned and ran, slamming the front door behind him as he raced into the storm.

37

Clayton

Beth tried to force her way past Clayton, but he reached for her arm again.

"We're not done yet," he growled. He wasn't going to let her leave without making sure she understood.

"He ran outside!"

"He'll be fine. I want to make sure you're clear on how things are going to go with us."

Beth didn't hesitate, slapping him across the face with her free hand, and he recoiled. When he let go, she pushed him backward with all her might, sensing that he was still off balance.

"Get the hell out!" she screamed. As soon as he steadied his feet, she slammed him in the chest again. "I am so sick of you and your family telling me what I can and can't do, and I'm not going to put up with it anymore!"

"Too bad," he shot back, the words coming naturally. "You don't have a choice. I'm not going to let Ben anywhere near that *boyfriend* of yours."

Instead of answering, as if tired of listening to him, she pushed away and strode past him.

"Where are you going?" he demanded. "We're not finished."

She pounded through the living room. "I'm going to find Ben."

"It's just rain!"

"It's flooding, in case you haven't noticed."

He watched her run out onto the porch, expecting her to find Ben there, but for some reason, she looked both ways and vanished from view. Lightning flashed, thunder echoing a moment later. Close. Too close. Clayton moved to the door and noticed that she'd headed to the far edge and was scanning the yard. Just then, he saw Nana approaching with an umbrella.

"Have you seen Ben?" Beth suddenly called out.

"No," Nana answered, looking confused, rain pouring around her. "I just got here. What's going on?" She stopped short at the sight of Clayton. "What's he doing here?" she demanded.

"He didn't go past you?" Beth asked, suddenly jogging toward the steps.

"It's no big deal," Clayton said, knowing he had to finish things with Beth. "He'll be back. . . ."

Beth stopped suddenly and faced him. All at once, Clayton noticed her anger had been replaced by something close to terror. The noise of the storm seemed to be suddenly very far away.

"What is it?" he asked.

"The tree house . . ."

It took only a moment to process the words, and then Clayton felt his chest constrict.

A moment later, they were both charging for the woods.

38

Thibault, Beth and Clayton

Thibault finally arrived at the kennel driveway, his boots waterlogged and heavy. Zeus kept pace alongside him, slowed only by the knee-deep water. Up ahead, he could see the car and the truck, as well as another SUV. As he approached, he made out the lights on top and knew that Clayton was at the house.

Despite his exhaustion, he surged forward, splashing hard. Zeus was bounding through the water like a dolphin skimming over the waves. The harder Thibault ran, the farther the distance seemed, but finally he passed the kennel office and angled toward the house. Only then did he notice Nana standing on the porch, aiming a flashlight toward the forest.

Even from a distance, she looked panicked.

"Nana!" he called out, but the storm kept the sound of his voice from reaching her. A few moments later she must have heard him, for she turned in his direction, catching him in the glare of her flashlight.

"Thibault?"

Thibault forced his way through the last few steps. The rain whipped around him and the waning light made it difficult to see. He slowed to a walk, trying to catch his breath.

"What happened?" he shouted.

"Ben's gone!" she shouted back.

"What do you mean, gone? What happened?"

"I don't know!" Nana cried. "Clayton was here and Beth came out looking for Ben . . . and then the two of them took off toward the creek. I heard something about the tree house."

A moment later, Thibault was sprinting toward the woods, Zeus at his side.

The rain and wind lashed the branches on either side of them, cutting their faces and hands. The path had been blocked by dozens of fallen limbs, forcing Beth and Keith to push through bushes and vines to get around them. Twice, Beth stumbled and fell; behind her, she heard Keith fall as well. The mud was thick and viscous; halfway to the tree house, Beth's shoe came off, but she didn't stop.

The tree house. The bridge. The flood. Only adrenaline and fear kept her from throwing up. In her mind's eye, she could see her son on the bridge as it suddenly gave way.

In the shadows, she stumbled again over a half-decayed tree trunk and felt a searing pain in her foot. She rose as quickly as she could, trying to ignore it, but as soon as she put weight on it, she crumpled to the ground again.

By then, Keith had reached her side and he pulled her up without out a word. Keeping an arm around her waist, he dragged her forward.

They both knew Ben was in danger.

Clayton had to force himself not to succumb to panic. He told himself that Ben was intelligent, that Ben would know danger when he saw it, that he wouldn't press his luck. Ben wasn't the bravest kid. For the first and only time in his life, he was grateful for that.

Even as they struggled through the underbrush, Beth hobbling beside him, Clayton couldn't ignore what he was seeing. Far beyond its banks, almost at their feet, he saw the creek, running wider, stronger, and faster than he'd ever seen it.

Thibault had been running hard, charging through mud and water, forcing himself not to slow but finding it more difficult with every step to keep up his desperate pace. Branches and vines snapped at his face and arms, scissoring him with cuts he didn't feel as he blasted through them.

As he ran, he ripped off his raincoat and then his shirt.

Almost there, he kept telling himself. Only a little bit farther.

And in the distant reaches of his mind, he heard the echo of Victor's voice:

There is more.

Beth could feel the bones in her foot grinding against one another with every step, sending flashes of fire throughout her lower body, but she refused to scream or cry out.

As they drew near the tree house, the creek widened even more, the current curling and whipping into circles. Brackish water broke into tiny waves around heaps of fallen branches along the fast-disappearing banks. The turbulent water was filled with debris, enough to knock anyone unconscious.

Rain came down from the sky in sheets. The wind toppled another branch, and it crashed to the ground only yards away. The mud seemed to suck the energy from both of them.

But she knew they'd reached the oak tree: Through the downpour, she could make out the rope bridge, like the ragged mast of a ship finally sighted through a misty harbor. Her eyes swung from the ladder to the rope bridge, toward the central landing. . . . The waters of the creek were racing over it, debris collecting against it. Her gaze traveled from the rope bridge to the tree house platform, taking in the awkward angle of the dangling bridge. It hovered only a foot above the water because the platform had nearly been ripped off the tree house's ancient structural support, clearly about to give way.

As if in a waking nightmare, she suddenly spotted Ben in the rushing creek, clinging to the rope bridge below the tree house platform. Only then did she allow herself to scream.

Clayton felt fear flood his veins as soon as he saw Ben grasping the fraying edge of the rope bridge. His mind raced frantically.

Too far to swim to the other side, and no time.

"Stay here!" he shouted to Beth as he raced toward the tree ladder. He scaled it and set off on the bridge at a run, desperate to reach Ben. He could see the tree house platform sinking. Once the force of the current touched it, it would tear away completely.

On his third step, the dry-rotted planks broke and Clayton felt himself smash through the platform, breaking his ribs on the way and free-falling toward the water. It was all he could do to grab the rope as he hit the raging water. He struggled to tighten his grip as he went under, his clothes dragging him down. He felt the current pulling at him, and the rope tightened. He held on, trying to get his head above water, kicking wildly.

He bobbed to the surface and gasped: His broken ribs exploded in pain, making everything go black for an instant. In a panic, he reached for the rope with the other hand, fighting against the current.

As he held on, ignoring the pain, branches rammed his body before spinning off wildly. The current crashed over his face, obscuring his vision, making it difficult to breathe, making it difficult to think of anything but survival. In his struggle, he didn't notice the pilings beneath the central landing lurch under the strain of his weight, beginning to lean with the ferocious current.

*   *   *

Beth hobbled to her feet and tried to walk. She got three steps before falling again. She cupped her mouth and shouted across the creek.

"Move along the rope, Ben! Move away from the platform! You can do it!"

She wasn't sure whether he heard her, but a moment later, she saw him start to inch out from beneath the platform, toward the harsher current in the center of the creek. Toward his father—

Keith was floundering, barely holding on. . . .

Everything seemed to speed up and slow down at exactly the same time when she suddenly saw movement in the distance, a little ways upstream. From the corner of her eye, she spotted Logan ripping off his boots and rain bottoms.

A moment later, he dove into the water, Zeus close behind him.

Clayton knew he couldn't hold on much longer. The pain from his ribs was excruciating, and the current continued to beat him down. He could catch his breath only in snatches, and he flailed against the death he suddenly knew was coming.

The relentless current was moving Thibault two feet down the creek for every foot he was moving across. He knew he could backtrack on land once he reached the opposite bank, but he didn't have that much time. Focusing his sights on Ben, he kicked with everything he had.

A large branch slammed into him, sending him under for a moment. When he surfaced again, disoriented, he saw Zeus behind him, paddling hard. He regained his bearings, then stroked and kicked with desperate effort. In despair, he saw that he hadn't even reached the center of the creek.

Beth saw Ben inching farther along the fraying rope bridge, and she dragged herself closer to the water's edge.

"Come on!" she shouted, sobbing now. "You can do it! Hold on, baby!"

In midstroke, Thibault collided with the submerged central landing of the bridge. He rolled in the water, spinning out of control; a moment later, he smashed into Clayton. Panicking, Clayton grabbed for his arm with his free hand, dragging Thibault under. Thibault flailed and felt for the rope, his grip tightening just as Clayton let go. Clayton clung instead to Thibault, clambering on top of him in a frenzied attempt to reach the air.

Thibault struggled underwater, holding the rope with one hand, unable to free himself from Clayton. His lungs felt as if they would explode, and he felt panic beginning to overtake him.

At that very moment, the pilings lurched again, the downstream weight of Clayton and Thibault too much to hold, and with a tearing sound, the landing gave way completely.

Beth watched Keith and Logan struggle just before the remaining ropes attached to the central landing snapped. Across the creek, the tree house platform tumbled into the creek in a massive eruption of water, and Ben was whipsawed downstream. In horror, Beth saw that he was still clinging to the rope attached to the central landing, which had spiraled into the current.

Zeus had been getting close to Logan and Keith when the central landing suddenly heaved like a seashell rolled up by the waves and crashed. Zeus vanished from sight.

It was all happening too fast—she could no longer see Logan or Keith, and only after frantically scanning the water did she spot Ben's head, a speck among the debris.

She heard Ben's high-pitched cries, and saw him fighting to keep his head above water. She rose again and hobbled forward, immune to the pain, trying desperately to keep him in view.

And then, like a dream come to life, she saw a dark, sleek head moving purposefully toward her son.

Zeus.

She heard Ben calling for the dog, and her heart suddenly filled.

She hobbled and fell, rose again and scrambled forward, then fell once more. At last she began to crawl, trying to see what was happening. She used the branches to drag herself forward. Zeus and Ben were getting smaller as they were carried downstream, but Zeus was getting ever closer.

Then, all at once, their two figures merged, and Zeus suddenly turned, heading for her side of the creek, Ben behind him, holding Zeus's tail.

"Kick, baby! Kick!" she screamed.

She hobbled and hopped and thrashed her way forward, trying and failing to keep up with the current. Ben and Zeus were getting farther away with every passing second. She strained to keep sight of them—they'd reached the center of the creek. . . no, past the center.

She kept going, fighting with every remaining shred of strength to keep them in sight, pushing forward, instinct taking over. Instead of pain, she felt her heart beating with every step.

Only a third of the way to the edge of the creek . . . the current getting slower . . . now a quarter . . .

She kept going, clawing at branches and pulling herself forward. They were lost in the foliage, and it took a few agonizing moments, but she found them again.

Almost there . . . allowing the relief to seep in . . . only a little bit farther . . .

Please God . . . just a little more . . .

Then they were there. Ben's feet hit first and he let go. Zeus surged forward and then reached ground as well. Beth lunged toward them as both Zeus and Ben staggered from the water.

Zeus collapsed as soon as he hit dry land. Ben crumpled a moment later. By the time Beth reached them, Zeus was on his feet, his legs trembling from exhaustion, drenched and coughing.

Beth went to the ground beside her son and sat him up as he began to cough in time with Zeus.

"Are you okay?" she cried.

"I'm okay," he panted. He coughed again and wiped the water from his face. "I was scared, but I had the picture in my pocket. Thibault said it would keep me safe." He swiped at his nose. "Where's Dad? And Thibault?"

At his words, they both began to cry.

Epilogue

Two Months Later

Beth glanced in the rearview mirror and smiled at the sight of Zeus standing in the bed of the truck, his nose to the wind. Ben sat beside her, rangier since his recent growth spurt but still not quite tall enough to rest his elbow comfortably out the window.

It was the first warm spell they'd had after weeks of miserably cold weather, and Christmas was coming soon, less than a couple of weeks away: The heat and storms of October had already become a distant memory. The floods had made national news. Downtown Hampton had flooded like many other towns in the region; in all, six people had lost their lives.

Despite the nightmare they had all endured, Beth realized that she felt a kind of . . . peace for the first time in recent memory. Since the funeral, she'd grappled with the extraordinary events that had led to that fateful day. She knew that many people in town wondered about the choices she'd made. Occasionally, she heard whispers, but for the most part, she ignored them. If Logan had taught her anything, it was that sometimes her faith in herself and her instincts was all she had.

Thankfully, Nana had continued to improve; in the days and weeks after "the accident," as she referred to it, Beth and especially Ben had leaned on her for her special brand of wisdom and her unfaltering support. These days, she sang regularly with the choir, found time to train the dogs, and was using both hands, limping only occasionally when tired. There had actually been a moment a couple of weeks back when both of them were walking exactly the same way. It was two days after Beth had had her cast removed—she'd broken four bones in her foot and had been in a cast for five weeks—and Nana had ribbed her about it, enjoying the idea of someone else being the invalid.

Ben had changed markedly since then, in some ways that Beth worried about and in others that made her proud. Surviving the ordeal had given Ben a newfound confidence that he carried with him to school. Or at least she liked to think so. Sometimes she wondered whether it was because of the photo he'd carried in his pocket. The lamination was scuffed and worn and beginning to separate, but he wouldn't part with it, carrying it with him everywhere. In time, she assumed he'd grow out of it, but who knew? It was Logan's legacy to Ben, and as such it held special meaning for him.

The loss had been hard on Ben, of course. While he rarely spoke openly about it, she knew he blamed himself in some way. And he still had occasional nightmares, in which he called out sometimes for Keith and sometimes for Logan. When Beth shook him awake, the dream was always the same. He was floundering in the river, about to go under, when he saw Zeus coming toward him. In his dreams, though, he grabbed for the tail, only to find that he couldn't grasp it. He would reach and fail again and again, only to realize that Zeus no longer had a tail, and he would watch himself—as if from someplace else—flailing as he sank slowly under the water.

When she reached the cemetery, Beth pulled into her usual spot. She carried two vases of flowers. First, as she always had when coming to this place, she went to the spot where Drake had been buried and took a moment to remember him before pulling a few weeds around the headstone and setting the flowers nearby.

Then she went to the other grave. She'd saved the larger floral arrangement for this one: It was his birthday, and she wanted to make sure he was remembered.

Zeus wandered here and there, sniffing and exploring as he usually did. Ben trailed behind, as he had ever since Zeus had arrived. Ben had always loved the dog, but after Zeus had saved him in the river, it had become impossible to separate them. Zeus seemed to recognize what he had done—or at least, that was the only way Beth could explain it—and in the dog's mind, they were now bound together. At night, he slept in the hallway outside of Ben's room. Stumbling to the bathroom in the middle of the night, Beth often spotted Zeus near the bed, checking up on his beloved companion as he slept.

Loss was complicated, and she and Ben both struggled with its aftereffects. She felt sometimes that their memories wreaked havoc with their grieving, for despite the heroism that marked their ordeal, their reminiscences were not always rosy. But when all was said and done, Keith Clayton would be remembered by her with unequivocal gratitude. She could never forget how he'd carried her when she fell that day. Or that in the end, he'd died trying to save their son.

That counted for something. That counted for a lot, and despite his other failings, that would *always* be how she chose to remember him. She hoped for Ben's sake that he would also come to remember him that way, without guilt and with the certain knowledge of Keith's love for him, so elusive in his life to that point.

As for her, Logan would be waiting when she got back home. He'd offered to go with her to the cemetery, but somehow she knew he hadn't really wanted to go. It was the weekend, and he preferred to spend the morning puttering around the grounds in solitude, repairing things and working on Ben's new tree house in the backyard. Later, they planned to decorate the Christmas tree. She was getting used to his rhythms and his moods, recognizing the quiet signals that telegraphed who he was. Good and bad, strengths and faults, he was hers forever.

As she pulled into the driveway, she spotted Logan coming down the steps from the house, and she waved.

She was his forever, too—imperfect as she was. Take it or leave it, she thought. She was who she was.

As Logan walked toward her, he smiled as if reading her mind and opened his arms.